Patriots

Steve Sohmer
PATRIOTS

RANDOM HOUSE NEW YORK

Library of Congress Cataloging-in-Publication Data
Sohmer, Steve.
Patriots / by Steve Sohmer—1st U.S. ed.
p.   cm.
ISBN 0-679-40207-1
I. Title.
PS3569.043P38   1991   813'.54—dc20   90-52927

Manufactured in the United States of America
24689753

First U.S. Edition

For my father, the best kind of hero.

I dare do all that may become a man;
Who dares do more, is none.

WILLIAM SHAKESPEARE
MACBETH I, vii

PROLOGUE: EARLY WARNING

The Cold War is now behind us.

PRESIDENT MIKHAIL S. GORBACHEV
SPEAKING AT STANFORD UNIVERSITY
JUNE 4, 1990

The White House
Monday, November 11, 1991
Veterans Day
7:04 A.M.

Air Force Major General Lucius Gaynor stood at the window of the elevated battle staff room; the fingertips of his left hand rested lightly against the glass. The glass was cold to the touch, but Gaynor was not aware of that. Behind him, his executive officer, Colonel Walsh, cleared his throat to press for a decision, but Gaynor did not hear him. Sixty feet above, the West Wing hummed with life; stewards served coffee, phones rang, and distinguished visitors paced waiting rooms, eager to pump the hand that held the reins of power. But five stories underground, behind the steel blast doors and concrete buttresses, only the soft hiss of filtered air stirred the shadows in the White House air defense room.

In the orange half-light beyond the observation window, NCOs and officers stood in silent twos and threes or sat rigid at computer consoles; like Gaynor, they were staring at the massive status board and plotting screen that overhung the front wall.

It was peacetime; the status board was dark. Alert panels that would flash a NORAD warning of an airborne threat against the United States and echo countermeasures were blank as windows on the night. Only the digital clock was lit; ticking past 12:04:16 Greenwich mean time—Zulu time—the worldwide standard of the American military. On the plotting screen beside the status board, a radar image of the mid-Atlantic coast from New Jersey to Virginia was projected in delicate green tracery; three dots of light maneuvered off the coast of Delaware.

Gaynor rested his palm against the glass, leaned his chin against the back of his hand, and squinted at the plotting screen. For almost two years, he had commanded the White House ADR as the personal appointee of the air force chief of staff. The position was sensitive and delicate—Gaynor was no random choice; he had *the profile*.

He was forty-nine, but prematurely gray—a tall and slender, quiet-spoken veteran who had earned his reputation for performance under fire with the 366th Tactical Fighter Wing at Da Nang. When the

Vietnam War was lost, Tactical Air Command had appointed him to the staff of Twelfth Air Force at Bergstrom. In 1985, he was named TAC's liaison to North American Aerospace Defense Command at Petersen Air Force Base in Colorado. That *curriculum vitae* gave Gaynor competence at every level of aerospace defense.

But his position in the White House was also symbolic; the commander of the ADR would be the senior member of America's armed forces to stand beside the president of the United States if Armageddon came.

Luke Gaynor had worn his country's colors for twenty-eight years. In all that time he had never seen anything like the three dots on the plotting screen.

No one had.

He lifted the receiver of the blue telephone and waited.

Upstairs at his desk in the Oval Office, President Samuel Baker wasn't taking calls. He was tired; he hadn't slept well. The shocking Soviet accusations that threatened to disrupt the Strategic Arms Reduction Talks in Geneva, the angry predawn meeting with Secretary of State Coleman, the furious Japanese protest over Hakodate—all the tumult of the fretful night had taken its toll. Now, Sam Baker was closeted with White House Chief of Staff Ted Harris and Press Secretary Ron Fowler, trying to evaluate reaction to Sunday night's presidential press conference and the announcement of the First Step disarmament initiative.

Fowler didn't have to sugarcoat it. "As expected—public reaction's very good. Editorials in the *Times* and *Post* are favorable—even the *Chicago Tribune.*" He handed the president a pile of telegrams and faxes. "Endorsements are pouring in from Congress—both sides of the aisle. With, of course, the expected handful of exceptions."

"Don't tell me—I can guess." Sam Baker flipped through the messages; they rang with buzzwords like "vision," "statesmanship," and "peace"; it was hard to imagine anyone in the free world who *wouldn't* embrace First Step. But any new White House program was bound to have detractors, and defense initiatives—particularly disarmament initiatives—always called out every naysayer and critic in the Congress, the Pentagon, and the press. When the strategic defense of the United States was at issue, all the professional patriots had to have their say. "Those opposed are Helms and Domenici, Symms, McCain . . ."

"And Whitworth," Fowler said. "You heard him on the *Today* show."

"Yeah," Ted Harris said. "And so did every yahoo and Red-baiter in the republic." Harris was sixty—a tall and flinty retired marine brigadier general and former national security adviser who still wore his white hair in a crew cut. In 1951, he had waded ashore at Pusan as a shavetail second *looey* to prosecute President Truman's Korean "police action." That muddy, bloody war had taught Ted Harris a profound lesson in military strategy in the nuclear age: if the president who had ordered the atomic bombing of Hiroshima and Nagasaki wouldn't let Doug MacArthur use nukes to prevent a Chinese rout of America's marines, no civilized nation would ever again use nuclear weapons in war. First Step was as much Harris's idea as Sam Baker's.

Harris screwed up his mouth like he wanted to spit. "Everybody knows Jesse Helms won't trust the Russians until they install Jesus Christ as general secretary and Billy Graham as foreign minister. But Whitworth . . . that one bothers me."

That one bothered Sam Baker, too. Simon Whitworth was chairman of the Senate Armed Services Committee and the Pentagon's best friend in Washington—but he was no hawkish firebrand; if anything, he was a reasonable man with a stubborn liberal streak. In their early years in Congress, Sam Baker and Simon Whitworth had led the opposition to the Vietnam War; they had been allies for twenty-five years.

The president set the sheaf of papers down. "Ted—what's your assessment?"

"What's there to assess? We've got a fight on our hands." Harris sensed the president's disappointment—and mistrusted it. Sam Baker was a deliberate, reflective man—generous in debate and slow to anger. What in lesser men might be indecision was, in this president, merely a nagging humanity.

"Mr. President—this is no time for waffling," Harris said. "If the conservatives want a fight, we've got to give them all they can handle."

Sam Baker sighed and nodded. "All right. What's the plan?"

Harris paced and spun it out. "Number one—send Scowcroft to the Hill. This morning. Right now. Two—get Boren, Pell, and Rudman in here for lunch, throw their car keys on the roof and don't let them go until they pledge allegiance. I'll call State and tell them we need taped endorsements from Kohl and Mitterand we can feed the networks. John Major has been raising hell since we briefed his ambassador on Friday, but—"

The phone rang; Harris broke off.

Sam Baker looked at the telephone on his desk; none of its buttons was lit. Then he realized the ringing sound was soft and muted, distant and remote as an echo from another room. It was an eerie sound, something like a distant trumpet—a sound he hadn't heard in seven years in the Oval Office.

Harris tapped the top right-hand drawer of the president's desk.

Sam Baker reached for the drawer, then hesitated. The blue telephone inside was the hot line from the White House air defense room—the phone they called the Nightmare Line. It was the phone that never rang.

He smiled at Fowler. "Ron, could you excuse us, please?"

When he had, Sam Baker opened the drawer and lifted the receiver. "This is the president."

"Good morning, sir. General Gaynor in the ADR. Could you meet me in the sit' room, please?"

"The . . . sit' room?" The ground-floor situation room was the communications center where the president and his advisers met in time of emergency.

"Yes, sir," Gaynor said. "If you please." He hung up.

Sam Baker set the receiver down. "Odd . . ." He looked to Harris. "Any exercises on this morning? War games? Anything like that?"

Harris shook his head. He didn't care much for Gaynor or any of the NORAD techno-soldiers; to them, war was an exercise in probabilities, fought by flying computers that occasionally had men attached. But Harris knew Gaynor wouldn't use the Nightmare Line to report an exercise.

So did Sam Baker. He shut the desk drawer, rose and clapped his hands against his flanks. "Well. Shall we see what Gaynor wants?"

He went out the side door to the hallway; Harris dogged him at the heels. "Sam, we can't wait on First Step. We can't sit back and let the opposition build."

"All right." They turned left down a short flight of steps. "Tell Scowcroft to go up and work the Hill. And set the Senate lunch." At the bottom of the stairs, the hall branched left to the navy mess, right to the situation room. "I'll call Dole and Wilson and—" The president fell silent when Harris touched his sleeve.

There was the usual white-on-red sign hung on the oak door of the situation room:

BRIEFING IN PROGRESS
AUTHORIZED PERSONNEL ONLY

But this morning, an armed marine sergeant stood beside it.

"Well," Harris murmured. "Formal today." The sergeant braced and yanked the door open.

Unlike the cavernous subterranean air defense room, the ground-floor situation room was small and intimate, low ceilinged, lit with flat fluorescent light. In its center stood a rectangular table and eight armchairs, each with its own encryption phone. In the communications annex, General Gaynor and Colonel Walsh stood staring at a radar monitor lit with an image of the mid-Atlantic coast.

The marine barked, "Ten-*hut!*"

Gaynor and Walsh braced.

"As you were," Sam Baker said. "General, what's going on?"

When the door closed, Gaynor said, "Good morning, Mr. President . . . Colonel Walsh."

Walsh flipped up the steel cover of his clipboard. "At 0600 this morning, a navy F-14 Tomcat fighter left Oceana Naval Air Station in Virginia Beach for a routine training mission. The pilot was Commander Charles L. Granger. His radar intercept trainee was Lieutenant Peter Dolman. Their flight plan took them into National Defense Operations Area W-506 southeast of Nantucket Island. At 0630, Commander Granger Maydayed a mechanical malfunction and made a forced landing at the Calverton Naval Weapons Plant airfield near Peconic River, Long Island."

"Excuse me, General," the president said. "But why does this concern me?"

"Sir, apparently the Mayday was a ruse." He nodded for Walsh to continue.

"Once on the ground, Commander Granger brandished a pistol and denied Lieutenant Dolman reentry to the aircraft. An unidentified crippled man took the lieutenant's place. At 0642 when service personnel attempted to intervene, Granger and his accomplice commandeered the fighter and escaped. The plane is now seventy miles east of Ocean City, Maryland, flying south on a course paralleling the coastline at a speed of five hundred twenty-five knots—roughly six hundred miles an hour at an altitude of forty-one thousand feet. The plane is armed with six Phoenix missiles, two Sidewinder missiles and cannon."

"Do navy fighters usually carry all that ordnance on training flights?"

"Well . . . no, sir." Walsh shifted uneasily. "We're investigating that."

The president looked to Harris.

"You've got fighters on alert," Harris said. "Intercept him."

"We tried that, Mr. Harris," Gaynor said.

Walsh flipped a page. "At 0653, NORAD Northeast Sector Control at Griffiss Air Force Base launched two alert air national guard F-16 Falcons from Atlantic City to intercept the F-14. When the Falcons attempted to approach Commander Granger, he first challenged them and then . . ." Walsh hesitated.

"Then *what,* Colonel?"

"Then he fired upon them."

Sam Baker straightened. "Fired upon them?"

"Yes, sir. A missile."

Harris whistled through his teeth.

"Has anybody talked to this nut?"

"He's not responding to radio calls."

"Where's he going?" the president said.

"We don't know, sir."

"Where could he be going?"

The officers stood silent. Then Gaynor said, "Cuba."

"A defector?"

"Sounds like it," Harris said.

"Sir," Gaynor said, "I'd like to remind the president that no naval aviation officer has ever defected or attempted—"

Sam Baker raised a hand for silence. "All right, General. But why bother me with this? Don't you have procedures?"

"Yes, sir. There are seven TAC and eight air national guard bases between the F-14's position and Cuba. We could intercept him from any one of them."

"And then what?"

"Talk him down."

Harris said, "Or shoot him down?"

All eyes went to Harris—then, quickly, to Gaynor.

"Yes," Gaynor said. "If necessary."

Now Sam Baker was beginning to understand why he had been summoned to the situation room. "Suppose we let him go to Cuba. Then demand they return the plane and crew?"

Harris shrugged. "Might get 'em back—might not. Nobody told that sonofabitch Castro the Cold War's over."

The president turned to Gaynor. "Anything on that plane we don't want the Russians to see? Special equipment? Secret gear?"

"No, sir. But—"

"All right, General. I understand." Sam Baker looked up at the flickering green image on the monitor. "Which one is he?"

Walsh tapped the screen. "That one." The dot of light blinked in the electronic darkness above the ocean. With each blink, it moved infinitesimally farther south.

Sam Baker stared at the screen; it was the worst possible day for an anomaly. The digital clock blinked to 1211 Zulu—7:11 A.M. in Washington—3:11 P.M. Moscow time. At that morning's briefings in the Kremlin, he knew translations of his First Step press conference had been passed around, analyzed, discussed. The same debate that had begun last night in the United States was starting now in Moscow; the same passionate legions of hawks and doves were squaring off— soldiers and conservatives on one side, liberals and reformers on the other—all patriots, all with unshakable convictions, all with soul-consuming doubts. Can the Americans be trusted? What is Baker's purpose? What's his real objective? How will NATO respond? The same caterpillars of fear and suspicion gnawed the leaves of the olive branch in Moscow as did here in Washington.

Sam Baker knew that halfway around the world, other eyes were scanning monitors like the one glowing in the White House situation room. Officially, the Cold War might be over, but the Atlantic coast-line of the United States remained one of the most closely watched borders in the world. Soviet Il-76 Mainstay warning and control air-craft from Cuba, Tu-95s from Riga, and KGB trawlers plying the Gulf Stream gave the Soviet Stavka generals in Moscow a rough approximation of the projection Sam Baker was looking at just now.

The president turned to Walsh. "Colonel, when will the Soviets spot the F-14?"

"They must have seen the missile track when he fired at the Falcons."

"What would they have made of that?"

"They'll think it was an exercise. A runaway missile that had to be aborted."

"And what will they think if he gets into a scrap with a couple of interceptors?"

Walsh didn't reply; he looked to Gaynor.

"Mr. President," Gaynor said, "this F-14 is armed with AIM-54C Phoenix missiles . . ."

"Yes? And?"

"That's the navy's long-range air-to-air missile, sir. It's accurate at almost a hundred miles."

"I don't see the significance."

Walsh rattled off the system profile. "With the AWG-9 fire control system in the F-14, the radar intercept officer can simultaneously track twenty-four aggressor aircraft. And simultaneously engage six in combat. He has five Phoenix missiles left."

"Are you saying we can't intercept this lunatic?"

"We can, sir. If we can jam his radar—"

Harris growled, "What do you mean—*if?* Don't we know how to jam our own radar?"

"Of course we do," Gaynor said. "But so do the men in the F-14. It's something of a paradox. To be sure of a kill, we'd have to send several planes. There could be a fight."

"With what outcome?"

"That would depend on the skill of the pilot and RIO in the F-14."

Now Sam Baker understood why his presence was required in the situation room. Sometime this morning—to preserve the honor of the nation's armed forces—he might have to order Americans into combat against one of their own; live young men, live ordnance, fiery sudden death. "Colonel, how many planes would we have to send against the F-14?"

"He has five Phoenix missiles left. We'd have to send six planes."

Harris wet his lips. "Uh-oh."

"And if there were a fight? How would you assess the outcome?"

"Obviously, we'd have losses."

"How many?" Harris demanded. "With what"—he loathed the word—"probability?"

"That's hard to say."

"Dammit, Colonel," the president said. "I want an answer!"

Before Walsh could reply, Gaynor touched his arm; when the general spoke, it was without emotion. "Five planes, eighty percent. Four planes, one hundred percent."

In the silence that followed, Harris whispered, "Jee-zus."

Sam Baker weighed the ominous statistics. "General . . . when does this decision have to be made?"

"To intercept the F-14 before it enters Cuban airspace"—Gaynor checked the digital clock; it read 1213 Zulu, 7:13 A.M.—"in the next fifty minutes."

He looked at the president, waiting. They all waited.

Sam Baker grumbled in exasperation; just at the moment when the most sensitive foreign policy issues demanded his undivided attention, he was being distracted by the ludicrous escapade of some runaway fighter plane. "Well . . . keep calling him on the radio. Maybe he'll turn back. Dammit, I'm not going to kill five men to keep some fool from defecting to Cuba!"

"No, sir." Gaynor's eyes drifted to the monitor.

Sam Baker followed his glance. The F-14 was off Wallops Island, Virginia, now and moving south; in the four minutes since the president had entered the situation room, the plane had flown another forty miles. Sam Baker glared at the dot of light. Of all the rotten luck, did it have to be *this* morning? He clenched his fists. "Who *is* this mad-man?"

"We're checking his personnel jacket now."

Head down, brooding, the president walked back upstairs to the Oval Office. Inside, Harris shut the door and leaned against it.

"Nice," he said bitterly. "Nice fucking way to start Veterans Day."

But Sam Baker sat silent at his desk, his back to Harris, staring out the thick, bulletproof windows. In the first gray light of wintry morning, he could see the hoarfrost glinting on the South Lawn's dormant grass; beyond the leafless branches of the Presidential Grove, the distant tip of the Washington Monument loomed bone white against a somber sky.

For the moment, NORAD would have to deal with the antics of the wayward F-14. Sam Baker had strategic problems to address. Harris was right; they had to move quickly to defuse congressional opposition to First Step. Massive new reductions of America's NATO forces would be welcome in Paris and Bonn, but they would be a hard sell in London and Rome and NATO headquarters in Brussels. Still, he had to get it done. For the sake of the country—for the sake of all countries—he had to get it done. His antagonists would be many and powerful: Simon Whitworth and the Senate Armed Services Committee, the diehard hawks in Congress, his own Secretary of Defense, and Joint Chiefs of Staff. The military would—

Abruptly, the president broke his line of thought. "Ted . . . you don't think that runaway fighter has anything to do with First Step?"

Harris looked up. "Funny . . ."

"What's funny?"

"I was just thinking the same thing."

AUTHOR'S NOTE

Patriots takes place during a thirteen-hour period that begins Sunday night, November 10, 1991, and ends at noon the following day. On those dates, American eastern standard time will be six hours earlier than European standard time. That is:

Noon in Washington ╤ 6:00 P.M. in Geneva

On Veterans Day, Monday, November 11, 1991, the times of sunrise and sunset will be:

	Sunrise	Sunset
Geneva	7:30 A.M.	5:08 P.M.
Washington	6:46 A.M.	4:57 P.M.

The reader is reminded that the United States and Soviet Union signed the historic START1 strategic arms reduction treaty on October 1, 1991.

Patriots

CALL TO ARMS

"The president is in a grave situation," Robert Kennedy said, "and he does not know how to get out of it. We are under pressure from our military to use force against Cuba. That is why he is turning to Premier Khrushchev for help. If the situation continues much longer, the president is not sure our military will not overthrow him and seize power. The American army could get out of control."

NIKITA S. KHRUSHCHEV
KHRUSHCHEV REMEMBERS

Sunday, November 10, 1991
The previous night

INI, BOLLING AIR FORCE BASE, WASHINGTON, DC

11:11 P.M. By the glow of a single streetlamp, the little brick building that sat among the trees on the north side of Castle Avenue looked like a tidy, center-hall Colonial house. But it was not a private home; it was INI—the offices of the Air Force Intelligence Agency's directorate of Research and Soviet Studies.

In his tiny office on the second floor, Lieutenant Colonel Richard Harding sat hunched at his desk, elbows before him on the blotter, hands cupping his face. He was forty-four, but looked older; a gaunt man, shrunken cheeked and pasty, his black hair thin and streaky across his scalp, his shirt hanging hollow from the knobs of his shoulders. It was Sunday night; tomorrow would be Veterans Day. Beyond Harding's open office door lay the deserted bull pen where INI analysts sat each workday, studying computer translations of Soviet military tracts, SIGINT intercepts of Soviet air force radio traffic eavesdropped by the National Security Agency, stolen Soviet air force operating manuals that supplied clues to the capabilities of their weapons systems, stolen maintenance manuals that provided hints about their reliability—everything from intercepted messages between the Soviet Strategic Rocket Forces command in Moscow and the director of their space shuttle program in Tyuratam to yellowed, blood-spattered love letters plucked by Afghani *mujahadim* from the corpses of Soviet advisers serving with the puppet Kabul government. Once, the work of INI had been the very stuff of air force intelligence; now the few remaining analysts were reduced to military archeologists cataloging artifacts of a soon-to-be-forgotten Cold War.

Just then, Richard Harding sat studying the transcript of President Baker's Sunday night press conference that had come in over the Pentagon's open fax line. There were no surprises in the text; Harding had stood with Colonel Petrovsky and the junior officers in the hushed INI conference room at eight o'clock that evening to watch the live broadcast. But the president's words in print gave them a finality no broadcast could convey. Now Harding felt it was his life—not sheets of heat-sensitive paper—he held in his hands.

He rose from his desk, locked the office door, and went to the row of filing cabinets. He dialed the combination that opened the last cabinet and dug back behind the files until he found the pint bottle of Stolichnaya. He took a long, hard swig.

Time was, the vodka would have burned his throat and belly; years with a bottle behind the files had turned that sensation into a numbing, sliding glow. Time was, he'd get a knot like a fist in his gut when he was afraid; years in a Vietcong prison had taught his mind to put its fear away in some sequestered, secret pocket. But the body never forgot how to be afraid. That was the great lesson he'd learned as a prisoner of war: the mind might believe in a life everlasting, a holy redeemer, a risen Christ who would cleanse the soul of sin and resurrect it to paradise in a world without end. But the body believed only in a beating heart, an unbroken skin. The body wanted to live. It sweated and gagged and grabbed at life when it felt life slipping away. Shame burned in Harding where the vodka did not. He locked the bottle back in its hiding place, sprayed his mouth with Binaca, took the fax, and went out the door and up the stairs.

In his office on the third floor of INI, Colonel Steven Petrovsky had just found what he was looking for in the printout of the daily computer activity log. He circled the entry and looked up as Harding entered. "Yes, Dick? What is it?"

"Transcript of Baker's speech came in over the open line, sir." Harding laid the pages on the desk.

Petrovsky didn't reach for them. "What about it?"

Harding shrugged. "Dunno. Thought you might want it for a souvenir."

Petrovsky stared at Harding; he could smell the liquor on his breath, could see it in his furtive eyes. He had often seen that frightened look on Harding's face at Chu My prison. Whenever they heard the door open at the end of the prison block, whenever they knew the Vietcong guards were coming up the corridor with their long bamboo poles and the beatings were about to begin again, Harding's eyes would betray his fear. It was a fear Petrovsky understood. When a man knows he is going to be beaten and has no escape, when he has been beaten so many times that pain has become a habit, the winnowing dulls his sensibilities. Warmth and cold become, somehow, irrelevant; hunger and thirst, a trivial itch; escape, a worn-out fantasy; freedom, an impossible dream. A man who has been endlessly, repetitively beaten first loses his appetite for sex, then for food, then for conversation. Only the eyes go on making contact; perhaps because in others' eyes they see the mirror of their own pain. Or perhaps because by seeing other victims they remember they are human eyes in a human body—not merely an organism whose only function is to feel pain.

Now, Petrovsky looked up at Harding with pity and compassion. He, too, was weary of the pain they had shared, weary of the decades they had carried the flag, weary of the duty that would burden them to the grave. Since the signing of the INF treaty in 1987, Steven Petrovsky had felt this day approaching. For three years, he and a trusted few had prepared against this moment coming on. At eight o'clock that evening—at the very moment President Baker stepped before the television cameras to proclaim First Step—Petrovsky had set the plan in motion. The call to arms was on its way to Granger. In a few minutes, O'Neill would knock at Lieutenant Russoff's door. The clock was running. The time of words was over. The time of violence was at hand.

"Well, we've got him where we want him," Harding said. "I mean . . . if we really want to do anything about it." He leaned across the desk and pointed to the bottom of the fax.

BRIT HUME, ABC-TV: Mr. President, any plan to ease the federal deficit by reducing Pentagon spending is bound to be popular with Congress and the public. But is it true that Secretary of Defense Zack Littman and the Joint Chiefs vigorously oppose your so-called First Step initiative?
THE PRESIDENT: Let me just say this decision was taken after full and deliberate consultation with the Secretary of Defense and the Joint Chiefs. Norm?
NORMAN SANDLER, UPI: Mr. President, when you speak of trimming billions from the defense budget—
HUME: Excuse me, sir, but ABC News has learned from a highly placed Pentagon source that Secretary Littman described First Step as—and I'm quoting here—"the most notorious retreat of American power since Saigon, 1975." Would you care to comment on that?

THE PRESIDENT: Brit, I'm not going to comment on innuendos or insinuations from "unnamed" sources in the Pentagon or anywhere else. Norm?

SANDLER: Mr. President—

HUME: Sir, did your Secretary of Defense call First Step "notorious" or not?

THE PRESIDENT: I suggest you ask Secretary Littman. Norm?

HUME: Sir, when we tried to contact Secretary Littman, his office said he was on one of his convenient "fishing trips" on a yacht off Eleuthera where he can't be reached.

PRESS SECRETARY FOWLER: Brit, you're out of order. Norm has the floor. Norm, go ahead.

SANDLER: Mr. President—

HUME: Mr. President—yes or no? Did you order Littman to the Caribbean so he would be unavailable to comment on First Step?

"Yes," Petrovsky murmured. "We've got him where we want him." He swiveled in his chair and fed the pages into the paper shredder. The machine hummed and went silent; the fax of First Step had ceased to exist. But when he swiveled back, the printout of the daily computer activity log lay before him, one entry marked in red.

"So," Harding said. "What happens now?"

"Now?"

Harding shifted from foot to foot. "Yeah. I mean—you know—what's next?"

Petrovsky looked at Harding; the man who trembled before him was a poor, gaunt memory of a soldier, good for nothing to the nation or himself. So many had come home like that—their youth squandered and futures fouled in a despicable, misbegotten war.

What was next was something Petrovsky would have to do himself.

He rose from his desk and walked to the window. Three miles upriver beyond the navy yard, the dome of the Capitol glowed and the Washington Monument glistened in the nighttime sky. Petrovsky stared at the panorama. Whenever the battle seemed unwinnable, whenever the words of his oath of commission seemed about to slip from memory, whenever he remembered Chu My prison and the caustic stench of terror sweats and dried piss in his trousers, he turned to that vision and it restored his soul.

"Steve?" Harding said behind him. "What do you think?"

Petrovsky stared at the Capitol; a sad smile bent his mouth. After twenty-six years of service to the nation, it was time to give his final order. "I think the sun will come up tomorrow."

Harding's breath caught. "Steve . . ."

"You have your instructions, Colonel."

But Harding hesitated.

Firmly, but not ungently, Petrovsky said, "Colonel, you have things to do."

"Yes, sir." Harding went to the door. When he looked back, Petrovsky was still standing at the window, but his head was bowed in an attitude of prayer or meditation. "God bless you, sir."

"God bless America," Petrovsky said. "And all the gallant men who serve her."

When the door closed, Petrovsky went to his desk and unlocked the bottom drawer. He took out the .25-caliber automatic pistol and chambered a live round. Then he clicked the safety into place and put the weapon in his pocket.

NATIONAL DEFENSE OPERATING AREA W-105A, FLIGHT LEVEL 420

11:16 P.M. Navy Commander Cholly Granger snapped off the instrument lights in the cockpit of the F-14 Tomcat and gazed up through the canopy into the darkness of eternity. His solitary fighter shot through the night, steering toward the horns of the rising crescent moon, riding an electronic arc to nowhere. Somewhere eighty miles east and eight miles below on the choppy, mutinous Atlantic, the aircraft carrier *Kennedy* was turning into the wind, making thirty knots, her two steam catapults drawn like bowstrings, each cradling an F-18 Hornet fighter ready to climb to the attack.

Granger pushed back in his ejection seat. He was forty-five—over-age and overgrade for flight time; every six months he had to scrap like hell to hang on to his job as an instructor pilot, to continue flying practice missions out of Oceana Naval Air Station in Virginia Beach. After twenty-three years of faithful service, that was how the navy rated him: not a combat squadron leader, but a weapons systems instructor—a decoy, a radar blip, a human drone.

Behind him in the backseat of the Tomcat, Granger's student radar intercept officer, Lieutenant Peter Dolman, sat staring at the blank, green-glowing radar of the AWG-9 weapons system. Granger did his best to forget Dolman was there; the boy was new and skittish. The AWG-9 was the partner Granger relied on; it was an amazing little beast. At altitude, its radar could distinguish a fighter-sized target 125 miles away. That gave the Tomcat an edge over any aggressor aircraft. The cardinal rule of aerial combat was *see your opponent first;* no fighter in the world could see farther than the Tomcat.

The Grumman F-14 had achieved a certain celebrity after costarring with Tom Cruise in Hollywood's *Top Gun.* But the Tomcat and its awesome AWG-9 hadn't been designed for cinematic dogfights wing-to-wing. The plane's radar and computers were designed to guide the AIM-54C Phoenix, the navy's most powerful and lethal air-to-air missile with a range of almost one hundred miles. Phoenix flew far and fast—Mach 5.5, forty-one hundred miles an hour—faster than any plane or weapon in the sky. The air force had nothing like the Phoenix for their fancy F-15 Eagle; their long-range missile was the thirty-mile Sparrow and the experimental AMRAAM launch-and-leave. After all, the air force Eagle had been designed for combat in the tight skies over Europe. Over water, over ranges of more than fifty miles, the Tomcat and its Phoenix were supreme—power incarnate, the glory of American naval aviation—the long, sharp, deadly claws of the fleet.

But this Sunday night Granger's Tomcat carried only recording instruments and a Sidewinder heat-seeking missile simulator with a five-mile range. Tonight, the combat was a game. What the AWG-9 saw would be recorded for video replay and analysis tomorrow.

On the threat warning panel to Granger's right, the yellow RECEIVE light winked on and, in the rear cockpit, the IFF blinked red. The Tomcat had entered the *Kennedy* battle group's radar cap. Seventy miles east, a junior naval officer—a weapons director seated at a radar console in the dark, orange glow of the battle staff room of the Aegis cruiser *San Jacinto*—had detected the F-14 as an unknown; now the Aegis computer was querying the Tomcat for an electronic password that would identify it friend or foe.

"Cholly—"

"I see it, Mr. Dolman. Ident."

Dolman pressed the button on the IFF transponder and a long string of digital signals streamed into the night. In the battle staff room of the *San Jacinto,* the information flashed on the weapons director's radar screen along with data on the altitude, bearing, and speed of the Tomcat.

Dolman's voice rippled with excitement. "Won't be long now."

Granger laid his head back, stared out through the canopy. Beyond lay only darkness—the barren, true-black ionosphere where stars burned as unwinking points of light. He often flew night training missions now, skimming the corridor between the earth's atmosphere and the endless vacuum of space at five hundred knots—five hundred seventy-five miles an hour. He could feel the steady hum of the General Electric turbofans behind him. The intercom was set for hot mike, and he could hear Dolman's eager breathing.

According to the rules of tonight's exercise, the AWG-9's radar was buttoned down to five miles; for all intents and purposes, they were flying blind. It reminded Granger of his old F-4 Phantom and the days he launched from the *Enterprise* across the Tonkin Gulf and crossed the coast of Vietnam at Thanh Hoa, turning north and west in search of targets on the jungle roads below Hanoi. In formation with other navy fighter-bombers, he would bump along above the clouds, hidden from the North Vietnamese anti-aircraft crews below. That was before the Russian-made SAM-2s and SAM-3s began exploding upward through the mist. Then navy pilots had to learn a whole new tactic of evasion; the SAMs forced them down where they were vulnerable to ground fire and every sortie became a lethal game of hide-and-seek through knotty, nameless hills.

Granger's headset crackled. "Hey, Cholly. What's the story?"

"Which story?"

"Like—where are they?"

"Keep your pants on. They'll be by."

Granger turned the intercom volume down and peered into the night. To the west, the bright, three-starred belt of Orion hung—Orion the hunter who had challenged the Olympian gods with violence and was slain by them. Here at flight level 420—at the threshold of eternity with the bowl of stars bending above him—Cholly Granger gazed into the ineffable cold perfection of the hunter's world and knew tranquillity.

These moments made it worthwhile staying on in a navy shamed by Vietnam. Naval aviation command had made it sound like training new flying officers was a noble undertaking; in a way, it was. But it was not what Granger had declared for when he first pinned on his wings. It was not the thrill of combat, the dry mouth, the cramping legs, the terror of the shrieking blood. It wasn't war. It wasn't what a warrior had steeled for.

Granger's mind drifted to the carrier battle group forty-two thousand feet below. Dimly in his imagination, he could see the two Hornet fighters crouching on the *Kennedy*'s deck, their nose wheels bowed like knights before a benediction, flaps at full extension like medieval armor, their afterburners gleaming lance points. Then with a sudden bellow of steam the mighty catapults shot forward, flinging the tiny fighters toward the horizon, accelerating them to 170 miles per hour in two heartbeats. The Hornets rotated stabilators, presented underbellies to the dark. They cleared the deck and settled downward toward the choppy waves. Then their wings were filled with air and they rose on a majestic cannonade and vanished in the night.

The Tomcat's radar scope was empty. Granger glanced at the RADAR LOCK light; it was dark. The Hornets had all the advantages in this fight; they didn't have to turn their tracking radars on and transmit the signals that would disclose their flight. They could leave their onboard radars in standby mode while the Aegis data-link vectored them unerring to their quarry. The thin ionosphere hissed past the Tomcat's fuselage at $-44°$ Centigrade. There was no other sound except the droning of the engines. There was no way the Tomcat crew could know the intercept had begun.

But Granger knew. Far down below, through miles of empty air his inner ear heard the challenge of the Hornets' roar. His imagination saw the dagger points of flame they trailed against the murky, star-striped sea. Slowly, he leaned forward against the heavy harness of the ejection seat, cocked his head, and lidded-down his eyes. There was no looking now; eyes could be fooled by night and distance. He must listen—listen with the hunter's ear, the ear that hears the owl's silent flight.

Once again, he felt the telltale pricking on his face and fingers. Once again, his left fist tightened on the throttles and his right index finger closed around the trigger on the stick. He was alone now, aloft in a globe of darkness that knew neither up nor down nor earth nor sky. Only blackness. And a hunter's heart.

Granger shifted his left hand on the throttles, thumbed the Tomcat's wing sweep control to MANUAL and eased it back. The hydraulic system moaned, the twin screw actuators turned, the white tape on the wing sweep indicator slid down toward fifty-five degrees. Slowly and unseen—the way a cougar crouches—the fighter's wings tucked inward toward its belly. The F-14 began to lose its lift, began to sink. Gently, Granger eased the nose down by degrees, tipping down into the jungle of the night.

"Cholly? Are we going supersonic?"

But Granger didn't answer. His hunter's ear was listening to the darkness. He closed his fist around the throttles and cocked his wrist; his right thumb clicked the weapons button on the stick from GUNS to SW to select the AIM-9 Sidewinder heat-seeking missile simulator. Then he toggled the MISSILE COOLANT switch to ON. Pumps in the Tomcat's port launch rail began streaming liquid nitrogen to the seeker head of the dummy missile under the left wing, supercooling its infrared detector to identify targets against the empty sky. Granger flipped up the red-and-white striped safety, toggled the MASTER ARM to DOGFIGHT. Now the Tomcat had bared its fangs. Granger's pulse beat in his temples and his breath was damp inside his mask.

"Cholly . . ."

Then Granger slammed the throttles forward and lit all five zones of the F-14's twin afterburners. With the explosive kick of a mortar shell, the plane lurched forward, slamming him back into his seat. Like a mad black stallion, the beast screamed through the sound barrier and rocketed downward into the night.

Dolman gasped, "Jesus Christ!"

"We're engaged, Mr. Dolman."

"Chrissake—engaged with what?"

Just then, the green dots that were the climbing Hornets flashed across his radar screen.

The radio crackled, "San Jacinto—Seeker-one calling a Judy! Tallyho, Cholly! Tag, you're it!"

Granger cut the throttles, rolled, and dived. He craned his neck and looked over his shoulder to the six o'clock position; the sky was empty—the Hornets had flown past. Somewhere in the darkness they were turning in a tight circle to meet the Tomcat with a loose-deuce or a bracket. This was the moment of decision; he either had to run or turn back into combat.

"Aw, come on, Cholly," Dolman whined. "Aren't we gonna fight?"

"Never turn to fight, Mr. Dolman. Only turn to kill."

Granger yanked the stick back hard and climbed; the G-meter clicked past 4.0—four times the force of gravity—and the belly bladder of his G-suit filled with air, hardened tight against his gut, forced the blood upward into his chest and brain against a blackout. Now they were flying straight up and accelerating in full afterburner. He punched the radar scan to fifty miles. Projected on the heads-up display before him, two green dots marked the Hornets turning back to meet him, twenty-five miles away and closing at eight hundred miles an hour. Granger rolled through an Immelmann, swung defiant in their path. Abruptly, the Hornets broke high and low.

Granger recognized the tactic; it was the prelude to a bracket: an offensive split that forced the lone intruder to choose between two defenders. Once the F-14 committed to attack one of the Hornets, the free fighter would swing into a pincer that would trap the Tomcat in its sights.

There were only two ways to defeat a bracket. One was to flee. The other was to get the first kill quickly, then turn and take the free fighter coming head-on with a nose shot before he had a chance to lock and fire. In this maneuver, speed was life, and lifetimes were measured in seconds.

Granger didn't hesitate; he threw the stick hard left and jumped the leader. They had only moments to find a radar lock and fire before the Hornet's wingman could reverse and lock on them. The G-meter in the Tomcat spun to 5.0 and the air bladders of Granger's G-suit inflated like a rock-hard football in his gut. "Lock him up, Mr. Dolman."

The green dot danced back and forth across the glass plate of the heads-up display as the Hornet banked and dived in a frenzy to escape. Granger slammed the nose of the Tomcat toward the deck. The G-meter spun backward to -2.0. The Tomcat's cockpit rolled wildly, over and over, as the two planes corkscrewed downward toward the ocean at a thousand miles an hour.

"Easy now," Granger whispered. "There he is. Easy now." In the back of his mind he could see the other Hornet, its afterburners lit to zone five, pulling 9Gs as it swung onto the Tomcat's tail. But Granger could see the flame of the leader's exhaust now. He hung on like death.

Through the intercom he heard Dolman panting in terror. Poor boy; it took more than flight training to prepare a backseater to fly straight down toward an ocean he couldn't see with the throttle jammed open and the Tomcat accelerating toward twice the speed of sound.

"Be ready," Granger whispered. "Be ready."

Dolman shouted, "I'm on him!"

The F-14 came screaming down toward the tail of the fleeing Hornet. The two jets thundered toward the sea at thirteen hundred miles an hour. Then Granger heard the high-pitched whistle of the Sidewinder's seeker head lock.

The sea was rushing up at them like a black stone barrier. Dolman screamed, "I got him! Lock on at a mile and a half!"

Granger squeezed the trigger on the stick. "Fox two!" In his heads-up display the AWG-9 flashed the simulated launch; the leader was dead. "Now, let's get—"

Then the Hornet's wingman shot past. "Fox two!" he shouted through the headset. "Have a nice swim, Cholly."

Granger throttled back, rolled, leveled off at fifteen hundred feet. "Dolman—ah, lordy."

Then the leader broke in. "Hey, Cholly? Where you goin'?"

Granger toggled the radio. "Gonna pick a cloud and have a meeting. Stand by."

"Ah, the stratospheric woodshed. Standing by."

Granger half turned in his seat. "Dolman, didn't they teach you to keep the bandit's wingman in sight?"

"Guess I got excited. Sorry."

Granger shook his head. "God protect the United States of America."

The crackle in his headset was the voice of Oceana Base radio. "Viper-one, this is Oceana Base. Over."

"Viper-one. Oceana Base, I read you loud and clear." Granger smiled. "Engler, haven't I told you never to call me here?"

"Hey, Cholly. Since when are you lookin' for a transfer?"

Granger plucked at the front of his flight suit where it was sweated to his chest. "Transfer? Not me."

"Yeah? Well what do you call this? 'Request for transfer denied. Your important mission to train and equip—' "

"Must be the wrong Granger."

"No way, José. Got your service number on the dispatch and everything."

Granger glanced at the clock on the right instrument panel of the cockpit; the sweep second hand was ticking toward 0424 Zulu—11:24 P.M. "Shove it in my mailbox. I'll straighten it out with NAVPERS on Monday morning."

"That's the thing. It ain't from NAVPERS—it's from the air force."

Granger stiffened. "Oceana . . . say again?"

"It's from the fucking air force! Now hear this: 'The sun will come up tomorrow.' " Engler laughed. "You believe that? The fucker signs off, 'The sun will come up tomorrow.' Don't know who this Colonel Petrovsky is. But he's got one screwball sense of humor."

Granger knew. And he knew Petrovsky's summons beckoned to his death.

147 MARSHALL AVENUE,
BELLE HAVEN, VA

11:25 P.M.   The black Ford slid through the cold Potomac fog, glided to the curb, and stopped. Its headlights winked off and the car sat motionless in the yellow cone of light beneath the streetlamp.

Then the driver's door thunked open and a man in the uniform of an air force master sergeant stepped out. He was a young man—in his thirties, tanned and blue-eyed, hair a streaky, burnished blond. He was almost pretty—a recruiting poster in his crisp blue slacks and military windbreaker. But there was a power in the way he moved and stood— all neck and upper arms and shoulders—a limber, silky, silent power.

For a moment, he stood peering down the street. But the wintry night was still. He slipped his flight cap on, went to the passenger door of the car, and yanked it open.

A woman stepped out and straightened the jacket of her uniform. She was younger than the man—in her late twenties. She wore the single silver bars of a first lieutenant and the nameplate on her breast read RUSSOFF. She was small, and her miniature hands were quick as they touched each button of her jacket. There was a strangeness to her.

She was both fair and dark. Her skin was ivory, but her hair was the shade of black that sops light in its blackness. She had the wide, high cheekbones of the Caucasus, but her jawline narrowed sharply to her chin with spadelike angularity. Her eyes were large and black as mourning. But their corners were slitted down by epicanthic folds that made them deepset, dark, and Slavic.

"Thank you, Browning," the woman said, and pushed through the sagging wooden gate into the rear garden of the house.

"See you to your door, ma'am?"

Without acknowledging, she took the stone path toward the night-light glimmering in the icy fog. The old flagstones had been tipped this way and that by time and the Virginia rain; the woman had to pick her way. She was tired; it was almost midnight and Sunday had been a frantic day. But her walk was straight-backed, the walk of an officer.

At nine-thirty that morning, word had begun to trickle down the Pentagon grapevine that President Baker had called a Sunday night press conference to announce a new disarmament initiative. By 10:00 A.M., Lieutenant Christy Russoff and the other staff of INI had been recalled from their weekend recreation to prepare internal assessments of First Step for the air force chief of staff.

In a curious way, Christy had welcomed the recall and the urgency it carried. It brought back the exhilaration of those bygone Cold War days when the nation still feared the barbarians from beyond the Urals, the Pentagon budget thrived, and jingoistic movie-goers cheered *The Hunt for Red October*. Christy had been at Bolling Air Force Base only six months when the Berlin Wall came down in December of 1989 and crushed the sense of purpose out of INI; without the Red Menace from the East, the directorate became a command without a mission. By November of 1991, Christy's Intel work seemed like endless rounds of shadowboxing with an opponent who had no stomach for a fight. Except for Colonel Petrovsky and Lieutenant Colonel Harding waiting out their last years to retirement, only junior officers and a scattering of NCOs and civilian clerks were left at INI; with less than four years of active service, Christy was third in the decimated chain of command.

The Sunday morning recall had given Christy a lift, set her adrenaline to pumping. All day long, she had huddled with other analysts in intensive consultation. At dinnertime, when she carried the draft assessments of First Step upstairs to Colonel Petrovsky's office, she was startled by the man's worried, haggard eyes. As Christy and the other staffers gathered in the conference room to watch the president's press conference, she understood her colonel's concern. The Cold War was over; the Persian Gulf was history; America's NATO armies were coming home. How far behind was the budget-cutters' ax for INI?

Now it was almost midnight and Christy was weary of strategic problems. Her shoulders ached to be rid of her bra straps and her underwear was sticking to her skin; she wanted nothing more than a shower, a few precious hours' sleep. Around her in the winter garden, tangled skeletons of jasmine and bougainvillea clung to the old brick walls; two willows bowed their bony branches, mysterious and damp. At the end of the flagstone walk, the little clapboard house sat, its night-light beaming a welcome through the fog. As Christy reached the first step to the porch, Sergeant Browning caught her arm.

Startled, she gasped, "Don't!" and tried to pull away.

But he stepped close and turned her to him. "Stop worrying. Nobody can see us here." With one powerful hand, he drew her into the dark beneath the willow tree.

Under the arch of naked branches, the Virginia night was dank and still. He held her close to him, and she could feel the body heat beneath his shirt. She could smell the cigarettes and coffee on his breath, and the rough grain of his chin brushed her cheek as he bent and pressed his lips on hers. She started to say no, but then his tongue was in her mouth. His hand went to her jacket, cupping her breast, pressing the cold cloth down.

"Every day it gets harder to keep my hands off you in public," he whispered.

"Tod, it's late. I'm tired. We're back on duty at 0600—"

But he was already tugging her skirt over her hips, bunching it about her waist.

"Tod, please. What if my grandmother—"

His kisses stopped her.

Wearily, she lay her head against his shoulder, let him have his way. He was a man and he had needs; needed to feel desired, much as she did; needed to feel the power of his sex; needed to feel that underneath her air force blues and first lieutenant's bars there was a woman who wanted him. Once upon a time, she had.

On her first day at INI, Sergeant Browning had conducted her through the small brick building—the library, the active files, the translators' cubicles, the word processing workroom. It was the summer of 1989 and the District of Columbia was sweltering. Christy was twenty-six then—a second lieutenant fresh from six months at the Air Force Intelligence School at Goodfellow and a year at the Naval Postgraduate School in Monterey. INI at Bolling was her first assignment; it was the fulfillment of a dream that had begun when she earned the ROTC scholarship that opened the doors of college. After five years of college and graduate school at Harvard, after almost two years of Intel training, she was an officer joining her first command. And as she toured the Research and Soviet Studies directorate that morning, the very air seemed tuned by light. The prissy air force blue burned vivid. The dreary translators' workstations glowed like windows on a new reality. The humdrum of the duplicating machines thrilled her like the sound of bugles going by.

And yet, as Christy followed Sergeant Browning down the narrow corridors, she found herself staring at the dark patch of sweat just above the belt of his trousers. Somehow she imagined she could smell that sweat and feel his hairy forearms hard against her naked back. Later, when he conducted her to the director's office and she stood before Colonel Petrovsky for the first time since the graduation exercises in Monterey, she could sense Browning's presence in the corner of the room. She felt his eyes on her, felt them undressing her the way airmen's eyes undressed female officers. And she was startled to feel the muscles in her back and belly shifting to accommodate him. It was as though some stranger were stirring inside her—someone she neither knew nor recognized—an intruder with a wicked smile.

Now, sequestered in the icy damp beneath the willow tree, she felt his hand peel back her pantyhose, felt the cold air prick her skin. And the intruder stirred again.

"I want you," Todd murmured.

When his finger touched inside her, the intruder slithered like a snake.

Working at INI that first summer of 1989 began as an adventure, became an agony. As Christy translated the Soviet army newspaper *Red Star* and the naval journal *Potemkin,* she felt her Cold War enemy was near. She could hear him breathing in the thicket of red crayon language and *Pravda* doublespeak. She could see his Slavic face—with brooding, dark, half-lidded eyes much like her own—staring back from *Sovinform* photographs. There in the Cyrillic text of his ideas—where lines of type stood black against the page like hedgerows—Christy waged a silent, unforgiving war.

While she did, Sergeant Browning sat at his desk outside her office managing the mail and phone calls, coordinating briefings, scheduling due dates for translations. Christy tried to discipline herself against his narrow hips, the silky blond hairs on his arms, the musky odor of his aftershave. He was an enlisted man, she an officer; the rules were strict, the punishment severe. She became concise and terse, stern with him and sterner with herself. It was no use.

Whenever he reported to her, she couldn't help noticing how long his lashes were, the way the shadows undulated through the dimple in his chin, the way his shirt pulled hard across his shoulders when he bent to the filing cabinet. She felt a predatory instinct, a mannish urge she couldn't comprehend or master, as if something in her woman's soul was flawed, perverted, bent. She could see him from her desk and hear his voice and watch him when he went to the computer terminal. Every time he put a printout on her desk, she had to press her knees together. Whatever he awakened inside her would not be still, would groan and rage, was frenzied to be satisfied. Each day at work became an ordeal of desire; each night alone, a vigil. Weekends when she didn't see him, she spent in hell.

She tried diversions, dated everyone who asked: college friends who worked as GS-12s in State and DoD; Lieutenant Nikolai Dubinsky, the Chicago boy who translated Russian maintenance manuals; Captain Zeeman, the dentist at the base clinic. She had a desultory, brief affair with a Venezuelan naval exchange officer, Captain Xavier Contreras, who worked in Manpower Deployment at the Naval Annex behind the Pentagon.

It was useless. And she knew why.

None of them was Captain Bryan.

Christy had first met Bryan when she matriculated at the Naval Postgraduate School in 1988. The institute was a collection of Spanish-style, tile-roofed buildings alternately washed by Pacific fog and California sun—a fascinating interservice hodgepodge of blue and green and khaki uniforms—where specialists from every branch of the military studied the technology of war. In the company of young-and-coming officers from the army, navy, air force, and marines, Christy spent an academic year in a curriculum that opened her mind to the complex and tyrannical realities of modern warfare. The school granted master's and doctorate degrees in a long list of martial esoterica. It also granted a Master of Arts in National Security Affairs—the specialty in which Christy was enrolled.

Beginning with an examination of the Survey of Strategic Bombing of 1945—through four decades of nuclear weapons development and deployment—Christy studied the philosophy and logistics of deterrence, the lethal cat-and-mouse game of strategic threat and counter-threat, the zero-sum equation of mutually assured destruction. She also learned the enigmatic rubrics of the subtlest of all military sciences—intelligence—in a complex, mind-bending sequence of classes.

NS3150 Intelligence Systems and Products
NS3151 Intelligence Data Analysis
NS3280 Nuclear Weapons and Foreign Policy
NS3450 Soviet Military Strategy
SE4006 Technical Assessment and Intelligence Systems
NS4280 Seminar in Nuclear Strategy and Deterrence
OS3603 Simulation and War-gaming

But of all the courses Christy undertook in her year in Monterey, the most complex, cunning and insidious went by the unremarkable title of NS4152 Problems of Intelligence and Threat Analysis. Colonel Petrovsky had introduced her to the officer who taught the course; the tall, fair-haired, gray-eyed Captain Bryan became Christy's ideal of an officer—her ideal of a lover.

On graduation day, it ended—suddenly, abruptly—the way affairs in the military end. They both left Monterey forever; Christy to Bolling Air Force Base and INI; Bryan to a counterintelligence assignment in Europe.

Christy remembered how they stood together one last moment in the bachelor officers' quarters foyer, suitcases clustered at their feet, a taxi honking in the street below.

"I'll miss you," Bryan said, gentle and reserved, the way the whole affair had been.

"I'll miss you, too." Then Christy caught herself. "No. That's not true. I'm dying. I'm standing here and breathing—but I'm dying."

Then Bryan's arms encircled her. And Christy knew she'd never feel that powerful embrace again. She raised her face and whispered, "I'll never love another man."

"Yes, you will. And you'll lead men into battle."

Christy felt the muscles in her back pull taut; that was her dream—the dream that was impossible. "When?"

"When we say our last goodbye." Bryan looked down at her with gray, impassive eyes. "On the day, remember me."

Then Bryan bent and kissed her. That last kiss was a wound that wouldn't heal; Sergeant Browning was a kind of sterile dressing.

By December of Christy's first year at INI the Cold War was ending and the days grew short. Late one afternoon, she called Browning to her office.

"Yes, ma'am?" He stood inside her door, head cocked to hear her order.

She rose and went around the desk and put the key to a motel room in his hand. Browning looked at the key, at her. Then he went out.

That night Christy lay in the darkened motel room, listening to the whine and rumble of the semis on the interstate outside, tensing when their surging headlights slashed the curtains, fighting down the throbbing in her chest.

It was after nine when she heard the key in the door; the sound was a needle in her gut. When the door swung open, he stood a moment with the hallway lights behind him—a hulking shadow, faceless, dark, and primitive. She clutched two fistfuls of the sheet beneath her chin.

When he shut the door, she lay suspended in the blackness. She could hear his breathing and the sounds of his undressing—first the zipper, then the tinkle when his buckle touched the chair. With each sound, her desperation ratcheted another click toward panic. When he lifted the sheet she gasped and stabbed her hand across her breasts; when he slid in beside her, her breathing stopped.

She squeezed her eyes shut, tried to block out all sensation. It was eternity before he touched her—a dry, hard, calloused palm that grated on her nipple. She wanted to scream, to flee. She felt choked and sweaty cold and sick to retching.

Then a woman's voice whispered, "Use me."

That made Christy's eyes flick open.

She searched the dark for the intruder. But there was no one. Only him. And a woman she had just begun to know.

All through that night he butted at her, eagerly and gruffly. She was docile, silent, yielding in a way she'd never been. All the yanks and hurts, the goading weight, the vulgar slap of flesh—the lunging ugliness of intercourse she had detested—became a darkling revelation. And even when he stretched her sideways with her knee against his neck, even when he lit the bedside lamp and gloated as he plunged into her helpless belly, even when he forced her on her face and jackknifed her thighs against her breasts—even then she knew he wasn't using her.

She was using him.

Two years had passed since that night in the motel room. Now Christy was a first lieutenant—an intelligence officer with her whole career before her. Yet she was risking everything in an affair with an enlisted man. She knew that she was doing wrong. But the intrigue excited her—the danger was erotic, an antidote to the post–Cold War drudgework of INI. And it was the intrigue, not Tod Browning's touch, that stirred the intruder slithering through the icy damp beneath the willow tree.

He panted, "Chris—I want you—"

"How much?"

He pressed her shoulder, tried to push her down.

But she stood rigid, fought him. "That's not an answer. Tell me."

Trembling, he moaned.

She pushed him away, straightened her clothing. "All right. In the house. Come on." Then she swept through the rattling tips of willow branches and marched up the porch steps without looking back.

He would follow.

From his vantage point in the misty shadows beyond the picket fence, Colonel Tom O'Neill watched the couple slip into the house and shut the door. He turned his wristwatch to the streetlamp's glow: 11:29 P.M.—0429 Zulu—5:29 A.M. in Geneva. Even now, the call to arms was flashing through the silent night above the North Atlantic. In a few minutes, the struggle would begin; the sun would come up tomorrow and by eleven o'clock it would be over.

But for the moment there was no hurry. O'Neill stepped back into the fog. The lieutenant was young and pretty; let her love while there was time.

She could not know what she had been trained for.
She could not dream her day had come.

30 ROCKEFELLER PLAZA, NEW YORK CITY

11:30 P.M.   Tom Brokaw settled behind the anchor desk, snugged his tie knot to his collar and stared out into the darkened newsroom. He was bone-tired. Sunday was supposed to be a day off.

That morning, he'd gone out the door of his apartment before first light and hit the FDR Drive north to the Deegan among the spotty predawn traffic. By sunrise, he was crossing the Tappan Zee Bridge to where the New York Thruway followed the west bank of the Hudson River into rural Ulster County. At 8:00 A.M., he was sitting in the pine-paneled Victorian dining room of the Mohonk Mountain House in New Paltz, chewing breakfast and planning the day's climb in the Shawangunk Mountains.

Rock-climbing was Brokaw's weekend passion; like the bicycle he rode down Fifth Avenue every workday when it didn't rain or snow, climbing was a way of keeping touch with the real world. To a news anchor who earned more than a million dollars a year, a climber's calloused hands and aching shoulders were a useful reminder that a man—even a world-famous television anchorman—is a human animal who emerges briefly from the dust only to return.

Brokaw was halfway up the east face of the craggy Adirondack shelf called the Trapps when the beeper on his belt sounded. From the radio telephone at the park ranger station, he reached Mike Marden, the president of NBC News, in his third-floor office at 30 Rockefeller Center.

"Mike—what's up?"

"President Baker's called a press conference for eight o'clock."

"Tonight?" Brokaw sighed; he knew what was coming.

"You're on with a half-hour *Special Report* at eleven-thirty."

"Can't Garrick handle it?" Garrick Utley anchored the Sunday *Nightly News*; he was a seasoned reporter, but he was no Tom Brokaw.

"Sorry, pal. Russert called from our Washington bureau. He thinks Baker's going to make a major policy statement on NATO."

"Doesn't Baker know it's Sunday?"

"That's the whole idea. He's trying to quash the instant analysis.

The newsweeklies and morning papers have already gone to bed. Monday's Veterans Day—perfect day for the country to be thinking disarmament."

"Anything on what Baker's going to say?"

"Blackout. Playing this one real close to the vest."

"Did Russert talk to Fowler?"

"Not returning calls."

"What about your White House buddy, Harris?"

"Ditto. And Secretary of Defense Littman is incommunicado. On one of his 'fishing trips' off Eleuthera, would you believe? The thing's been orchestrated like a symphony."

Brokaw grumbled; since the rapprochement with the Soviets began, the president and his top defense official were constantly at odds over cuts in Pentagon spending. Littman's fishing trips to the remote Caribbean island of Eleuthera were a standing joke among the Washington press corps. Brokaw checked his watch. "Want to grab some dinner if I get back to town on time?"

"Wish I could," Marden said. "Got my in-laws here all day. Buy you a belt at the Festival when you get off the air?"

"Done."

Now it was 11:30 P.M. and Brokaw sat at the anchor desk, trying to focus bleary eyes on the lighted rectangle of the TelePrompTer. The last bars of John Williams's NBC News theme were building to a crescendo in his earphone. Somewhere in the darkness a stage manager's voice was counting, "In five . . . four . . . three . . . two . . ."

Brokaw looked up at the TelePrompTer, blinked his eyes clear, and took a beat as the music rang out. Then the stage manager waved his hand and the copy began to roll.

BROKAW
(on camera)
Good evening. I'm Tom Brokaw with an NBC News *Special Report*. At an extraordinary Sunday night press conference President Baker stunned the nation and our European allies . . .

In the control room the TD shouted, "Roll VTR-1!" and a tech in the tape room next door hit the PLAY button.

. . . with an announcement that he had ordered American troop strength in NATO reduced to fifty thousand men . . .

The TD counted down, "Four . . . three . . ."

> . . . and had offered the Soviets a zero-option agreement that would eliminate sea-launched nuclear cruise missiles from the arsenals of both nations.

(cue tape)

OVAL OFFICE, THE WHITE HOUSE, WASHINGTON

11:31 P.M.   It was just then—just as Tom Brokaw was turning his head to cue the videotape of the president at the White House press room podium—that Ted Harris and Sam Baker settled into the two wing chairs before the television set at the far end of the Oval Office. The networks' late news specials were "must" watching; the Sunday night broadcasts would set the tone for the public debate of First Step that would begin on Monday morning.

"Looks like Brokaw's playing it straight," Harris said. "Let's check out ABC." He zapped the set to channel 7. Ted Koppel sat at the anchor desk before the chromakeyed image of Congressman Les Aspin, chairman of the House Armed Services Committee. "That answers that. Going for the jugular."

Sam Baker folded his arms across his chest; Koppel was one of the great questioners—a television news provocateur who would probe hard to find flaws in First Step.

"In the warm afterglow of improved Soviet-American relations and the stunning victory of Operation Desert Storm," Koppel said, "President Baker has made it plain he wants U.S. forces out of Europe *now*. But why is the president so eager? America's commitment to NATO has kept the peace on that continent for forty-five years. Can we really be certain the Soviet Union has abandoned its historic commitment to world revolution? Or has America's federal deficit and pressure from our international trading partners replaced NATO as the balance of power?"

Koppel turned to Aspin. "Mr. Chairman, is First Step—as President Baker would have us believe—a courageous first step toward permanent European stability? Or is it, as some senior military analysts allege, a first step toward a Europe in which Russia is the only superpower?"

Harris muttered, "Sonofabitching demagogue."

Sam Baker put his hand on Harris's. "Easy, Ted. Aspin can handle that."

"The American people want reductions in our military spending," Aspin said. "President Baker promised he could achieve that—once the START1 and European security treaties were in place."

The intercom sounded; Harris rose and crossed to the president's desk, sat down and picked up the phone. "Yes? All right. Send him in." He hung up. "Whitworth's here."

"Good."

"Now, the president has his treaties," Aspin said. "The last Soviet troops will be gone from Germany by 1993. Gorbachev says the Cold War is over, and our Japanese bond holders are demanding a peace dividend."

The door of the Oval Office opened. Senator Simon Whitworth, Chairman of the Senate Armed Services Committee, stepped inside. Like Sam Baker, Whitworth was an old man—over seventy—in an old-fashioned three-piece suit. A watch hung in his breast pocket from a thin gilt chain in his lapel. He stood just inside the door, his back ramrod straight.

Aspin said, "As long as America retains a sufficient nuclear missile deterrent to neutralize any Soviet strategic threat, First Step is a good idea whose time has come."

Harris snapped off the television set.

Sam Baker rose. "Simon, thank you for coming at this hour."

"Not at all, sir."

Stiffly, they shook hands. Then they took the chairs before the fireplace.

The president nodded at the television set. "You saw that?"

"Yes."

"If Les Aspin can support First Step, why can't you?"

"I'm not the only man in Congress who opposes First Step, Mr. President."

"I know that, Simon. But if we don't seize this opportunity—"

"Mr. President, you're rushing things."

Sam Baker sat back. "Simon, I'll ask you point blank. Will you go along with an American NATO garrison of fifty thousand men?"

"No."

"Why not?"

Whitworth measured the president. "Mr. President, I campaigned for you twice. And I respect you. But First Step is dangerous. And I oppose it."

"Is that what you're going to say on the *Today* program tomorrow morning?"

"If they ask me, yes."

"What makes you so sure I'm wrong?"

"Mr. President," Whitworth said softly, "what makes you so sure you're right?"

The president turned to Harris. "Ted, could you excuse us, please?"

When the door closed, Sam Baker's tone changed. "Dammit, Simon, you know as well as I do there are no guarantees. We have to make the hard choices now or we'll never get the budget deficit under control."

Whitworth laced his fingers. "Talk plain, Sam. What are you asking me to do?"

"Back me. Give First Step a chance. Call it a reasonable doubt. We'll work through it together."

"I can't."

"Simon, the country's wallowing in recession. We've got to stop wasting billions on an army that will never fight in Europe and nuclear cruise missiles we'll never use. Think of your own state. Think of the farmers who—"

"I am thinking of them. And of their children." Whitworth reached out, put his hand on the president's knee. "Sam, forgive me for saying this. You and I—we're old men now. We feel the future slipping through our fingers."

Sam Baker started to reply. Then he hesitated.

Whitworth was right. Sam Baker was the president. But he was also old and near the limits of his power. From 1984 to 1989—through the last six dogged years of the Cold War—he had borne the nation and the Western allies in pursuit of fleeting peace. In December of 1989— just when Sam Baker's patience was exhausted at grasping after ghosts—a crack had miraculously appeared in the Iron Curtain; throughout the free world, governments and peoples were swept with hope that a millennium of global peace and international cooperation had begun. Then in rapid succession a brutal series of events in the Middle East had dealt the world—and the American economy—a numbing blow.

By the spring of 1991—in the face of spiraling economic pressures—Sam Baker found he had alarmingly little room to maneuver. If he lowered interest rates, he would fuel inflation. If he strengthened the dollar, he would exacerbate the nation's ruinous imbalance in foreign trade. War jitters had curtailed consumer spending and sent unemployment soaring. But the president could not move his administration too quickly toward austerity, because that might jar investors' fragile faith in the stock market; if that happened, there could be an economic aftershock that would sweep the country into a depression.

First Step was a breakthrough idea, a miraculous prescription for the nation's fiscal ills, a wonder drug that promised quick relief without harmful side effects. America's NATO forces represented almost half the Pentagon's annual budget—$150 billion. And NATO *was* a Cold War hangover, a vestigial counterforce to a threat that no longer existed. Clearly, the one best way to cut the Pentagon budget without paying a price in preparedness was to reduce the American presence in NATO, reallocate some military assets to a new rapid-deployment force and pocket billions in savings.

In economic terms, First Step was a tourniquet that would stanch the flow of the nation's precious resources.

In geopolitical terms, it was a timely masterstroke.

And yet as Sam Baker sat in the wing chair in the Oval Office, he knew Simon Whitworth was not entirely wrong; in military terms, First Step was a calculated risk.

And a risk was *always* a risk.

"The Soviet Union is going through its greatest period of instability since the revolution of 1917," Whitworth said. "We can't forget what history has taught us about governments in turmoil. The collapse of the Weimar Republic after the First World War brought the Nazi brown-shirts to power in Germany. In the past ten years, political unrest has triggered military coups from Cambodia to Chile to Nicaragua to Zaire. Every time the social order of a nation dissolves into chaos, it's the army that steps into the vacuum."

"Simon, what are you saying?"

"I'm saying *stop*, Mr. President. Stop what you're doing. The Russian government isn't stable. If Gorbachev falls and the conservatives seize power, anything could happen over there. The Soviet military could get out of control. There could be civil war. First Step is dangerous. You're moving too fast."

In the silence that followed, neither man stirred.

"Simon, is that your final word?"

Whitworth straightened his spine. "I'm sorry, Sam," he said.

In his cubicle beside the Oval Office, Ted Harris sat at his desk, arms folded, brooding. The flickering blue light from the television set carried the image of Sam Baker at the press room podium.

THE PRESIDENT

Under the terms of the START1 treaty, we and the Soviet Union retain a sufficient strategic missile deterrent to guarantee the security of our respective nations. Now, it remains for one side to take a first step toward reducing its massive standing armies. I believe this nation should take that first step—boldly and without equivocation—by reducing our NATO forces to reasonable peacetime levels. If we and the Soviets are to continue down the path of peace together, this nation must take that first step now.

It was a reference to reducing America's NATO forces that had triggered Secretary of Defense Zack Littman and the shouting match at the National Security Council meeting in the White House's Roosevelt Room on Friday.

"Fuck our Japanese bond holders!" Littman shouted.

Sam Baker slapped his open palm down on the table. "Mr. Secretary, you forget yourself!"

"The hell I do!" Littman got up from his chair and stomped away from the table. He was a combative, slick-haired, knobby little man—an NRA member and meat-hunter from Wyoming. He had been a partner in Sam Baker's Washington law firm. He had been best man at Sam Baker's wedding. He was the best friend Sam Baker had—would ever have—and he was a tough little sonofabitch who could eat nails with the army. He was a man whose opinion Sam Baker could not ignore.

"Give the Soviets a START treaty," Littman said. "Give them billions in economic aid. Hell, give them the fucking Washington Monument if you want to. But, goddammit, don't back away from NATO!"

Secretary of State Arthur Coleman sighed. He was a pragmatist like George Schultz before him—cool headed, goal directed, a doer; he was a man who measured progress by achievement, not rhetoric. "Zack, you know the strategy as well as we do. The START treaty leaves us an effective strategic missile deterrent. Now we've got to cut our conventional forces in Europe and shift the burden of NATO to the Europeans. Either we do that or we go on spending until the Japanese cash in their bonds and buy the White House and kick us out on our ass."

Littman stood in silence as the good-natured chuckling washed over him. The financial cost of America's commitment to NATO had become the bugbear of the budgeteers. Since the triumph in the Persian Gulf, every congressional attack on the federal deficit began and ended with the half of the Pentagon budget that went to maintain an enormous force of men and weapons in Europe. By contrast, the nation's strategic missile deterrent—its land-based Peacekeepers and submarine-based Tridents—required low manning levels, little maintenance and less than ten percent of Pentagon spending to keep the weapons operational. To the economic planners of the 1990s, the intercontinental ballistic missile was a far more attractive and cost-effective deterrent than an American armored division in Germany.

"Look, gentlemen," Littman said. "We can't stake the strategic defense of the free world on half the ballistic missile warheads we had in 1990. Whatever your beloved START treaty didn't eliminate, it ratified, including research and development. The Soviets are building two new generations of intercontinental missiles—the SS-24 and SS-25. They're modernizing their SS-18 and planning—"

Brent Scowcroft, the president's national security adviser, didn't wait for him to finish. "And we're deploying the Trident II. So what?"

"Brent, you have an uncanny knack for never seeing the forest for the trees."

"Drop dead, Zack," Scowcroft said.

Vice President Charlie O'Donnell put his hand back through his shaggy white hair. "Zack, what are you saying? That deterrence doesn't work?" O'Donnell was a red-faced bear of a man who had spent his whole life in Congress; he had been Speaker of the House when Sam Baker chose him as his running mate in 1984. Charlie O'Donnell knew more about ward-heeling than strategic weapons, but he was no fool. "Strategic nuclear weapons have kept the peace for forty-five years. Europe hasn't had a continuous peace like that since the eleventh century."

"Sure, the deterrent works, Charlie. But only as a backup to our armies." Littman came to the end of the table and rested his palms on it. "Gentlemen, listen to me. And listen carefully. The end of the Cold War isn't the end of the journey—it's just another crossroad. The intercontinental ballistic missile you're so fond of is the dumbest weapon since the arrow. Once launched, it flies on a fixed trajectory to a fixed target. Its capacity to terrify the enemy is based on just that—its dumb, blind power to thunder into the sky and level cities seven thousand miles away. But its dumbness eliminates our options.

Fire one missile"—he held a finger in the air—"fire one missile and
you bring down a rain of Armageddon on the entire world."

Slowly, Littman began to walk around the table. "But our conventional forces are men. They can think. They can react to the unex-
pected with judgment." He stopped and rested his hand on the back
of Secretary Coleman's chair. "Once our NATO armies are disbanded
. . . once our air bases in Europe are turned into shopping centers and
go-cart tracks . . . once we've eliminated the human element from our
strategic defense, we will have no strategic defense."

"Zack, stop it," Scowcroft said sharply. "This is sophistry. We'll
have the missiles."

"The missiles can't be fired."

"What? Of course they can be fired. Jesus Christ. . . ." Scowcroft
turned his face away.

Littman leaned across the table. "Look at me, Brent." And when
he did, Littman said, "The missiles *cannot* be fired. And I'll tell you
why. Because if, god forbid, the day ever came when we had to fire
them, who would push the button?"

He looked at the president; then he pointed at him. "You?"

He pointed at O'Donnell. "You?"

He pointed at Coleman. "You?"

The three sat uneasily under his stare.

"No, gentlemen. We cannot stake the strategic defense of the free
world on a weapon no one in this room, no one in his right mind, no
one but a madman would employ."

Littman stood, waiting for a reaction. There was none.

"All right, Zack," Sam Baker said. "You've had your say. Sit
down."

"Mr. President—"

"I said, sit down!"

Littman went back to his seat.

"You're the one who's lost sight of the stakes we're playing for. This
is not a military issue. It's a political issue. And it's the most important
political issue of our time." Sam Baker pushed his chair back. "If we
want the Cold War dead and buried, we've got to help Gorbachev stay
in office and keep the pressure off him."

The president rose and paced toward the end of the room. "You
didn't talk to the man when we went to Moscow. You don't know
what he's going through." He glanced at Littman. "You think *we've*
got money problems with Congress and the Japanese? Gorbachev's
trying to start a consumer economy from scratch before the lid blows

off in his republics. He's *got* to cut military spending. Hell, the reform governments in the Warsaw Pact did him a favor by kicking his tanks out. They're making his troop reductions for him. The man couldn't keep two hundred fifty thousand soldiers in Eastern Europe even if he wanted to."

"And what happens if Gorbachev gets bounced?" Littman wasn't backing down. "In 1960, Khrushchev announced bigger cuts than Gorbachev. He said the same thing you're saying now—once they built the rockets, their air force and navy lost their importance. Khrushchev mustered a million men out of the Soviet army and pulled fourteen divisions out of the Warsaw Pact. Four years later, he was locked in a dacha on the Black Sea without a telephone and Brezhnev was building an army of five and a half million men and fifty-three thousand tanks."

Coleman snorted. "Are you saying Gorbachev's in danger of a coup? Come on, Zack—every time anyone in the Politburo disagrees with him, they wind up running a tree farm in Siberia."

"Arthur, be realistic. A ten-year-old can see the man's skating on thin ice. His famous *perestroika* hasn't accomplished anything for the average Russian except to triple the price of sausage and cheese. *Glasnost* cost them their Eastern European empire and got Boris Yeltsin elected president of the Russian SSR. Gorbachev had to send twenty thousand troops to Baku to keep the Azerbaijanis from seceding. He's flirting with civil war in Armenia. He had to send tanks into Vilnius and shoot down innocent civilians to keep the Lithuanians in line."

"You're making my point," Sam Baker said. "The Red Army acted without authorization in Lithuania."

"No, Sam. You're making *my* point. What happens if the Red Army decides Gorbachev needs a permanent vacation in the Crimea?"

No one moved to reply. It was *the* question. And every man in the room dreaded the answer.

The Soviet government had a long and twisted history of tension with its military. When Lenin had attempted to expropriate grain from the peasants in 1921, sailors at Kronshtadt had mutinied. The insurrection spread through the Soviet Baltic fleet and threatened to engulf the fledgling communist nation. When Lenin ordered the Red Army to quell the rebellion, more than ten thousand soldiers died. Fifteen years later in 1936, Stalin unleashed a series of purges that systematically exterminated ninety percent of the USSR military leadership. Even today the borders of the Soviet Union and the Red Army's own munitions depots were not guarded by regular troops but by the secret police of the Ministry of Internal Affairs—the dreaded MVD. The vaunted Soviet Strategic Rocket Forces' nuclear keys, codes and triggers were controlled not by Red Army generals, but by the KGB. Now the Soviet Union was going through its greatest time of economic and political upheaval since 1921—and the specter of the Kronshtadt mutiny dogged the Politburo's heels. At the Communist party conference in Moscow in July, the glowering brown-suited generals of the Soviet Stavka and the six million troops they commanded had emerged as the driving force behind the hard-line conservative effort to control Gorbachev and his reforms.

A military coup by the armed forces of the United States might be inconceivable. But to the Soviet Politburo—to the heirs of Lenin, who had lost ten thousand soldiers suppressing the Kronshtadt mutiny— the Red Army was a ferocious guard dog that might someday again turn on its master.

"Mr. President," Littman said, "if Gorbachev's political situation deteriorates, if his generals decide to take things into their own hands, if the Politburo loses control of Soviet armed forces . . . there could be hell to pay. You pull our troops out of NATO and I guarantee you a neutral Europe under a Soviet thumb by the year 2000."

The room was silent.

Then, softly, Sam Baker said, "We'll have to take that chance, Zack. The reality is we can't afford to keep them there."

Littman looked down the table. The consensus was against him, and it was unshakable. "Mr. President, listen to me." There was desperation in his voice. "We can't afford not to."

Now, Ted Harris sat alone in his office waiting for the intercom to summon him back into conference with the president. He knew what Sam Baker would tell him: that Simon Whitworth would do everything in his power—everything the Senate Armed Services Committee chairman could do—to thwart, delay, confound, stifle, hamper, impede, and ultimately dash First Step. It would be a fight—a desperate fight. But it was a fight that must be won.

147 MARSHALL AVENUE,
BELLE HAVEN, VA

11:41 P.M. She had Russian eyes. The school children in Trenton, New Jersey, had called her Piggy Eyes and Squinty. The words had stung, had sent Christy Russoff running to her grandmother in tears. But the taunting had ended when Christy reached her teens. Then her baby fat turned into breasts and hips, and something erotic began to smolder in her black, half-lidded eyes. Then the girls began to envy her straight black hair, the milky skin that never pimpled. And the boys began to call.

Now, by the dim light of the bedside lamp, Christy lay in the tangled aftermath of sex—the damp sheets coiled across her thighs, the bedroom resonant with Tod's heavy breathing, and the yammer of Tom Brokaw from the television set that had drowned his grunts of ecstasy. She lay supine, her tangled hair strewn like coal dust across the pillow, her pubis black and shiny with perspiration. Between the fringes of her eyelashes, through the narrow slits of epicanthic folds, the night-light glistened on an inward darkness.

She had the sense of her vagina. Three days each month when she was ovulating, she could feel her ovaries—two taut burning knots between her hipbones. On winter mornings when she shrugged her shift around her ankles and the cold air touched her body, she could feel her nipples tighten. Only Tod and Tampax reminded her of her vagina.

It was the way he took her—ramlike, like a goat. He was the kind of lover women crooned for: masterful, thorough, tireless, unfettered, venturesome, and hard. She'd had to grow in sex to encounter him at all his levels. But, somehow there was no art to it. Because there was no guile. He was as blunt in bed as he was in the office; he was no Captain Bryan.

While she and Tod had coupled—while the television droned Tom Brokaw's rehash of the president's press conference so her grandmother could sleep on undisturbed—Christy's mind had drifted back to her first night in Bryan's arms in Monterey. The seduction had begun in her second week of classes—first intellectually, then in the way of counseling and friendship, then with a touch, a hint, a look, a sigh. And then one rainy night beside a flickering driftwood fire—against all military law, against her oath, against all logic—she had let Bryan guide her to the narrow bed in the BOQ. There, Christy had found a delicacy that surpassed her understanding. There, in a quiet that made every breath a peal of thunder, with a touch like pearls in oil, with a patience that mocked her lust and tormented her desire, Bryan had brought her to orgasmic paroxysms unlike any she had known. Together, they had made that year in Monterey a conspiracy of love.

Discovery would have meant a formal reprimand, dismissal from the school, the ruin of their careers and, worse, irrevocable separation. By stealth, by pretense, and deception they had survived and carried on. Fear of detection had driven them together as much as lust, had taught them to communicate with glances, to express a world of secrets with hints and feints and innuendos. Even more than her classwork in intelligence, the illicit affair had trained Christy's mind to stealth and cunning. By graduation day, intriguing had become a habit, collusion an erotic vice.

Now Tod slept. The television chattered on. Outside Christy's bedroom the Virginia suburb lay still and dark in the embrace of wintry night. And Christy dreamt of the elegant, towheaded Bryan—the gray, impassive eyes beside hers black as anthracite, the fair hair white against the blackness of her own, the gentle arms that could engulf her smallness and the—

"*Marianka? Marianka, eto ty tam?*"

Christy sat up abruptly at the sound of her grandmother's voice outside the door.

Tod stirred and mumbled, "Wha—"

Christy clutched his arm and held him silent.

"*Marianka, ty tam? Gde ty?*" Her grandmother's voice was anxious, almost fearful.

Christy swung her legs down, pulled her robe about her shoulders. "Tod, get dressed. Hurry!"

He grabbed his trousers. "What's the—"

"*Marianka! Polkovnik O'Neill xochet govorit s toboi!*"

Christy froze.

Tod stopped fumbling with his belt. "Chris, what is it?"

"Quiet!" Quickly, Christy tied the bathrobe at her waist. As brightly as she could, she called, "*Vot ya zdes, Babushka,*" and opened the bedroom door a crack.

Her grandmother stood in the hallway—a weathered Slavic woman in an embroidered caftan, her pale skin carved deep with years, her eyes, like Christy's, slits of darkness.

"*Babushka? Chevo on khochet.*" Then Christy stiffened like a rod.

Behind her grandmother, Colonel Tom O'Neill stood staring.

Christy blinked and caught her breath and realized she had stepped into a nightmare.

" 'Evening, Lieutenant," O'Neill said. "Sorry to disturb you." He was an aging Irishman with florid, pudgy cheeks and quick blue eyes and quicker laugh; a week after Christy had reported to INI, Colonel Petrovsky had introduced them. There was something fatherly about O'Neill and Christy liked him. But he wore three slashes of campaign ribbons that retold the agony of Nam.

Just then Tod's face appeared in the doorway. "Hey, Chris. What's—" He stopped dead with his uniform shirt half on.

Christy's grandmother gasped; her hand went to her mouth.

O'Neill roared, "Step out here, you!"

Barefoot, tucking his shirttail into his trousers, Tod pushed out into the hall. O'Neill looked him up and down, and there was acid in his greeting. "Good evening . . . *Sergeant.*"

Tod braced. "S—sir."

Christy drew a breath, drew up her courage. "Sergeant, go back into the bedroom."

O'Neill glared at her. "You're at attention, Lieutenant!"

"Yes, sir." Her eyes lay steady on O'Neill's and her voice was calm, authoritative. "Sergeant, this doesn't concern you. Go back into the bedroom—*now.*"

Confused, Tod looked back and forth between the officers.

Then an odd smirk turned the corner of O'Neill's lip. "All right, Sergeant. Go on. Get dressed."

Tod stepped into the bedroom and shut the door.

For a moment, O'Neill studied Christy, then he nodded, satisfied. "Colonel Petrovsky told me you were bold." He took an envelope from his jacket pocket. "Your colonel has an errand for you."

"Now, sir? Tonight?"

"Right now."

Christy unfolded the typewritten message and scanned the instructions. Her eyes fixed on the last sentence above Petrovsky's signature. "And I should tell her—"

"Her," O'Neill broke in sharply. "And no one else. That is an order. Do you understand?"

Christy started at the harshness in the colonel's voice. O'Neill's quick blue eyes were still and hard; behind them, she could sense a tension in his neck and shoulders.

"Do you understand?" he said again.

"Well—yes, sir."

O'Neill smiled and put his hat on. "Then goodnight, Lieutenant."

He nodded to her grandmother. "Sorry for the inconvenience, ma'am." He went down the hall and let himself out.

Christy stared after him. Then she glanced back down at the last sentence of Colonel Petrovsky's order.

The sun will come up tomorrow.

Strange.

Hi Robert!

4 RUE CHARLES CUSIN, GENEVA, SWITZERLAND

5:45 A.M.   The embassy courier who yanked the rusty bellpull of the old brick townhouse did not know what the envelope contained. Nor did the sleepy concierge who peeked through the grating in the tall oak door. But she took the envelope directly upstairs and rapped at the bedroom door. Jake Handlesman was already wearing his yarmulke and tallis over his pajamas in preparation for his morning prayers; he set aside his leather pouch of phylacteries, opened the door, and accepted the envelope. He knew what it contained.

After forty years as a strategic arms negotiator, it was hard to hit Jake Handlesman where he wasn't looking. He was too well connected, had amassed too many favors owed, had plowed too many back channels to be taken unawares by a policy decision as crucial as First Step—no matter how the administration conspired to keep it secret. For more than a year, he and certain others had privately weighed the options facing a president squeezed between a recessive economy and the rising cost of the nation's defense. A month ago, as the president moved toward a decision on First Step, discreet measures had been put in place to prevent a foreign policy fiasco. Last night—while the other members of the START delegation sat anxiously watching the president's press conference on CNN at 2:00 A.M. Geneva time—Jake slept a fitful sleep. Now, the messenger had come. For Jake Handlesman, the envelope contained no news.

He shut the door and locked it—the punctilious habit of all men who live their lives amid state secrets. Then he flicked on the bronze art nouveau lamp and sat in the circle of light on the edge of the bed. He was an old man—over seventy—with yellow, rheumy eyes and a beard the color of dirty snow. In pajamas, old blue slippers, and his careworn, threadbare tallis, there was an air of the ghetto about him: his skin waxy as mottled parchment, his breathing halt with decades of muttered prayers, his yarmulke floating on a scruff of wispy hair. It seemed as though eternity waited at his shoulder, impatient, marking time.

Jake tore the double seals of the envelope, put on his half-frame reading glasses, and gingerly leaned against the pillow. His back had begun to ache again; for two weeks now it had troubled his sleep. He gently settled himself, held the document under the lamp, and tilted his head to ease the words of the president's opening statement into focus.

PRESIDENT BAKER: Under the terms of the START1 treaty, we and the Soviet Union have set a timetable for reducing our respective arsenals of strategic nuclear missile warheads by as much as fifty percent. The implementation of this treaty will dramatically reduce the threat of nuclear war. It has already opened a new era of superpower cooperation and set the stage for reducing our conventional forces.

Jake sighed and shook his head; politicians not only made history, they rewrote it. President Baker had begun his preamble to First Step by making the START treaty's fifty percent reductions sound like a miraculous new panacea of peace. In fact, it was old George Kennan who had first championed the fifty percent formula in 1981 when he had accepted the Albert Einstein Peace Prize. Jake smiled at the irony; in 1947, George Kennan had authored America's first Cold War manifesto—the Doctrine of Containment—the principle of armed encirclement that had remained the belligerent policy of the United States toward the Soviet Union until 1989. Who could have imagined the architect of the Cold War would live to win a peace prize named for the mathematician who had fathered the most lethal weapon in history?

But, then again, who could imagine that a species that had contrived the means of its own annihilation would invest trillions of dollars to perfect the weapon? Paradox upon paradox; all roads through the nuclear maze began and ended in paradox.

Jake's eyes drifted upward from the telex to the intricate nineteenth-century plasterwork on the bedroom ceiling. Even if fifty percent reductions could be achieved, what made the Kennan formula a Holy Grail? Between them, the Americans and Soviets had fifty thousand nuclear warheads: twenty-four thousand strategic, twenty-six thousand tactical. If each side reduced its strategic stockpile to a verifiable twelve thousand, could the world sleep fifty percent safer? Of course not. Even *fifty* warheads delivered against key urban targets in either country would effectively terminate the political lives of those states. It was not megatonnage but the capricious affairs of men that made the massive city-killer strategic nuclear missiles the ultimate menace; relations between the superpowers could cool again as suddenly as they had warmed. Behind the START protocols and grinning politicians lay an ominous new paradox: the weapons START1 did not eliminate, it tacitly affirmed; both superpowers still retained the capacity to exterminate the human race. The Soviets and Americans might have achieved a new level of understanding and cooperation during the Persian Gulf crisis, but in the polite and quiet atmosphere of the Geneva negotiating rooms their merciless struggle for nuclear supremacy ground on.

After forty years of arms negotiations, Jake Handlesman knew it was not the *number* of warheads that steadied the strategic teeter-totter popularly known as the balance of terror, it was the disposition of the weapons, their launch platforms, their relative capacities for destruction. *That* was what made strategic arms negotiation so delicate and dangerous even in a post–Cold War world; the Americans and Soviets were like two men on a perfectly balanced seesaw with their legs dangling a thousand feet off the ground. Neither could increase his mass without raising the other's level of terror, for if either achieved a clear advantage, the urge of the stronger to attack might become irresistible, just as the panic of the weaker to act preemptively might become overpowering. Paradoxically, neither could unilaterally dismount without causing both to fall through the same tyranny of logic. All the two men on the seesaw could do was talk, reason, negotiate— and inch in equal increments toward the fulcrum. Only then, when they had embraced at the center, could they creep down toward safety.

It had taken Jake a long time to understand the rubrics of the nuclear paradox even though he had been among the first eyewitnesses to the power of the bomb. In early 1945, he had been a recent Harvard M.A. in Russian Studies with a heart murmur—a tiny systolic *whoosh*—that made him 4-F and unfit for military service. The State Department had Jake working as a procurement clerk when a rudimentary card-sorting machine discovered his facility in Russian, Japanese, and a smattering of Romance languages and assigned him to the staff of the United States Survey of Strategic Bombing. What first appeared to Jake a tedious, make-work junket from bomb crater to bomb crater was to become a life-shaping experience.

From the moment Jake stepped out of the C-47 transport onto the windy, bomb-pocked airfield in occupied Yokota, he experienced a panorama of the cruelty and violence of modern warfare few men have known. By day, the survey members assessed the havoc bombs had wrought in Japan's physical and social fabric. By night, they deliberated and debated. The survey's conclusions would profoundly change the course of world military history, for what they discovered among the ruins of Japan was not the destructive power of the new B-29 bombers, but a horrific vision of the future.

On the survey team's third day in Hiroshima, Jake broke away from the group and climbed a hillside north of the port and spent the afternoon sitting against the charred trunk of a single, standing tree and looking out across the irradiated rubble of the city. That quiet afternoon staring into hell convinced Jake there had been *two* wars in the Pacific.

The first—the old-fashioned, conventional war—had begun at Pearl Harbor on December 7, 1941, and ended on August 5, 1945.

The second—the world's first nuclear war—began on August 6 at Hiroshima and ended three days later at Nagasaki.

Jake was twenty-five years old. Yet he understood that this *must* be the last nuclear war in history. Because it would surely be the longest.

When the survey report was prepared at the end of 1945, Jake was assigned the chore of gathering the scientists' evaluations of the two nuclear bombing sites, consolidating survey members' interviews with survivors, and drafting the summary section entitled "The Effects of the Atomic Bombs." To James Forrestal, who was appointed America's first Secretary of Defense in 1947—and to his successors for forty-four years to come—Jake's closing paragraph would be gospel:

Does the existence of atomic bombs invalidate all conclusions relative to air power based on pre-atomic experience? In the survey's opinion, many of the preexisting yardsticks *are* revolutionized. The problem of control of the air, should we be attacked, is of paramount strategic importance. The most intense effort must be devoted to perfecting our defensive air control. But we must also accept the probability that, however effective our air defense, some enemy planes or guided missiles may be able to evade our defenses and attack us.

The threat of immediate retaliation by a potent striking force of our own should deter any aggressor.[1]

[1]Report of the United States Survey of Strategic Bombing, U.S. Government Printing Office, 1946.

Jake's final sentence was history's first propounding of the Doctrine of Deterrence. He was, himself, the father of the paradox.

When the Strategic Bombing Survey team disbanded in 1946, Jake resigned his post at the State Department with the feeling of a job well done. Through Movietone newsreels and still photographs in *LIFE,* the public had begun to grasp the horrendous danger of the new nuclear weapons. Enlightened minds in the Truman administration were already using the report of the Survey of Strategic Bombing to lobby for an end to A-bomb research and development.

Jake had been offered an instructorship at Harvard and a place in the doctoral program in Russian Studies. By 1948, he was deep into a search for a subject for his thesis when he found a telegram from the State Department tucked into his pigeonhole in the faculty lounge. The fledgling United Nations was about to take up the question of a permanent ban on nuclear weapons and American Ambassador Bernard Baruch wanted Jake for his staff. Jake eagerly accepted.

He applied for the first of many leaves of absence that would characterize his dual careers as teacher and arms negotiator, and threw himself into his United Nations assignment with vigor, only to discover to his astonishment that the American delegation had been instructed to *resist* the ban. Instead of joining in a worldwide effort to outlaw the bomb, the Truman administration had decided to maneuver for an American monopoly over nuclear weapons and technology; the United States government's obsession with deterrence had begun. Truman's short-sighted policy legitimized the Soviet Union's drive for an atomic weapon of its own and triggered the frenzy of nuclear weapons development that would become known as the arms race.

For Jake, the Baruch episode was the beginning of a vocation that was to bedevil the rest of his life with ambiguity and frustration. Jake was no starry-eyed utopian; he understood nuclear weapons could not be uninvented. He could even argue that low-yield tactical nuclear weapons might have a rightful place in modern defensive arsenals. But the superpowers' growing inventories of offensive intercontinental missiles loomed over mankind like a death warrant. Through four decades divided between the ivy-covered walls of Harvard and negotiating tables in Helsinki, Geneva, Vienna, and Madrid, Jake felt like a man chasing a ball rolling downhill.

Now Jake lay on his bed holding the transcript of the president's First Step press conference and brooding. He had been present at the creation—an eyewitness to the unconscionable inhumanity of nuclear war. For more than forty years, he had worked tirelessly, selflessly in arms control. And, in the end—by the bitterest of ironies—his life's work to purge the world of strategic nuclear missiles had only succeeded in permanently perpetuating their existence. The vaunted START1 treaty and First Step were the final nails in the coffin, because they proclaimed to the world that the two great superpowers intended to rely on their strategic nuclear missiles to keep the global peace for generations to come.

The phone rang.

"Jake? Are you awake?" It was Drysdale, the CIA delegate on the American START team.

"What is it, Rufus?"

"Jesus Christ! Did you see Baker on the tube last night?"

Jake heard the shock and fury in the man's voice; clearly, the Central Intelligence Agency had left even its most trusted operatives in the dark about First Step. "I'm reading the transcript now."

"It's unbelievable! Unthinkable!"

"Indeed," Jake said softly. "It will create some difficulties."

"Difficulties! For crying out loud, you know as well as I do—"

"Rufus. This phone is not secure."

"Oh, yeah—right. Look, Mulholland's office called. There's a plenary session at the Soviet mission at eight-thirty to discuss this crap. I'll see you over there."

Jake hung up; but his hand lay still on the receiver. Drysdale was right; the fools in Washington had finally done it. The Doctrine of Deterrence now celebrated its final triumph over reason. Yes, the winds of freedom blowing through the Soviet Union and Warsaw Pact were dispersing the threat of blitzkrieg from the East. But the safety of mankind still wobbled precariously atop a mountain of nuclear warheads.

Now, in one shameless burst of mendacity, President Baker had sacrificed any hope of eradicating intercontinental nuclear missiles to short-term economic utility. First Step was no muddle-headed blunder; it was a new vision of disarmament—a manifesto for a future where nuclear deterrent missiles policed the strategic peace—a final and irrevocable declaration that the balance of payments outweighed the laws of logic. Jake sighed in despair. Was the President of the United States a fool who didn't understand the danger?

No. President Baker understood.

And Jake knew what was in the president's mind, what he was counting on, what gave him the Dutch courage to adopt such a pernicious policy. He remembered walking the windy plains of South Dakota east of the Black Hills where the fathers of the nation peered down from the granite heights of Mount Rushmore across thousands of acres of scrub-treed prairie. There, buried in massive concrete coffins, protected by barbed wire and vicious sentry dogs, America's Minuteman and Peacekeeper missiles waited—gigantic motors fueled and ready, their launch crews alert, their plutonium warheads slowly radiating out their half-lives of a thousand years. *They* were what President Baker was counting on to replace the nation's shrinking armies as the defenders of the state—the same false hope Jake had conjured in the summary of the Strategic Bombing Survey of 1945— the old idea that had shadowed him like a filthy beggar these many years.

An odor touched Jake's nostrils and they twitched. He raised his head.

In the stillness of the shadowy, predawn bedroom, he could sense another presence now. It was there before him, standing silent in a darkened corner, waiting, unbreathing, but filling the narrow room with the rancid stench of winding cloths and putrefaction.

Jake turned and stared into the shadows. He saw the interloper now: a tiny corpse that wouldn't die, its arms and legs burned puckered scarlet, flesh hung like rags from blackened bones. Silently, it shuffled toward him with its halting gait and bony smile, two desiccated hands extended in supplication. And Jake recognized the specter, even though it had no face.

It was deterrence—Jake's private nightmare—the cursed legacy he had willed an unsuspecting world.

Savagely, Jake seized the telex paper and tore it into pieces.

The real progeny of Hiroshima and Nagasaki was his own monstrous, misshapen child.

NCO DORM, BOLLING AFB, WASHINGTON

11:52 P.M.   In the NCO dormitory at the western end of Bolling, Technical Sergeant Polly Kulikov sat at the desk in her bedroom. She was wrapped in a towel, her hair still wet from the shower. She was trying to concentrate on the computer printouts before her, trying to ignore the screech and boom of Led Zeppelin from the bedroom next door, and doing her best to watch her television set with half an eye. While the rest of the INI staff had been clustered in the conference room watching the president at eight o'clock that night, Polly had been downstairs at her computer terminal running nonsensical errands for Colonel Petrovsky. Now, she was trying to catch the last few minutes of Tom Brokaw's report on the president's First Step press conference. The reporter's question-and-answer session was one hell of a show.

NORMAN SANDLER, UPI
Mr. President, as far as Congress is concerned, do you expect your controversial First Step proposal to—

THE PRESIDENT
Now don't start hanging labels on First Step. Someone holding a microphone calls First Step "controversial," and right away we have a controversy and the Soviets think we're lunatics. We have an adequate nuclear deterrent force—thousands of strategic missiles and bombers to protect us and our allies. We are safe. And when Congress has an opportunity to review this proposal, I'm sure they'll find it acceptable. Terry?

TERRY HUNT, AP
Mr. President, if that's true, why would Secretary Littman call First Step "notorious"?

THE PRESIDENT
Terry, I've already said I have no intention of commenting on allegations from unnamed sources.

BRIT HUME, ABC
Mr. President, did Secretary Littman call First Step "notorious" or didn't he?

PRESS SECRETARY FOWLER
Brit, you're out of order.

HUME
Ron, I'm trying to get an answer—

FOWLER
You're out of order and if you don't sit down I'm
going to have the Secret Service remove you. Excuse me, Mr. President.

THE PRESIDENT
Lesley?

LESLEY STAHL, CBS
Mr. President, do you honestly expect America's
military to accept First Step without a fight?

Suddenly, the bedroom door burst open. Polly slapped the pad of
computer printouts shut so fast she almost lost her towel.

Her suite-mate, Sergeant Dana Pavlov, was standing in the doorway in bra and panties, her blaring ghetto-blaster under one arm
flooding the bedroom with rock 'n' roll and a bottle of J.T.S. Brown
uplifted like a torch, looking for all the world like some randy Statue
of Liberty. *"Dayte mne vashi oustalye, vashi bednye, vashi zatolkanye
massy. . . ."*

Which translated through a veil of alcohol as "Give me your tired,
your poor, your huddled masses. . . ."

"Dana, give me a break."

"Hey, Polly, if you solve all the problems of INI tonight, what are
the rest of us going to do tomorrow?"

"Can it, Dana."

"Whiskey make you frisky."

"Fuck off, Dana."

"Potseluy menya v zhopu!"

"Kiss mine."

It was a relief when Dana slammed the door.

Polly dropped back into her desk chair, switched off the television,
and peered out into the wintry darkness. The massive Defense Intelligence Agency loomed in the fog, its sleek aluminum flanks gleaming
in the glare of the streetlamps. Polly shuddered and tightened the knot
of the towel where it folded between her breasts. She pushed her
glasses up her nose and flipped back to her place in the stack of
printouts. This was her third tour in air force intelligence and the first
time she had ever taken classified files out of a secure area.

She probably wouldn't have printed and taken the files at all if
Colonel Petrovsky's handwritten instructions had not seemed so peculiar. First, there was the practical joke: send some navy fighter jock

a message turning down his request for transfer to the air force. She thought, *Boys will be boys.* Then Petrovsky wanted a program written to someone else's computer.

Polly sent the burlesque message, then sat down at her console to transmit the program. She typed her access code, then the instruction dial DSN *#487-5058,* and hit the return key.

The computer responded > *dialing,* and she heard the digital tones and the distant ringing. Then the ring clicked silent and the computer flashed > *connection* complete and the challenge > *ID#?*

She typed the ID number on Petrovsky's handwritten sheet and hit the enter key. Instantly, the computer responded > *PASSWORD?* She carefully typed *password = mpf33722* and the computer responded > *logon33722.* Polly typed the short program.

> copy con:autoerase.bat
> erase 068043371*.*
> erase 120674292*.*
> erase 070088815*.*
> erase 112854546*.*
> erase autoerase.bat
> disconnect
> ^ Z

The computer responded > *one file copied,* and Polly typed the command to execute—*run autoerase.bat.*

But before she hit the enter key and ran the program, something made her pause. DSN was the Defense System Network, with hundreds of prefixes and thousands of numbers. Polly shouldn't have recognized the prefix 487, but she did; it was the prefix code for Randolph Air Force Base outside San Antonio—the base where she had done her first computer training.

Polly pulled out the DSN phone directory, leafed to Randolph, ran her finger down the list to extension 5058. It was unlisted. That was odd. She turned back to the computer screen, stared at the two entry keys. Her Intel training was churning curiosity into suspicion.

She couldn't decode the ID, but the password was a log-on code for an mpf—a master personnel file—identified only as 33722. The sequence Polly had typed instructed the Military Personnel Center computer to create a program that would erase four active duty personnel dossiers and then itself, leaving no clue to who had entered the Randolph computer system. The only incriminating record would be the posting in the INI computer's daily activity log; only someone here at Bolling could find that, and only if he knew what he was looking for.

Polly stared at the eight lines glowing on the screen. How could Colonel Petrovsky have gotten hold of two highly classified numerical keys to the air force personnel mainframe?

Then it occurred to Polly that what she was doing was no longer a practical joke. It was a crime. And her complicity was already permanently recorded in the INI daily activity log. Before she executed the command that erased the four active duty files—permanently erased four names, ranks, service numbers, and careers from the MPC computer's memory—she printed the dossiers on the Laser-Jet beside her terminal and took them with her.

Now it was after midnight and the four dossiers lay on the desk before her. She knew two of the men: 068043371 was her boss, Colonel Steven Petrovsky; 120674292 was his exec, Lieutenant Colonel Harding. She didn't recognize the other two names—Colonel Thomas M. O'Neill and Sergeant Terry Watkins. Polly bent over the printouts, scanning the four careers for the common thread that might lead her to an understanding of what she had done. On the notepad at her elbow she had written:

LIFERS
NAM
CHU MY

That was all the four air force men had in common: all were careerists; all had served in Vietnam; all had been POWs in a prison named Chu My. Polly yawned and tossed her ballpoint pen on the desk and leaned back in her chair and stared listlessly at the half-eaten turkey sandwich on the plastic tray. When you got right down to it, she really didn't give a damn why Petrovsky wanted the four dossiers erased. She flipped the printouts closed, pushed her chair back from her desk to rise, and threw a last glance at the blank screen of the television set.

Abruptly, she stopped stock-still.

Sitting dark and silent, the television screen looked exactly like the video monitor of the computer in her office. Polly remembered the four erase commands blinking on and off as four names and careers vanished from the memory of the air force. She remembered Lesley Stahl's question to the president. She remembered thinking Lesley Stahl was right; the military *wouldn't* accept First Step without a fight.

And then, quite suddenly, it occurred to Polly Kulikov that she had become an accessory to mutiny.

It was a thought so harrowing, so fantastic and bizarre, that it wasn't until something moved in the reflection on the blank screen that she looked back and recognized the officer standing just inside her bedroom door.

She flung her chair back, leaped to her feet, clutched the towel closed about her bosom. "Get the hell out of here!"

But Colonel Petrovsky stepped forward, and there was menace in his step.

Polly edged backward. "You stay away from me."

His eyes drifted to the stack of printouts on her desk. Before he could move, she reached down, grabbed one of the dossiers, held it up in his face. "That's right. I made copies. What the hell is going on?"

Petrovsky didn't answer.

"It's First Step, isn't it?" she said. "This has something to do with First Step."

His eyes turned hollow, trapped. Polly hated that stupid look in a man. Her voice turned mocking, full of scorn. "The sun will come up tomorrow. What a sad little joke you are. . . ."

Petrovsky reached into the pocket of his uniform.

"You're a traitor," she snarled. "You're all traitors. And you'll all hang for—" She broke off when he raised his hand. "What the hell—"

There was a soft *pock* when the .25-caliber pistol fired through its silencer and a *tick* when the bullet nicked the edge of the printout. Polly's head snapped back; she caught herself, and glared at Petrovsky. Then her heart beat and blood spurted through a tiny black hole above her left eye and splashed the paper in her hand. That was the last thing Polly saw. Her eyes rolled up and she collapsed to the floor like a limp piece of string.

Steven Petrovsky had seen people brain-shot before; he knew the woman's heart would beat for fifteen minutes. He stooped, quickly tore the towel from her body, and wrapped it about her head. Then, while the sound of Led Zeppelin thundered through the walls, he dragged the body toward the footlocker at the end of the bunk.

AMERICAN FESTIVAL CAFÉ,
ROCKEFELLER PLAZA, NEW YORK CITY

12:11 A.M.   Tom Brokaw slumped off the escalator and swung through the revolving door into the shadowy interior of the brasserie. Scattered here and there among the tables, drowsy couples whispered over coffee; a tipsy group of Japanese businessmen shared a smutty laugh.

In the deserted bar, the lights were ruddy dim and the air sweet with whiskey and cigars. A waiter with sleeves up and necktie down was stacking chairs upended on the naked cocktail tables. Mike Marden was waiting at the rosewood rail with two double scotches. In 1988, Marden had been editor of the Minneapolis *Tribune* when the management of General Electric recruited him to the presidency of NBC News; his lazy shock of premature white hair gave him the look of a latter-day Carl Sandburg.

"Luck." Marden downed his drink and signaled for another. "Long day?"

Brokaw drank, then leaned against the bar with both hands. "The longest."

"Want a car to take you uptown?"

"No, thanks. Rather walk. Got some things to think about."

"Know what you mean. By the way, I called Tom Capra . . . asked him to open the *Today* show with a live Gumbel interview with Senator Whitworth. What time you planning to get to the office in the morning?"

"Eight-thirty maybe."

"Good."

They stood side by side, staring at the gleaming rows of bottles.

"Got a real strange feeling about this First Step thing," Brokaw finally said.

"Me, too."

"Same feeling I had when Nixon said we'd won the Vietnam War and he was bringing the troops home to peace with honor."

Mike Marden sighed. "Me, too."

THIRD STREET SE, WASHINGTON

12:21 A.M.   Tod was still shaking. "What the hell are we going to do?"

Christy slouched beside him in the front seat of the car, her heavy-lidded eyes half-open, musing as the ghostly tenements of Washington's southeastern ghetto slid past them through the fog. This was the forgotten Washington; the ugly urban underbelly far off the tree-lined commutation routes between the Virginia hunt country and Capitol Hill. Arson-blackened windows in derelict buildings gaped over the street like silent screams. The curbs were littered with carcasses of cars raped for parts by frantic junkies. On the sidewalks, trash cans lay akimbo and stinking garbage rotted in the chilly damp. In the doorways, street people huddled against the frost like animals.

Christy stared dully out the window. She was tired; she needed sleep. But the Intel officer inside her could not shake a nagging sense of strangeness. Colonel O'Neill's midnight visit was singular, peculiar. Then there had been the tension in the man, the apprehension in his eyes, the curious language of Colonel Petrovsky's order, the—

"Chris, I'm talking to you. What do we do?"

She shook off the reverie. Junior officers obeyed orders; it was not theirs to reason why. "Do about what?"

"That colonel—he saw me in your bedroom! What if he reports us?"

"He won't."

"How do you know?"

She didn't, but somehow, she did. "Because I know."

"But what if he does? Goddammit, Christy, it's fraternization! It's a court-martial offense!"

"Tod, he won't report us."

But he wasn't reassured. "Who the hell was that guy anyhow?"

"Some old soldier buddy of Petrovsky's. Works in the White House ADR."

"*The White House?* Aw, Jesus."

She touched his sleeve. "Tod, please. Let's just find the address and—"

He wrenched his hands on the steering wheel. "Easy for you to say."

Christy lowered her eyes; it *was* easy for her to say. She was an officer, he an enlisted man. To her, the officer corps was a ladder to responsibility and prestige. To him, it was a monolith of cold, implacable power. There was a towering bar of rank that separated them even in the moments when their bodies were joined in the most intimate embrace. It was a barrier she could not bridge for all the tenderness in the world.

She remembered the day that wall began to rise between her and other people—in Cambridge, Massachusetts, during the fall semester of 1983. She had gone down to breakfast at the Harvard Union that morning and sat at the usual round table for ten in the big bay window that looked out on Lamont Hall and the yard. She never had to sit alone at that table very long; a pretty, dark-eyed nineteen-year-old girl did not sit alone for long in the Union, even at breakfast. But, that morning, though she sat almost an hour dawdling over bran muffins and the *Globe,* no one sat beside her. No one sat in any of the nine empty chairs around the table. Even though the Union was crowded by eight-thirty, Christy sat alone.

Before she caught the bus to her ROTC class at MIT, she stopped in the ladies' room to smarten her uniform and set her flight cap. Two girls chattering over their makeup fell silent when they saw her, gathered their paints and brushes, pushed the sleeves of their sweatshirts up past their elbows, and slipped out the door. Christy looked after them, puzzled. Then, she turned to the mirror. The image there transfixed her.

The woman in the mirror was not just another teenager in jeans and sweatshirt. She wore the cool, trim, military blues of the United States Air Force ROTC. She was an officer cadet. She was different.

On the dot of nine, Colonel Alexander Saroyan came through the door of the lecture hall at MIT. He was a short, small man of fifty—sweet faced and wry, a Vietnam-era pilot who had spent three years flying KC-135 Stratotankers out of RAF Fairford before his appointment as commander of the MIT ROTC program. He smiled and said, "Good morning."

The class rose and braced. "Good morning, sir."

"As you were." Saroyan turned and went to the blackboard. "I meet this class only twice—today and at commencement. And I write on the blackboard only once." Then he printed five words:

COMMÁND

LOYALTY

DISCIPLINE

INTEGRITY

INITIATIVE

"You have many things to learn in ROTC but none more important than the definitions of these words." He put a check mark before "command."

"Command is the lawful authority that a superior exerts over a subordinate. And—provided a commander's order is lawful—it must be obeyed without hesitation." His chalk *skreeked* at the second check. "Loyalty is the allegiance subordinates owe to their superiors. You may not agree with your commander's decision, but you must accept it and relay it to your subordinates as if it were your own." *Skreek.* "Discipline is the cement that binds a military force together. It is discipline that ensures stability under stress."

He looked at the blackboard and back at the cadets. "Then we come to integrity. Which embodies uprightness, sound moral principals, truthfulness, honesty." Skreek. "And, lastly, initiative. Taking action in the absence of orders—*that* is the sign of a true leader."

He put the chalk down in its tray, walked away from the blackboard, and stood looking back at what he had written. "For an air force officer, nothing—absolutely nothing—comes before these words. Except three things. Would anyone care to say what those are?" He scanned the silent faces of the cadets. Then a lone hand went up in the back of the room.

"Yes?" Saroyan craned his neck and squinted. "Cadet . . .?"

"Russoff, sir." Christy got to her feet.

"Tell us, Miss Russoff, what three things come before these words?"

"Duty-Honor-Country."

"Very good, Miss Russoff. I see you've been reading your *Air Force Officer's Guide.*"

"No, sir. My father was in the air force."

"And is he retired?"

"No. He died in Vietnam."

Half a dozen curious faces turned back toward Christy.

"Then I suppose you know a great deal about officership already," Saroyan said. "Please come down and write those three words on the board for us." He offered her the chalk. And when Christy began to print the words, he touched her shoulder.

"Bigger," he said. "Bigger."

Now Christy slouched in the front seat of Tod's car and listened to the dull thumping of the tires on the potholed street. She looked at her watch—12:23 A.M. That wouldn't seem so late if she were coming home from a party. But she wasn't coming home from a date like other young women. She was in uniform and under orders. That was the air force—it took, it gave. It had taken her parents and orphaned her. In return, it had given her compensation, an education, a way out of the Trenton slums. It had taken something of her womanhood; in return, it had given her a uniform and a career. It was a life she had chosen. And yet, somehow—like the affair with Captain Bryan—it had chosen her. Tonight, Duty-Honor-Country not only came before the code of officership, but also before a good night's sleep. Bryan had been right. *It's not just an adventure, it's a job.*

Tod slowed the car to creeping, craned his neck to catch a house number through the fog. "Man, I don't know . . . you sure you got the right address?"

Christy stretched against the stiffness in her shoulders and held Colonel Petrovsky's order in the light of a passing streetlamp. "1104 Third Street Southeast. Another block or two."

"What's this life-or-death mission anyhow?"

"Pick up some woman named Mrs. Mary Watkins."

"Who's she? Petrovsky's girlfriend?"

"Dunno."

"And? After we pick her up? What then?"

"Take her to Andrews Air Force Base. To the security police detention facility."

"You're kiddin'. Lemme see that." He reached for the sheet of paper.

Sharply, she pulled it away.

"Hey, what's the matter with you?" he said.

"There's a message in here I'm not supposed to show to anyone else."

"Come on." He snorted, reached again.

"Tod, please, it's an order." She stuffed the paper in her purse and snapped it closed.

He hit the brakes; the car juddered to a stop. "Are you serious?" He stared at her. "Jesus, you *are* serious. Hey, Chris. Getting a little carried away, aren't you? This is chauffeur service, not a secret mission behind enemy lines."

She put her hand on his. "Let's do what we have to and go home, all right?"

He sat a moment, glaring. "You always have to do it by the book, don't you?" Then he swung the car in toward the curb and stopped.

He climbed out, went around, and opened Christy's door. They stood together on the shiny wet asphalt of the street, looking up through the fog at a haggard tenement.

"Well, let's get it over with." Tod took her elbow.

Christy stepped back. "I have to go alone."

"In there? You're kidding me." Together, they stared up the tenement steps. Beyond the cracked glass of the front door, a dangling bulb hung in the garbage-cluttered foyer.

"Tod, I don't like this any more than you do. What I have to say to her is private. It's official business. Please understand."

Irritably, he pulled himself up to attention. "Yes, ma'am."

"Tod, don't."

But he stood rigid, eyes glaring, while she went up the steps and inside. When the door closed behind her, he leaned against the car, staring down the street, exasperated.

Inside the murky entry hall, the stink of urine was thicker than the chilling fog outside. Christy opened her purse, found a hankie, pressed it against her nose and mouth, scanned the row of mailboxes; they hung nameless, ripped ajar, dangling from rusted hinges. She pushed her hankie back into her purse, stepped through the inner door to the lobby, and froze.

At the bottom of the stairwell, three teenage boys were hunched in heated conversation; a drug score was going down. Abruptly, the fat one looked up.

"Well, lookie here. . . ." The three boys stepped apart.

"Whoo-ee!" the one with the earring said. "Hey, mama. Good you could fall by."

Christy glanced back out the front door. Tod was leaning against the car, his back to her, smoking; two wood and glass doors separated them; both doors opened inward against her.

"Hey, baby!" The fat one stepped forward. "You just in time for the party. Lemme host you some *blow.*"

Christy turned to face him. "Stay where you are."

The fat boy laughed; he had yellowed teeth and one gold cap. "Well, listen to sister! Honey, you—"

Christy pushed her hand deeper into her purse and squeezed the hankie. "Move away from those stairs."

Earring opened his arms to her. "Oh, sure, baby. We just gonna fade—"

"Do it now."

"The fuck we will!" The fat one clenched his fists and started toward her. Christy set her feet and flexed her fingers in her purse.

The third boy—the one in the leather raincoat—caught the fat one's arm. "Cool it, Speed." He nodded at Christy's hidden hand. "She's got a piece, man."

The three boys tensed. Christy stepped aside, nodded once toward the door. "Walk."

"Fuck you, baby. We ain't goin' nowhere."

"Just walk easy out that door and keep on going."

The fat one raised an angry finger. "Little army cunt—"

Raincoat shouted, "Shut up, Speed! She gonna blow your head off!" He eyed her uniform. "And she'll do it, too." He opened his hands. "Don't mind him, Cap'n." He grinned and sauntered toward her. "He's fried out on dust. He don't—"

Softly, Christy said, "One more step and I'll drop you where you stand."

Raincoat's smile evaporated.

Earring grabbed his sleeve. "Come on, bro. Let's mosey." And when Raincoat wouldn't move, he shouted, "Man, use yo' fuckin' head!" and yanked him toward the door. Raincoat glared as Earring dragged him out.

The fat one stopped with the door ajar. "Hey, Cap'n—true what they say 'bout army pussy?"

Her dark eyes stared him down. He laughed once, and went out. Christy took her hand out of her purse and straightened her jacket.

Then she became aware of the beating of her heart.

It was steady, measured, slow.

She thought of Colonel Petrovsky. He was right—she *was* bold; there were times he knew her better than she knew herself. Christy stood at the bottom of the stairwell, looking up at the flights that spiraled into the blackness. Petrovsky had given her an order, and they both knew she would obey.

She climbed out of the light.

4 RUE CHARLES CUSIN, GENEVA

6:27 A.M. Jake rose from his bed and bitterly flung the scraps of the telex into the wastebasket. There were some human needs for which even questions of the world's survival must wait. On his old blue slippers, he padded to the bathroom and snapped on the light. One thing about Switzerland of which he never wearied: the cleanliness. A hundred years of bathers had worn the white enamel in the bottom of the antique footed tub to a thin bluish haze. But the tub was impeccable and pristine, as was the bidet and toilet. Jake opened the fly of his pajamas, bent to relieve himself.

He was accustomed to the burning and dark fluid now. When he was younger, he would stare at the ruddy stream, trying to remember if the murky redness curling in the bowl was darker than it had been last month, last week, had been yesterday. Now he understood darkness was darkness. Black was black. And the darkness of eternity would be a void of silent, endless night.

He flushed the water and snapped off the bathroom light. He was due at L'Hôtel des Bergues for breakfast at seven o'clock. He would have to hurry and his back had begun to ache again and he had not yet finished his morning prayers.

But as he entered the bedroom, the soft glow of predawn light through the window caught his eye. He turned, drew apart the curtains, squinted at the first dim light glazing the undersides of the clouds above the lake. It would be sunrise in an hour.

Jake stared at the feeble glow. It occurred to him that, two hours from now, the same sun would rise over London. Two hours after that it would rise over Santa Maria in the Azores and, two hours later, over Recife and Rio. He imagined the carpet of morning, spreading slowly westward as the earth turned first Asunción and St. John, then Bogotá and Boston to the same frayed edge of light. He thought of that light simultaneously touching the tip of the Washington Monument and the twin crosses atop the towers of Iglesia Santo Domingo in Lima, Peru. The same light would soon be falling on the tomb of George Washington at Mount Vernon, of Simon Bolívar in Caracas, of Carlos Fonseca-Amador in Managua.

Jake cinched the leather thong of the tefillin about his forehead and softly chanted the Hebrew words, ". . . thou will imbue me with thy wisdom . . . by thy might thou will cut off my foes. . . ."

Then it occurred to him that the sun rising over Rue Charles Cusin was setting half a world away over Auckland and the frozen vastness of the Bering Sea. The sunrise over Columbus's gray Azores would be sunset for the Mud Men of Port Moresby and the Ainu of Hokkaido. So God had decreed: half of mankind must dwell in darkness so half might live in light. "And God said, Let there be light. And there was light. And God saw that the light was good. And he separated the light from the darkness."

Jake shook the words of Genesis from his head; it was an abomination to meditate upon the Torah before the morning prayer was complete. He wrapped the splintering leather of the retsuah tightly three times around his middle finger and chanted, "I will betroth you to myself forever. . . ."

But the daemon tapped him on the shoulder. Was it not, then, ordained by God that half of mankind must huddle in darkness so half may glory in light? Yes. He knew that to be true. A lifetime of teaching and arms negotiation had taught Jake that all existence divided itself between light and dark. Where there was intelligence, there would always be both prodigies and fools; where there was money, there would always be egregious excess and soul-searing penury; where there was food, there would be gluttony and famine; and where there was power, there *must* be master and slave. Three thousand years of Abraham's example, two thousand years of Christian love, seventy years of Marxist-Leninism had not tipped the balance from the haves toward the have-nots. And four decades as an arms negotiator had taught Jake Handlesman that, where there was infinite, lethal thermonuclear power—the very power in which he imagined Jehovah must have wrapped Himself when He willed the stars to flame—where such power existed in the hands of man, there, too, must be master and slave.

Nodding, chanting, Jake stood looking at the sky and murmured the obligatory words of Exodus 13. "Remember this day, in which you came out of Egypt, out of a house of slavery; for by a strong hand the Lord brought you out. . . ."

Yes, yes. A strong hand.

"And when your son asks you in time to come: What does this mean? You shall tell him: By a strong hand the Lord brought us out of Egypt, out of a house of slavery." ✓

Jake looked down at his own hand, bound in the leather of the retsuah; it was an old man's hand, the sallow skin thinning to reveal the living sinew underneath; soon, too soon, the skin would release the soul within to return to its Creator. And yet, wrapped in the Law, it was still a strong hand. "And when Pharaoh made difficulties about letting us go, the Lord slew every first-born in the land of Egypt." His was a hand that might yet lead the world out of nuclear bondage.

Mechanically, Jake's lips recited the ancient prayer. But his mind drifted back to that afternoon in Hiroshima when he had sat alone against the barkless, blackened tree and looked down on the nuclear desolation as Moses might have looked down from Mount Sinai on the abominable idolatry of the tribes. Forty-six years later, Jake had come to understand he was not a Moses, but an Aaron—a caster of the golden calf.

The president was standing in the shadow of Jake's idol when he spoke his First Step folly. Jake saw him clearly now. The president of the United States was standing at a podium. Before him stretched the awesome bowl, the boundless amphitheater of television, one gigantic room where all the peoples of the world gathered in their billions. Behind the president, stood row on row of grave, gray-suited men. Jake knew their faces, knew their names: all the well-intentioned fools who had led America's defense since the bombing survey of 1945— Forrestal and Kennan and the architects of containment; John Foster Dulles, McElroy and the champions of massive retaliation; four decades of McNamaras, Lairds, and Schlesingers, Harold Brown and Kissinger and Weinberger and Cheney—all the ghostly ranks of true believers in deterrence, standing behind the president in a great arcing semicircle of the damned.

And behind them all, Jake saw another figure.

Silent it was. And black as death. Stupendous, brute, and massive— like a huge Babel that rose as an affront to heaven and blocked the very sun. It towered above the billions, engulfing all in murky shadow—a dread, dumb ballistic missile god.

Yes, yes. Jake nodded, prayed, wrung out his heart in the sacred words, and begged forgiveness. He was old and sick to dying. As his sins admitted of no penance, his affliction admitted of no cure.

But even in his passion, he could see that fate had brought him to the final paradox of his career. Today, in one infamous act of disobedience, he would do as his namesake Jacob had; he would confront the evil angel of deterrence hand-to-hand. Even as he knew he would stand before his Creator on the Day of Judgment—even as he realized it must mean ignominious disgrace—Jake Handlesman knew he could not . . . must not . . . would not let chaos triumph.

First Step had to be stopped.

At any cost.

Jake broke off his morning prayer and stared through the mist at the first dim halo of dawn beyond the mountains. What was the sun itself but a huge thermonuclear furnace that burned day out of night?

Dimly through the feeble light he heard the ram's horn's song— eerie, breathy, primitive. Yes, yes. The sun was rising on a day of battle. Jake and others who understood the danger had prepared against this day. There would always be ideals for which men must die, as there were words and pillars of fire that summoned men to their death.

He murmured, *"Yisgadal v'yiskadash . . ."*

He stood in the window before the sunrise and chanted the prayer for the dead.

1104 THIRD STREET SE, WASHINGTON, DC

12:29 A.M.   Christy paused on the sixth-floor landing to let her eyes adjust to the darkness. The tenement hallway stank of chicken; behind one of the peeling, graffiti-spattered doors, someone was blowing a blues harmonica and the sound was full of lonely distance. She picked her way to the door marked 62, pulled herself up straight, and knocked. Silence. She knocked again. At last, she heard someone stir behind the door; then three locks clicked in sequence and the door cracked open on its safety chain. A wedge of light painted Christy's face.

A wary voice said, "Whaddya want?"

"Mrs. Mary Watkins?"

"I said, whatcha want, girl?"

"Mrs. Watkins, I'm Lieutenant Russoff. I'm to say to you"—the awkward words came haltingly—"The sun will come up tomorrow."

The door slammed shut.

Startled, Christy stood in darkness. She raised her hand to knock again.

Then the chain released, the door swung open, and Mrs. Watkins stepped into the hall. She was a middle-aged black woman in a worn cloth coat with an old knit bag over her arm—a poor woman trying to make her poverty presentable. By the doorway light, Christy could see the woman's eyes were dun and rheumy, the eyelids heavy like her own.

"Little young for this kind of thing, ain'tcha, girl?" The woman bent and studied Christy's face. "What you say your name was?"

"Lieutenant Russoff."

"Russoff?" She eyed Christy with suspicion. "You Russian or what?"

"I'm . . . American."

"Yeah, right." Mrs. Watkins snorted. "And you just following orders. Just like the rest of them." She snapped the light and slammed the door. Then she pushed past Christy to the stairs. "Come on, bitch. Let's do the dirty deed."

Christy stared after her, astonished.

ORDER OF BATTLE

Patriotism as practiced in the air force is based upon the conviction that preservation of the American system of life—with its noble traditions, free institutions, and infinite promise—is at once the highest practical morality and the most enlightened self-interest. Patriotism springs from deep knowledge that this land, this people, are in truth the hope of the earth.

THE CODE OF THE UNITED STATES AIR FORCE,
AIR FORCE OFFICER'S GUIDE (27TH EDITION)

19 RUE JEAN PÉCOLAT, GENEVA

6:30 A.M. The electric clock clicked once, then filled the darkened bedroom with its snide buzz. Sara Weatherby rolled over in the four-poster bed, groped the clock, and slapped it silent.

She lay that way, her hand on the clock, her drowsy, waking eyes staring up into the faded canopy. The high-ceilinged rococo bedroom was dark except for the purple spines of dawn that filtered between the velvet curtains. The warmth of the mattress and pillow beckoned Sara back to sleep. She shut her eyes and let her shoulders settle into the familiar topography. Then the man beside her threw a lazy arm across her shoulder and her eyes opened and she realized she was not alone.

Sara sighed, slipped out from under, softly swung her legs free of the quilt, and perched on the edge of the thick feather mattress, neither asleep nor awake, gingerly waiting for consciousness and the memories it might contain. Her head throbbed at the temples and her sour stomach rolled; dimly, she remembered the ristafel dinner at the apartment of the Dutch military attaché, the saté and the peanut sauce, the bawdy laughter and the endless toasts with icy pink genever. She hiked the spaghetti straps of her blue silk teddy, took hold of one of the carved mahogany bedposts, and eased herself to her feet.

Abruptly, the man sat up in the bed.

Sara smiled at him and yawned, "Mor-ning." She chewed the musty sleep-taste in her mouth and scratched her hip. "Wanta coffee?"

The man just stared.

With a fingernail, Sara picked the sleep from the corner of her eye, blinked and focused on him; he was in his twenties, swarthy, with close-cropped hair and a black mustache squared neatly as a Band-Aid.

"How do you take it?" she said.

He blinked at her without comprehension.

"Cream? Sugar?"

Disoriented, he scanned the room.

"Hey, you okay?"

"Nie mowie po Angielsku," he said. *"Gdzie to jest?"*

"I'm Sara." And she thought, *Jesus Christ—a Polack?* Then she remembered the cab ride home, the dusky hand of the Polish air force captain groping her skirt. She remembered the giggling and drunken shushing as they struggled arm-in-arm to climb the stairs, his hips grinding against her buttocks as she fumbled with her key. She remembered him lying on the bed, facedown and fully clothed, snoring while she struggled to undress him. Then her mind took mercy; that was all.

Sara leaned against the carved pillar, rested her forehead against the back of her hand, and laughed softly in her throat.

"Co jest az tak smieszne?" he demanded.

"Nothing." She shook her head and sighed.

"Gdzie jestem?"

"This is my apartment." She put one finger to her lips. "Now shush. 'Nuff happy patter. Just stay where you are."

"Co masz no mysli?"

"Stay." She gestured with two downturned palms as to a dog. "Just . . . just stay."

Chuckling, shaking her head, she made her way into the kitchen. She was thirty-nine and she had the achy walk of a woman who was running out of dreams.

Her orange cat jumped up on the cluttered kitchen counter and pawed impatiently as Sara passed. "In a minute, McKenzie. What is it with everybody today?"

She struck a match, lit the burner beneath the kettle and prepared two cups of Café Hag. But when she went back into the bedroom, the four-poster was empty, the bathroom door was closed, and she could hear the shower running. She shrugged and set the man's cup on the sill beside the bathroom door. But when she turned toward her closet, something caught her eye.

The jacket of his uniform lay in a crumpled heap on the floor beside the bed. She bent and picked it up, ran her eye along the two rows of campaign ribbons: two unit citations, jump school, flight school honors, helicopter training, basic training honors . . . a very athletic little man. Too bad he'd been too drunk to . . .

Sara's eyes snapped back to the helicopter training ribbon; it was always worn to the left of the flight school ribbon.

On this uniform, it was to the right.

In sudden fury Sara flung the jacket to the floor, yanked the bathroom door open and shouted, "SONOFABITCH!"

The man in the shower let out a startled cry.

"Sneaking bastard!" Sara ripped the shower curtain aside.

The man fell back against the tiled wall, fists clenched, wide eyes blinking through the spray.

Sara cocked a finger at him. "You hit me and I'll rip your dick off! OUT! Out, you motherfucker!" She grabbed the taps and spun them shut. "Out! Before I call the *polizei!*" She stuck her face in his. "*Polizei!* You get me?"

She stormed out of the bathroom, snatched up his uniform and underwear, strode to the front door, yanked it open, and began flinging his clothes out into the hallway.

The man rushed from the bathroom, pulling a towel about his waist as Sara flung his shoes out the door one after the other. He grabbed her wrist. "Crazy *beetch!* What you doing?"

She twisted free of him and shoved the door wide open. "Get out of here you KGB fuck!"

Suddenly, the man cracked her across the face. Sara went sprawling, hit the side of the bed as she fell and landed hard on the floor. The man took a step toward her.

Sara reached up, pulled the drawer of the nightstand open, drew her .22 Beretta automatic. The comedy was ended. "Hit me again I'll blow your balls off."

The Russian froze. *"Amyereekanskee hore."*

"KGB fuck!"

Checked, he spat contempt at her, and stamped out the door.

She scrambled to her feet. "Gimme my towel, you creep!"

He stopped on the landing, glared red-faced at her and her pistol. The door across the hallway opened on its safety chain and a startled eye appeared in the crack.

"Take your *vucking* towel!" The Russian tore it off and flung it at her.

Sara lurched forward with both hands and slammed the door. Then she leaned against it and laughed until the tears streamed down her cheeks. In Geneva, the Cold War was not *quite* over—thank god.

ANDREWS AIR FORCE BASE,
CAMP SPRINGS, MD

12:54 A.M.   The black Ford rolled into the glare of the twin spotlights and stopped before the sentry booth at the main gate of Andrews Air Force Base. Christy peered out the backseat window. Beyond the chain link fencing and barbed wire, the nightbound landscape wore an eerie camouflage of wintry fog. Taxiway beacons glimmered ghostlike in the mist; beyond the runways, the massive hangars brooded, abandoned to the night. Christy rubbed her eyes against the numbing grip of sleep. She was exhausted. Her uniform clung cold and damp against her body. She needed a hot shower, a good night's rest. But she was under orders and she could not shake a whispering sense of apprehension.

An air force security policeman wearing a sidearm and carrying an oversized flashlight leaned in at the driver's window. Tod held out his ID. The SP checked it, pointed the light through the back window of the car. Christy held up her ID, squinted as the beam swept her, then Mrs. Watkins. The light snapped off.

"Proceed." The SP stepped back.

"Base security HQ?"

"Straight ahead." The policeman saluted. Tod drove on.

The SP headquarters was a low brick building; behind it, a cinderblock compound was fenced and lit by four halogen spotlights. The compound might have been the garage of a motor pool except for the barred and wire-covered windows that identified it as the detention facility of the Unified Washington Military District.

Tod parked the car, stepped out, and opened Christy's door. As they waited for Mrs. Watkins to emerge, his look said, *What now?* and Christy's headshake answered, *I don't know.*

"We'll be a few minutes, Sergeant."

"Yes, ma'am."

Inside, the booking hall was chilly reinforced concrete, the floor a dismal green linoleum, the overhead fluorescent lights recessed in cages. Behind the counter, a master sergeant sat poring over a copy of *The Sporting News.* The man was in his forties; the nameplate on his right breast read JEETER. Across his left breast spread a trail of campaign ribbons that wandered back to Vietnam, to combat, capture, and internment. He didn't look up at the sound of the door, didn't notice when Christy stopped before the desk, didn't raise his eyes until she said, "Excuse me, Sergeant. . . ."

Jeeter started, blinked. When he spotted her insignia he yawned, "Sumpin' I can do for you, L'tenant?" Then he saw Mrs. Watkins standing behind her. "Aw, come on now, L'tenant. You gotta be kiddin'. Visitin' hours are 1000 to 1400. Y'all come back t'morrow, heah?"

"But I was—"

Then Mrs. Watkins said, "My man, I hear the sun'll come up tomorrow."

Slyly, Jeeter smiled. "Yes'm, now that you mention it, I do believe it will." He plucked the order from Christy's hand and crumpled it into the wastebasket. Then he picked a ring of keys from a peg and opened the door behind the counter. "Y'all follow me."

But Christy stood where she was. Her mind flashed *compartmented information.* She and Mrs. Watkins had been given a password and partial instructions—standard military procedure to ensure the secrecy of a high-risk mission. But why build such melodrama into a simple errand? It made no sense. None of it did.

Mrs. Watkins pushed past Christy toward the door. "Little toy soldiers," she muttered. "Lord, have mercy."

"L'tenant," Jeeter said and leaned on the knob, "y'all comin' or not?"

Uneasily, Christy followed Jeeter and Mrs. Watkins out the back door into the harsh glare of the spotlights, and down the narrow concrete path between two tall barbed-wire fences. Where the path ended, the detention block sat squat and grim. Jeeter unlocked the last cell door and creaked it open. Inside the gloomy cubicle, a black man in air force prison coveralls sat on the edge of a bunk. Christy could see he was a big man, muscular and strong.

Mrs. Watkins gasped. "Terry—"

The man looked up.

"Oh, God. Terry!"

He stood with a clank of chain and Christy could see his wrists and ankles were manacled.

And then Mrs. Watkins was across the threshold, her arms wide to embrace him, her kisses and her sobbing sweeping over him. Christy stood in the doorway. In spite of herself she felt her heart go out to—

Suddenly Watkins turned toward the darkest corner of the cell and shouted, "Sons of bitches! Does she have to see me chained up like a dog?"

Christy's eyes darted toward the shadows; three uniformed men stared back. She stiffened, pulled herself up to attention. "Good evening, sir."

"Good evening, Lieutenant," Colonel O'Neill said and stepped into the fall of lamplight through the open door. "Thank you very much for delivering our guest."

"Will . . . that be all, sir?"

Then a chair scraped the floor and another man rose from the shadows. "Not quite."

Christy's eyes widened; the man was Colonel Steven Petrovsky, director of INI. Behind him, she recognized Lieutenant Colonel Harding.

Petrovsky turned his chair to the unpainted wooden table. "Mrs. Watkins, won't you have a seat?"

But the woman clung to her husband.

"Mrs. Watkins, if you please."

At last Watkins eased his wife toward the chair. Slowly, never letting go of her husband's hand, she sat.

Petrovsky smiled at Christy. "Lieutenant, would you and Sergeant Jeeter kindly wait outside?"

Christy stepped back from the threshold. As Jeeter swung the door closed, Watkins shouted, "Bastards! Did you have to drag my wife into your nightmare!"

The steel door slammed shut in Christy's face.

" 'Scuse me, L'tenant. . . ."

Christy looked back; Jeeter tapped his breast pocket.

"Smoke 'em if you got 'em," she said. Then she sat on the bench beside the door—bewildered.

L'HÔTEL DES BERGUES, 33 QUAI DES BERGUES, GENEVA

6:58 A.M.   Mikhail Yurievitch Lermontov sat at a table in the ground-floor café of the old Hôtel des Bergues studying his newspaper by the predawn glow through the frosty window. His bony shoulders were hunched against his neck and his glasses perched on the tip of his nose like a sparrow on a twig. Galled by his own forgetfulness, his right hand tapped his yellow pencil on the tabletop.

"Oui, m'sieur?"

Lermontov looked up; the sleepy waiter stood beside him, leaning on his broom.

"Que voulez-vous, m'sieur?" the waiter said. He was a small man in a long white apron that touched the tips of his patent leather shoes; by the razor cut of his beard, Lermontov could tell he was one of those French who lived in Annecy and drove across the border each day to work in Switzerland. Since 1946, Lermontov had been a member of the *nomenklatura*—the trusted few—the handful of Soviet citizens who worked within the privileged archipelago of Communist party enclaves that dotted the drab cities of the USSR. By accident of birth, by dint of hard work, by wit, by achievement, by guile, and by luck, he had survived a revolution, two wars, four years of Stalin's dreaded *Yezhovshina,* a decade of Khrushchev's government-by-crisis, fifteen years of Brezhnev's stagnation, and the turmoil of Gorbachev's *perestroika.* Unlike so many millions of his unfortunate countrymen, Lermontov had led a charmed life. He had traveled in the West since the first Soviet strategic arms negotiating team was dispatched to Helsinki in 1969; he had been among the first Soviet negotiators to sit across the table from Americans Gerard Smith, Paul Nitze, and Jake Handlesman. Still, Lermontov had never become accustomed to the idea that Europeans could live in one country and commute daily to jobs in another.

He shrugged. *"Rien."*

Testy, the waiter patted his broom on the marble floor. *"Arrêtez ce* tap-tap-tap, *monsieur. S'il-vous plaît."*

Lermontov looked at his pencil. Before he could say *Pardonnez*— the waiter stalked away.

Lermontov smiled; the French were sulky because they lost the war. *And the Russians,* he thought, *because we won.*

He sipped his coffee and turned back to the crossword puzzle in his *International Herald Tribune.* He was a tall and slender man with a long, attenuated face and massive, deep-set eyes that recalled the Rublyov icons in Blagoveshchensky Sobor. He was deep in his seventies and had the pale skin of a Great Russian—dry and chalky, fine as white linen—and the shadow-lines of age were rough and ragged as if a hasty hand had drawn impulsively with charcoal. In the purple dawning light, the mottlings of his years lay on his cheeks and brow like coats of tempera, as if each season of his life had left its own patina; each accretion delicate, transparent, hiding nothing of the past, a chronicle accrued of troubled times. Once he had been a virile and athletic youth, a soldier who had worn a saber and commanded a brigade. Now, seven decades had bowed him bible-backed and he looked fragile and remote, like those pensioners one sees crabbing up and down the streets of Paris—elderly veterans in black suits and black bow ties, carrying an umbrella on a sunny day, ribbons won in long-forgotten battles pinned above their hearts. That was the final destination of every veteran's journey, and those who awaited the last bivouac were the same in Paris, Moscow, Amsterdam, Vienna, and New York. They shared the weary eyes and shuffling gait; their blood bonfires quenched and comrades dead; enemies extinct; orators silenced and slogans forgotten; searching as an old mind turns out its pockets for a misplaced word, groping to recall the cause that moved their feet in the days when their marching shook the world.

Mikhail Lermontov was an old soldier, but he was not a pensioner. The *Tribune* crossword puzzle was the dainty perquisite of a negotiator on the Soviet START delegation in Geneva. He looked up and smiled as a rumpled, bearded man in a blue suit and dotted blue bow tie sat down across the breakfast table. *"Zdravstvuyte."*

"Zdravstvuyte, Misha," Jake said, and unfolded his napkin into his lap. "What's in the paper? Good news?"

"Great excitement. 'Strong dollar humbles franc.' The speculators are doing a killing."

"Making a killing. My friend, you should have been a capitalist." Jake motioned to the waiter. *"Café complet."* The waiter nodded curtly, shuffled off in no great hurry. "And the puzzle?"

Lermontov tapped his pencil on the newspaper. "These days, they make so many puns . . . very difficult."

Jake adjusted his glasses. "May I?"

Lermontov leaned forward, held the newspaper where Jake could study it. When they were leaning together, Lermontov whispered, "First Step is a blunder. Surely you see that."

Jake nodded, intent upon the puzzle. "We must make the best of it." Then he brightened. "My friend, I think I can help you. May I?" He took Lermontov's pencil. But as he printed the letters, he whispered, "Remember Afghanistan and Kuwait. We both pay for our history lessons in blood."

They shared a private, worried look.

Then Jake turned and looked out the window toward the lake. South and east, the clouds that wreathed the Alps were underlit in flame against the glory of the dawn. "Still, on a morning like this it's hard to believe there's violence in the world."

Lermontov chuckled. "My friend, you should have been a boulevardier." He set the newspaper on an empty chair as the waiter returned with Jake's coffee and roll. "You sit here with the CIA watching you . . ."

Lermontov nodded right. A serious young man at the next table quickly averted his eyes.

"The KGB watching me . . ."

At a table on the left, another serious young man went quickly back to his breakfast.

"The *Bundespolizei* watching all of us . . ."

At a table near the door, a middle-aged Swiss raised his copy of *Neue Zürcher Zeitung* to conceal his eyes.

"And you can still say it's a beautiful morning?"

Jake put his hand on Lermontov's. "At least they're not in an alley in Montevideo, slitting each other's throats."

Lermontov stared at Jake; his eyes softened. There was much they shared. "Yes. At least we may be thankful for that." He cleared his throat, raised his coffee cup and, loud enough for all to hear said, "*Mir.* Peace." He held his cup aloft, turned a defiant eye on the other tables one-by-one; none dared meet his glance.

Jake lifted his coffee cup. "*L'chaim,*" he said.

But the red glow of the rising sun glimmered darkly in his eyes.

DETENTION CELL #6, ANDREWS AFB, CAMP SPRINGS, MD

1:00 A.M.   Terry Watkins was in a fury. His wife clutched his arm, trying to restrain him. "You slimy motherfuckers! What's she doing here?"

O'Neill set a calming hand on Watkins's shoulder. "Terry, have you thought it over?"

Watkins shrugged the hand off, went back to the bunk and thumped his butt down. "You know, they keep us mighty busy in Leavenworth, Colonel."

"Have you, Terry?"

"Yeah. I've thought about it."

"And?"

"And nothing. I'm through doing your dirty work."

Harding sneered. "You're doing thirty years to life. That's what you're doing, asshole. Sonofabitch never had the guts to—"

Watkins leaped to his feet, lurched forward like a tethered animal; his ankle chains clanked taut. "Take these cuffs off, I'll show you who's got guts!"

"At ease." Petrovsky raised his hand. "Everyone, relax."

The men fell silent.

Petrovsky picked a speck of lint from the front of his uniform. "Terry, we've been counting on you. We'd like to see you free." He looked down at Mrs. Watkins. "Mary wants you free. Don't you, Mary?" The woman's face went slack. Petrovsky reached out, gently stroked her hair. "Don't you?"

"Keep your fucking hands off her!"

Petrovsky took his hand away. "All right, Terry. No need to shout." He walked around the table, stood before Watkins's bunk. "We brought Mary here to help you make your decision."

Watkins looked at his wife; her fearful, hopeful eyes stared back at him. "A pardon?" he said.

"No. You'll be out. That's all. But you *will* be out."

"And be a hunted man for the rest of my life?"

"Either that, or you're back on a plane to Leavenworth at noon tomorrow. It's up to you."

Mrs. Watkins gasped, "Terry—"

Watkins put a finger to his lips. His eyes were gentle. "Mary, shush."

Petrovsky said, "For the last time, Terry. Are you with us?"

Watkins stroked his wife's face. There were tears on her cheek—tears of fear and hope and the fear of hoping. Watkins said, "Colonel, I'll go to hell first."

Petrovsky smiled. "We've been to hell. Remember?"

The two men stared eye-to-eye. Then Watkins slouched back on his bunk and turned away. His wife lowered her head against the back of his hand.

"All right," Petrovsky said. "If that's your decision. No hard feelings." He dug a pack of Wrigley's spearmint from his pocket. "Stick of gum?" Watkins ignored him. Petrovsky tossed the pack on the table, turned, and nodded. Harding rapped once on the steel door.

Outside in the darkness, Sergeant Jeeter tossed his cigarette away; Christy scrambled to her feet as he pulled the door open.

"Lieutenant, give them half an hour in private," Petrovsky said as he passed her. "Then see Mrs. Watkins home."

"Yes, sir." She stepped back as the three officers went by.

Christy stood and watched the men walk away down the narrow

path between the fences, in and out of the hot slashes of the spotlights. It was a strange, displaced image: three officers, the cruel barbed wire, the savage lights—all fogbound in a pall of wintry night. Somehow, it was not an image of Andrews Air Force Base or Washington but an image from a prior time and distant, angry place—an outpost on the verges of a war.

Then Christy realized the three officers were in step. Their thick-soled shoes snapped at the pavement in a rigid, driving cadence.

They were not walking; they were marching.

And for the first time she felt the icy chill of night creep through the fabric of her uniform, crawl over the pores of her skin, coil about her legs like a serpent.

Behind her, Jeeter slammed the steel door shut.

Involuntarily, Christy's hand went to her throat.

PLACE DES NATIONS, GENEVA

7:38 A.M. Jake left his taxi at the Place des Nations—he always did when the weather would allow—and took the long walk up the hill to the American mission as his morning constitutional. East of the lake the peaks of the Alps were brilliant daybreak saffron in the rising sun. He passed the smart white eight-foot walls of the Soviet mission compound; the uniformed Red Army corporal who kept the gate raised his hand in recognition. Jake nodded back and quickened his steps toward the American mission just up the hill.

Isolated behind concrete barriers in two diplomatic missions three hundred meters apart on the Avenue de la Paix and Route de Pregny, the Soviet and American START teams had spent the past nine years debating thermonuclear insanity while a new world evolved around them. The sudden waning of the Cold War in the winter of 1989 had provided a remarkable experience for Jake and the other American negotiators—men who spent their days in edgy wrangling over the minutiae of missile counting rules and megatonnage and then went home to televised images of mobs cheering the return of democracy to Budapest and East Berlin. Jake had followed the dispatches from the State Department, read the detailed reports in the *International Herald Tribune* and *The New York Times*. But the blow-by-blow accounts of communism crumbling from Bulgaria to Nicaragua—bulletins that filled free men and women with hope and joy—were to

Jake and the other strategic arms negotiators like reading the sports pages, intriguing but of no real consequence. Somehow, the START negotiations were immune, buffered from the worldwide renaissance of freedom, isolated in their own dismal reality, insulated against the peal of liberty's bells. By November of 1991, Jake understood the phenomenon: what happened in the world of men meant nothing to the bomb.

Where the Avenue de la Paix became the Route de Pregny, Jake stopped before the double gates of the American mission compound and held his pass close to the thick, bulletproof window so the guard could compare his picture with his face. The locking mechanism on the turnstile clicked; Jake pushed through and walked up the driveway. There was a catering truck parked at the top of the drive, and men in white coveralls were off-loading cocktail tables and red plush chairs for the Veterans Day cocktail gala that afternoon. The housekeeping staff was busily hanging crossed American and Soviet flags in the windows of the west wing lobby.

Jake never walked that last short hill without a touch of sadness. It had come to this: the airy steel and glass six-story building surrounded by a wall of concrete barricades and wire; uniformed and armed marines in the foyer operating the metal detector and X-ray scanner that were de rigueur. Such were the precautions required to protect American diplomats from the frustrated rage of the Third World. Jake ran his identity pass through the card reader; when the red light went out, he pushed through the glass inner door and took the elevator to the fifth floor.

His secretary, the maidenly, menopausal and persnickety Miss Green was waiting in his anteroom. "Good morning, Doctor." She held out his mail.

Jake muttered, "So it is," and shuffled through the pile of faxes and interoffice memoranda. As he did, his nostrils twitched; Miss Green wore Opium; the perfume's cloying odor infested the air of his reception room like an evil spirit.

She handed him the phone list and gave her usual recitation while he scanned it for himself. "Matson called from NATO Brussels. Said it's urgent."

"Call back tomorrow."

"Your friend, Mr. Singer from *The New York Times* . . ."

"Decline. Politely."

"The Misses Abrahams invited you to Montreux for a Wednesday lunch."

"Enchanté."

"And Dr. Feidus confirmed your appointment at ten-thirty."

Jake looked up, remembering. "You'd better cancel."

She sniffed. "We canceled last week. At your age, health is everything."

That put a twinkle in his eye. "Is it?"

"Yes." She nodded toward his office. "And 'Major Cool' is waiting for you."

"Really?" Jake handed back the mail and went to his office door. Then he stopped and looked back at Miss Green. "Health is not everything. Even at my age." He opened the inner door and went inside.

The room was drably functional, its prefabricated walls hung with the standard-issue posters from the USIA—the Statute of Liberty, the Grand Canyon, Niagara Falls—sentimental, jingoistic kitsch. Jake loathed the room; it had all the personality of a Ramada Inn. An army major stood near the sliding door that opened onto a tiny balcony. Five floors below, the glass cupola of the terrace lounge they called the Winter Garden glistened in the morning sun.

"Good morning, Major. To what do I owe the pleasure?"

"Good morning, Doctor," Sara said.

She turned to face him, and despite himself, Jake flushed. Major Sara Weatherby had been his aide for more than two years; yet, he still felt the same excitement each time he saw her. In every man, there is a slumbering life of fantasy to which one living woman holds the key; most men live out their lives without ever meeting her. The first time Jake met Sara, he knew she was the one.

He was aware of her reputation: maddeningly brilliant, something of a tart. But she was also beautiful beyond imagining. Her hair was ash blond, so pale and fine it was almost white. She had gray eyes— large and lifeless—the most impassive eyes he'd ever seen; the first time he'd felt their gaze, he knew he would wring his soul to kindle fire in those eyes. But he was old and she was young. She was also tall—five eight or five nine—taller than he. Under the snug green jacket of her uniform, her breasts were high. They said she had her jackets tailored to better display her figure. They said she was promiscuous; one met a number of men who claimed they'd had her. But in all the time Sara Weatherby had been his aide, Jake had never seen that side of her—although he speculated under certain circumstances he might find it most beguiling. In the office, she was correct and curt and flawless; they called her Major Cool.

Jake went to the sliding door, looked down at the Winter Garden and the bare thicket of the woods beyond the concrete barricade. In the distance, the lake glistened and the snow-peaked Alps loomed awesome and serene.

"Major, have you noticed what a lovely day it is?"

"Sir?"

"Have you noticed the mountains are filled with light, and that you're a pretty woman?"

"I beg your pardon, sir?"

"Just today, why don't you say, Hi, Jake, it's great to be alive."

Sara said, "Ambassador Mulholland is awaiting a call from the president. He'd like to speak with you when they've finished. Will that be all, sir?"

Jake sighed and shook his head. "Yes, Major. That will be all."

OVAL OFFICE, THE WHITE HOUSE, WASHINGTON

1:47 A.M.   President Samuel Baker sat wearily on the couch before the crackling hickory logs in the fireplace. His press secretary Ron Fowler sat across. Ted Harris leaned against the mantelpiece, fists driven down into the pockets of his trousers.

"All right," Harris said. "Starting tomorrow morning, we're on the offensive. Whitworth's on *Today;* we'll get Scowcroft on *Good Morning, America.*"

"No go," Fowler said.

"Why the hell not?"

"Arledge says they've got a Vaclav Havel exclusive and they're doing Eastern Europe."

"What the hell does he think First Step is about? Eastern Cincinnati?"

"We've got Dan Moynihan on the CBS *Morning News* and Bob Packwood Monday night on Larry King. I think we can . . ."

Sam Baker's mind drifted away from the conversation. He was tired. He used to mock President Reagan for dozing during cabinet meetings; now he felt only compassion for the man. Being president of the United States *was* the hardest job in the world—it was too hard for an old man—and yet it was a job that should be left only to old men after life had taught them tolerance and patience and their aging bodies reminded them every morning how close they stood to Judgment Day.

In a way, Monday, November 11—Veterans Day—would be Sam Baker's day of judgment. At breakfast tables, over morning papers, in commuter trains, in car pools, around office coffee machines . . . Americans would begin debating his First Step disarmament initiative. In Elks club bars, in police ready rooms, at workout spas, and in the supermarket checkout line . . . everyday Americans in everyday places would begin debating the future security of their nation. It was one of the wonders of democracy: free people freely debating the policy of their elected leaders—free to agree or disagree. And Sam Baker knew it was their view—the view of the man in the street, not his own—that would finally shape the destiny of the United States.

Ron Fowler droned on, listing the broadcasts and magazines, the authorities the administration would parade before the media to answer questions and allay concerns about First Step. Sam Baker sighed; when the prize was public opinion, that was how the game was played. The professional communicators, the spin doctors, the phrase-makers had to hit the interview trail with their stock of fact, rhetoric, and hyperbole. Sam Baker didn't like it, but he had no choice. The opposition was small and scattered, but they were distinguished and articulate men who would argue their positions well.

"All right, Ron. Thank you." Sam Baker looked to Harris. "Where are we on allies?"

"Coleman leaves Tuesday for Brussels. John Major is demanding a meeting—"

"A summit?"

"No. Just a belly-to-belly by December third."

"He feeling any better about First Step?" Sam Baker already knew the answer.

"He wants to cut your nuts off."

"He'll have to wait his turn."

"That's what I told him."

Sam Baker chuckled. Then he clapped his hands down on his knees. "Well. If that's the lot, I think I'll hit the hay." He rose, and so did Fowler.

But as the president started for the door, Harris said, "What about your call to Geneva?"

Sam Baker tapped his forehead. "Almost forgot. Can't you handle it?"

"I think you'd better."

"The cruise missile thing's a detail."

"Not to the START guys," Harris said. "You'd better talk to

Littman, too. You know how the navy feels about anything that limits force projection since the Persian Gulf."

Sam Baker put his hand to his mouth to cover a yawn. "All right. Get them on the phone."

Ambassador Craig Mulholland, chief of the American START delegation, sat at his desk in his office on the second floor of the Geneva mission, scribbling marginalia on the First Step briefing paper that had come by secure fax from the State Department's Office of Strategic Affairs; the document contained the talking points for the morning's plenary at the Soviet mission. Mulholland was fifty-five, a thick-lipped, big-nosed man, a career diplomat who'd served through four administrations before his patronage of Ambassador Richard Burt had landed him at START. After three years of El Salvador, the Duarte charade and jungle war, Mulholland was glad to have a quiet posting off the firing line. But as he studied the talking points of First Step, he was worried.

His intercom sounded. "Mr. Ambassador, the president is calling on the secure line."

"Thank you, Dorothy." Mulholland punched the code key on the encryption phone console on his desk. The display blinked once; then the legend *The White House* appeared. "Good morning, Mr. President. I mean . . . good evening."

"Getting to be morning here, too," Sam Baker said. "Craig, you got the briefing paper on First Step?"

"Yes, sir. I have it in my hands."

"Well, there's not much to it. We need a zero-option on sea-launched nuclear cruise missiles to make the NATO cutback work."

"Yes, sir." Mulholland checked that point.

"So you'll need to work out an INF-style agreement for on-site inspectors in navy yards and no-notice inspections on naval battle groups at sea. Can do?"

Mulholland circled that one. "I don't know, Mr. President. Navy yards are one thing. But boarding parties on the high seas . . . that may be tough."

"Just make the Soviets understand that if they don't agree, the Senate won't buy the package. And our NATO troops stay where they are."

"Yes, sir. I'll try."

"Who's your technical team leader on verification?"

"Jake Handlesman."

"Never met the man. What's he like?"

"An old-timer. Shrewd. Tough. Goes all the way back to Helsinki 1969."

"Is he too tough?"

"Secretary Littman says he's the right man."

"I see." Sam Baker weighed that. Each of the key departments—State, Defense, the Joint Chiefs, and the CIA—had its picked men on the negotiating team, experts looking after that department's particular interests. The picked men fought for their priorities, back-channeled reports to their bureaucratic bosses. It was an awkward system, even a divisive one, that had evolved over the decades. But, in a democracy, it was the only way to win consensus. And without consensus, no strategic arms agreement could survive the scrutiny of Congress.

Another line rang. Harris went to the president's desk, punched in and lifted the receiver. He motioned to the president. "They're getting Littman now."

"All right, Craig," Sam Baker said. "Do your best. Get me something I can take to the Hill."

"I'll try, sir."

The president held the disconnect down. "Stay on the line, Ted." Then he hit another button. "Hello? Zack?"

Zack Littman stood in a corner of the teak-paneled stateroom of the motor yacht *Odalisque*. His black satin bow tie hung loosely from the open collar of his ruffled shirt, and the jacket of his tuxedo lay across the foot of the double bed. Outside the open porthole, paper lanterns bobbed in the Caribbean breeze; he could hear the syncopated rhythms of recorded Latin music from the lounge a hundred feet astern. Behind him at her dressing table, his wife Clara sat in her blue sequined evening gown, removing her pearls.

"Yes, Mr. President?" Littman said.

"How's the yacht, Zack?"

"It's a block long and there are separate saunas for men and women. Does that answer your question?" He looked back at Clara; they shared a smile. "You know, Sam, there are days when I begin to think the critics of Pentagon spending aren't all cranks."

"You take good care of those aerospace barons. They vote, too, you know."

"Probably six times each."

The president forced a smile. Zack Littman was his oldest friend; it had hurt like hell to send him away incommunicado while First Step was breaking. But it had to be done. Even so, it was hard for Sam Baker to hear the distance in Littman's voice; beyond the embarrassment of another "fishing trip" to Eleuthera, First Step had opened a gulf of permanent dissonance between them.

"Clara and Louise enjoying the holiday?"

Littman looked lovingly toward his young wife. "Clara's practicing her Spanish." She waved at him in the mirror, laughed soundlessly, and shook her head. "And Louise thinks we shouldn't hurt the fish. Actually, we haven't hurt many."

"Look, Zack, I won't keep you long. I just got off the phone with Mulholland. Give me your opinion. Will the Joint Chiefs go along if we can cut a deal with the Soviets for permanent on-site inspectors at navy yards and no-notice boarding parties on warships at sea?"

Littman straightened. "Mulholland can get that?"

"He's going to try. But will the Pentagon sit still?"

"The air force and army might buy in. The navy will fight it tooth and nail."

"What does the navy know that we don't?"

"They've been shot at. We haven't."

Sam Baker sighed; the professional soldiers would go on fighting the Cold War for years after it was over. "Have you talked to Powell?"

General Colin Powell was the first black chairman of the Joint Chiefs of Staff: handsome, charismatic—a model soldier and a perfect "Beltway general."

"I talked to him this afternoon."

"And? What did he say?"

Littman grumbled. "What do you think he said? He said, 'Yes, sir.'"

In other words, Powell and the Joint Chiefs would support First Step. They had no choice. But neither had they any appetite. "All right, Zack. Call him again in the morning. Tell him to get the navy aboard. Tell him it's important."

"You're the boss."

"And say goodnight for me to Clara."

"Sure. The same to you."

Littman pressed the disconnect. For a moment, he stood with his finger on the button. In spite of everything he had said and done, the president had announced First Step; now he was moving to implement it. Within days, both superpowers would begin taking irrevocable steps toward restructuring their defense establishments. And the world would begin drifting into an age when thermonuclear intercontinental missiles—not men—kept the strategic peace.

A movement from the dressing area caught Littman's eye. He turned and looked back. Clara was just stepping out of her dress; in spite of all that was preying on Littman's mind, the sight aroused him. Clara was almost thirty years his junior, a trophy wife, a passion that had come to him long after he had thought his passions spent. She saw him watching, discreetly turned her back as she unhooked her bra.

Littman stared. Why did women do that? Turn away? Or had she just begun to do that one day and he hadn't noticed until now?

"Clara . . . turn around." And when she did, he could see how motherhood had transformed her figure; her breasts had matured and softened, no longer pointed up the way they had. Her nipples were pronounced and heavy-tipped from nursing. But he still adored her.

"Zack?" She raised a forearm to cover herself. "What is it?"

"Did I tell you that I love you?"

She smiled shyly. "Not since yesterday."

He held the receiver tighter. "I love you, Clara."

"I love you, too." She opened her dresser and took out the plastic bag that contained her diaphragm and jelly, went into the bathroom, and shut the door.

Littman waited until he heard the sound of running water. Then he punched another number on the telephone.

"I'll be with the ambassador," Jake said as he passed Miss Green's desk. "And in plenary session at the Soviet mission until ten."

"Don't forget. Doctor's appointment. Ten-thirty. And the Veterans Day gala at four o'clock."

"No, Miss Green. I won't forget." But when he reached for the doorknob, the phone rang.

"Doctor, the Secretary of Defense is calling."

"I'll take it inside." Jake went back into the inner office, locked the door, and picked up the receiver.

"How are you, Mr. Secretary?"

"Jake, this First Step thing is—"

"Taken care of."

"Jake, I'm worried—"

"It's taken care of, Mr. Secretary. I assure you."

There was silence on the line. Then Littman said, "All right. Good-night."

Jake looked out the window at the blazing sun, at its vast energy pouring down on the surface of Lake Geneva. "On the contrary—good morning."

DETENTION CELL #6, ANDREWS AFB, CAMP SPRINGS, MD

1:51 A.M.   Terry Watkins stretched back in his chair so that his coveralls pulled taut across his lap. Then he zipped his fly. He could still feel the creeping damp shining off the cinder-block walls like cold light, but now he had a good, warm glow in his joints and he didn't feel so angry anymore.

His wife stood with her back to him, irritable, adjusting her clothes. "That what they brung me for? To *do* you?"

It had been seventeen years since he'd had her; tenderly, he watched her dress. Poor thing, she was losing her figure. The lusty curves that once proclaimed her sexuality—the swelling of her buttocks, the brackets of her hips—had lost their timbre. Now the flesh of her hips had ridden upward toward her waist; her buttocks had grown slack and flaccid. And when she had unbuttoned the front of her dress, it startled him how low her nipples rode. Soon those upward-downward countercurrents would neuter her figure and she would be a middle-aged woman, slab-thighed, slab-sided, dull, undifferentiated flesh. Petrovsky was nothing if not shrewd; seeing Mary this way honed the sting of imprisonment. Terry Watkins was confronted all at once with his wife's soul in a stranger's aging body.

"Dammit, Terry, you answer me!"

"They brought you here because Petrovsky wants me to run an errand. And they left you here"—he sighed—"to give me a taste of being free."

She went to him, knelt beside his chair, and clutched his arm. "Can they do that? Set you free?"

He brushed her hair back from her forehead. "Don't think about it, Mary."

But her tears were welling again, pooling and quivering on her lower lids. "Terry . . ."

"I said . . . *don't.*"

She shook her head and her tears spilled through her lashes and down her cheeks. She caught one with the tip of her tongue as a little girl might, and her eyes wandered the cell as though she were lost. "You don't know how it is with me. I got no hope. No way. All these years . . . had nothin' but welfare checks and . . ."

He eased down off the chair, knelt with her. The concrete floor was freezing and rough against his knees, but her warmth came through his coveralls. He took her face in his hands and the steel chain of his manacles hung across her throat like a necklace of sorrow. "Don't you know I love you?"

"Then do it. Do what Petrovsky wants."

He lifted his arms up and over her head, put the manacled hoop of his wrists around her, held her to him. Now the very chains that imprisoned him seemed to bind them together. His voice was gentle, indulgent, as though speaking to a child. "Mary, listen to me. I know they look like the guys I soldiered with. They're not. They're changed. The country treated them like they lost the Vietnam War. For eighteen years, they've been stuck in little make-work jobs. They're angry. They're dangerous."

She looked up at him, blinking through her tears. "What do they want you to do?"

He shook his head. "I can't tell you."

Angrily, she wiped her eyes. "That how it is with us now? Secrets between us?" She tried to pull free, to rise.

He held her. "Mary, if they thought you knew, they'd kill you."

For a moment, she stared at him. "You call what I'm doin' *livin'*?"

He pressed her closer. "How'd I rate a wife like you?"

On the low wooden bench outside the cell, Christy sat in the glare of the halogen lights, clutching her arms across her chest for warmth, staring up at the gleaming points of barbed wire, watching her steamy breath rise. The November night was silent. In the wood beyond the road, there was no whispering of insects, no crickets' chirp, nothing to distract her from the sighs and whispers beyond the steel door.

A few feet down the walkway, Sergeant Jeeter stood, one boot cocked against the fence behind him, smoking and staring out toward the taxi lights of the deserted runway. When the sounds of lovemaking had begun, he leered and seemed about to make a joke. But he thought better of it when Christy's eyes admonished him; their slitted darkness gleamed authority.

It had been a long learning curve for her—learning to control men with a glance, to order them about. It had not come easy; taking orders was one thing, giving them another. She had completed the cycle of officership courses at MIT; those lectures had taught her the style—precise, concise, and unequivocal. But nothing in her undergraduate training had prepared her to issue real-world commands in the real world of the air force. That, she'd learned from Captain Bryan.

When Christy reported to the naval school in Monterey after almost a year on active duty, she was still afraid enlisted men resented her and her authority.

"Why?" Bryan said. "You have the rank."

"But I'm a woman. They know I'm not a real soldier. When the shooting starts, they'll fight. I won't."

"Don't be silly. When you give an order they don't see a woman. They see a uniform."

"I don't see uniforms."

"What do you see?"

Christy lowered her eyes. "I see men."

"Do you?"

"Yes."

"And do you like it? The power to command?"

Christy hesitated; Bryan was wise. "Yes."

"Is it . . . erotic?"

Christy lay her head on Bryan's chest. "Yes."

"I envy you," Bryan said and smiled. "Remember, men taking orders from a woman isn't as unnatural as it sounds. They all had mothers." Christy shut her eyes and felt the strong hand brush her hair. "The rest will pass."

It never had. Even now, enlisted men were more than uniforms to her. They were bigger, stronger, more experienced and tougher. They were real soldiers; they could fight. Christy could not ignore that; she didn't want to; three years on and it was still erotic—not the men, the power. It was on the parade ground, when a thousand heels hit concrete in unison; it was doing push-ups in the gym when her muscles screamed for oxygen; it was during survival training when she crouched in muddy water with a bayonet in her fist; it was in those moments when it was her sweating, straining body—and other bodies—that made up the corps; it was then she felt a soldier.

It *was* about bodies after all. War was when minds had failed and bodies had to arbitrate. That was the paradox her life had become. To the United States Air Force, anatomy was destiny. She was a soldier in every way except the way that counted; the door to combat was forever shut against her sex.

At their first interview at MIT in 1986, Petrovsky had asked her, "Why Intel?"

"Because women aren't permitted into combat."

"And Intel?"

"It's the one way I can fight."

Petrovsky had made good on the promise he had made to her that day—on all his promises. He had arranged a year's delay in her call-up to active duty that allowed her to complete her master's in Russian Studies. He had endorsed her applications to Air Force Intelligence School and the Naval Postgraduate School in Monterey where she earned a second master's in National Security Affairs. He had even given her the letter of introduction to Captain Bryan. And he had asked for nothing in return—only loyalty. There were moments Christy wondered why.

She knew she was pretty in an exotic, Slavic way. Petrovsky was a bachelor—a gentle, quiet man who'd never married. She must have been attractive to him. And yet there was never any hint in him of anything but warm formality. She admired him for that, and for the chance he'd given her to fight the only way she could.

But she had been born too late. The Cold War was over. Soon INI would be a memory—a footnote to the history of a war that never happened, a war without glory, her war. Soon Petrovsky and O'Neill and Harding—even Captain Bryan—would be shades like her father: ghostly warriors fading into memory, remembered only by discarded unit insignia gathering dust in the corners of museums.

And yet, tonight Petrovsky had given her an order with implications that seemed to test the boundaries of military law. Christy sat, remembering the image of three officers marching into the night. She was an intelligence officer and—for some reason she could not fully comprehend, her flesh prickled with an intuition of impending battle.

Sergeant Jeeter dropped his cigarette and crushed it out. "It's 0150 and then some, L'tenant."

Christy shook off the reverie and stood. "All right. Open up."

Jeeter put his ear to the steel door of the detention cell. Then he looked at Christy, smirking. "Nothing' movin'. Guess they had it off."

"Open the damn door, Sergeant."

"Yes'm." He pulled the bolt and swung the door ajar.

The image in the cell made Christy stiffen. Watkins and his wife were kneeling on the floor as though in prayer, arms wound about each other, heads lowered to each other's shoulder.

Watkins looked up, glaring. "What the hell do you want?"

"I'm sorry. Time to go, ma'am," Christy said.

Watkins pressed his wife closer. "I love you, Mary. You're all that keeps me going. Please try to understand."

"I'll try," she said. "I love you."

He kissed her tenderly.

"Okay, Watkins. 'Nuffa that." Jeeter jerked the prisoner to his feet. Watkins bent and helped his wife up, watched Jeeter lead her out the door. Then Watkins leaned over the table, picked up Petrovsky's pack of chewing gum. He winked at Christy. "Thanks, kid."

She started at the familiarity.

"Relax." Watkins smiled. "No war on yet." And Christy saw him plop down on the bunk before the door slammed shut between them.

SOVIET MISSION, 15 AVENUE DE LA PAIX, GENEVA

7:54 A.M. "NATO will reject it outright," Abakov said. He was the party political officer on the Soviet team, an arrogant, self-righteous little Marxist from the Caucasus, an oily, quasi-educated *apparatchik* from Kirovabad and a lieutenant colonel in the KGB. It was said he had gypsy blood. The other Soviet delegates sat in silence; they didn't like Abakov, particularly when he might be right.

"Conventional NATO force reductions are not our concern," Viktor Karpov said. "Only the sea-launched nuclear cruise missiles. If President Gorbachev agrees to their elimination, our duty will be to see the policy implemented." He was a natty, dark-eyed patrician and chief of the Soviet delegation; by treaty, his status, like Mulholland's, was ambassadorial. His opinion had to be respected—but not necessarily by the KGB.

"If, and I say *if*"—Abakov waved his index finger—"*if* we agree to a zero-option on sea-launched nuclear cruise missiles, what then? Conservatives in their Senate will form committees and make television speeches. Reactionaries will get up on their hind legs and shriek, Appeasement! And we'll have SALT II all over again."

"With respect, Sergei Iosifovitch," Admiral Grushkin said in his courtly manner, "SALT II has been respected although unratified. Has it not?"

In the far corner of the room, Lermontov sat quietly beneath a window, listening with half an ear, his face turned toward the light, eyes half closed, basking in the warmth of the early morning sun. In the Kremlin, the Politburo had only begun to consider President Baker's proposal on sea-launched nuclear cruise missiles, yet Abakov had already rejected it. Even after six years of *perestroika,* the KGB still thought of itself as a separate government of the USSR. How difficult it was to govern a nation with a legacy of seventy-five years of secrecy and repression.

Even so, it amused Lermontov to listen to such open debate outside the small surveillance-proof room in the mission basement known as the bubble. But one of the paradoxes of arms negotiations was that there were few if any secrets. Spy satellites gave each side an accurate accounting of the numbers and dispositions of the other's major weapons systems. Espionage, *The New York Times,* and simple logic provided corroboration and details. In any event, the arsenals had to be discussed with frankness; if not, how were negotiations to proceed at all? Lermontov put on his eyeglasses and unfolded his *International Herald Tribune.*

"Be that as it may," Karpov was saying, "my instructions this morning are to discuss the American proposal to decommission all sea-launched nuclear cruise missiles."

"What about verification?" Abakov said. "What about that? How do we verify? And how do they? By surrendering the sovereignty of our vessels on the high seas?"

Lermontov smiled; on that point, Abakov was right beyond dispute. Massive intercontinental ballistic missile silos were visible to military satellites; their numbers could be verified without on-site inspection. But the sea-launched cruise missile—the so-called *slick-em*—was an eighteen-foot-long miniature robot jet airplane that flew at subsonic speeds fifty feet above the surface of the earth. It could carry a 200-kiloton nuclear warhead and was guided by a powerful computer and exquisitely detailed mapping system that allowed it to pick its way in and out of valleys, fly beyond its target and double back, perceive threatening aircraft, take evasive action, and return to its original course. The stunning pinpoint accuracy of the American navy's cruise missiles—and the destruction their conventional explosive warheads wrought on Baghdad during the Persian Gulf war—had come as a harrowing and unnerving revelation to the generals of the Soviet Stavka Command. Clearly, the nuclear armed TLAM-N land-attack *slick-ems* of the American Sixth Fleet could reach and destroy every Soviet military and civilian target west of the Urals. And the tiny *slick-ems* could be secreted in submarines or any surface ship larger than a frigate. Even if a zero-option on the missiles were agreed, verification would be impossible without on-site inspectors at both countries' naval bases and the right to conduct unannounced boarding of naval vessels on the high seas. In that respect, the elusive, lethal *slick-em* was the crowning paradox of forty-five years of strategic arms development. Unless the two rival nations agreed to surrender naval sovereignty, neither the weapon's existence nor its nonexistence could be verified.

"Sergei Iosifovitch," Lermontov said wearily, "zero is the only state we *can* verify."

All the faces in the room turned to Lermontov. "If we agree a thousand *slick-ems* on each side, how do we assure ourselves the Americans don't have a thousand and one? Cruise missiles can be hidden, moved, repainted. But if we agree to zero, even one becomes a violation."

"Thank you, Mikhail Yurievitch," Karpov said. "Now, as to our agenda for today. . . ."

Lermontov didn't have to hear the rest of this morning's instructions. He had heard them a thousand times: identify, clarify, define, examine hypotheses, probe for options, and then report to Moscow and await instructions. Workaday, repetitive, but necessary in this game of millimeters.

Lermontov turned his *Tribune* to the light, adjusted his glasses, and stared at the rows of definitions printed alongside the puzzle. He had first begun working American crossword puzzles when he matriculated at the Institute of Foreign Affairs after the Great Patriotic War; his instructors had used the puzzles to test their students' vocabularies by requiring them to work in pen against the clock. The weekend *Tribune* puzzle was still a challenge but a challenge he enjoyed. When negotiations were in session, he could always ask Jake Handlesman for help when he was stumped—as he had been this morning—for an eight-letter word for "peril." He could always count on Jake. He looked fondly at the heavy letters his old friend had printed in the squares. Then Lermontov realized the crosswords didn't fit. And then he saw that Jake had printed

HAKODATE.

MISSION PLANNING ROOM, OCEANA NAVAL AIR STATION, VIRGINIA BEACH, VA

1:59 A.M.   Commander Cholly Granger, the F-14 training pilot, stood at the counter in the silent AirOps building, filling out a log-and-load sheet with a blue navy pencil. Lieutenant Robert Niles, the yawny black duty officer shuffled out of the kitchen, stirring his mug of coffee. "Hey, Cholly, hear the Tomcatters off the *Kennedy* gave you a 'Winder up the ying-yang. You gettin' too old, bro'. These kids startin' to push you around."

Granger looked up; the embarrassment of the intercept had made it back to Oceana before he had. He smiled and handed the form to Niles. "Never laid a hand on me."

"Yeah. Right." Niles swung his leg over his chair like he was mounting a horse; then he ran his eye down the requisition. "Lessee what we got here. F-14. Check. Two AIM-9M Sidewinder. Check. Six—what's this—six AIM-54C Phoenix?" He laughed. "Come on, Cholly-man. Can't draw stores like that 'less we're goin' to war."

"Never can tell, Bobby. Some people say the sun will come up tomorrow."

"Yeah. And some people—" Then Niles broke off; he stared at Granger. "Tomorrow?"

Granger nodded once.

Softly Niles said, "Hallelujah, brother." He signed the authorization and handed it back.

3314 P STREET, GEORGETOWN

2:02 A.M.   Senator Simon Whitworth shuffled out of the bathroom, switched off the light, and shut the door. The yellow glow at the end of the hallway told him his wife Margaret was awake and reading. He hesitated. After forty-three years of marriage, he could hide nothing from her; there was no concealing the fact something was preying on his mind. Better to think of a way to tell her the truth without upsetting her.

But he knew there wasn't one. He sighed and padded down the hall.

Margaret was sitting up in bed, her bright corona of red hair framing her face against the pillow, her knees pulled up under the covers, a copy of *Emperor of America* cocked against them. Her gilt-framed reading glasses were perched on the tip of her nose and her lips were parted, engrossed in the unfolding story. She was a great reader; Whitworth had always admired that in her. She was different from the other prom-trotters he had courted in Charleston when he had come home from the Marianas after V-J day. Margaret Mavis Delacourt had the whitest skin and reddest hair of any woman he had ever seen. But she was shy about the freckles on her arms and bosom. Simon Whitworth had learned to love freckles as he had learned to love her. Now she was a grandmother six times over who raised money for worthy causes, coached the wives of newly elected senators on capital

etiquette, and still found time to read three newspapers every day—
every word, cover to cover, even the sports. Whenever Simon Whitworth prayed, he reminded God to take him first; there was no way
his heart could beat on after hers was stilled.

Margaret looked at him over the tops of her reading glasses,
watched him shuffle across the room to his edge of the bed and sit,
a fragile, weary man in striped pajamas, an old prisoner under life
sentence to the state.

"Simon," she said softly in her delicate South Carolina drawl. "It's
after two, hon. You have to get your rest if you're going on that
program in the morning."

"Yes, dear." But he sat where he was.

Margaret reached out and rested her fingertips against his back. She
could feel the warm life beating under the well-worn pajamas. Once,
a lion had inhabited that body; now, an elderly man sat beside her on
the bed, an aging champion in his twilight years, vulnerable in his
decline. Softly she said, "They're going to ask you about First Step,
aren't they?"

Silently, he nodded.

"And you don't approve?"

"First Step is dangerous." He looked back at her. "I must speak
out."

She took her glasses off. "Then do it, Simon." She stretched her
open palm toward him.

He took her hand in his; it was small and fragile, darkened where
the blots of age commingled with the freckles. "Peg, what if I'm
wrong?"

"Are you?"

"I don't know." He turned to her, and she could see his eyes were
haunted. It was a look she hadn't seen since he'd served with Peter
Rodino on the House Judiciary Committee that had voted the im-
peachment of Richard Nixon.

Margaret set her book and glasses on the night table. "Are you
afraid you'll make enemies?"

That made him smile. "I've got enough enemies to last three lifetimes." He squeezed her hand and let it go, bent to ease his slippers
off. Then he lay back and swung the covers over his legs. "I've stood
against the hawks. I've stood against the Pentagon. But now I'm
standing against disarmament."

She slid closer to him, laid her head on his shoulder. His joints were
bony beneath the cloth—brittle but still hard. Gently she whispered,
"What is it, Simon? Why does it vex you so?"

"I'm on the wrong side, Peg. I'm on the side of madmen and warmongers."

She shut her eyes and held him close. "Whatever side you're on is the right side, Simon."

"Mother, I hope so. In God's name, I hope so." He snapped off the light.

SOVIET MISSION, 15 AVENUE DE LA PAIX, GENEVA

8:05 A.M.   Jake Handlesman had the floor. "You have military attachés in embassies and consulates all over the United States. Your KGB has operatives in every port city with a major naval installation. They can take taxis to our bases for inspection."

The American interpreter began the translation into Russian.

While he spoke, Jake sat back, looked down the length of the room. Even the architecture of their mission betrayed the Soviets' ambivalence toward their past. The dormitories and the office block looked like a modern college campus—functional and spare. But the grand salon of the ambassador's residence was a vestige of the years between the wars, decorously columned and parqueted, its soaring ornate ceiling leafed in gold—a cream-colored glory of Stalinist pretension. Above the conference table, a garish Venetian chandelier hung like an inverted Christmas tree.

Beneath its glitter, the mahogany table was a welter of electronic calculators, dossiers and faxes, reference charts and books, laptop computers, scattered coffee cups, and half-empty glasses of orange juice. The Soviets puffed away at Marlboros and Gauloises, the Americans at their pipes and Cuban cigars. With the garden doors sealed tight against November's chill, the room was close and stuffy. The START teams had been meeting this way since 1982, and protocol had long ago relaxed. The men had their jackets off and ties loosened, all except Mulholland and Viktor Karpov, each in a dark Italian suit.

Jake, Lermontov, and eight other American and Soviet negotiators sat opposite each other—five on a side, each team a mirror image of the other. The ambassadors—Mulholland and Viktor Karpov—sat center with their translators and stenographers flanking them. To the left sat an armed forces delegate in civilian clothes: on the Soviet side, Admiral Vassily Grushkin, former vice commander of the Northern

Fleet; on the American side, Major General Arnold Fuchs, a SAC two-star from Omaha. To the right sat a representative of state: on the Soviet side, KGB Colonel Abakov in his foreign ministry *apparatchik's* black suit and tie; on the American side, Jason Whittaker—a sandy-haired former Rhodes scholar and journalist who had joined the State Department under Carter—an aging yuppie who had written the definitive book on New England watercolorists in the Edwardian Age. To Whittaker's right at the end of the table sat Jake, with Lermontov opposite. At the other end sat two spooks from the CIA and KGB, colorless balding men who looked like Mr. Peepers but would probably slit each other's throat in church. The Russian was named Zinov. Period. That was all the Americans knew about him, except that he had a direct line to KGB Director Vladimir Kryuchkov's office on the second floor at Number 15 Dzershinsky Square—the building they called the Lubyanka—and his job was to watch Abakov as Abakov watched the other Soviets. The CIA representative was Rufus Drysdale. He was one of those dull-eyed southerners who was smart as hell but still said "nigra" for effect. Behind the negotiators and against the walls sat half a dozen aides with notebooks open on their laps. Behind Jake sat Major Sara Weatherby.

When the American interpreter finished his translation, Karpov replied in Russian. When he had done, the Soviet interpreter read back his shorthand notes.

"The continental United States is not the issue. If a zero-option on sea-launched nuclear cruise missiles is to be realized, the American naval battle groups are the issue. Your Trident submarines. And your forward bases."

Mulholland nodded to Jake. The formal statements of bargaining positions, the central dialogue between the sides was always conducted by the delegation chiefs. Even when the floor was open for debate, subordinates waited for permission to speak.

"Gentlemen, gentlemen. . . ." Jake shook his head. "We're talking about decommissioning and destroying our entire arsenal of nuclear *slick-ems.* And dismantling the assembly plants and test facilities. Once these are gone, are you suggesting we'd stake any part of our defense on untested missiles that might have been hidden for years in the holds of ships?"

"It is not beyond the realm of possibility," Abakov said caustically. "Even for the nation that invented planned obsolescence."

Grushkin leaned close to Karpov, began to whisper in his ear; whispering and note passing provided a continuing undertone to the discussion.

"Sergei," Jake said. "I'm describing an environment in which *slick-ems* can't be maintained or tested. What American president would rely on a weapons system that couldn't be updated or tested?" He looked to Karpov. "Viktor, talk to this . . . this paranoid."

"Jake," Mulholland said.

"All right, all right." Jake gave Abakov a tiny bow. "Excuse me, Sergei Iosifovitch."

Abakov nodded once. Jake's intemperate language had been a breach of protocol; the etiquette of negotiations required the dialogue at the table to be polite, disciplined, elliptical. Whenever tempers flickered and argument replaced debate, the adversaries were expected to rise and move to a corner of the room. Everything they said could still be overheard but was unofficial; it was not recorded by the two stenographers.

"Now, as to verification," Drysdale began.

Zinov interrupted him with one quick sentence in Russian. Delegates on both sides shifted uncomfortably. Each of the security representatives spoke the other's language like a native, but they persisted—even during open debate—on their infantile game of prerogative and translation.

The Soviet interpreter said, "Verification is not on our agenda today."

"I beg your pardon," Mulholland said. "I'm afraid it has to be. Implementation of First Step is impossible without proper verification procedures. Surely you recognize that?"

"That may be," Abakov said. "But it's not for discussion *today.*"

"Sergei, are you willing to discuss First Step or not?"

"Why do you think we're convened this morning?"

"Then you have to let us set the agenda."

"Mr. Ambassador—"

Karpov leaned over and set his hand on Abakov's arm. He smiled at Mulholland. "First Step is your proposal. We will hear your agenda. Please . . ."

Mulholland nodded down the table to Jake.

"We must have permanent, on-site inspectors at all Soviet naval bases," Jake said, "including your overseas installations at Cam Ranh Bay, Aden, Guinea, Angola, and Pinar del Río. In addition—"

Abakov snorted. "You'll have to talk to Fidel about Pinar del Río." The Soviets laughed.

Jake ignored that. "And an equal number of no-notice inspections on our respective navies' warships at sea."

Grushkin, the vice admiral, cocked his head. "Pardon me . . . an equal number? Dr. Handlesman, perhaps you forget we have four carrier groups, and you have fourteen? We have two hundred seventy-five capital ships; you have five hundred sixty-five." He raised his bushy eyebrows. "Do I take it you are prepared to accept no-notice inspections on your Trident submarines?"

"Absolutely," General Fuchs said with a wry smile. "If you can find them."

"Oh, we can find them, General."

"Maybe."

Jake raised one finger. "Excuse me, did I forget to mention Cyprus?"

That was the last straw.

"Bozhomoi!" Abakov pushed his chair back, abruptly rose and marched to the end of the room. He didn't wait for Jake to join him. "It is impossible!" Away from the table, there was no caveat against emotion—or theatrics.

Jake slowly got to his feet. "We have inspections under INF—"

"At two restricted sites in each country. This crazy plan requires dozens!" Abakov was turning nasty. "Your president said he was prepared to move immediately to reduce your NATO forces if we agreed to negotiations on sea-launched cruise missiles. *Spasibo!*" He kissed the tips of his fingers and flared them open. "Let him begin his troop withdrawals. We'll see what we shall see."

"Sergei, you know our troop withdrawals are linked to the zero-option on the missiles. And no zero-option is possible without adequate verification."

Abakov sneered. "Does your president now decree *our* negotiating positions as well as his own?"

Drysdale stood up. "We gotta have verification. And you know it. Now, cut the crap and cut the cards." He sat down.

"Excuse me, please," Karpov said. Then he spoke a paragraph in Russian. He knew when to use the time for translation to dissipate the heat.

Karpov spoke slowly, as did the interpreter, who took his cue. "According to our information, President Baker's statement of last night did not mention the elaborate inspection protocols which you now demand as a precondition for implementing First Step. We do not understand why we are confronted with this ultimatum today."

Mulholland opened his hands. "Viktor, we all know verification is a prerequisite. The president was on television. He was speaking . . . in broad strokes."

Karpov squinted. He turned to his interpreter, and they whispered about the translation of "broad strokes."

At the far end of the room, Abakov threw his hands up. "In any case, we cannot allow an army of American inspectors on Soviet soil. It's impossible."

"If *glasnost* is possible, this is possible," Jake said with a wry smile.

"I tell you it is not!"

"Why? Because your general staff doesn't want Gorbachev and his *perestroika* Politburo to know the numbers of weapons they've actually deployed?"

Admiral Grushkin got to his feet; that was extraordinary. He and General Fuchs made it a point of honor never to lose their tempers. But since the brutal military crackdowns in the Baltic republics, the growing tension between the Soviet government and the Red Army had become a biting embarrassment. "You give your Pentagon three hundred billion dollars a year and you think you know where every dollar goes? *Eto vzdor!*"

"Admiral, please," Mulholland said. "Civilian control of the military is absolute in the United States. President Baker is Commander in Chief of America's armed forces. All officers and servicemen must obey his orders."

Then, softly, Lermontov said, "With respect, Mr. Ambassador . . ." Every eye went to his end of the table. "With respect, my friend, you are naïve. You don't control your generals any better than we do." The room went still and silent. "We must have inspectors at your naval base in Naples. Subic Bay. Bahrain." Then, almost as an afterthought, he said, "And Hakodate."

"Ha-ko-datay?" Mulholland said.

Fuchs leaned in beside him. "Navy oil depot in Hokkaido, Japan."

Mulholland didn't recognize the name, but everyone else at the table did. In September of 1976, the Soviets had suffered a Cold War security catastrophe when Lieutenant Viktor Belenko landed his top secret MiG-25 interceptor at Hakodate and announced to startled Japanese customs agents he was seeking political asylum. The advanced warplane was returned to the Soviet government a week later. But not before American aeronautical experts had studied its capabilities and pinpointed the vulnerabilities of the new Red Air Force superfighter. To the Soviets, the name Hakodate carried the same disturbing connotations as Bay of Pigs for Americans.

Mulholland shook his head and chuckled. "Mikhail, we have a

treaty with the Japanese, which excludes nuclear weapons—even our nuclear-powered ships—from our bases on their islands."

"Yes," Lermontov said wearily. "We are well aware of your many, many treaties."

It was a gentle but stinging insult; the men stirred uneasily.

Softly, Karpov began, "Mikhail Yurievitch—"

"Mr. Ambassador," Lermontov said, and he looked at Mulholland with steady, piercing eyes. "Presidents come and go. But generals"—he searched for the word—"endure."

The delegates sat in uncomfortable silence.

LINCOLN BEDROOM, THE WHITE HOUSE, WASHINGTON

2:17 A.M.   For his money, Sam Baker liked old flannel. Old, well-worn flannel pajamas—the kind where years of toasty nights and lazy Sunday mornings had worn the grit out of the cotton so it was pliable and soft as an old man's promise. He liked the English style of bedroom slippers, too: oversized and lined with thick white fleece and loose at the heel so they flapped behind him when he walked. And he liked a terry robe—the kind you could leave on the bathroom radiator in winter, so when you stepped out of the shower it was waiting for your shoulders like the warm caress of a good woman. He liked that sort of homey thing.

But as he lay rereading the transcript of his First Step press conference—lay on the great, eight-foot rosewood Victorian bed in the Lincoln bedroom—he was all tricked out in silks: natty maroon silk pajamas from Giorgio's, a gray silk paisley robe from Sulka, and leather half-slippers from Brooks Brothers that didn't have a heel at all. Every time he turned a page, his silks hissed like the petticoats of a high-class prostitute. And the leather-lined slippers made his feet perspire. His head housekeeper, Shirley McIlhenny, had seen to all of that. He was the president—but not to her; to her, he was an old man, a widower who wanted looking after. Shirley had come to the White House under Jack Kennedy. In Shirley's time America had six first ladies. But the White House had only Shirley.

Sam Baker first caught sight of Shirley when he'd moved into the White House on January 21, 1985. She was unpacking for him—standing over an open suitcase, holding two fingers of one hand to her lips and slowly shaking her spume of strawberry blond hair. From that day onward, the third-floor family quarters became a place of mystery. Things appeared and disappeared. The first to go were his favorite flannels and slippers. In their place appeared creamy silk pajamas, a dandy's silk-lined robe, and creaky new leather slippers that were his proper shoe size—unflappable and no fun.

One Sunday morning in the first year of his first term, he had been dawdling over coffee and croissants in the Lincoln bedroom the way he liked to do, snuggled in a Morris chair and catching up with the week's sports in the newspaper. The bedroom door had opened and two smartly dressed young men entered, lugging a trunk between them. They nodded a silent greeting and set the trunk down alongside the tall pier glass where Mrs. Herbert Hoover used to do her pompadour every morning. Then they stood like two toy soldiers—one with a tape measure hung around his neck and a nub of soap in his hand, the other holding an open box of straight pins. Sam Baker couldn't imagine who the hell they were.

At last he put his newspaper down. "Can I help you, gentlemen?"

"No, thank you, sir," the blond young man said in an English accent. "When you're done . . ."

Sam Baker said, "I see," but didn't.

The young men smiled.

Then the door opened and Shirley marched in the way she did. "Good morning, Mr. President. You've met Mr. Selton and Mr. Harmon. Now, finish your breakfast, sir. Remember, Oscar Wilde said 'Never keep your tailor waiting.'"

Sam Baker motioned her to his side and whispered, "Tailor?"

"Yes, sir." She leaned closer. "Mr. Selton makes suits for—" She hummed the first four notes of "Rule Britannia" and raised her brows.

Sam Baker's eyes widened. "The queen?"

She tsked him. "H . . . R . . . H," she whispered, mouthing each letter as though it were a state secret.

Well, it took Sam Baker a few moments to put "H.R.H." together with Prince Charles, and when he did he couldn't remember what Charles's suit had looked like when he'd met him (maybe that was a good thing).

"English suits," he muttered. "Not exactly patriotic."

Shirley crossed her arms, imperious. "President Nixon drank French Bordeaux. Nancy Reagan wore Valentino underpants and Chanel No. 5. An English cut will suit you very well." She nodded to the two young men.

Then they had Sam Baker up before the pier glass in his pajamas, and Mr. Selton was stretching his tape measure here and there and reeling off numbers to Mr. Harmon, who was writing like the dickens. Every three months from that day forward—regular as the *Super Chief*—the two Englishmen would materialize in the Lincoln bedroom to fit the best suits Sam Baker had ever owned, the kind of suits he'd never dreamed of owning. The kind of suits he'd never dreamed *anyone* had dreamed of owning.

One day, he'd found a new handful of Turnbull&Asser ties in his closet. He confronted Shirley. "Who's paying for all these fancy doo-dads?"

"Never you mind."

"Now, just a second, madam. There are laws against buying personal items with White House money."

She gave him the same look he'd seen on the face of his mother the first time he'd told a lie. "You're paying."

"I am?" *That,* if anything, was worse.

"Your trustee. And we don't want to hear another word about it."

Sam Baker called the banker at First Virginia who looked after his investments in a blind trust while he held the presidency. "What's all this finery been costing?"

"I'm sorry, Mr. President," his banker said gravely. "That information is classified."

That was what it was like to be the president; the damn woman was holding him prisoner in his own dressing room. Shirley was always up and dressed by the time he came down to breakfast. And she never went to bed before he did. And if an urgent message woke him in the night, she was always dressed and standing in the hallway with the Secret Service when he came downstairs. For a while, he thought there must be three of her.

So when Sam Baker realized someone was tapping at the bedroom door at two-thirty in the morning, he assumed it was Shirley with a cup of herb tea.

He set the transcript aside and pushed himself up on one elbow. "Come in, Shirley."

But it was Ted Harris—all smile and crew cut, no jacket, tie off, sleeves rolled up—carrying a domed silver platter from the kitchen and grinning like a kid pulling a Halloween prank. "Room service!"

"For Pete's sake, Ted. Why aren't you home in bed?"

"Thought I'd bunk in Stalag 17 tonight. You know . . . just to be around." Stalag 17 was the nickname of the subbasement dormitory where the Kennedys and Robert McNamara had passed restless nights during the Cuban missile crisis. But whenever anyone slept down there, it was no joke.

"Then I got to feeling peckish," Harris said. "So I raided the fridge. Join me?"

The president sat up and rubbed his hands together. "I'm famished. Whatcha got?"

"Ta-da!" Harris raised the dome. Under it were two gleaming cocktail glasses. "Gin on the rocks with a pair of olives." He handed one to the president, sat down on the chaise across the room, and kicked off his shoes.

Sam Baker held the glass up in the light, admiring its cool gray frosting. "What would I do without you?"

Harris gave that serious consideration. "You'd be teaching public administration at VMI."

Sam Baker chuckled. "I'll drink to that." And when they had, he settled back into the pillows. "You know, there are days when I wonder why any kid would want to grow up to be president." He looked at Harris. "Are we going to get through this, Ted?"

"We got through Panama. And Desert Storm. We'll get First Step done."

"But are we *right* to get it done?"

Harris stopped, his glass halfway to his lips. "Sam, don't start that again."

"I'm no military strategist. You're no analyst. The strategic balance is so complicated. . . ."

"Sam. We've heard from the experts."

"Yes. The experts," Sam Baker said bitterly. "Remember what Kennedy said about listening to the experts during the Bay of Pigs? Ted, we're trying to balance economics and defense when they have nothing to do with each other."

"That's politics, Sam. The art of the practical."

"It's also compromise."

"Oh? And since when is compromise a dirty word?"

"When it becomes expedient . . . and dangerous."

"Sam, First Step isn't an expedient. It's indispensable and you know it."

Sam Baker sighed; Harris was right. The end of the Cold War was only the carrot; the nation's dismal economic reality was the stick. Reducing America's NATO forces was an obvious, quick, and popular way to realize billions in savings.

Harris yawned and checked his watch. "Sam, stop debating with yourself and go to bed. We're doing what we have to. Reducing our NATO armies, keeping a presence in the Persian Gulf, building a rapid-deployment force, and hanging on to the strategic missiles to keep the peace. First Step is the right idea at the right time. We've already had dozens of calls from Congress and telegrams from all over the world. And they're running ten to one in favor."

"What about the Soviets? Suppose Gorbachev won't go along with the zero-option on sea-launched nuclear cruise missiles?"

"He's got to go along. He wants us out of NATO more than we do. The Soviets can't afford their conventional armies any more than we can."

"But the Soviets are different from us, Ted. This is a big, open-hearted country. With a constitution that's lasted two hundred years. The Soviets have fought a revolution and four wars in this century. Including Stalin's gulags, they've lost fifty million dead. Now they're having a second revolution."

"All the more reason they can't keep six million men in uniform."

"But their general staff's frightened by the changes in the Warsaw Pact. They're suspicious of a united Germany in NATO. Fear and suspicion twist men's souls." Sam Baker glanced down; beside the bed stood a rocking chair—an exact replica of Lincoln's chair in the presidential box at Ford's Theater. Sam Baker never sat in that chair; no one did. "It's not the Politburo I'm afraid of. It's their generals. What if they turn on Gorbachev?"

"You mean revolt?" Harris snorted. "Sam, you're not serious."

"You saw them on television at their party conference. All those Soviet generals in their brown shirts, scowling at Gorbachev's speeches, watching him, glaring at him."

Harris cocked his head. "Whitworth got to you, didn't he?"

Sam Baker sighed. "Yeah. He got to me."

The president rose and went to the window and drew back the green velvet curtain. Between the White House and the old Executive Office Building, West Executive Avenue lay fogbound and silent under the streetlamps' glow. Secret Service agents sat at their posts, reading or dozing. Official Washington slept well tonight. *Everyone*, Sam Baker thought, *but the president.*

"It's not just Whitworth, Ted. It's Littman. My own Secretary of Defense. And the Joint Chiefs."

"They're warriors, Sam."

The president let the curtain fall. "They are also patriots."

"Sam, Sam," Harris chuckled and shook his head. "We've got the strategic missiles and the bombers for deterrence. We're safe. You said so yourself."

"Yes. I did. But *are we?*"

"Don't be ridiculous. No civilized nation would use nuclear weapons for anything *but* deterrence."

"I'm not talking about nations. I'm talking about men. What if someone like Khaddafi ever got his hands on the bomb? What if Israel hadn't bombed that Iraqi nuclear reactor in 1981? Where would we have been if Saddam Hussein had the bomb when he invaded Kuwait?"

The two stared at each other.

Then Harris said, "We'd have been up shit's creek. Period." He took a long swig of his martini. "All right, Mr. President. I'm going to tell you the truth about First Step. And it's a truth you may not want to hear." He set his glass down. "The only people who can be sure we're right are the people who will write the history of this republic a hundred years from now."

"And will there be people in a hundred years to write our history?"

Harris smiled and opened his hands. "Sam, don't get maudlin. Nobody wants to die."

419 M STREET SW, WASHINGTON

2:28 A.M.   The gooseneck lamp was lit, but the cluttered bedroom lay in shadows: the fretful unmade bed, the scattered socks and underwear, the closets out and shoes and candy wrappers helter-skelter. In the Pullman kitchen, Colonel Tom O'Neill sat at the Formica counter in undershirt and shorts, holding a ballpoint pen and staring down at a blank sheet of yellow paper. A bottle of whiskey and a tumbler stood at his elbow; he took a long swig.

He was cold and tired; he felt as though he hadn't slept for days. The strain showed in his face as he rubbed his thighs against an inner chill. He looked at the desk calendar. Sunday, November 10. He put pen to paper. Then he stopped and checked his watch. It was almost 0230. It wasn't the tenth anymore; it was Monday, the eleventh. It was Veterans Day. O'Neill put the pen back down and slouched in his chair.

Every year since he had been repatriated, Tom O'Neill had always followed the same routine on Veterans Day. He would leave early for the drive across the Memorial Bridge to Arlington National Cemetery and park his car in the lot below the visitors center. Then he would take the long walk up the hillside, following a route that took him past the graves of Phil Sheridan and Bull Halsey and Claire Chennault, to find a seat before the amphitheater filled. There, he waited while the massed flags and the ranks filed in—the army, the navy, the air force, the coast guard, and marines. He sat patiently among them while the Secretary of Defense laid a wreath at the Tomb of the Unknowns, while the twenty-one guns sounded their salute and a lone trumpeter played taps. Then the band would strike up the grand old tunes— "America, the Beautiful" and "Shenandoah" and "The Battle Hymn of the Republic." At last, the band would play "The Star-Spangled Banner" and, among the thousands, O'Neill would rise and raise his voice in song while jets from Andrews streaked overhead, rolling thunder across the graves. It was a sentimental ritual. Yet it was a ritual that restored his soul.

But this Veterans Day there would be no ritual, no restoration for Tom O'Neill. With First Step, there would be no tunes of glory to stir his heart again; he had been summoned to the flag and he would answer, even though it was a certain rendezvous with death.

He turned the calendar facedown on his desk. Then, in a bold hand, he wrote the date. And, below it . . .

Last Will and Testament of Thomas Michael O'Neill.

PENNSYLVANIA AVENUE SE, WASHINGTON

2:30 A.M.   Christy sat in the back seat of the Ford, staring out at the fogbound streets of Washington. Like the shrouded city in the mist, the night had become a puzzlement: Colonel O'Neill's midnight visit and Colonel Petrovsky's order, the curious password and compartmented information of the errand, the senior officers in the detention cell, Terry Watkins's angry shouting—all of it bizarre, mysterious, disturbing.

Christy sighed and settled deeper in her seat. At least it would soon be over; in a few minutes she would be headed home to sleep and—

Suddenly, Mrs. Watkins reached forward, caught the epaulet on

Tod's jacket. "Take a left here, will you, fly-boy." Tod swung the car down K Street.

"Don't you live on—"

"Yeah. But I ain't goin' home. I'm gonna . . . stay at my sister's." She looked at Christy. "That okay?"

"Of course."

Mrs. Watkins eyed her. "How old are you, honey?"

"Twenty-eight."

"Know why my husband's in jail?"

"No."

"Five years he was a POW. When he got back, they made him a gunny instructor. One day, he thought some kid was razzing him 'bout Nam. He gave the kid a burst. Ever seen them kind of guns they have in bombers?"

Christy shook her head.

"First shot killed the boy. The rest was just . . . I dunno. . . ."

"Despair?"

"Yeah, I 'spoze. Ones that were prisoners so long. Some never made it all the way home." She sighed with painful resignation. "You ever lonely, hon?"

"Sometimes."

"I been lonely twenty years." Mrs. Watkins tapped Tod's shoulder. "Stop here."

He swung the car to the curb before a decrepit ghetto house—one of a long row of slatternly, slack-roofed shanties huddled in an arroyo between two abandoned tenements. Tod got out, went around to the rear passenger door and pulled it open.

"Goodnight, ma'am," Christy said. And then, "Mrs. Watkins—"

"Yeah?"

"Just . . . I'm sorry."

It was the tenderness in Christy's voice that stopped Mrs. Watkins. Tod stood at the curb, holding the door open, waiting to help her out. But the woman leaned close to Christy, caught her by the hand. "Lissen, girl. You take this car and that boy out there and you start runnin' right now. You run and don't look back. And you don't stop. Until you know it's over."

Christy blanched. "Until what's over?"

"Until they're all dead. Or all heroes. Ain't nothing else for any of them anymore."

Then Mrs. Watkins let go Christy's hand, slid off the seat, stepped out the door, went quickly up the steps to the house, and rapped the knocker twice. The door opened and a white man in grimy overalls and undershirt stood yawning and scratching his belly. Then he kissed Mrs. Watkins, roughly pulled her to him, palmed her buttocks, and led her inside. The door slammed closed.

Tod spit on the sidewalk. "What a bimbo!" He lit a cigarette. "What the hell was she jabbering about? Her husband shot up some recruit with a twenty-millimeter canon? Jesus Christ."

But Christy sat, dumbfounded, shaken, staring at the house.

"I tell you," Tod muttered. "This man's air force. What a loony bin." He slid into the driver's seat and checked his watch. "Well, it's after 0230. We're on duty at 0600. Want me to take you home?"

Christy didn't answer. She was staring at the shanty, but she was seeing the night, the barbed wire, the slashes of searchlights, and three men marching as if to war.

"On the other hand . . ." Tod reached back and touched her knee. "There's a motel in Anacostia—"

Abruptly Christy pulled away.

"Hey, what's with you?"

"I'm sorry, Tod. I just . . ."

"What did that woman say to you? When she was getting out? Was she telling you to run away?"

Christy shook her head.

"Run away from what? Christy, I heard her. She said something about dead heroes."

Christy set her jaw; again, the gulf of rank yawned wide between them. "I can't discuss it."

"Goddammit, Chris! Stop playing soldier and tell me what's going on!"

"Tod, I told you, *I don't know!*"

That did it. He wrenched the key in the ignition; the engine roared to life. "Okay. Where to, Lieutenant?"

"Tod—" She leaned forward to touch him, but he stepped hard on the gas pedal; the acceleration shoved her back.

"I said *where to,* dammit?"

She needed a quiet place, a place where she could think. "The O-club. I'll catch a little sleep there."

His harsh eyes found hers in the rearview mirror. "O-club it is."

PISTOL RANGE, OCEANA NAS,
VIRGINIA BEACH, VA

2:46 A.M.   The chain drive whirred and the paper target slid down the darkened range, ducking in and out of shafts of yellow incandescent light. At the firing station, a figure waited in the shadows. As the target passed the twenty-five-foot mark, the man opened fire: eight shots—rapid, unhesitating.

The target reached the firing station; the chain drive thunked and stopped. The range fell silent. Cholly Granger leaned into the light. Eight bullet holes punched a tight group through the belly of the target.

He pulled the paper target down, balled it, threw it in the wastebasket. Then he removed the empty slide from his 9-mm automatic pistol, slipped in a loaded one, chambered a live round. He eased the hammer down and flicked the safety on.

Then he snapped the overhead off and stood a moment in the pitch-black range, as though preparing his eyes—and his soul—for the darkness to come.

AMERICAN MISSION, 11 ROUTE DE PREGNY,
GENEVA

8:52 A.M.   Ambassador Craig Mulholland flung the door open and marched into his office. Jake and Sara followed.

"Shut the damn door."

Sara did, and leaned against it.

"What the hell was the meaning of that?" Mulholland glared at Jake. "You purposely provoked that row."

Jake sat in the chair before the desk, tamped the tobacco in the bowl of his pipe, and put a match to it. "I provoked nothing."

"Snide old bastard Lermontov insults the president. Calls me a liar. Says our treaties are no good. And you sit there and say it was nothing?"

"Lermontov was negotiating. So was I."

"Goddammit. I think your negotiating set First Step back six months!"

"Not at all." Jake exhaled a cloud of thick, blue smoke and swung his pipe into the corner of his mouth. "I told Lermontov permanent on-site inspectors and no-notice boarding parties were indispensable to implementing the zero-option on *slick-ems.* He told me he could get some form of agreement from their Supreme Naval Command . . . provided we can get our Joint Chiefs to open our forward bases. And he told me in such a way that Grushkin wouldn't get apoplexy and that little *stukach,* Abakov, would report they were being tough on us."

Mulholland started to respond, then caught himself. He stared at the bearded old man and his aide.

Gently Jake said, "Mr. Ambassador . . . please," and motioned him into his chair with the tips of his fingers.

The bluster went out of Mulholland; like a deflating balloon, he settled behind his desk. "Is that true?"

Offhand, without looking back at her, Jake said, "Weatherby?"

"That's correct, sir," Sara said.

"And will they force the issue of inspectors at our forward bases?"

"Yes, Doctor."

"And will we agree?"

"We can't."

Still smiling at Mulholland, Jake said, "Why not, Major?"

"Hakodate."

"Hakodate?" Mulholland snapped. "Goddamn it, what the hell is so important about Hakodate all of a sudden?"

Sara said, "Stores and handling equipment for nuclear TLAM *slick-ems* were secretly installed in the port arsenal at Hakodate at the beginning of June."

Mulholland waved an angry hand. "Dammit, that's not true! We've got an anti-nuke treaty with Japan. Besides, there's no way to tell a cruise missile is nuclear or not without unscrewing—"

Calmly Jake said, "What makes you so sure the missiles at Hako-date are armed with nuclear warheads, Major?"

"The cruiser *Valley Forge* and six support ships were stationed there last month."

"To cover which targets?"

"Komsomolsk, Vladivostok, and the SS-11 ICBM complexes at Svobodnyy and Olovyannaya."

"Nonsense!" Mulholland was losing his temper. "There could be a dozen reasons for transferring that battle group."

Jake chuckled and shook his head. "Mr. Ambassador, your first mistake in negotiating with the Soviets is assuming you know more than they do." He tamped his pipe. "And the second is assuming your leaders have told you the whole and absolute truth."

Mulholland stared at them, shaken.

67 CHANDLER ROAD, SPRINGFIELD, VA

2:58 A.M.   Lieutenant Colonel Richard Harding stepped into the foyer of the house, quietly shut and locked the door. The hall was darkened, but a blue light flickered in the living room and he could hear the hiss of static. He lowered his head and slumped down the hall.

Through the archway to the living room, he could see his wife, Fat Beth, asleep in the velveteen Barcalounger, her feet hanging out the bottom of the floral chintz muumuu she wore day and night, her frazzled bleached-blond hair splayed across her pillow. On the floor a pizza box gaped among the empty cans of Bud. The television screen flickered with hash.

Harding stood in the archway, feeling like he wanted to spit. Then he went inside and snapped the television off.

That roused her. "Wazzat?" Blinking, Fat Beth pushed up on one elbow; when she saw him, she sagged back in a lump. "Oh . . . it's you."

"What are you doing home? All the bars closed? Or did you get lucky early?"

"What the hell do you care? At least I don't have to watch fuck films to get my jollies."

Harding pulled his tie down and unbuttoned his collar. "Told you I'd be working late."

"Yeah. Sure." Bone-stiff and tipsy, Fat Beth levered herself out of the chair and tottered toward the kitchen.

Harding watched, disgusted. "You waddle like a pregnant cow."

Her laugh crackled like small arms fire. "Listen to him. The major domo from Oklahomo." She stopped in the kitchen doorway and steadied herself against the frame. "What kept you late at the office, dear? New issue of *High Society* out today?"

"Shut your drunken mouth."

He pushed past her into the kitchen, went to the refrigerator, and yanked it open. The shelves were gray with mold, filled with old milk cartons, desiccated chicken in plastic wrap, vegetables decaying into mush in Saran Wrap shrouds. He settled for a can of beer, slammed the door against the stink, and pulled the tab.

She poked him hard in the back. "You were gonna stay twenty-five and make your star. Well, two to go. And you're still a light colonel."

Harding sucked his beer and leaned against the counter. "Don't start that crap again."

Fat Beth put her hand through her frizzy hair. "I could have had any one of them back then. Jimmy Adams was in your class. Now he's a four-star and CINCPACAF. Know where *his* wife lives? In a fancy ranch house on Hickam. Not in some godawful shack in Noplace, Virginia."

Harding slugged his beer and wiped his mouth with the back of his hand. "If you weren't such a drunken slob, maybe you'd have made the contacts she did. Maybe you'd have helped me up the ladder the way the other air force wives support their men."

"Helped you? Helped *you*?" Beth snorted. "Help a monkey learn the alphabet." She pushed away from the door and came weaving toward him. "Three years I waited while you were in that Vietcong prison. Three years I dreamed of standing on the runway, watching my hero come down the steps of a MAC plane. And what did I get for waiting?" Disgusted, she stared him up and down. "A walking corpse who can't get it up. A tin soldier who lost his war, but can't make a living any other way."

He slammed the beer can on the counter. "We didn't lose the war!"

"Oh, no. Pardon *me*! Not the precious air force. The boys in blue didn't lose the war. It was those dirty hippies and the politicians." She screwed her mouth up. "Don't sling me that bullshit again! It makes me want to puke!"

"It *was* the politicians! They gave up! They lied to us about winning peace with honor. Then they brought us home to shame. Like the little rats were embarrassed we had lived to tell the tale!"

"They should have been." Her voice dripped acid. "I was."

With a sudden bellow of rage he leaped at her and seized her by the throat, flung her back through the archway to the dining room, lurched after her, and bent her backward onto the table.

"Kill you—bitch!"

She pounded at his face with both her fists and tried to scream, but his hands closed down her windpipe. The table rocked beneath their writhing bodies. With an explosive *crack!* a leg collapsed, hurling them to the floor amidst the crashing glass and china. She dug her nails into the carpet and tried to crawl away. But he swung his leg across to straddle her, his two thumbs drilling into her throat. Her eyes bulged out as though their retinas would burst, and spittle sprayed from her mouth as she gasped for air.

Then her hands fell limp against her sides.

Harding hunched his shoulders forward, bore down squeezing; his fingers turned white with exertion. Then, abruptly, he released his grip and stared at her, panting.

Fat Beth raised a hand and paddled feebly at her throat. "Scum-bag," she rasped. "Can't even do that right."

OFFICERS' CLUB, BOLLING AFB, WASHINGTON

3:05 A.M.   The low, brick officers' club sat dark atop the rise where Theisen Street dead-ended at Westover, its parking lot deserted, a single night-light burning above the stairs. The black Ford slid up to the curb and stopped. Christy stepped out, shut her door, and leaned in at the window.

"Tod, about tonight. I—"

But he tromped the gas and roared off toward the NCO dorm without a word. Christy watched the taillights of the car brighten at the Duncan Avenue stop sign, watched the smoky exhaust curling in the cold; when Tod turned the corner, the red rectangles vanished in the wintry night.

Then Bolling was still. Christy stood on the curb, holding her arms across her bosom against the chilly damp, listening to the silence. Westward and below, streetlamps dotted the soft slope toward the Potomac; by their dim glow she could make out the humpbacked silhouette of the base commissary. Beyond on Luke Avenue stood the bowling center and, across Defense Boulevard, the BX, the barber shop, the sewing center, the florist. It had been almost thirty years since low-rise apartments and offices had replaced Bolling's runways and hangars. The air base was a suburban village now; no bright wings tilted skyward from its arms. Some summer days, Christy would open her office window and listen to the rumble of civilian DC-9s and 727s taxiing at National Airport across the Potomac. Then she'd shut her eyes and imagine the whining turbofans powered flights of F-15s trundling down the vanished Bolling runways, whispering rumors of war.

But now even National Airport lay deserted. The air was hushed and thick with frigid fog. Washington slept. The darkest moments of the night crept on.

Christy turned, opened the door to the club, and went inside.

In the shadowy reception room, the night manager—a towheaded boy who didn't look like he was out of his teens—was slouched in a leather armchair reading *Penthouse* and smoking. He looked up absently as Christy entered. But when he saw her lieutenant's bars he crushed his cigarette, stuffed the magazine under a cushion, and scrambled up.

"Sorry, ma'am. I mean . . . excuse me, ma'am."

"Any fresh coffee?"

"It was fresh at dinner."

Christy smiled. "Just black."

He headed for the kitchen. And when he returned, she carried the cup and saucer up the darkened hallway toward the lounge; at the door she stood a moment, peering into the shadows. Then she went inside.

The lounge was arched and Gothic, cluttered with leather couches and overstuffed armchairs—the kind of aging, well-worn leathers that have lost their sheen and grown soft as chamois with the decades. Christy liked this room particularly well; it had a scent of men. Even when the room was empty, she could hear the old blue jokes and sturdy laughter, see the men sitting as they did—knees apart, heads thrown back, hands clasped behind their necks, the way her father must have sat when he was alive.

She did not remember her father, except from photographs: a dashing air force major, his wavy hair combed straight back, leaning against a hangar door, hands in the pockets of his flight jacket, jawing the stem of his pipe with the confident grin of a cavalier. Christy was three years old when her father was reported KIA during a bombing mission over Haiphong. Four months later her mother went into the bathroom, shut herself in the shower stall, and drank a measuring cup of lye. Her grandmother never told her how her mother died; when Christy was a high school junior, she went to the Trenton *Times* and looked up the story in the microfiche index. It appalled her; otherwise, she felt nothing. But in the lounge at the officers' club, somehow she always felt her father near.

Before she had matriculated at the Naval Postgraduate School, Christy had avoided O-club lounges. She'd felt unwelcome; the clubs had seemed a man's domain. It was Captain Bryan who first took her into the lounge at Monterey.

"You're as much an officer as they are," Bryan said.

"It doesn't seem . . ."

"A woman's place?"

"No."

"Why do you accept their valuation of you? Why don't you make them see you for what you are? Do you want to be an intelligence clerk your whole career?"

Christy's breath caught at the dread thought. "I want to be a soldier."

Bryan took her by the shoulders. "Then remember: gender is a garment. Inside every man there is a woman. Inside every woman, there's a man."

Christy looked up at the serene, gray eyes and couldn't doubt them.

"And inside the man in every woman—"

"What?" Christy said.

"—there is a warrior."

Now Christy stood in the shadows of the lounge at Bolling, remembering Bryan's hands on her shoulders. They were powerful hands; if only they could have infused their power into her. . . .

A line of glass display cases stood along the far wall of the lounge; Christy knew them well. In each, a mannequin in period uniform was labeled with the name of an officer who had won the Congressional Medal of Honor or Air Force Cross. She sipped her coffee, walked along the row, admiring them. One by one, the uniforms and planes marched backward through the history of twentieth-century aerial warfare: the F-15 Eagle, F-4 Phantom, F-86 Shooting Star, the old twin-engined P-38—all the way back to Sopwith Camels and flying suits with jodhpurs.

Christy stopped before the last case. The Air Force Cross glinted on the mannequin's breast. Below, the citation read

FOR EXTRAORDINARY HEROISM IN MILITARY OPERATIONS
AGAINST AN ARMED ENEMY OF THE UNITED STATES.

It always braced Christy to read those words. They spoke to her. They were why she'd joined the air force. Not to escape from Trenton and its creeping urban blight. Not because of the scholarship that enabled her to complete her education. Not even for the uniform, the responsibility and respect, the prospect of a bright career; those were only the reasons she gave her grandmother and friends—the reasons she listed on her ROTC application. The real reason she had joined the air force was to carry the flag in battle.

But between her years in ROTC and her call to active duty, the world had turned. The Cold War was over; the triumph of Desert Storm was history. She had missed her war, had lost her chance to be a warrior. She was superfluous, irrelevant; an intelligence clerk relegated to an obsolete command. Tonight she was no more than a uniformed messenger.

She remembered one winter night in Monterey. There was a fire on the hearth in Bryan's apartment in the BOQ; Christy had lain beside it in her terry robe, thumbing her copy of *Customs and Courtesies* by the flickering orange light. She had stopped at the color plate of the Air Force Cross, stopped to admire it and dream. Then she heard ice cubes tinkling in a whiskey glass and realized Bryan was standing over her.

"Pretty bauble, isn't it?" Bryan said.

"Beautiful."

"Would you like to win one?"

"No woman ever has."

"Does that mean no woman ever will? Perhaps you'll be the first." Bryan knelt beside her, took the book and held the photograph of the medal against Christy's breast. "You know, I think it suits you."

Hurt, Christy turned away. "Don't make fun of me."

"What we do isn't about medals. . . ."

"I know, I know. Duty-Honor-Country."

"And sacrifice."

"And what do you get to show for that?" Christy demanded.

"Knowing those you honor, honor you. A medal's just a chunk of painted brass tied up with ribbon. You'll see that for yourself someday." Bryan set the book aside. "What is it, love? What do you have to prove?"

"That I'm a soldier. That I'm as brave as they are."

Gently Bryan brushed the hair from her brow. "Just because men are bigger doesn't make them braver. You're as brave as any man."

"How would you know?"

Bryan smiled. "You're brave enough to have an affair with me. Besides, being a woman is an asset."

Christy rolled over on her back. "How?" Her terry robe fell open and the firelight glistened on her thighs.

"Men always underestimate a woman's strength. Learn to exploit that to your advantage." Bryan eased Christy's knees apart and began to stroke her. "You don't feel the need to prove yourself when we make love, do you?"

"No." Christy put her head back, shut her eyes, and let the warmth of Bryan's touch pool out and inundate her body.

"Men do. They're prisoners of their sex in bed as well as war." Then Bryan swept her up and kissed her. "Do you know I love you?"

Christy tensed; the warmth drained out of her. "I . . . hope you do."

"Be brave enough to believe that. The rest will follow."

Now Christy looked down the long row of display cases in the Bolling O-club. The heroes who had worn those uniforms had all been combatants. And all combatants were men. Would her moment—would any woman's moment ever come? Or were there promises that even Captain Bryan couldn't—

Christy raised her head.

She remembered Mrs. Watkins's face, her grim, prophetic eyes.

All dead . . . or all heroes.

Strange.

The whole night had been strange—a world pulled inside out like a sock. Petrovsky. Harding. O'Neill. And a prisoner named Watkins and his wife.

The sun will come up tomorrow.

Yes, Christy thought. The sun *would* come up and she would have had precious little sleep. She turned toward one of the welcoming leather couches.

But, as she did, her eye caught her reflection in the glass front of a display case. She stopped and stared; a bedraggled, weary woman stood before her—more wet cat than officer. Christy set her coffee down, yanked her jacket straight and pulled herself up to attention.

That was better. Even Captain Bryan would approve. Christy snapped a sharp salute.

On the glass front of each case, her image floated like a ghost—her face rigid, eyes clear—loyal to the calling of the dead.

BACHELOR OFFICERS' QUARTERS, OCEANA NAS, VIRGINIA BEACH, VA

3:41 A.M. Commander Cholly Granger took the last handful of navy-issue socks from the dresser drawer, tucked them neatly one by one into the corner of the suitcase and snapped it closed. He set the suitcase on the floor and looked around the tiny bedroom of the BOQ.

The closet stood open, empty. The dresser was empty, as was the medicine cabinet in the bathroom. He was moving on.

He sat down on the bed. His olive green flight suit was laid there and, beside it, his 9-mm automatic pistol and little leather jewelry box. He unsnapped the box and turned it over. A jumble of campaign ribbons tumbled out onto the stiff wool blanket.

With his fingertip, he gently turned the decorations upright. The first set of shiny gold wings he had earned at Pensacola. The green and yellow Vietnam service medal with its three red stripes like bloodstains. The Air Medal ribbon with Strike Flight cluster. The lozenge of the Purple Heart and golden POW decoration. The red, white and blue Silver Star for valor they'd pinned on when they brought him home.

Granger scooped the ribbons up, weighed them in his hand; they were light as air. He remembered the crisp fall day his father had taken him pheasant hunting in the scrub where Union Flat Creek joined the quick Palouse and cascaded down the Rockies westward to the sea. He was ten years old, and the 20-gauge he shouldered was almost as tall as he. It was his father who had given him the wisdom of the hunt, had trained his ear to hear the silent night flight of the owl. They walked abreast in the sullen brush of autumn, hearing the crackle of dry grasses going down, listening for the telltale cackle of the pheasant, watching for his bright plume against the sere.

Then, with the rumble of coal cascading down a cellar chute, a small plane arced into the valley, its wings edgelit in flame.

"Pa, lookit!"

It was a T-37 jet trainer from Fairchild AFB west of Spokane, practicing aerobatics in the chinks and gorges of the Rockies' flanks. It was the first jet plane Granger had ever seen. It shot past like a hawk, dropping thunder on him. He had to wrench his neck to see it pass.

"That plane din't have no motor, Pa."

"Has a jet inside that pulls the air and pushes it behind."

"What keeps it up?"

"God holds the pilot in his hand."

Now Cholly Granger sat in the silent BOQ bedroom, holding his own life gathered in his hand: the thrill of pinning on his wings; the sweaty terrors of night combat missions; the suffering in Chu My's bamboo prison. And, worst of all, the deadly drudgework of the dull years since the war. So it all came down to this: one last chance to make it matter. And he would. Even if it cost him the last honor due and owing from the navy—a coffin covered with a flag.

Granger took his flight suit on his lap, unzipped it to the waist and turned back the flap that would cover his left breast. Then he pinned his ribbons inside where they would rest against his heart.

8 RUE JEAN-JACQUES PRADIER, GENEVA

10:56 A.M.   Doctor Hans Feidus shook his head. "Vell," he said, "I give you another tube salve. And powder for der sitzbath. That's all I can do." He snapped off the examining light, swung the fixture back against the wall. He was a German Jew who had escaped the Holocaust in 1942 and settled in French-speaking Geneva; he and Jake communicated in a patois of English-German-Yiddish. Over the years Jake had consulted Feidus they had become friends.

"I understand," Jake said. "Thank you, Doctor." Gingerly, he slipped his shirt across his back and began the buttons.

"You should have seen someone."

"Back then, who knew?"

"*Ja. Ich verstehe.*" Feidus scribbled a prescription and set it on the examining table. "*Kaffee?*"

"Thank you."

Feidus went to the door and opened it. "*Friedl, zwei Kaffee, bitte.*" He went out and left Jake to dress.

Indeed. Who knew? Jake's back had first begun to trouble him in 1947; first, a stiffness as though his skin were too tight about his ribs; then a soreness like a sunburn; then a jagged weeping wound along his spine. He consulted a dermatologist in Brookline—a man named Goldstein, who had been a classmate at Harvard before the war.

"Contact dermatitis," Goldstein said and wrote him a prescription for a tube of the new hydrocortisone. When the lesion did not respond, he changed his diagnosis—"Could be a staph' infection"—and gave Jake a prescription for a new drug, aureomycin. What followed was a long and frustrating time of pills and protocols. That was when Jake first began to feel the burning when he urinated; he wondered if the infection was venereal. While his sexual experience had been limited, some of it had been (so to speak) professional. He summoned up his courage and asked Goldstein.

"What?" Goldstein said. "On your *back*?"

In the end, the young doctor threw up his hands. "I'm sorry, Jake.

I've never seen anything like it." In 1948 in Brookline, Massachusetts, no one had. It was not until the summer of 1953 that events corrected Goldstein's diagnosis.

Jake had become engaged to a woman who taught classical philosophy at Radcliffe. Her name was Rebecca Ashkenazy; she was the daughter of a distinguished, orthodox-but-assimilated Jewish family of real estate developers in Swampscot. Becca was a virgin. After they became engaged she let Jake have her. He had never had a virgin, never had a woman with less sexual experience than he. It was a month before he realized she had never had an orgasm, another month of trying to explain the phenomenon to her, a third of patient coaxing and manipulation until she achieved. She was multiorgasmic; one night in his faculty rooms, she bared her nails against his back. He screamed in pain and groped the bedside lamp on. Becca started to apologize, then saw her bloody fingers in the light; Jake's flesh had come away like putty.

Then, of course, he knew.

There would be no more women in his life. No marriage. No children to carry on his parents' names. No domestic bliss of bungalow-with-picket-fence-and-Chevrolet that was the postwar American dream. He was to have none of that. The engagement broken, he settled down into a waiting game with his mortality. Now, thirty-eight years later, they had entered endgame, the final gambit; the clock had run its course.

When Jake had tied his tie and slipped his jacket on, he went into the consultation room and took the chair before the desk. Feidus was thumbing a thick textbook.

"Well. What's the prognosis?"

Feidus looked at him over the top of his glasses. "*Nu?* You have to ask?"

"Just like to know how long I have. That's all."

"*Gott* will tap you on the shoulder when he wants you."

"Yes. But when?"

"No man can know."

Jake waited for another answer.

Feidus let the cover of the book fall closed. "A few months."

"How many?"

"I said there is no certainty."

"Doctor." Jake wet his lips. "I'd rather you weren't quite so . . . circumspect."

"As you wish. A month or two. Not more."

Jake's smile stiffened.

"Have you children, Doctor Handlesman?" Then Feidus caught himself. "No. Of course not. I beg your pardon."

The door opened and the nurse set two demitasses before them and went out.

Jake took the creamer and poured for both of them. "How . . . how will it happen?"

Feidus stirred his coffee. "You have no kidneys left. Little by little, the disease shuts down the tubes and blocks the drainage. You void more blood than urine now."

"I've noticed."

"At a point, the urine is not drained at all. Then, very quickly . . ." He opened his palms, then turned them over, placed them downward on the desk.

"I see." Jake's voice trembled. "And what . . . will it feel like?"

"*Ach.*" Feidus waved the question away.

"I'd like to know."

"Lethargy. Light-headedness. Brief periods of dizziness, then blackouts. Followed by coma, heart failure, and death."

Jake's voice was pinched. "And . . . will my mind be clear?"

"I think so." Feidus smiled gently. "Actually, it will be quite painless."

"But *will* my mind be clear?"

"*Ja, ja.* And then a day will come when you remember you have an important appointment. Or you must make an urgent call. But you will not remember where to go for your appointment. Or whom you must call. And then you will look about your office or your bedroom for something to remind you, and realize you do not recognize the place or know why you are there. When that happens, you must prepare."

Outside the office window the great bell of Notre Dame in the Place des 22 Cantons began to toll eleven.

"When that day comes . . ." Feidus broke off.

Slowly, the great bell tolled. The eleventh hour. Of the eleventh day. Of the eleventh month.

Jake turned his head and listened. At the American mission on the Route de Pregny, he knew the bustling preparations for the afternoon gala had abruptly stopped; the marine guards had paused in their duties, stood rigid at their posts. At American NATO bases from Torrejon in Spain to Iraklion in Crete, honor guards stood before flagpoles as the colors were lowered to half-staff. And there were other ceremonies, Jake knew. At the Arc de Triomphe in Paris, President Mitterand stood among the massed dignitaries and battalions as the

Flamme Eternelle flickered out. Jake could see the gray, great men of France—bareheaded, bowed, the restless winter breezes ruffling their sashes of honor. Behind the politicians, smart young soldiers stood rank-on-rank, their brasses and their weapons gleaming, grave boyish faces set. But it was not for these that Paris held its breath.

Behind the debonair brigades and fretty horses of the cavalry, in bleachered knots and swales or slipshod rows along the curbs they stood—old men in long black winter coats, some with faded ribbons pinned above their hearts, faces pale, hair grayed, eyes staring into nothingness, as men's souls will stare forever when they have been washed in blood and steel.

The final bellstroke tolled. Across the continent, old warriors and young stood in silence. It was the moment of the veterans.

Jake cleared his throat. "You were saying, when that day comes . . . ?"

"On that day, do not lie to yourself," Feidus said. "You will not get well."

"Denial has never been my vice, Doctor. I assure you I have prepared." Jake put a hundred-franc note on the desk and rose. "And now . . . I recall I have an important appointment. *Auf Wiedersehen.*"

OCEANA NAS, VIRGINIA BEACH, VA

5:01 A.M. Slowly, to the dull rumbling of the heavy chain drive, the towering hangar doors crept apart, dwarfing the figures of three men who stood on the tarmac of the taxiway under the horns of the crescent moon. The chief petty officer flipped through the pages on his clipboard. Lieutenant Dolman yawned and scratched the stubble on his chin. But Cholly Granger stood unmoving, clear-eyed, clean-shaven, erect, holding his flight bag and helmet, waiting.

In the center of the hangar under the glaring fluorescent lights, a solitary F-14 Tomcat stood—a brute, mean, needle-nosed, twin-engined beast with a gleaming aluminum skin, its wings tucked back in seventy-five-degree oversweep like a hunting arrowhead. Two massive white Phoenix missiles hung from the wing pylons; a slim, white Sidewinder missile was fixed to each pylon's side rail. Inboard, two bulging external fuel tanks were mounted beneath the engine nacelles, each holding nineteen hundred pounds of JP-5. Four more Phoenix were mounted on pallets bolted beneath the fuselage. Washed in the cold green light, the Tomcat crouched, the image of power, violence, death.

"Check the serial numbers on the ordnance, Commander?"

"Go to it, Lieutenant," Granger said.

Dolman and the CPO bent, ducked beneath the wing and out of sight. Granger could hear them.

"Should have two AIM-9M Sidewinders. Serial number AIM9M120695 . . ."

Granger unzipped his flight bag. Inside was his spare torso harness, his 9-mm automatic pistol. He slipped the pistol out, wedged it down into the thigh pocket of his G-suit, and zipped the pocket closed.

"And we should have six AIM-54C Phoenix. Serial numbers AIM54C73365 . . ."

Cholly Granger walked back to the open hangar door and gazed east into the star-spangled sky. At the horizon there was only darkness. But now it was the darkness before dawn.

EXUMA SOUND, WEST OF ELEUTHERA, THE BAHAMAS

5:04 A.M. The steward rapped lightly at the stateroom door. When there was no answer, he rapped again and waited. Finally he used his key, unlocked the door, and softly swung it open. He set the tray with the steaming cup of coffee on the nightstand and switched the lamp on low.

Secretary of Defense Zack Littman rolled over, blinked his eyes open.

"Five o'clock, Mr. Secretary," the steward whispered. "Mr. Vander Pool and Mr. Finchley are at breakfast in the lounge."

Littman yawned and nodded. Beside him in the bed, Clara shifted in her sleep and curled her arms tight about her pillow. Tenderly Littman smoothed the covers over her. Then he swung his feet down to the cold teak floor. "Why are aerospace executives always such devout fishermen?"

"I'm afraid I wouldn't know, sir."

Littman yawned again and scratched his chest. "The sacrifices a man makes for his country. . . ."

SOVIET MISSION, 15 AVENUE DE LA PAIX, GENEVA

11:11 A.M.   Mikhail Yurievitch Lermontov sat at the foot of the small oak table in the basement room that was the bubble of the Soviet mission. At the head of the table KGB Colonel Abakov sat, a platter of smoked fish and brown bread before him. One of Abakov's goons—a simian, balding Uzbek with bushy eyebrows—leaned against the far wall.

"Hakodate? Yes, a brilliant stroke, I quite agree," Abakov said and rolled a slice of salmon on his fork. "But, you'll admit, Professor, an extraordinary serendipity." He stuck the forkful of fish in his mouth and a wedge of buttered brown bread after it.

Lermontov never liked sitting in the bubble; it was a room within a room. The interstices between the walls were filled with rubber bumpers interlarded with sheets of aluminum foil and wiring that emitted an inaudible electronic curtain. Nothing said or done within the bubble could be heard by electronic surveillance from the outside world.

The Soviet mission compound was a macrocosm of the Russian mind. American negotiators lived in hotel suites or in apartments rented by their government. But the Soviets lived and worked together behind an eight-foot concrete barricade. Their office blocks and dormitories were connected by underground tunnels so their movements could not be monitored by watchers with binoculars in taller buildings. The delegates' offices were spartan and the cells they called their bedrooms worse. It was like living in a monastery of the damned. But the inner sanctum—the sanctum sanctorum—was the bubble; no heresy spoken within its confines could be heard by man or God.

"I should think you'd want to verify," Lermontov said.

"But we have, comrade." Abakov wiped his chin with the back of his hand. "Do you think the Organs are asleep, Mikhail Yurievitch? Certain Japanese comrades are already preparing a small demonstration."

That made Lermontov raise his head. It was the omnipresence of the KGB one feared the most; in hours they had verified the presence of American cruise missiles in Hakodate and passed the word to agitators in Tokyo and Osaka.

"And yet . . . a certain curiosity remains," Abakov said, "as to how you came by such startling and welcome news."

"I have my sources."

"Yes." Abakov sneered his disdain. "The Jew, Handlesman. We were well advised to encourage you to nurture that friendship. Were we not?"

Lermontov slouched in his chair. "Very well advised."

Abakov began rolling another slice of salmon with his fork. "And yet, forgive me, Professor, but one's mind spins on. In your opinion, what motive might Dr. Handlesman have for sharing this delightful tidbit?" He popped the salmon in his mouth and swilled his glass of tea.

"I cannot say."

"Curious, is it not?"

"Most curious."

"Perhaps he will have more to say to you at their Armistice Day reception this afternoon?"

The two men stared. Then Lermontov said, "Perhaps." To the KGB, every Soviet citizen was either an informer or informed upon. That was Lenin's legacy; hereditary national paranoia. "If this interview is concluded . . ."

"Yes, yes." Abakov waved his fork in dismissal. "No doubt you have important things to do."

Lermontov rose, went to the door and waited.

Abakov took another sip of tea. Then he waved his fork again. His goon unlocked the door; even after six years of *perestroika,* the KGB were bullies. Lermontov nodded and went out.

In the courtyard of the compound, the four black Fiats that shuttled the Soviet START delegation between embassies were parked along the driveway. Their KGB drivers lounged beside them, hats pulled down, smoking and sniggering together. Lermontov showed his pass to the uniformed corporal at the gate, walked out into the Avenue de la Paix.

Instantly a sense of freedom filled him.

He walked down the hill to the Place des Nations, stood a moment at the corner, watching the Citroëns and Mercedes wheeling through the square. Then he took the #8 bus downtown to the Place de Cornavin.

The city center was busy with well-fed Swiss—mothers and toddlers bundled against the November cold, portly burghers with their ubiquitous umbrellas, teenagers in Nike shoes rushing this way and that. Lermontov walked the Rue du Mont-Blanc toward the lake, letting his eyes wander over the endless clutter of advertising signs for Coca-

Cola, Gauloise, and Fernet-Branca. Even in the teeming, traffic-clot-
ted streets, the air smelled pure.

But Abakov's question nagged. *What motive might Dr. Handlesman
have for sharing this delightful tidbit?* All morning Lermontov had
been worrying about the same thing. He checked his watch, turned
right along the Quai des Bergues.

Lermontov had first met Jake Handlesman at the SALT talks in
Helsinki in 1969. Those early negotiations had all the spontaneity of
a religious ritual: the delegates rigid and uncomfortable across the
table from each other, text and responses repeated as by rote, a kind
of clockwork gavotte of step and parry. Lermontov remembered how
Jake sat so calmly in his chair, never crossing and recrossing his legs
as Paul Nitze did, or tugging at his forelock as Gerard Smith used to
do when he was paragraphs ahead of the translation. Jake sat, making
notes and doodling, bow tie balanced on his Adam's apple, a wistful
smile peeking through his beard.

Then, one day, as the delegates were rising for recess, Lermontov
caught a glimpse of the scribbles in Jake's spiral pad; they were the
movements of chessmen, transcribed into two columns according to
the Standard Algebraic Notation. "Excuse me, Doctor," Lermontov
said. "Do I discern that you play chess?"

"Yes. Do you?"

"A bit."

Jake eyed the Russian. "Is that a fair assessment or a preliminary
position?"

The two negotiators smiled.

The next afternoon, they lunched together in the canteen as protocol allowed. Lermontov brought his portable chessboard with the flat,
magnetic counters printed with the symbols for chessmen. The two
were well matched; both played the hypermodern game. They opened
1 P-QB4, Kt-KB3; 2 Kt-QB3, P-K3; 3 Kt-B3, P-B4; 4 P-K3, B-K2.
On the fourteenth move, Lermontov played P-QR3 and Handlesman
responded KtxKt, which led to 15 RxKt and Kt-B3.

Lermontov looked up. "Aha! Keres versus Smyslov. Zurich, 1955."

"1953," Jake said, with obvious delight. From that moment, for
twenty years, their friendship grew.

In January 1989, after much haranguing of the bureaucracy of the
Soviet Institute of Foreign Affairs, Lermontov had arranged for distinguished Harvard Professor Handlesman to visit Moscow in the
spirit of *glasnost* and deliver a series of lectures entitled "Prospects for
Detente in the Nuclear Age—An American Perspective."

It snowed heavily during the week preceding Jake's arrival and the freezing city's streets were all but impassible. Lermontov fretted that the turnout for Jake's lectures might be sparse. On the contrary, the hall was packed: more than a hundred *aspirantiy* and *candidatiy* from the institute, almost every member of the faculty, dozens of *apparatchiks* from the foreign ministry and KGB. As Lermontov looked down from the podium, he understood; the opportunity to gaze upon an American nuclear strategist was as aphrodisiac as the power of the weapons themselves.

Lermontov's welcoming remarks began with a recitation of Jake's long career. But he concluded his introduction by describing Jake as something more than an arms negotiator: a true visionary, a global thinker and, above all *nevya debrenza*—a friend of reason. In response, Jake did not disappoint the multitudes.

Jake's lectures, which spanned four successive evenings, were delivered in impeccable Russian spiced with quotations from Marx and Lenin, Generals Zhukov and Malinovsky and, of course, First Secretary Gorbachev. In characterizing detente in a nuclear age, Jake conjured many images, but two were particularly memorable.

The first was a ghastly specter of nuclear winter, of a world shrouded in perpetual twilight, buried under snows as merciless as those that banked the doors of the institute that night.

The second image, which concluded the final lecture, was a vision of the Arctic Circle and the Bering Sea, a landscape of permafrost and silence and yet the one place on earth where the American Seward Peninsula and the Soviet Chukotskiy Poluostrov seemed to grope toward each other through the frozen fog.

The alternatives were clear, the lectures a profound success. On the closing night, a messenger delivered a large bouquet of roses to the rostrum with a note of thanks from the foreign ministry. Jake raised the bouquet above his head as the audience applauded.

"Pust' vsegda pobedat tsveti nad snegam," Jake said. "May flowers triumph over snow." The students cheered.

The next morning, as a tacit indication the Politburo approved the lectures, it was arranged for Lermontov to escort Jake to luncheon at the restricted Central Committee canteen at 5 Nikitnikov Ulica. But by way of showing his own appreciation, Lermontov arranged to hire a private room at the Sandunovsky *banya* as a surprise.

Jake was curious when Lermontov stopped along the way and bought two bunches of birch twigs from an old man sitting on the pavement beneath the soaring columns of the grand prerevolutionary building. And Jake raised his head and sniffed as the first whiff of herbs reached them as they climbed the stairs. But when the matron

handed them locker keys and Lermontov began to undress, the air of
expectancy went out of Jake and he seemed apprehensive and uneasy.

Bundled in great thirsty towels, each carrying a liter bottle of cold
beer and a slender birch bough, the two men entered the tiny, white-
tiled private steam room on the third floor and shut the heavy wooden
door. Lermontov tossed a bucket of cold water on the heated rocks
in the corner, and the room swelled with rosemary-scented steam.
They sat on the low tiled shelf and let the steam roll over them, their
bodies glistening in yellow light.

"Your lectures will be much discussed and long remembered,"
Lermontov said.

"Thank you."

The old Russian sat back, rested his shoulders against the tile. "Will
we live to see the day when strategic missiles are a memory?"

"I used to hope so."

"And now?"

"Now, I wonder."

"I wonder at the madness of man," Lermontov said.

Then Jake lowered his head and rested a hand against the slick tiled
wall to steady himself.

"My friend—" Lermontov touched Jake's knee. "Are you unwell?
Perhaps it's too hot?"

Jake forced a smile. "No. I'm all right."

Lermontov shook out his birch branch and handed it to Jake. "Will
you oblige me?" He turned his back and Jake realized Lermontov
wanted to be switched.

"Do not hesitate," Lermontov said. "It is the heart of the ritual."

Jake obliged him as best he could, clumsily switching the bough
across Lermontov's back until his skin glowed healthy pink and
dripped with perspiration.

"Now, your turn." Lermontov made a circling gesture with his
finger.

"No, thank you, Misha. I think not."

"But it's the best part. It brings color to the skin."

"No, really—"

"We only share this with our closest friends. You will offend me."

"As you wish." Jake shrugged his towel off and turned around.

Lermontov stood and shook out the birch bough. But when he
raised his hand to strike, his eyes fell upon the lesions spread across
Jake's back.

In the light suffusing through the steam, Lermontov could see the
blackened central ridge that ran upward along the backbone and

the splotchy red and purple wounds that uncoiled like tentacles to the shoulder blades. Beads of perspiration seemed to ooze out through the hundred yellow pustules that dotted the raw flesh like maggots. What Lermontov looked upon was a map of hell.

Slowly he lowered the birch branch.

"So you see," Jake said.

Shaken and pale, Lermontov sat beside him. "My friend . . . forgive me."

Jake took his hand. "It is of no consequence. But, then again, it is a private matter."

"Of course. Do you take treatment?"

"There are no treatments."

"And is there—"

"No. No cure. No hope."

"I see. May one ask . . . ?"

Jake looked at him with wistful, wizened eyes. "Hiroshima," he said.

In the aftermath, two naked old men sat among the clouds that swelled within a pure white room. But the room was no longer in a Moscow *banya*; it had unlinked itself from time or place, and hung suspended in the endless instant of eternity. In the detonation of that word, they knew each other, knew themselves, knew their purpose on the earth as only God could know them.

"There was a tree," Jake said, "that looked down over the devastation. One afternoon, I sat, leaning against that poor, irradiated tree."

Slowly Lermontov raised his hand to his forehead. Through the steam, Jake could see tears in his eyes. Then Lermontov touched his own sternum, and Jake realized the Russian was making the sign of the cross.

"What is it, Misha?"

"I was thinking of the crucifixion of our Lord."

Jake smiled. "That is the Christian metaphor."

"And for a Jew?"

"For a Jew . . ." Jake stroked his beard. "A Jew would say . . . the tree was the Tree of Knowledge. And the penalty for plucking at its fruit was mortality."

"As Adam was banished from the garden. . . ."

Jake shook his head. "Adam's punishment was not that he was banished. His punishment was that he was a man, and he remembered paradise."

★ ★ ★

Mikhail Yurievitch Lermontov stood at a busy street corner on the Quai du Mont-Blanc looking out at the midday sun gleaming on the waters of Lake Geneva. Why had Jake Handlesman given him Hakodate? Because he knew that shred of information was enough to stall First Step for weeks or months or even years. But why?

Or would Adam, in one infamous act of disobedience, return in his rage of exile and put his maker's garden to the torch?

OFFICERS' CLUB, BOLLING AFB, WASHINGTON

5:45 A.M. The night manager stood in the doorway, holding a steaming mug of coffee, debating how best to wake the officer who lay sleeping under the trench coat on the leather sofa in the darkened lounge. At last, he reached down and switched on a table lamp.

Abruptly Christy sat up, her eyes wide open, suddenly awake. "Wha—what is it?"

"Sorry, ma'am—0545."

"Already?" She sagged back against the cushions.

"Thought you might like a cup of fresh before I go home."

Wearily, Christy pushed up on one elbow, took the mug, and mumbled, "Thanks."

"And I sort of need my coat."

She looked down at the raincoat covering her legs. She smiled and held it out to him.

"You have a good day, ma'am," he said.

"You, too." She took the mug in both hands, shut her eyes, and sniffed the warm good-morning of the coffee.

The manager stopped at the window and peered out through the venetian blinds; it was still dark outside. "Sun'll be up in an hour."

The words hit Christy like a blast of frigid air. She stopped with the mug halfway to her lips. *The sun will come up tomorrow.*

"Well, goodnight . . . I mean, good morning, ma'am." He went out the door.

Christy sat up and looked about the room. The memories of last night flooded over her—Petrovsky's order and the trip to Andrews and Mrs. Watkins's warning. Now, the mannequins in the display cases had lost their camaraderie, seemed a gathering of strangers, men capable of evil acts as well as good. There was no more lying to herself;

something was gnawing at the Intel officer inside her and would not be still. All her training had taught her to obey orders without question; last night, she had obeyed. This morning, the questions would not keep.

An odd clicking caught her ear.

She rose, slipped on her shoes, went to the door and listened. Through a vaulted archway at the far end of the hall lay the billiard room; she had passed it many times but had never been inside. She stood a moment, listening to the intermittent clicking. Then she went down the hall and stopped at the threshold.

The long, low room was dark and deserted except for one set of lights above a billiard table at the rear. A man in a colonel's uniform stood at the table; he was a tall man, and graceful; there was a kind of easy elegance about the way he moved and held his billiard cue. He had a dignity of bearing, but there was also gentleness and patience in him. Christy didn't recognize him. Then she did.

She stepped back from the door.

Without looking up, Colonel Petrovsky said, "Good morning, Lieutenant."

Christy straightened. "Good morning, sir."

"Come in, please, won't you?" And when she approached the table, he said, "You had a busy night. Get some shut-eye?"

"Some."

"I'm sorry we kept you up so late."

"I didn't mind."

"I'm sure." He walked to the far side of the table and surveyed the positions of the three scattered balls. "Get Mrs. Watkins home all right?"

"Yes, sir."

"Did she talk to you about our meeting with her husband?"

"No, sir."

"May I ask, what did you talk about?"

"She told me about her husband's crime."

"I see. And what was your reaction?"

"Naturally, I was shocked."

"Naturally." Petrovsky chalked the tip of his cue. "A lot of them couldn't adjust."

"I'm not sure maladjustment is an excuse for murder. Sir."

He stopped chalking and looked at her. "You're a steely woman, aren't you?"

Christy hesitated. But there was no malice in him. "Yes, sir. I suppose I am."

"You always say exactly what you think. You always do your duty as you see it, don't you?"

"I try to."

"The whole world could come crashing down around you, and you'd still do your duty, wouldn't you?"

"I . . . "

Petrovsky smiled. "I think you would." He laid his cue stick on the table. "Come with me." He turned toward the end of the room. She followed. He had a long, easy stride; she had to walk quickly to keep abreast.

"How long were you at Harvard, Lieutenant?"

"Four years undergrad. One more for my master's in Russian Studies."

"All courtesy of the air force?"

"Yes, sir."

Petrovsky stopped before an isolated display cabinet in the far corner of the billiard room. Unlike the exhibits hallowed in the lounge, this cabinet was cluttered, dirty, ignored. It was filled with memorabilia of the Vietnam War. On the wall beside the cabinet, a scattering of framed photographs and newspaper clippings hung at cockeyed angles, undusted and untended.

Petrovsky drew his index finger across the front of the cabinet, then rubbed the grime between his thumb and fingertip. "Mementos of a war America would like to forget." He pointed at one of the framed clippings on the wall. "Can you reach that, Lieutenant?"

Christy lifted it from the nail and brought it down. Under the glass was a yellowed article from *Pravda*. In the grainy photograph beside the Russian text, a squad of grinning Vietcong guerrillas leveled AK-47s with fixed bayonets at a ragged group of American prisoners of war.

"Can you translate the headline?" Petrovsky said.

" 'Heroic Vietcong Forces Subdue Reactionary Criminal Invaders'."

"Indeed." He pointed at one of the prisoners. "Recognize him?"

Christy squinted at the young black airman in the tattered flight suit. His eyes stared back, fearful and confused. He was unmistakably Terry Watkins.

"That's how Terry Watkins lived for five years in a VC prison," Petrovsky said. "Can you imagine what that was like? Can you imagine living in a cage in a jungle prison for as long as you were in college?"

"No, sir."

"All the time you were studying the glories of military history and learning to march in an ROTC parade, Terry Watkins was in Chu My prison learning war." Petrovsky touched her shoulder. "Try to imagine what that was like. The isolation, the loneliness, the beatings. Imagine you're in captivity. There's no escape. Your enemy is brutal, ruthless—practicing every kind of physical and psychological intimidation. Your government has abandoned you, has turned its back on you and your war. Imagine all that and look closely. What did Terry Watkins learn in five years in Chu My prison?"

Christy shook her head.

"That man is the only creature capable of evil," Petrovsky said. "And modern weapons multiply his capacity for cruelty without end." He nodded toward the doorway. "Those neat uniforms and mannequins in the smoking room aren't war. This"—he rapped a knuckle on the glass—"this is war. This is the dark nature of man."

Christy peered into the faces of the seven American prisoners in the photograph. Behind their hollow eyes and stooping shoulders she could sense a resignation that was not surrender—but an understanding born of pain. It was as though—

Suddenly, she jabbed a finger at the photograph. "That's you! And . . . and Colonel Harding. And Colonel O'Neill."

Petrovsky took the clipping from her hands and stared down at it. "Chu My prison. Class of 1973. You might say we all learned together." He smiled softly. "It's a strangely liberating feeling—the moment you accept that you've been abandoned and doomed to die. It lets you see things as they really are. Well"—he handed the clipping back—"that was long ago and far away. Hang that, Lieutenant. But don't forget it." He turned, walked toward the billiard table.

For a moment, Christy stood staring after him. Then she hung the article in place and followed.

Petrovsky picked up his cue. "Did you see the homecomings of our Vietnam POWs? The televised repatriations? Quite different from the way the heroes of the Persian Gulf were welcomed—wasn't it?"

"Yes, sir."

"Those sickly men, their patriotic little speeches. Wives and children waiting obediently behind red velvet cordons to embrace those ghosts of soldiers." He chalked his cue and set the cube down on the rail. "The government told them they'd won peace with honor. And they believed it. For a time." He looked at her. "You heard the president last night. What was your assessment?"

"Assessment, sir?"

"First Step. Think it's a good idea to stake the strategic defense of the free world on intercontinental nuclear missiles?"

The bluntness of the question surprised Christy; junior officers did not evaluate policy. They obeyed policy. She hesitated.

"Don't be shy, Lieutenant."

"No, sir. I wouldn't do it."

"Why not?"

"We'll lose our options. If some strategic threat arose—"

"We'll still have the deterrent missiles."

"The missiles can't be fired."

"Can't be fired?"

"No, sir. Not without escalating into an exchange that would exterminate all human life. Deterrence only prevents a sneak attack in peacetime. If tensions mount and war becomes inevitable, the logic flip-flops. The launch of a single missile forces an all-out exchange."

Petrovsky smiled. "I've never heard that said more clearly or succinctly." He cocked his head. "Did Captain Bryan teach you that?"

Bryan's name made Christy stiffen. She'd always wondered if Bryan had told Petrovsky about their relationship in Monterey. "Well . . . yes, sir."

"And what is that moment called?" Petrovsky said. "The moment when the deterrent changes from a safeguard to the trigger of annihilation? Do you remember?"

"It's called *Point Paradox*."

"Exactly." Petrovsky folded his arms and leaned back against the edge of the table. "You wrote your thesis on the Cuban missile crisis, didn't you?"

"Yes."

"And do you remember what Kennedy said that made Khrushchev and his Politburo blink? The threat that made them back down?"

"Well . . . yes, sir. He said—"

Petrovsky raised his hand. "I'm sure you do, Lieutenant." He nodded, satisfied. "You never disappoint me. Now . . . what must be done about First Step?"

"Done, sir?"

"We have a curious situation, wouldn't you agree? The president says the terms of START and our improving relations with the Soviets justify massive NATO force reductions. But you and I know First Step will put the nation and our allies in jeopardy. You're an Intel officer. What must be done?"

Puzzled, Christy groped, "I suppose . . . the Senate . . . if they don't ratify—"

"But suppose they do? They're not strategists. They're only politicians. What then?"

"Then . . . First Step will be law."

"Yes, a law we must obey. Now, I ask you again. If First Step is to be stopped, what must be done?"

"Well . . . nothing can be—"

"Seven good men could stop it," Petrovsky said. Then he added softly, "Or women."

Christy felt the slender hairs prickle on her neck. In the harsh vertical light of the billiard table lamp, the lines of age were etched deep about the colonel's eyes and mouth, grained-in the way the wind cuts rock. She thought of the picture of the young Petrovsky among the seven prisoners of Chu My. It was as though she were seeing the whole man for the first time, seeing beyond the patina of the elegant, peacetime soldier. Christy felt her fingertips begin to tremble. Behind Petrovsky's smile and reassuring eyes, the warrior within was old and battle-scarred—hardened, tempered, steeled. About them, the room, the club, the base, the nation lay in darkness. There were but two of them and whispers that hinted of conspiracy.

Petrovsky turned and went to the far side of the billiard table. He moved the three balls to the corners of the cloth. "Do you know how billiards is played, Lieutenant?"

"No, sir."

"The object is to make your cue ball strike both other balls. Now, how would you make this shot?"

Christy looked at the three balls spread at the extremities of the long, green cloth. "I don't know, sir."

"Remember your training. Sometimes to achieve an objective, you have to be oblique, play the angles, do the opposite of what your enemy expects. Look again."

Christy leaned over the table, studying the lay of it. "I don't see—"

"Didn't Captain Bryan teach you? Always find the framework." He touched the tip of his cue to the center of the green fabric. "Look again."

She stared down at the three balls, the empty yards of green felt, and padded cushions. And in her mind the lines of force began to weave a pattern. "What if . . . the cue ball hits the red ball. Then there . . . and there . . . and there. And here and here. Five cushions and the second white ball."

"Excellent, Lieutenant. You have a remarkable deductive mind. You'll make a fine commander someday."

Christy looked up at Petrovsky; this was not about billiard balls and they both knew it. "But that's only theory, sir. It's also a question of execution."

"Yes. It is." He bent over the table, stroked his cue ball. It rolled along the path Christy had described: striking the first object ball, then ricocheting off five banks, finally rolling up to kiss the second cue ball.

"That's right," Petrovsky said. "It *is* only a question of execution." He put the cue down and came around the table. Then, softly and in Russian, he said, *"Framework, Marianka Petrovna."*

The language and her name and patronymic startled her.

"Perceive the framework. Recognize the plan. Know your place in battle."

She answered him in English. "Women have no place in battle."

"There is always a place in battle for a warrior." Then he smiled and returned to English. "Do you know what day this is?"

"The eleventh. Veterans Day."

"Tell me, did Captain Bryan ever talk to you about the men of Chu My prison?"

Before she could answer, he turned sharply at the sound of hurried footsteps in the hall.

Lieutenant Colonel Richard Harding stood panting in the archway, hair tousled, jacket unbuttoned, tie askew. "Steve—"

Gently Petrovsky said, "Colonel, you're out of uniform."

Harding's eyes fell on Christy. Embarrassed, he brushed his hair down with his palm, pulled his necktie straight.

"What is Lieutenant Russoff to think when—"

"Sir, I'll run the errand," Harding said.

Petrovsky straightened.

"The errand. I can do it, Steve. Please. Give me a chance."

Christy looked back and forth between the men. There was such haste in Harding's voice, such desperation.

Then Petrovsky said, "Yes, Colonel, I believe you can." He turned to Christy; again the gentle light came on in his eyes. "I've enjoyed our talk, Lieutenant. Now, will you please excuse us?"

"Yes, sir." Christy went to the archway. But as she went out, she looked back and caught a glimpse of Petrovsky and Harding.

They were embracing.

AMERICAN MISSION, 11 ROUTE DE PREGNY, GENEVA

11:52 A.M.   Lieutenant Colonel Robert Wilding, commander of Marine Security Detachments/Europe, stood on the sixth-floor landing of the American mission and pressed his ear against the door. From within the reference library, he could hear the dim tapping of plastic keys. He turned the doorknob slowly. Silently, the bolt drew back. He eased the door ajar and squinted through the crack.

The library was small and dusty; its steel-stacked rows of books and files were shelved at random, chock-a-block spine-in and -out, and scattered helter-skelter on the floor. This was the dead-letter office of arms proposals—gambits and countergambits, tenders and ripostes— the whole long skein of negotiations that wandered like so many broken trails of bread crumbs through the dark forest of ballistic missiles. All the documents gathered in this room had one thing in common: all had been rejected. Now they were abandoned to molder until another generation's historians came to sift the causes of their own time's peace or war in this burial ground of hope.

Wilding stepped inside and shut and locked the door behind him. Then he leaned back against the wall, held his breath, and listened. The plastic tapping stopped, and then began again. Wilding hunched down, slid stealthily along the stacks toward the sound.

Around the corner of the last steel bookcase, beneath a window yellowed and opaqued with soot, a blond army major sat at the lone computer workstation, deftly paging through a printed reference with one hand, simultaneously punching through the computer's index with the other.

"Figured you'd be up here," Wilding said.

Sara looked up, then back to her computer. "Hello, Bob. What brings you to Geneva?"

"Annual reconnaissance."

"On Veterans Day?"

"Figured I might get a dance with you at the gala this afternoon. How about a hello kiss?"

"I'm busy."

He bent over her shoulder and tried to read the data scrolling up the screen. The scent of her hair twinged his nostrils. "What are you working on?"

"Cross-checking *slick-em* verification memoranda from the '88 and '90 technical conferences. Nothing that would interest you."

Wilding leaned forward, nuzzled the back of Sara's neck. "Does that mumbo jumbo turn you on?"

She ducked her head aside. "Go away, Bob."

"I called you last night."

"Sweet," she said without sounding like she meant it.

"Where were you?"

"I went to Annabelle's for dinner. We got to talking. I stayed over."

He chuckled in his throat. "I love it when you lie to me." He nuzzled her again. "How about tonight?"

"I'm busy."

"How about now?"

"Bob, I'm working."

"Are you? Or are you chicken?"

That made her turn her head. Wilding was tall and muscular, a sandy-haired career marine in his early forties. But his face was odd and angular—lantern jawed and heavy boned—the consequence of massive reconstructive surgery after the North Vietnamese repatriated him at the end of the war. Sara always wondered what he might have looked like before the interminable beatings had disfigured him beyond recognition. He might have been an all-American boy.

"Right here. Right now," Wilding said, and started to unbutton the jacket of his uniform.

"Don't be ridiculous." Sara tossed her hair and turned away.

"No one ever comes up to this rat hole but you." He slipped his jacket off, hung it over the computer screen.

"Stop it, Bob." She shoved the jacket aside; it tumbled to the floor.

"Hey. Easy on the class-A's." He picked the jacket up, brushed the dust from the rows of campaign ribbons and set it gently on the window sill. Then he undid his tie and started on his shirt buttons.

"Bob, quit it or I'll call a guard."

"You forget—they work for me." He peeled off the shirt and hung it on her chair. There was a long, jagged scar, a craggy ridge of white, hairless flesh that curved along his right side from his armpit to his navel. To its left and right, two rows of dots marked the puncture wounds of sutures. He kicked off his shoes and undid his belt.

"Bob, I'm warning you. . . ."

He unzipped his fly, unhooked his trousers, stepped out, and set them on the sill.

She tried to glare her disapproval. But all at once she couldn't keep from laughing. "You're insane. This is the—"

He caught the elastic waistband of his Jockey shorts.

"Bob!"

"There's only one way you're going to get rid of me."

"You're crazy."

He slipped the Jockey shorts down and kicked them away and stood there in his socks—blond, muscular, and hardening. "Am I?"

Sara sighed; theirs was the classic overseas military affair, a fragmentary series of off-and-on coincidental meetings at conferences and TDYs. She knew what to expect: desultory kisses, hasty foreplay, a kind of joyless, momentary lust that flared an instant and then returned to darkness like a candle quenched in fear. They all made love like that—the POW survivors; they called it love and thought it was. If for no other reason, that was why she couldn't deny him.

She pushed her chair back, stood, and let him take her in his greedy arms. He put his hand behind her neck, pressed her head down and pressed her lips against the scar.

She bared her teeth and bit down on the ridge.

He murmured in her hair, "You like that, don't you? Why? Because it's hard?"

She didn't like the wound—she hated it. Sometimes when he held her mouth to it, she bit so hard he bled. Even then he felt no pain; the nerves within the scar were dead. It was a double paradox; the Vietcong jailers had saved his life to torture him for information, but when they beat him, the scar was the only part of him that didn't feel the pain.

At last, Wilding released her and stood watching while she unbuttoned her blouse. "Everything," he said, and stroked himself.

She unfastened her skirt. "Everything?"

"Everything."

When she stepped out of her panties, he moved forward and took her in his arms. She shut her eyes and let him grope between her legs.

He was panting. "Know why I love you?"

"I didn't know you did."

" 'Cause you're a wicked little bitch. Come here." He swiveled the chair to her. But when she moved to sit, he turned her, made her kneel on the seat instead, her knees wedged open, feet apart and soft breasts hanging down. The window's fall of light glowed on her tiny waist, on her lean flanks humping back to meet him.

Wilding wet his fingers, stroked her from behind, then pushed and entered. Sara's hands shot forward, catching the cold steel shelving of the stacks. Despite herself, she groaned.

"Tight today," he whispered and cupped her breasts. "So you weren't lying about Annabelle. . . ."

"Yes, I was."

"I like it when you're tight." He thrust again. "You feel me?"

She teased. "A little."

He began the rocking rhythm, and her old brass bangle bracelet tinkled against the metal shelf. He stopped abruptly.

"I said *everything.*"

She opened her eyes and looked at the bracelet. It hung from her wrist, a memento mori, a rebuke. "I never take that off."

He butted deep and hard, a challenge. "Not for anyone?"

She groaned against the pain and arched her neck. "Not anymore."

OCEANA NAS, VIRGINIA BEACH, VA

5:56 A.M.   By starlight, the F-14 Tomcat bumped down the taxiway, and turned toward the white lights that marked the active runways. The cockpit canopy was up; Cholly Granger sat in front. Behind him, his student RIO, Lieutenant Dolman, was on the radio. "Oceana tower, this is Viper-one."

The radio crackled back, "Oceana tower, Roger. Viper-one, you are cleared runway two-zero right, wind calm."

Granger tapped in on the radio. "Engler, we've got external tanks and heavy ordnance. We'll wait for one-one right."

"Okay, Cholly. Stand by."

"Standing by."

Granger eased the throttles forward. Like a black angel of death, the F-14 swung into position at the runway's end. With the hiss of a serpent, the canopy locked closed.

VETERANS' ADMINISTRATION MEDICAL CENTER, NORTHPORT, LONG ISLAND, NY

5:57 A.M.   Willie Logan moaned in his sleep and churned the covers. The gown he wore was sweated to his chest and back; the bedclothes were a tangled mass of perspiration. His body lay in the darkened hospital room, but his mind was somewhere in the noon sky over Ban Don, Vietnam.

"Bandit . . . I have a bandit one o'clock. Heads up, Cholly. I got him . . . I got him. . . ." Logan tossed and flung the sticky sheet aside. "Fox one! Missile running true. Hold it . . . hold it . . . I have a bogey. . . . Wait! I have incoming missile! Six o'clock. Dive, Cholly! DIVE!"

Suddenly Logan sat upright, eyes wide open, cheeks glistening with sweat. "We're hit!" he shouted. "Cholly! Eject! Christ, my legs! Cholly, I can't get out! Cholly, eject! CHOLLY!"

With one great spasm, he flung himself out of the bed. His head thudded on the linoleum and he lay panting on the floor. The tangled sheets slithered down, enveloping him like a shroud.

The room lights snapped on. A young VA nurse stood in the doorway. "Mr. Logan!" She rushed to kneel beside him. "Mr. Logan, are you all right?"

He moaned and clutched her hand. She eased him upright against the side of the bed.

Logan was gasping; sweat streamed down his face and neck. "Okay . . . I'm okay. . . ."

Night supervisor Marge Kessler stood sneering in the doorway. She was a retired navy nurse, a dark-and-burly, wire-haired, big-breasted woman. Her jowly face was painted with a cruel, sardonic smile. "What's the problem? Did he piss his bed again?"

"Marge, he fell!"

"For chrissake . . ." Kessler stamped across the room, stood over Logan, and glared at him with contempt. "What's the matter, sailor? The bogeyman make you pull the plunger?"

The young nurse cradled Logan's head. "Marge, honest to god!"

"Aw, cut the hearts and flowers, kid. This basket case has been in and out of here since '73." She bent to help Logan up.

He wrenched away. "Keep your hands off me, Kessler."

"Yeah? And how you gonna get back into bed, tough guy?" She kicked aside the loose flap of the gown; his legs had been amputated at midthigh. "Come on . . . *hero.*"

She seized one arm; the young nurse took his other. Together, they heaved Logan back into bed. Kessler punched up the pillows with her fist. "Plenty of guys came home in pieces. They learned to use their artificial arms and legs. But not this prima donna."

"Marge!"

Kessler yanked the sheets up over him. "Plenty of guys went home in plastic bags. I zipped a lot of them closed." She leaned over the bed, stuck her face in Logan's. "Who gave *you* a guarantee, Mac?"

"Fuck you, Kessler."

"Wouldn't you like to try." She snorted and threw his blanket over him. "I'll see you on the parallel bars in fifteen minutes. And, mister, you better come to play." She stalked back to the door and shot one last vicious glance across her shoulder. "Creep!"

OCEANA NAS, VIRGINIA BEACH, VA

5:59 A.M.   In the dark at the end of the runway, the frigid night air was alive with the whine of idling turbofans. Invisible in the darkness, identified only by the rhythmic pinging of its navigation strobes, the F-14 Tomcat waited, brakes locked, wings set wide at twenty-three degrees, trailing-edge flaps at full extension for takeoff.

In the cockpit, Cholly Granger punched the computer to double-check the analog clock on the panel. The digital display flashed 1059:48Z for Zulu—Greenwich mean time. The clock was correct.

Around the corner from the prime minister's residence at Number 10 Downing Street, in the middle of the wide, windy boulevard of Whitehall, a workman stopped his wire brush and looked down from the scaffolding which embraced the monument to the dead of Britain's wars known as the Cenotaph. Across the street on the curb before the Georgian facade of the Foreign and Commonwealth Office, a bent old man in a plain cloth coat stood bareheaded in the wintry chill, an arthritic hand raised to his brow in an open-handed salute. The tattered ribbons of decorations on his breast fluttered in the wind. The workman smiled at the old man; then his eyes followed the speeding traffic south to Parliament Square, the Albert Tower, and Big Ben.

The voice of Oceana tower crackled through Granger's headset. "Viper-one, you are cleared for takeoff."

"Roger, tower. Hey, Noel . . ."

"What?"

"Just . . . see you sometime."

"Sure you will. Happy landings, Cholly."

Granger eased the throttles forward. The convergence nozzles on the F-14's twin tail cones flexed outward and the blue flames of the afterburners stretched into graceful points. Slowly at first, then gathering itself, the F-14 bumped forward down the runway, riding the thunder of its turbofans. One by one, then in groups, then in an unbroken white streak, the runway lights flashed past the cockpit.

In the backseat, Dolman ticked off their ground speed. "Eighty knots . . . one-twenty . . . rotate. . . ."

Granger eased the stick back; the stabilators jabbed downward into the rising draft. Gently, the fighter's nose tilted skyward. Then the nosegear clunked up off the tarmac and Granger pulled hard on the stick.

At precisely 1100 Zulu, the first stroke of Big Ben fell.

With a banshee's cry of vengeance, the Tomcat screamed into the predawn sky.

BOLLING AFB, WASHINGTON

6:00 A.M.   Yawning and shivering, Christy came out the door of the O-club and started down the hill toward INI. The sky was somber black; the air had turned to prickly, freezing damp, thick with river mist that rolled before the icy breeze off the Potomac.

Bolling was already stirring. Two ranks of security police in sweaty gym suits came toward her up Brookley Avenue, running lockstep double-time, in and out of the yellow light of the streetlamps, their sergeant chanting cadence.

> Girl took off her pretty dress.
> Traded it for Oh-Tee-Ess.
> Sound off!
> One! Two!
> Sound off!
> Three! Four!

A few of the grunts grinned and winked at Christy as they passed.

> Girl became an office-suh.
> When we screw I call her "sir."
> Sound off!
> One! Two!
> Sound off!
> Three! Four!
> Cadence count!

One, two, three, four. . . .
ONE, TWO! THREE, FOUR!

Their tramping feet and voices faded into the darkness. Christy stood looking after them, her cheeks burning.

She went up the concrete steps to the little brick building that housed the INI directorate, punched the access code for the digital lock, and waited until the bolt clicked open.

Inside, the office was stirring to life. Sleepy NCOs and civilian clericals were pulling data from USAFE HQ in Ramstein, Torrejon AFB in Spain, and RAF Bentwaters in Britain. By 0655, anything hot had to be on the secure fax lines to the Pentagon to make the morning stand-up for the Joint Chiefs.

Christy zigzagged through the warren of workstations toward her office at the far end of the ground floor. Tod was waiting with a cup of coffee and a handful of dispatches.

"Thank you, Browning."

"May I speak with you, Lieutenant?"

They went inside her office and shut the door. Christy keyed her access code into the computer on her desk. Her E-mail electronic mailbox lit with a one-line message:

```
Dinner my place tonight? Dubinsky.
```

She shook her head and punched the erase key. The message vanished.

Tod sat on the edge of her desk, thumbing the dispatches. "Your grandmother called this morning, borderline hysterical because you hadn't come home."

"God, it was so late I didn't call." Christy reached for the phone.

He caught her hand. "What about it?"

"About what?"

"That funky errand Petrovsky had us on last night."

"Tod, forget about last night." She pulled her hand free, picked up the receiver, and began to dial.

"I was going to. Then I saw this in your in-box." He dropped one of the dispatches on her desk.

"What's that?"

"Copy of a telex from Petrovsky to some navy fighter jock named Granger. Turning down his request for transfer to the air force. Petrovsky had Polly send it last night and route a copy to you."

Christy shrugged. "Some kind of joke." Through the receiver, she could hear her grandmother's phone ringing.

"Yeah, Petrovsky's a real comedian."

Christy glanced down at the telex. The last sentence caught her eye.

```
The sun will come up tomorrow.
```

Her grandmother's sleepy voice said, *"Da?"*

Christy slapped the receiver into its cradle and grabbed the dispatch. A hollow opened in the bottom of her stomach. "Tell Polly I want to see her."

"Not in yet. What—"

"Soon as she gets in. Now, let me work."

Tod stiffened. "Yes, ma'am." Then he went out the door and slammed it.

By the time Christy realized how she'd sounded, he was gone.

CONVENT OF ST. MARY-IN-THE-WOODS, ARLINGTON, VA

6:03 A.M. Colonel Tom O'Neill climbed heavily through the darkness, following the puddles of light beneath the knee-high mushroom lamps. At the top of the hill, the stolid, brick Victorian convent sat creped in mourning, black against the blackness of the sky. From its upper stories, curtained windows stared down inscrutably, betraying no secrets.

Above the pair of arched oak doors a weathered wooden Jesus hung beside the night-light, his sacred heart ignored by nuns in black and novices in white who scuttled, singly and in silent pairs, down the shadowy cherry walk toward the glowing portal of the red brick chapel. O'Neill watched the nuns, their faces eclipsed within their cowls, hands buried in their sleeves, their chaste, black lace-up shoes shuffling in quick, obedient steps. He understood their haste, their single sense of purpose; he, too, had taken orders but of a different kind. He yanked the bellpull, took off his hat, tucked it under his arm, and went inside.

The narrow, vaulted entry hall was lit by an ornate bronze chandelier; the marble floor was bare and scrubbed and reeked of piny disinfectant. A curving stone stairway descended from the second floor to embrace a lime-streaked medieval statue of Saint Christopher bearing a pensive infant Jesus, his eyes a pair of empty, blinded sockets. To the right, along the wall, a wooden rack contained three rows of pigeonholes, each neatly labeled: SISTER PETER JAMES, SISTER SIMON MARK, SISTER PHILOMENA, and the rest.

O'Neill checked his watch. He was about to step outside and ring the bell again when he heard keys jangling above him. When he looked up, a busty, gray-haired matron was tramping down the stairs.

"What is it?" she said without a greeting.

"Sister Mary Patrick."

"What about her?"

"I'm her father."

The matron looked him up and down. Then she unlocked a side door and snapped on a light. "You wait in here."

O'Neill went into the reception room; it was narrow as a crypt, and just as damp. On the threadbare oriental rug an old oak table held a single lamp, a Bible, and a peremptory hand-lettered sign that read NO SMOKING.

But what caught his eye was the painting hung above the carved stone fireplace. It was a descent from the cross after Caravaggio—the black and umber and vermilion laid on with a will. Generations of soot and sun had dulled the lacquer to a murky brown. And yet the swooning of the flaccid body, the attenuated arms, the blood-black wounds of the stigmata made O'Neill clench his fingers to his palms. The painting was a copy, and a poor one. But within its compass—in the droop of Jesus' lifeless head—the grip of death was real.

The bolt sounded. When O'Neill turned, the door was open and a nun stood staring. Her cowl framed her sallow face, the hollows of her eyes; her skin was pasty white, her lashes and her eyebrows colorless. It was the sort of face that stared down from the granite pediments of great cathedrals—blank, ageless, old, older than he, older, somehow, than the Commandments.

"Daddy!" She laughed and hurried to his arms.

He embraced her.

When she stepped back, she held him at arm's length and scanned his face. "Daddy, you look tired."

"I'm fine."

"What is it? Is something wrong?"

"Here. Sit with me." He led her to the wooden bench beneath the Pietà.

"I can't stay, Daddy. It's my day to ring the bell for morning prayer."

"I won't keep you." O'Neill took her hand in his. It had been four years since she'd put on the plain gold wedding ring. Yet every time he saw it, he felt a pang of loss. "Kate, do you remember when you were a little girl, sometimes we'd talk about conscience?"

"Yes."

"And I always said follow your conscience, Katherine Anne. Whatever happens. No matter what your friends might say."

"I remember." She stared at him. And he could see the nun in her preparing to hear and know the worst. "Daddy, what is it you came to tell me?"

"I have to do something, Katie. Something you may not understand." He wet his lips. "Something that may make people shun you."

"Daddy . . ."

"And I just want you to know. This thing I do . . . it's an act of conscience."

She looked at him and he could see the patience in her. She had a nun's eyes now; the all-forgiving eyes that measured men's souls against the pillars of eternity. "Have you talked to Father Bill?"

"No."

"Will you?"

"If that will make you feel better."

"I'm not saying that for me. Will you see him?"

O'Neill nodded. Then he clutched her fingers. "But I want *you* to know I'd never—"

Softly, she broke in on him. "Daddy. I am not your judge."

She stood. "Now, I must go. I love you, Daddy." She smiled at him, that fleeting smile in which she was a girl again. "God bless you." Then she left him without looking back.

O'Neill sat staring at the closing door. Then he wiped his hand across his mouth and took his hat and went into the foyer. He slipped the slim envelope that contained his will into the pigeonhole marked SISTER MARY PATRICK. Then he went out and down the walk toward his car.

And the bell tolled his stride.

ILE ROUSSEAU, GENEVA

12:06 P.M.   On a weathered wooden bench behind a rusty iron railing, Jake Handlesman sat looking eastward past the busy traffic on the Pont du Mont-Blanc, out across the waters of the Rade de Genève to where the quiet body of the lake glistened in the sun against the distant cyclorama of the Alps.

Jake liked the little manmade pentagonal island park the Swiss called Ile Rousseau, thrust as it was from the Pont des Bergues into the cold Rhône flowing westward into France. It was a park of paradoxes—a tiny, preserve of birch and elm, a summer refuge for the thrush and finch, an eye of quiet in the roiling wintry city.

He liked it, too, because it was named for Jean-Jacques Rousseau—a man whose very life was paradox. As an undergraduate, Jake had read Rousseau's *Confessions;* he had not believed a word. Rousseau was the moralist who had authored *Du contrat social.* But he was also a libertine who fathered five children by a chambermaid he never married—a rogue who delivered each newborn infant to a foundling hospital and admitted he felt no guilt abandoning his children. Rousseau was an equivocator who affected the style of a pauper and intellectual, but strove his whole life for acceptance among the aristocracy. He was a self-aggrandizing pedant who sought to place his works under God's protection by laying them on the altar at Notre Dame in Paris but was frustrated by an iron gate he had not noticed on previous visits to the church. Rousseau curried and then ruined a friendship with the brilliant encyclopedist, Diderot. He was vilified by David Hume and ignored by the other great thinkers of his time—Voltaire, Kant, and Edmund Burke, even Montesquieu.

And yet—a hundred years before Marx—it was Rousseau who argued man is born good, and that discord stems from inequities of wealth and privilege. After the French Revolution, in one final paradox, Rousseau achieved in death the recognition he had sought in vain throughout his life. The old hypocrite's bones were reinterred in perpetual glory in the Pantheon in Paris, while his ideas lived on to change the world.

Now Jake sat in the park named for the great equivocator, knowing that by revealing the secret of Hakodate, he, too, had become an equivocator whose life was doomed to close in infamy.

He looked up as Lermontov sat down beside him. "I congratulate you on your performance this morning," Jake said.

"As I do you on yours." Lermontov laid the portable magnetic chessboard open on the bench between them.

Jake adjusted his glasses and bent to examine the position as they'd left it. "Me? What did I do?"

"You were absolutely convincing."

Jake baited with a pawn to bishop three. "Was I? About what?"

"About your commitment to First Step." Lermontov took pawn with pawn. "About wanting to eliminate the *slick-ems.*"

"That's why we're here. To eliminate weapons."

"That's not why you're here. Now, you're here to defeat First Step."

"My friend, you overestimate my capabilities." Jake captured pawn with bishop.

"Why did you give me Hakodate?" Lermontov moved his queen to bishop-two.

Jake shrugged. "In the beaten way of friendship. . . ." He took knight with knight.

"You knew reports of American nuclear weapons in Japan might delay First Step for years." Lermontov captured Jake's knight with his queen.

"Even unconfirmed reports?"

"We have corroboration." Lermontov leaned forward and his voice was pinched with apprehension. "There will be demonstrations. A protest from the Japanese foreign ministry. Your intention to honor your treaties will be challenged by our military. All your treaties."

Jake studied the position of the chessmen. "Possibly."

"Our generals will argue—if the Americans disdain their treaties with Japan, why should we believe they will keep their word to us?"

"You have Gorbachev's ear. Advise him."

"Believe me, I will do my best," Lermontov said.

"If you knew Hakodate was incendiary, why did you use it?"

"As a patriot I had no choice. You know that."

There was a twinkle in Jake's eye. "A forcing move?"

"A cunning move. But why?"

Jake caught Lermontov by the hand. "First Step is dangerous. You said so yourself this morning. It permanently ratifies the existence of strategic nuclear missiles. Misha, have we come all this way to lock-step now together into hell?"

The two old men stared at each other. Then Jake released the Russian's hand. "You don't recognize the game, do you?"

Lermontov's eyes narrowed. "Should I?"

Jake tapped the chessboard. "Réti versus Bogoljubow. New York, 1924. Your move, I believe."

INI, BOLLING AFB, WASHINGTON

6:08 A.M.   Zigging and zagging, Christy hurried through the half-empty bull pen, clutching Petrovsky's dispatch to Granger. Two years ago—before the end of the Cold War—every desk had been occupied and active. Now most of the desks stood deserted, their computer terminals shrouded and silent, including the desk plaqued T/SGT. POLLY KULIKOV.

Christy knocked on the office door behind Polly's desk and pushed inside. Lieutenant Nikolai Dubinsky was bent double in his desk chair, laughing out loud. He was twenty-six, crew cut, and dark eyed, three months Christy's junior in grade and one of the few men left at the directorate; the rumor mill had it that no combat command would take him. He looked up at the sound of the door.

"Hey, Rice Crispy. Want to hear a good one?" Dubinsky held up the amusement page of *Red Star,* the Soviet army newspaper.

"Nicky—"

"Stalin used to say that in the West people exploited each other. But in the Soviet Union it was exactly the opposite. Ain't that a great one?" And he laughed again.

"Nicky, have you seen Polly?"

"Nope. How 'bout that dinner?"

"What time is Polly on duty?"

"0600, like the rest of us slaves. Which would make her"—he checked his watch "—eight minutes late. Whaddya say, Chris? Chicken cacciatore and all the Chianti you can drink."

"Have Polly call me as soon as she gets in."

"Lunch, maybe?"

Christy stepped out of his office, shut the door, and stood against it; Nicky Dubinsky had a one-track mind—and he wasn't any better cook than lover. She looked down at Granger's FPO address on the dispatch in her hand. Then she went back up the hall to her office, shut the door, and dialed a number at the Naval Annex in Alexandria.

The proper voice with the Spanish accent said, "Naval MPC. Captain Contreras speaking. Not a secure line."

"¿Xavier? Christina aquí."

At once, the man's tone mellowed. *"Buenos días, cara mía. ¡Tanto tiempo! ¿Por qué te escondes? Miles de años sin te verte. . . ."*

"*Xavier,* do a working girl a favor. . . ." She punched up the E-mail facility on her computer.

AMERICAN MISSION, 11 ROUTE DE PREGNY, GENEVA

12:09 P.M.   Major Sara Weatherby stood at the window of the sixth-floor library, buttoning her blouse and staring out past the tracery of spiny frost that coated the glass. Behind her, Wilding pushed his tie knot tight against his Adam's apple and leaned in, nuzzling her ear.

"How'd you get so good?"

"Years of practice," Sara said and walked away.

"Hey, what kind of answer is that?" Wilding cinched his belt. "You're supposed to say, Bobby, you're an inspiration. . . ."

She sighed in irritation. "Am I?"

That stopped him. "If you feel it." Then, softly, he said, "Had a lot of men?"

She snapped her skirtfront straight. "Are we going to have that conversation *now*?"

He smiled that hurt little smile of his. "Not if you don't want to."

"Look, Bob. I was married. I've had lovers. You're one of them. I'm not a virgin. Over and out."

He touched her shoulder. "See you tonight?"

"I said I'm busy."

She flicked the computer off and walked out the door.

37°35′N × 75°35′W, ALTITUDE 8,000 FEET

6:10 A.M.   The Tomcat climbed through the darkness east of Chincoteague, Virginia, leveled off at eight thousand feet, steering northeast at five hundred knots on heading 045, boring into the black corridor between sky and open water. In the cockpit, Cholly Granger eased the throttles to eighty-five percent military power, the cruise setting for the General Electric turbofans. At altitude, the eastern horizon showed the first thin trail of indigo; overhead, it was still starry, endless night.

Granger thumbed the intercom. "Dolman, select Hampton on the TACAN."

"Yes, sir." In the rear cockpit, Dolman punched the plane's automatic direction finder to the preset for channel 83.

The TACAN locked on the beacon, Granger toggled in the autopilot, and settled back in his seat. Beyond lay open ocean, the North Atlantic Control Area, and beyond that, the Military Operations Area where the carrier *Kennedy* was conducting combat training exercises. "Dolman, go to PDS on your radar and max detection range. Set defense alert perimeter at one hundred twenty miles. And run your missile-on-aircraft test sequences, please."

"Now, sir? Got at least half an hour before—"

"Just," Granger sighed, "one time, Dolman. Follow an order."

"Aye-aye, sir."

THERAPY ROOM, VA MEDICAL CENTER, NORTHPORT, LONG ISLAND

6:11 A.M.   Willie Logan strained forward in his wheelchair, bent, and pushed the steel doors open. Then he rolled into the chilly therapy room. Marge Kessler, the sharp-tongued nursing supervisor, looked up from her desk.

"Well. Here he is—Mr. Wet Dreams."

"Fuck you, Kessler." Logan rolled past her. "I don't have to take that shit from you." He rolled to the far end of the room, pivoted the wheelchair, and locked the brakes. Then he leaned heavily on the armrests, swung himself onto a bench, and pulled his dead thighs after him. A Puerto Rican orderly waited with Logan's artificial legs.

Kessler stood. "Yes, you do, Mac. As long as you want the VA to pay your bed and board here, you'll take anything I dish out. And don't you forget it." She nodded to the orderly. "Buckle on his stumps, José."

"*Me llamo Luis.*"

"Just do it, asshole."

INI, BOLLING AFB, WASHINGTON

6:12 A.M. Christy sat hunched forward, elbows on her desk, staring at the E-mail matrix on her computer screen. The legend in the upper left-hand corner read:

       Granger, Charles L. CMDR 066349900

The rest of the screen was blank.

Alongside her computer, the day's briefing calendar, her translation work, the thicket of interagency requisitions marked ASAP all lay untouched. Christy was staring at the computer screen, but she was thinking about Colonel Steven Petrovsky. She was beginning to wonder if he had broken the law.

The office door opened; startled, Christy looked up.

It was Tod. "Excuse me, ma'am. Didn't mean to—" He shut the door and his tone changed. "Hey, why so jumpy?"

"Has Polly—"

"Nope. But"—he grinned and laid a slip of paper on her desk—"I got her phone number out of the recall roster."

Christy snatched it and reached for the phone.

Tod sat on the edge of the desk. "You're welcome." And while she dialed, he leaned over Christy's computer and pivoted the monitor so he could read the screen. "What's this?"

"Thought I'd run a service record check on that pilot, Granger. The one Petrovsky sent the message to."

"He's navy. How you gonna do that?"

"Called Contreras over at their Annex."

Tod's face hardened; he knew Christy and the Venezuelan had been lovers. "Him again?"

"Tod. That's ancient history. I asked him to E-mail Granger's record over here."

"And?"

Christy tapped the screen. "That's it—name, rank, and service number. Someone erased the rest last night."

"Whoa!" Tod pulled a face. "Talk about a great way to get your butt thrown in the brig!"

But by then Christy was listening to the repetitious ringing of Polly's phone. "Dammit. Why doesn't she answer?"

MASTER BEDROOM, THE WHITE HOUSE, WASHINGTON

6:13 A.M. Sam Baker came out of the dressing room, buttoning the front of his shirt. "Well? What did Fowler find out?"

Harris sat on the chaise longue at the far end of the bedroom, balancing his coffee cup and saucer on his knee. "NBC's opening the *Today* show with an interview with Whitworth and replaying part of it on the *Nightly News*. The old man's going for maximum exposure."

"Do you blame him?"

"Yes, Sam. I do."

The phone rang; Harris lifted the receiver. He held it out to the president. "Mulholland."

"Good. That means he's got the *slick-em* deal done."

"Told you the Soviets had to go along."

Sam Baker took the phone. "Hello, Craig. I hope congratulations are in order."

In his office at the American mission in Geneva, Ambassador Craig Mulholland stood behind his desk. His jacket was off, his sleeves rolled up and necktie loosened. "Mr. President, something very disturbing surfaced at the negotiating session this morning."

Sam Baker heard the tension in Mulholland's voice. He waved Harris to the other phone; silently, Harris lifted the receiver.

"Mr. President," Mulholland said, "do we have a nuclear *slick-em* depot at Hakodate?"

"Where?"

"Hakodate. In Japan."

"Absolutely not."

"Mr. President, *are you certain*?"

Puzzled, Sam Baker looked to Harris.

"Dammit, Sam." Mulholland was struggling to control his temper. "I can't do this job if you keep me in the dark!"

"Now, hold on, Craig—"

But Mulholland wouldn't hear it. "When I took on this negotiation we agreed—direct access and full disclosure. Now I'm sitting here in Geneva with egg on my face! And I ask you again: do we have sea-launched nuclear cruise missiles in Japan?"

"Just a moment." A sudden chill ran through Sam Baker. He slapped his hand over the mouthpiece. "Ted, get Zack Littman on the line. Right now." He uncovered the phone. "Craig, I'll call you back."

Sam Baker hit another button on the phone. "Katherine, have General Gaynor come up here. On the double." He hung up and stared at Harris. "The fools. The stupid, arrogant fools. . . ."

THERAPY ROOM, VA MEDICAL CENTER, NORTHPORT, LONG ISLAND

6:14 A.M.   Hand over hand, Willie Logan dragged himself along the parallel bars. And with each staggering step, the knee and ankle joints of his plastic legs clicked and groaned. The Puerto Rican orderly hovered beside him, ready to catch him should he fall.

At the far end of the bars Marge Kessler stood, hands on hips, a malicious smile curling her lip. "Back off there, José. Let our hero stagger along under his own power."

Logan was sweating, gasping. "You're a bitch, Kessler. You know that? A real brass-balled bitch."

"Oh, give it a rest, Logan. You'll have us all in tears."

Suddenly Logan stumbled. He tried to regain his balance, but pirouetted in a tight spiral until his right hand bent double on itself. Then he lost his grip and fell hard on his face on the rubber mat.

"Goddammit!" He pounded the mat with an impotent fist. "Goddamn you, Kessler!"

She stood over him, sneering. "You've really got to improve your attitude, Mr. Logan."

"Fuck you, Kessler! Fuck you, cunt!"

"Don't you know the sun will come up tomorrow?"

Logan lay as he was, prostrate and still on the cold rubber mat. Then he looked up—straight into Kessler's steely eyes.

INI, BOLLING AFB, WASHINGTON

6:15 A.M.   Christy sat, holding the receiver; the monotonous ring droned off and on. At last, she slammed the receiver down.

Tod leaned against the side of her desk. "Still no Polly?"

Christy shook her head.

He tapped the E-mail matrix on the computer monitor. "What say you tell me what this is all about?"

Without answering, Christy punched the print command, took the sheet of paper with Granger's name and service number from the printer, picked up the copy of Petrovsky's dispatch, and started for the door.

Tod said, "Hey—where you going?"

"To see Colonel Harding."

Christy opened the door; abruptly, Tod pushed it closed. "To see Harding about what?"

"Tod, you know as well as I do. Something weird is going on."

"What?"

"I'm not sure. But I'm going to report it."

"Report what?"

"Whatever's going on."

"What's that?"

She was losing her temper. "Dammit, I don't know."

"Then what are you going to report?" He leaned against the door and held it closed. "Chris, this is the air force. You want to report something, you put it in writing. In triplicate. You stamp it, date and time. And you put it in the interoffice mail."

"This won't wait."

"What won't wait?"

She sighed with exasperation. "Tod—"

"You go see Harding, he'll say"—Tod sucked in his cheeks, aping the gaunt lieutenant colonel—"er . . . see here, Lieutenant. What's this all about?"

"Someone at the navy MPC erased a personnel file."

Tod was play-acting. "Could be a glitch, Lieutenant. Don't like to admit it, but a bad sector does crop up on a GI disk every now and then. Suggest you have the navy file a CIR—leave it to the high-tech boys. Have a nice day, Lieutenant." He flipped a salute with his fingertips. "That's the air force, Chris."

"What about Polly?"

"If she's late for work, that's between her and her supervisor."

"Tod, open the door and get out of my way."

He took her arm. "Christy, if you think you know what's going on, dammit, tell me."

She pulled free. "Sergeant, get out of my way or I'll call the security police!"

Tod straightened as though she had slapped him in the face. "That's how it is?"

"That's how it is."

"Well, if Harding kicks you out on your butt, don't come crying to me." He pulled the door open.

She gathered herself and marched up the hall.

MASTER BEDROOM, THE WHITE HOUSE, WASHINGTON

6:17 A.M. Sam Baker sat on the edge of the bed, holding the telephone receiver. On the chaise, Ted Harris sat holding the extension. General Gaynor stood near the door, hands clasped behind his back.

"Good morning, Zack," Sam Baker said. "Sorry to drag you away from the fish."

Zack Littman—in whites, deck shoes, and marlin harness—stood in the dayroom of the yacht *Odalisque,* holding the portable phone. From the fantail he could hear the high-pitched screech of running line as his host played a sailfish. At the buffet behind him Clara poured herself a cup of coffee. "That's all right, Sam," Littman said. "I'm not catching anything but a cold."

"Zack, I have General Gaynor here with me. He's just received confirmation from the Joint Chiefs that we have a nuclear *slick-em* depot in Hakodate."

Littman hesitated. Jake had been right; it *was* handled. "So what? The Japs don't know it."

"The Soviets threw it in Mulholland's face this morning."

"Bad luck," Littman muttered. Clara looked over at him.

"I want you to do something about those missiles, Zack," Sam Baker said.

"Mr. President, the deployment of our *slick-ems* is not covered under START or any other treaty with the Soviets."

Sam Baker was beginning to lose his temper. "But they *are* covered under our no-nukes treaty with the Japanese. For god's sake, we're not kids playing marbles! You moved nuclear cruise missiles within a hundred miles of Soviet territory without my approval and in clear violation of a long-standing treaty with our most important trading partner!"

That silenced Littman.

"Zack, for weeks now, you've been resisting First Step every way you could. Carrying on at NSC meetings. Stirring up the Joint Chiefs. Do you deny that?"

"I've made no secret of how I feel about First Step, Sam. Not with you, not with anyone."

"Well, if you feel so damned strongly about it, be a man. Resign! Run for office yourself. Fight me in the open."

"By the time I did that, Mr. President," Littman said softly, "it would be too late."

Each was silent, weighing those words.

The president lowered his voice. "Zack, you get those missiles and that equipment out of Hakodate by tomorrow. I'll tell Mulholland to say they were being transshipped or something."

But Littman wasn't cowed. "Mr. President, I don't think we should let the Soviets push us off our own bases."

"Your exception is noted!" Sam Baker slammed the receiver down.

Zack Littman snapped off the portable phone and slowly set the receiver in its cradle.

Clara touched his shoulder. "Zack? What's wrong?"

"He's making too many concessions. He's sending the Soviets the wrong signal."

"Maybe he wants to prove to them how much we want a lasting peace."

"The way to peace is through strength. The only way."

Their six-year-old daughter Louise bounced through the doorway, carrying her Raggedy Ann; a long, floppy bow of bright pink ribbon was tied in the doll's woolly hair. "Daddy! Daddy! See my dolly!" She stood at Littman's knee, held the doll up in both her hands.

Littman stooped to the child, gently cupped her tiny face. Then he looked back at Clara. "I want our children—and our grandchildren—to live free."

"Don't you think President Baker wants the same thing?" Then Clara saw the desperation in her husband's eyes.

"He has no children."

INI, BOLLING AFB, WASHINGTON

6:18 A.M.   Christy pushed through the door into Lieutenant Colonel Harding's reception room. Sergeant Dana Pavlov looked up and smiled.

"Hey, Lieutenant. What can we do for you?"

"Dana, did you see Polly this morning?"

"Nope. Musta slept in."

"I need to talk to Colonel Harding."

"No can do, Lieutenant. He left for downtown at 0600."

"Downtown?"

"Said he had to run an errand for Petrovsky." Dana chuckled. "Ain't that a laugh? Lieutenant Colonel running errands. Probably want to do his own typing next week."

She grinned. But Christy couldn't see the joke.

OVAL OFFICE, THE WHITE HOUSE, WASHINGTON

6:20 A.M.   Secretary of State Arthur Coleman paced angrily between the desk and couches. When Sam Baker entered, Coleman stopped and said a sharp, "Good morning, Mr. President." Ted Harris shut the door.

"All right, Arthur," Sam Baker said. "What's so damned important?"

"It's on your desk."

A translation of a letter lay atop the president's leather correspondence folder; the Japanese original of the official diplomatic protest was attached. Sam Baker scanned the letter, passed it to Harris, then sank into his chair.

"Now, Sam—" Coleman came across the room with his finger raised. "I don't want an argument. This time he's gone too far."

Coleman stood over the president; there was blood in his eye. "Sam, he's got to go."

"Arthur, sit down."

"No." Coleman leaned forward and rested his palms on the desk.

"An hour ago, we received that letter from the Japanese government, alleging we had stationed nuclear cruise missiles at Hakodate. Naturally, I phoned Kaifu to assure him it wasn't true. Fifteen minutes ago, I got an urgent call from the JCS telling me it is. Sam, either Littman goes or I resign. There is no third alternative."

Sam Baker studied Coleman's face. He was in his fifties, a pudgy, balding man who always had a suntan. He was the most effective secretary of state since George Shultz because—like Schultz—he never lost sight of the objective, never lost his patience, never bent the truth. Sam Baker had never seen him this angry.

"Arthur, I will—"

"What?"

"I will consider it."

"Then consider this." Coleman turned and went to the door, and pulled it open. "Colonel? If you please."

An army colonel entered, stood inside the door, and braced. He carried a briefcase. Sam Baker glanced at Harris, who leaned back against the wall, head cocked with apprehension.

"Mr. President," Coleman said, "this is Colonel Neil MacDonald of Army Intelligence."

"Good morning, Colonel. Please, be at ease." The president indicated a chair.

"Thank you, sir."

"In the matter of Hakodate," Coleman said, "I believe you have a report, Colonel."

"Yes, sir." MacDonald opened his case and drew out a slender file in bright blue covers. "Mr. President, we believe we have the source of the Soviets' information about Hakodate."

Sam Baker shot a look at Harris; his eyes narrowed.

"As you know, sir, army intelligence and the CIA routinely conduct surveillance at the START talks in Geneva. Both sides. The Soviets and our own negotiators."

"Yes, I'm well aware." Sam Baker abhorred the idea that American diplomats had to be watched. But after the Bloch affair in 1989, he had approved increased appropriations for surveillance at all overseas missions.

MacDonald said, "For some time, we have conducted a close surveillance of Dr. Jacob Handlesman."

The president looked up sharply. "The man who works on verification?"

"Littman's man," Coleman said flatly.

Sam Baker sat back; the drama before him was becoming ominous.

MacDonald flipped back two pages in his file. "Beginning at the Helsinki SALT negotiations of 1969, Dr. Handlesman formed a personal friendship with a Soviet negotiator named Mikhail Lermontov. In January of 1989, Lermontov arranged for Handlesman to deliver a series of lectures at the Soviet Institute of Foreign Affairs in Moscow. With the concurrence of the CIA, the Arms Control and Disarmament Agency approved the trip. They even paid for his ticket."

"And? What did Handlesman say?"

"What he said was not important, sir. We were giving him a chance to cement his relationship with Lermontov in the hope it would pay us a dividend one day."

Sam Baker's lip curled in distaste. "Was Handlesman aware of your . . . investment?"

"No. If you'll forgive me, sir—when you bait a trap with cheese, you have to leave room for the mouse."

Sam Baker sighed. He deplored espionage; the Cold War might be over, but spying remained an essential element of realpolitik. "All right, Colonel. Continue."

MacDonald flipped forward a page. "When Handlesman returned from Russia, we placed an undercover operative on his staff to monitor any unofficial dialogue he might have with Lermontov and the Soviets."

"Does Ambassador Mulholland know that?"

"No, sir. To protect our operative, we report only on a strict need-to-know basis." MacDonald took a dispatch from the file and handed it to the president. "This morning, our operative reported a suspicion that Handlesman had leaked the Hakodate information to the Soviets through Lermontov."

Sam Baker scanned the E-mail communiqué. "Suspicion based on what?"

"What's the difference?" Coleman said. "Could be woman's intuition for all I care. The point is, it makes sense. It fits. To the Soviets, discovering American nuclear missiles at Hakodate is . . . is like us finding Soviet missiles in Cuba." Then he boiled over. "Goddammit, Sam. Littman put those missiles into Hakodate and conspired with Handlesman to leak it to the Soviets to wreck First Step!"

Harris leaned away from the wall. "Pardon me, Mr. President. Perhaps this would be an opportune moment to excuse Colonel MacDonald. That is, if he has nothing further to report."

"Thank you, sir," MacDonald said. He took the dispatch from the president, folded his file into his briefcase, and went out.

When the door closed Sam Baker rose and walked slowly to the fireplace. He was tired; he'd had three hours' sleep, had awakened to Mulholland's angry phone call, the disastrous news about Hakodate, and the argument with Littman. "Arthur, listen to me very carefully. If you're telling me the Hakodate leak is Zack Littman's idea and Handlesman's doing . . . you're accusing two men of treason."

"Sam," Coleman said. "That is *precisely* what I'm telling you."

The words hung between them.

Sam Baker stood quietly and let the history of his friendship with Zack Littman pass before him: their law office on Vermont Avenue, his wedding and Littman his best man, their fanciful late-night conversations about how they'd change things for the better if they ever led the nation. The whole long, glorious history of their friendship played before him . . . and played out.

Softly, without looking back at Coleman, he said, "Arthur, do you believe in First Step?"

Coleman looked to Harris. Harris opened his hands and shook his head; both were aware of the president's doubts. "Sam, that's not the point," Coleman said.

"Then what is?"

"The point is you're the president." Then Coleman said, "Good morning, sir," went out the door, and shut it quietly behind him.

Harris was seething. "That sonofabitch Littman. If I ever see his ugly face again . . ."

Quite suddenly Sam Baker felt bone-worn and weary, as though the air had left his lungs and the string his legs. He put his hand out, steadying himself against the mantel.

Harris stepped toward him. "Sam? Are you all right?"

"I'm fine . . . fine." He ran his hand back through his hair. "Ted, what do we do?"

Harris grumbled. "What can we do? Tell the Soviets those *slick-ems* aren't nuclear and get them the hell out of there."

". . . Lie to them?"

"Yes, Sam. Lie to them. And then get the FBI and CIA into the Littman-Handlesman leak and plug it—for good." Harris reached out and took the president's arm. "Sam, this is no time to be prissy. We've got to fight fire with fire."

Sam Baker nodded. Harris was right; too much was at stake. The new atmosphere of cooperation between the United States and the Soviet Union was still fragile, vulnerable, untested. Reports of American nuclear missiles at Hakodate must have rung like alarm bells through the upper echelons of the Soviet Stavka Command. "All right. Brief Mulholland. And instruct the Joint Chiefs to have those missiles removed from Japan with all deliberate speed."

"Consider it done." Harris started for the door.

"And, Ted . . ."

"What, Sam?"

"I suppose . . . you'd better call Judge Webster and Attorney General Thornburgh. Ask them to come here as soon as possible."

"Right away." Harris opened the door and went out.

Sam Baker stood alone in the Oval Office. At his feet, woven into the carpet as it was into the fabric of his life, lay the great seal of the president of the United States. In one claw, the eagle clutched the olive branch of charity and peace. In the other, its talons closed upon the bolts of justice and retribution.

MEMORIAL BRIDGE, WASHINGTON

6:24 A.M.   The scattered Veterans Day morning traffic hissed through the icy fog, headlights and taillights linking the cars into a liquid snake. On the District side of the bridge a few cars swung down the tight spiral to Rock Creek Parkway; the rest coiled toward Constitution Avenue and the long rank of federal buildings north of the Mall. Beyond, the Capitol dome loomed above the mist—aloof, immutable, austere.

The taxicab carrying Lieutenant Colonel Richard Harding swung away from the traffic flow, stopped under a streetlamp at the corner of Twenty-third and Constitution. Harding's hands trembled as he paid the cabbie; he wiped at the cold sweat on his neck as the taxi drove away. Then he straightened his jacket where it bulged over the 9-mm pistol hidden in his belt, and walked the curving pavement.

To his right, the District was beginning to stir under the early morning haze: shadowy joggers patted out a soft cadence between the streetlamps lining the Reflecting Pool; vans rumbled to and fro on Seventeenth Street. To Harding's left, the steps of the Lincoln Memorial lay bare and empty, silent, still.

Alone behind his massive colonnade, Lincoln sat in a pale fall of yellow night-lights, sat in repose, in glory. Harding stopped and looked up at the great, craggy head. There was much calm, much resolution about the statue as it held vigil over Washington. Harding peered into the face of Lincoln; from the sockets beneath the heavy brows, a darkness stared back. Three fingers of Lincoln's right hand rested on the fasces of the law; his left hand seemed to be closing to a fist.

Harding turned and walked on, following the sloping footpath downward into Constitution Gardens. There, in the glow of stumpy, low-voltage lamps, an angled wall of black granite stood gaping like an open grave. Harding followed the path to its lowest point and stopped where it jinked back and upward.

At the nadir and the nexus, the tapered wings of black stone yawned about him like a shroud. At his feet lay the findings of the wind: pine needles, desiccated flowers, limp paper flags. By the lamplight he could read the rows of graven names—Brent A. McClellan, George F. Douglass, Curtis J. Wein—that stretched in both directions to the vanishing point. And as Harding stood reading, he could feel the cold breath of the granite and the earth behind the wall.

Dimly, drifting like a ghost above the ranks of chiseled letters, he could see his own reflection—a pale figure in air force blue, a vestige, a nagging memory of a war ill-begun, desultory in prosecution, infamous in blood-price, buried in unhallowed ground. Soon, very soon, he would be among the names. He would smell their sweat and hear their bawdy laughter, hear the sweet clang of metal at the call to lock and load. Soon, he would be among the dead who had gathered to the service of the flag. His mind embraced the ending of his life. But his hand shook uncontrollably as he wiped the fearful perspiration from his chin. His body could not help itself; his body wanted to live. He could feel a wave of panic gathering somewhere deep inside him. He had feared this moment, feared his resolve might crumble when the moment came. He struggled to control his trembling hands, the tremors that knifed down his legs. For an eternity he hung between his duty and his fear. Then the wave of terror broke across his soul, sweeping all before it.

He turned from his mission, fled back the way he came. Through the ground fog that enveloped the Vietnam War Memorial, the dead sighed in despair.

Harding was halfway back up the path when a rustling in the trees caught his ear.

On the bluff above him, three young men stood watching. One held an M-16 assault rifle; the second carried an M-60 machine gun across his shoulders like Christ bearing His cross. The leader seemed about to shout a challenge. Harding stopped abruptly, tensed.

Then he realized they were bronze.

They were dead men coming off their last patrol, eyes glazed with horror, limbs exhausted with the deathwork, bones and hearts grown cold. Their stare was not a greeting, but a challenge. Harding knew what they expected of him.

He wiped the perspiration from his mouth, turned toward the Capitol, his duty, and his fate.

INI, BOLLING AFB, WASHINGTON

6:26 A.M.   Christy walked slowly through the busy ground-floor bull pen. When she passed Tod's desk he rose and fell in beside her.

"Well? Did you see Harding?"

"Out. Went downtown at 0600. Polly in yet?"

"Nope." He touched her sleeve to stop her. "Hey. Forget the wild-goose chase. Come on—I'll buy you a coffee."

But she stood staring at the dispatch and blank service record in her hand. "Dammit, I'm going to see Colonel Petrovsky."

"Aw, come on, Chris—"

"Tod, something's going on. Something strange. People are breaking all kinds of rules. People who know better."

Tod took her elbow, eased her around the corner into a quiet corridor. And when they were out of sight of the rest of the office, he said, "Listen, Christy, I may just be some two-bit sergeant, but I'm warning you. Don't poke the system. The air force has a real funny way of reacting when it gets poked. And when you go outside the chain of command, it has a nasty habit of hitting back."

"I'm going through the chain of command. Harding's out of the office and—"

"Christy. Let it go."

"No!" She turned and started up the hall.

He dogged her at the heels. "So what are you going to say to Petrovsky? Where do you get off sending me on some crazy errand in the middle of the night? With a weird woman who turns tricks while her husband's in the slammer?"

She ignored him and marched toward the stairs to Petrovsky's office.

"You gonna chew Petrovsky out because he wasted two bucks of the taxpayers' money to send a practical joke to some navy zoomer? Or you going to complain Polly Kulikov is"—he glanced at his watch—"twenty-six minutes late for work?" He caught her arm. "You go to Petrovsky with that, they'll lock you in a rubber room!"

Nicky Dubinsky turned into the hallway. "Hey, Lieutenant Bright-Eyes. Heard from Polly yet?"

Abruptly, Tod and Christy stepped apart. "That will be all, Sergeant."

"Yes, ma'am." Irritably, Tod stalked away.

Dubinsky stood watching Tod disappear around the corner. "You know, I got a hunch there goes an airman who hankers after taking you on some *very* special maneuvers." He snorted. "Every goon would have his day."

Christy started up the stairs.

"Still time to sign up for chicken cacciatore tonight," Dubinsky called after her.

She stopped and looked down at him. "Nicky, why don't you stick your chicken—"

"Uhn-uhn-uhn." He grinned and wagged a finger. "Conduct unbecoming."

Christy caught herself; Dubinsky was right. She smiled her best smile. "Nicky," she said. "Fuck off."

AMERICAN MISSION, 11 ROUTE DE PREGNY, GENEVA

12:27 P.M.   Chief negotiator Craig Mulholland sat at his desk, listening intently to the voice on the telephone. Jake sat across. Major Sara Weatherby stood at the far end of the room, looking out the window.

"Yes, sir," Mulholland said into the receiver. "I will, Mr. President. And I hope I didn't sound—no, not at all. Thank you, Mr. President." Mulholland hung up.

"Hakodate?" Jake said.

Mulholland nodded, shaken.

"How many missiles?"

"He didn't say."

"Sixteen," Sara said without looking back at them. "And four W-69 replacement warheads."

Mulholland turned, gaping.

Sara glanced at him and shrugged. "The usual preconfiguration."

Jake stroked his beard. "And I suppose we're to tell the Soviets it's all a mistake?"

Mulholland shifted uncomfortably. "The official position . . . is that the missiles are not nuclear—"

"Naturally."

"—and being transshipped to Korea."

Jake sighed and shook his head; it was as he and Zack Littman had anticipated. Now, lie would beget lie, and in the end, mistrust would slither out and throttle the good intentions of First Step. Of all human emotions, suspicion was the most virulent; even the deepest passion of love was not immune to its bore-worm. Often when he prayed, Jake wondered why a loving God had created man a social animal and yet implanted in him a bottomless capacity for mistrust; perhaps—like the vermiform appendix—the instinct was a vestige of primitive proto-man, a bloodline of the jungle law of the survival of the fittest.

Or, perhaps did the Creator delight in the perverse and paradoxical nature of His creation?

Mulholland leaned across the desk. "Look, Jake—the missiles are being embarked tomorrow at 2100 our time. Is there some way we could slip that information to the Soviets . . . informally?"

"What's the difference how we lie to them?"

"Well, none maybe. But I denied it in front of everyone. I don't know. Credibility."

"I could drop it to Gregor Slotkin," Sara said.

"Who?"

"Their air force liaison."

"You have that kind of relationship with him?"

"They'll verify with their Cosmos satellites anyhow. I don't see this as much of a crisis, gentlemen." She turned back to the windows.

Awed, Mulholland looked to Jake. "Where did you find her?"

Jake shrugged and smiled. "She found me."

INI, BOLLING AFB, WASHINGTON

6:28 A.M.   Christy knocked once, then opened the door to Colonel Petrovsky's reception room and stepped inside. This was the big-time air force: massive oak and leather furniture, crossed unit flags with battle pennants, and Petrovsky's stern-faced sergeant-secretary, Lulu Shaughnessy, *not* looking glad to see her.

"Yes, Lieutenant?"

Christy fingered the dispatch and blank service record in her hand. "Lieutenant Russoff to see—"

"Got an appointment, Lieutenant?"

"No. But—"

"Colonel's not to be disturbed till 0800. Thank you." Lulu turned back to her work.

Christy gathered herself and stepped up to the desk. "I have to see the colonel immediately. It's urgent."

The woman looked at Christy over the top of her half-frame glasses. "Is it?"

"Yes, Sergeant. It's damned urgent. If that's any of your business."

With a steady, surly look, Lulu lifted the receiver. "Excuse me, sir, Lieutenant Russoff to see the colonel. Yes, sir. I told her. She says it's urgent." Lulu hung up, gave Christy half a nod toward Petrovsky's office, and turned back to her typewriter. Christy went to the door, took a deep breath, opened it, and stepped inside.

In the paneled inner office, Colonel Petrovsky stood behind his desk, feeding a stack of papers into the shredder, his back to the door. "What's so important, Lieutenant?"

Christy didn't answer.

Petrovsky stopped his shredding and looked over his shoulder. Then he put his papers down. "All right, Lieutenant. What is it?"

A peculiar sense of uneasiness came over Christy. Somehow she felt the colonel was looking through her—as if he knew what she would say before she said it. "Sir . . . I felt I should speak to you about certain . . ."

"Certain what?"

"Certain irregularities."

"Which *irregularities*?"

Christy hesitated. Tod was right; lieutenants *didn't* poke the system. Now—standing before Colonel Petrovsky's desk—she felt ridiculous. There could be a hundred explanations for everything that had happened, and every one of them conformed to military law.

"Lieutenant, if you're going to waste time, please do it somewhere else."

Christy looked toward the door. Her instinct was to turn and walk through it. But a sense of duty bound her to stay. "Sir, last night, when I took Mrs. Watkins to the detention facility at Andrews . . ."

"Yes?"

"Visiting hours are 1000 to 1400."

"And?"

"Well, it's irregular for you and Colonel—"

"Lieutenant, many men who served in Vietnam had difficulty read-justing to peacetime life. It's not uncommon for senior officers to commit themselves to rehabilitating these men. Is that all?"

"Well, yes, sir. That is, no, sir. Sergeant Kulikov—"

"—is running an errand for me this morning. As is Colonel Hard-ing. I understand you've been to his office, too."

"Well . . . yes, sir."

"May I ask why?"

"I . . . I asked a friend at the navy MPC to run a service record check on one of their instructor pilots. His record was erased. All that was left was his name, rank and service number."

For a moment, Petrovsky stared at her. Then softly he said, "Which instructor pilot?"

Christy held up the computer printout; the paper trembled in her hand. "Granger. Commander Charles L."

A curious look passed Petrovsky's face, as though he were trying to hide a smile. "Why did you request the file of that particular officer?"

"Because you had Polly route me a copy of the dispatch you sent him. It's the same message I took to Mrs. Watkins. The sun will come up tomorrow."

Petrovsky took the papers from her hand and leaned back against his desk. "Christy . . . you are involving yourself in something beyond your purview and your understanding. And if you pursue it, you may face serious consequences. You may even endanger your life."

Christy's face went slack.

Petrovsky eyed her, measuring. "Does that frighten you?"

"Well, I . . ."

"Does it?"

She lifted her chin. "No, sir."

Petrovsky smiled. "I didn't think it would." He turned back to his desk. "That will be all, Lieutenant. Dismissed."

Obediently, Christy went to the door. As she pulled it open, the paper shredder began to hum again. When she looked back, Petrovsky was feeding the dispatch and printout into the machine.

40°15′N × 72°10′W, FLIGHT LEVEL 220

6:30 A.M.   To the east, the sky was pre-dawn royal blue; four miles below, the dark Atlantic rolled. Cholly Granger checked the time—1130 Zulu. Then he slid his left hand off the throttles and flicked the engine ramp switches up to STOW. On either side of the Tomcat, the rectangular air intakes flexed up and open, and unstable air swirled into the compressors. The twin turbofans hesitated, then coughed. The F-14 lurched, nosed down and began losing altitude.

Through the intercom, Dolman said, "Cholly? What's up?"

"Feels like compressor stalls. I'll try the throttles."

Granger pushed the throttles forward. The engines surged, then choked again. "We got a problem."

"Uh-oh."

"Hold your water." Granger punched the radio preset for New York Center. "New York Center, this is Alpha-Delta-203 out of Oceana, declaring an emergency."

In the massive New York Center air control room in Islip, Long Island, controller Tom Cuzzimano sat before one of the long rows of large, round radar screens. He punched in on the radio. "New York Center. Roger 203. What's your situation?"

"Got some kind of engine problem. Need a place to set down fast."

"Are you heavy or light?"

"Loaded. Over."

"Designated emergency set-down for naval aircraft in your sector is Calverton Field at Peconic River, Long Island."

"I know it, New York."

"Turn left to heading three three zero. We'll notify Oceana."

"Roger."

"Good luck."

"Same to you."

491 M STREET SW, WASHINGTON

6:31 A.M.   Colonel Tom O'Neill eased the cardboard box down from the top shelf of his bedroom closet, carried it gently to the

Pullman kitchen counter, and opened the lid. The box was filled with beads of plastic foam.

Gingerly, O'Neill pushed his fingers through the foam until their tips touched the cold steel object within. He raised it from its resting place and held it in the light.

The gleaming cylinder was the size of a mechanical pencil, but tapered and sealed at both ends. Two short wires protruded from its tip—one red, the other black. O'Neill laid the cylinder on a handkerchief, wrapped it carefully, and slid it into the inside breast pocket of his jacket.

Then he set the box on the floor beside the wastebasket, snapped off the lights, put on his hat, and went out.

40°42′N × 72°40′W, ALTITUDE 8,000 FEET

6:32 A.M. Granger swung the F-14 in a slow bank to the west. Behind him, Dolman was on the radio.

"Roger, New York. AD-203 descending to five."

At his radar console in New York Center, Tom Cuzzimano watched the dot of light that was the F-14 dropping westward on heading three three zero. His supervisor Milt Epstein hung over his shoulder, chewing an unlit cigar.

"Alpha-Delta-203, come left to heading three two six," Cuzzimano said. "You are cleared for a high-key SFO into Calverton."

"Roger, New York. Tallyho." Granger pressed down on the gray landing gear lever in the left vertical panel; the Tomcat's hydraulic system moaned, the doors under the fuselage clunked open, and the gear rotated downward. On the panel, three miniature pictures of wheels clicked into place, indicating the struts had locked. Granger slid the flaps controller to full and eased the throttles forward to bring up the power. The long I-shape of the runway lights swung toward the needle of the Tomcat's radome.

"Contact Calverton tower on 234.4," Cuzzimano said. "Happy landings, pal."

"Roger."

Cuzzimano pulled at his ear. "Wouldn't want to dead-stick a fighter onto that old field with live missiles strapped to my belly."

Epstein chomped down on his cigar.

INI, BOLLING AFB, WASHINGTON

6:33 A.M.   Christy stepped into her office, silently shut the door, and leaned against it. Tod was waiting for her.

"Well? Did you see Petrovsky?"

Christy didn't answer. She could not shake the strangeness of the conversation in Petrovsky's office; it was almost as if the colonel were daring her to follow her suspicions.

"Chris? What happened up there? What did Petrovsky say?"

"It wasn't what he said. It was the way . . ." Then she shook off the confusion. "Tod, we've got to find Polly. Whatever's going on, it's illegal. I'm sure of that now."

"What?"

She seized his hand in both of hers. "Petrovsky and O'Neill. And that navy pilot—Granger. They're all involved in something—"

Tod pulled free, stepped back. "What if they are? What's that to you?"

She squinted at him as though she couldn't understand the question. "What do you mean? I took an oath to defend this country. Just like you did. Now, are you going to help me find Polly or not?"

CALVERTON FIELD, PECONIC RIVER, NY

6:34 A.M.   The Tomcat flared to a perfect landing on the concrete runway. Granger stepped lightly on the brakes and pulled up the wing spoilers to slow the plane to taxi speed. To the east, the morning star burned bright above the first glow of dawn; on the ground there was only shadowless gloom.

"Class-A grease job, Cholly," Dolman said through the intercom. "Engines seemed to work fine on final."

Granger steered the plane toward the taxi pad. "Guess the problem is intermittent."

"Those are the toughest ones to track."

The massive warplane taxied in among the Piper Cubs and Cherokees tied down near the hangars. Beyond stood the buildings of the Calverton Naval Weapons Plant and Grumman factory where Tomcats and other military planes were assembled. A scattering of curious ground crewmen were gathered in the half-light, hands covering their ears against the high-pitched scream of the turbofans. Two of the crewmen rolled a set of metal steps to the side of the canopy as the plane came to a stop. They plugged in the field's auxiliary power unit. Then Granger shut the engines down.

The canopy hissed open as the crew chief clambered up the stairs. "Morning," he said and stuck his hand out to Granger. "Phil Brown."

"Morning, chief." Granger unsnapped the buckles of his harness and climbed out. Dolman swung out behind him.

"Engines give you a scare?"

"Some." Granger scanned the eastern sky; sunrise was less than fifteen minutes away.

"Lucky you were in the area. A service crew will be here any time now. Want some coffee, men?"

Dolman said, "Yessir!"

"Go ahead, Lieutenant," Granger said. "I'll keep an eye on things."

Dolman followed the crew chief down the stairs. Granger stood at the top, scanning the driveway behind the hangars. He checked his wristwatch. 1135 Zulu. He was on time.

AMERICAN MISSION, 11 ROUTE DE PREGNY, GENEVA

12:35 P.M.   The large conference room in the west wing of the American mission was decorated with crossed Soviet and American flags in preparation for the Veterans Day gala that afternoon. But there was no gaiety around the long oak table. The two negotiating teams sat in gloomy silence as Soviet Ambassador Viktor Karpov concluded his prepared statement and the Soviet translator began to read back his notes.

"Reports of a formal protest by the Japanese foreign ministry regarding the stationing of American sea-launched nuclear cruise missiles at Hakodate appear to indicate a grievous and provocative violation of the United States' long-standing nuclear exclusion treaty with Japan. Coming at this time, these reports raise serious questions regarding American intentions to comply with the zero-option provision of the proposals referred to as First Step. Therefore—"

Mulholland broke in. "Viktor, I've already given you assurances. Those missiles are conventional, not nuclear."

From his vantage point at the far end of the table, Jake watched the delegates on both sides shift uneasily; breaking in on a formal statement was simply not done. Worse, everyone in the room knew Mulholland's assurances were lies.

"Mr. Ambassador," Karpov said softly. "With respect, we cannot accept that statement at face value. I'm sure you understand."

"But the missiles are being shipped out tomorrow."

"May we inspect them before they leave Hakodate?"

Mulholland slouched in his chair. "I'm sorry. That's between us and the Japanese."

"I, too, am sorry." Karpov nodded for his interpreter to continue.

"Therefore, on instructions of our government, we regret to inform you that we must request an indefinite postponement of further discussions of First Step until this matter has received the most careful review. We remain ready to consult on other strategic arms issues."

Mulholland could not hide the desperation in his voice. "But we'd planned to move ahead on First Step immediately."

"Yes," Lermontov said. He stared across the table, stared hard at Jake. "The plans of mice and men . . ."

Jake stared back—eye for steely eye.

The missiles of Hakodate had scored their first kill.

OVAL OFFICE, THE WHITE HOUSE, WASHINGTON

6:38 A.M. "Craig, I'm as sick about it as you are. I'll get back to you as soon as we have a solution." Sam Baker slowly lowered the telephone receiver to its cradle. For a moment, he stood alone in the Oval Office and let the shock wave of Hakodate roll over him. His own Secretary of Defense—his dearest friend—might be guilty of high treason. And unless some means could be found to reopen discussions of First Step with the Soviets, the proposals and their promise would wither and die.

The president went to the window, drew back the curtain, and stared out through the thick bulletproof polymer panes. By the hazy glow of the dawn sky, he could see the little clump of trees that stood before the West Wing: the delicate, heartsick magnolia Jack Kennedy had planted beside his beloved rose garden; the bent-branched linden of Franklin Roosevelt; the lonely willow oak of Lyndon Johnson, and the stiff pin oak of Eisenhower. Beyond them, alone and to itself, stood the tree that in centuries to come would dwarf the others and over-shadow the White House itself: the giant sequoia planted by that master of pretense and ill-proportion, Richard Nixon. Sam Baker stared up into the tangle of leafless branches; the trees of the Presidential Grove were gathered in the dawn's early light, silent witnesses over him, custodians of the judgment of the ages.

There was a sharp rapping and the door behind him opened. It was Ted Harris. "Well? What did Mulholland say? Did the Soviets buy our explanation about Hakodate?"

"No." Then Sam Baker turned—jaw set, eyes burning with determination. "Ted, get Fowler in here. And get Coleman on the phone. Goddammit!" He clenched his fists. "I'm not letting First Step go without a fight!"

INI, BOLLING AFB, WASHINGTON

6:39 A.M.   Lieutenant Nicky Dubinsky straightened. "Can I help you, sir?"

"Have you seen Lieutenant Russoff?" Colonel Petrovsky stood in the middle of the ground-floor bull pen, holding a copy of *Red Star.*

"She and Sergeant Browning just went out."

"I see. Well." Petrovsky flicked the newspaper. "I'll just leave this on her desk."

"Would you like me to—"

"No. That's all right."

Petrovsky stepped into Christy's office and shut the door. He dropped the copy of *Red Star* into the wastebasket. Then he pulled open the bottom drawer of the desk. Behind the files lay a box of Tampax, a hair brush, packets of pantyhose, a stack of old theater programs—a young girl's private things.

Petrovsky thought then of the graduation ceremonies at the Naval Postgraduate School in Monterey—how he had sat with Captain Bryan among the other visiting dignitaries and faculty members while Christy's name was called. Together they had watched her stand, walk to the rostrum, and accept her master's degree in national security affairs.

Petrovsky had leaned close to Bryan. "Will she do?"

"She won't just *do.* She's perfect."

"Perfect as a lover?"

Bryan's eyes hardened. "Careful, Steve. She's too important. And she's mine."

Now Steven Petrovsky stood looking down into the drawer, peeping into the privacy of a dark-eyed young officer he would never really know but upon whom he and Bryan had hung the very purpose of their lives and the lives of others, perhaps even the life of the United States.

He took the automatic pistol with the silencer from his pocket and set it down among Christy's private things. Then he shut the drawer.

CALVERTON FIELD, PECONIC RIVER, NY

6:40 A.M. In the shadows atop the metal stairs, Cholly Granger stood leaning against the open canopy of the F-14. By the halogen lights on the peaks of the hangars, he could see Dolman on the tarmac below, standing with the chief and ground crewmen, sipping coffee and chatting.

Then a car came bumping down the service road behind the hangars. Its headlights flashed twice.

Granger bent, unzipped the pocket in the leg of his G-suit, drew the 9-mm automatic pistol, released the safety, and thumbed the hammer back. "Attention, please. Attention on the ground!"

Beneath him conversations broke off, faces turned upward, eyes squinted at him through the gloom.

Granger's voice was firm, commanding. "Everyone—lie down. Right where you are. Hands behind your heads."

Dolman came to the bottom of the stairs and set one hand on the railing. "Cholly, what—"

Granger leveled the pistol at him. "At ease, Mr. Dolman. This is not a drill."

Open-mouthed, Dolman backed away.

"Hey, Commander." Brown flashed a big smile. "Don't you think you're—"

Granger fired the pistol into the air; a foot-long burst of yellow flame spit from its barrel and the report reverberated among the hangars. The men beneath him gasped and ducked.

"Now! On the ground! Everyone!"

They hit the deck.

An old gray Chevrolet rolled out across the taxipad, in and out of the glare of hangar lights. It slid up and stopped beside the stairs beneath the F-14. The driver's door opened and Marge Kessler stepped out. Without a glance at Granger, she went around to the passenger door and pulled it open. Willie Logan swung his crutches and his legs out.

Kessler helped him stand, helped him make his way clumsily across the tarmac to the stairs. Logan stopped there in the beams of the car's headlights and turned to Kessler, his eyes filled with confusion and gratitude. "Why you?"

Kessler shrugged. "I guess . . . I just don't want to see what we did go to waste."

Awkwardly, clutching the crutch against his side with his elbow, Logan raised his right hand in a salute.

Kessler took a step back, braced, and saluted. There were tears in her eyes. "Godspeed . . . Lieutenant Logan." Then she snapped her arm back to her side.

Logan turned and looked up the stairs. Granger stepped forward. "Need a hand, Willie?"

"I can make it."

Logan started up. It was a bitter, painful struggle as he swung his plastic legs in clumsy arcs, clunked from one step to the next. Sweat beaded on his forehead as his beefy hands pulled him up the metal stairs.

Granger watched him moving upward through the shadows. It had been ten years since he'd seen Logan; the man's hair was almost white and ragged age lines furrowed his straining face. Granger could see the pain etched there as Logan struggled upward in his desperate pride. He remembered the long journey through the jungle, carrying the bleeding, incoherent man while the VC prodded at his legs and buttocks with sharpened bamboo stakes. It was five days before they reached the prison at Chu My; by then, the black stink of Logan's gangrene was ingrained in Granger's tattered flight suit and coated his mouth and pores. But he hadn't let Logan die. And when the VC doctor cut away the pulpy, fungus-eaten legs, Granger had jammed the block of hardwood between Logan's teeth and endured his screams as though they were his own.

Granger bent and reached out his hand.

Logan shook his head and smiled. "Not this time, Cholly."

A horn sounded in the distance. Granger's eyes snapped up. Two pairs of headlights swung down the service road behind the hangars—a blue Grumman service truck and crew van.

"Time, Willie," Granger said. "We got to go."

Logan sat on the edge of the cockpit, reached under his belt, and unbuckled the leather harness. "Won't be needing these." The prosthetic legs clattered from his trousers, tumbled down the steel stairs and crumpled in a pile on the tarmac below. Logan swung into the rear seat of the cockpit. Granger dropped the flight bag with the spare torso harness into his lap.

"Don't know if that'll fit."

"It'll have to do." Logan yanked Dolman's helmet on.

Granger swung into the pilot's seat. He waved the pistol at the men on the ground below. "Pull those stairs, chief!"

The chief and crewmen scrambled to their feet.

"Everybody!" Granger shouted. "Watch the blast!" He snapped the switch that engaged the starter unit and pushed in the black-and-yellow handle that disengaged the brakes. Then he toggled the engine crank control; the port engine turned over, moaned, and caught. He toggled right as the service cars pulled onto the taxi pad. With a hiss and a whine, the starboard engine of the Tomcat fired.

"Pull that APU, chief!" Granger shouted. Two ground crewmen scrambled to unhook the umbilical from the auxiliary power unit and roll it aside. Slowly the F-14 began to taxi.

As it did, a foreman and a work gang began climbing out of the vehicles. Dolman ran across the tarmac to the foreman, shouting to be heard over the scream of turbofans. At last, the startled foreman understood Dolman's frantic jabber; he shouted an order to his men. They dropped their tools and rushed toward the plane. But Granger swung the blast of the fighter's exhaust at them, hurling them backward, sending men and tools, hats and coffee cups flying. When the hurricane of the fighter's exhausts hit the tethered Piper Cubs and Cherokees, they tore free of their mooring cables, flipping end-over-end like toys.

Granger swung the Tomcat to the bottom of the runway. He snapped his harness latches and locked the tube of his G-suit into the pressure valve.

"How you making out with that torso suit, Willie?"

"Almost there."

A ground crewman jumped into the van and started it; he raced across the infield toward the center of the runway, trying to block the takeoff roll of the fighter. Granger checked his flaps and gear and eased the throttles forward.

Behind him, Logan said, "Where we headed, Cholly?"

Granger took a last look at the instruments. He raised his eyes to the runway lights, the dawn glow beyond. "Haven't you heard? We're bound for glory."

Then he slammed the throttles forward. At 1142 Zulu the F-14 screamed down the runway and flashed into the sky, leaving confusion behind it on the ground.

NCO DORM, BOLLING AFB, WASHINGTON

6:42 A.M.   In the dawn shadows, Tod's black Ford rolled into the parking lot before the NCO dormitory and ground to a halt. Christy was out her door before he had the headlights off. He had to hustle to catch up with her.

"Chris, wait. Maybe you're right. Maybe something screwy's going on."

"Well," she said and kept on walking. "Thank you."

"If it is, let's do it by the book."

"What does that mean?"

"Call the OSI."

"And do what? Make an appointment? For when? A week from now?" She stopped and caught his sleeve. "Tod, whatever they're up to is going to happen soon. By the time the OSI gets into it . . ."

"What?"

"I don't know. But I'm going to find out. Now, are you coming in with me or not?"

He looked up at the dorm, then shook his head. "No way. I'm not serving out my hitch in Leavenworth."

"Then wait here. I'll be back." She pushed through the door.

At the far end of the second-floor corridor, a drowsy bay orderly was vacuuming the carpet.

Christy stopped before the door marked T/SGT. POLLY KULIKOV and knocked. No answer. She knocked again. Nothing. Exasperated, she tried the door; it was locked. She looked down the hall.

"Airman." And when the woman couldn't hear her over the sound of the vacuum, she shouted, "Airman!"

Abruptly the woman snapped off the vacuum. "Yes, ma'am?"

"Have you seen Sergeant Kulikov this morning?"

"No, ma'am. She ain't come out."

"Do you have the key to this door?"

"Ma'am?"

"Airman, am I speaking English?"

"Yes'm."

"Then do you have the key for this door?"

"Ma'am, we're not supposed to—"

"Dammit! Unlock this door right now!"

While she did, Christy stood over her, impatient. "Now, go back to your work."

Muttering, the woman wandered away down the hall.

In Polly's bedroom the air was thick with stale food and cheap perfume. The lights burned and the bed had not been slept in; on it, clothes lay neatly stacked as though someone was preparing for a journey. Polly's desk was strewn with scattered papers; Christy picked through them; nothing; dead end. She looked about, frustrated, stymied. As she turned to leave, her eye fell on the carpet. A tiny trail of black spattered dots led from the desk; she let her eye follow them to where they ended at the footlocker beside the bed. A curious dark stain had soaked into the carpet, cutting a black arc around one corner of the trunk.

Christy bent to the stain, brushed it with her fingers. The stain was tacky and the carpet stiff. Christy looked at her fingertips; they were streaky red. It was a stain no woman past puberty could mistake. It froze her fingers like the fire of dry ice.

Christy stared at her fingers. All her instincts, all her training told her she had come to the place where the road divided. From where she stood, one path led to safety, the other spiraled downward into chaos. Her next step would be a retreat or a first step into battle. She had to choose. But she hesitated.

Why *was* this her personal crusade? Why shouldn't she leave it to the Office of Special Investigations?

She knew the answer; Captain Bryan had taught her why. *Always do your duty as you see it, as though the fate of the nation rested upon you—because it does.*

Quickly Christy bent to the locker, unsnapped the toggles, and threw back the lid.

Crammed inside—her head half-wrapped in a towel, her arms and legs hunched to her bloodless body as though clutching herself against a deepening cold—Polly Kulikov gazed up with the wide-eyed stare of a frightened child. But there was no luster in her eyes; the corneas were dry and dusty. And the blood from the fatal bullet wound in her forehead had run down her cheek and dried like a black scarf about her throat.

A spike of nausea hit Christy like a kick in the gut. A spasm clutched the muscles in her legs. She lurched up and back against the wall, arms stretched wide against the swirling vertigo, gasping for breath to keep from fainting. Cold sweat surged up out of the pores of her breast and back. She hung that way—pinned to the wall like an insect by the spear of revulsion—gulping air and panting against her retching.

Her first thought was to call for help. Her eyes fastened on the telephone on Polly's desk. She thrust herself away from the wall, lunged at the telephone, and seized the receiver in both her hands.

Then—suddenly—she caught herself.

She was close to hyperventilating, on the verge of panic. She had to get a grip on her emotions. She had to think.

She looked at the receiver in her hand. An emergency call would bring the security police. The SPs would follow procedure and call the OSI. Christy knew what that meant: hours of cooling her heels in an interrogation room while some dull-eyed investigator babbled a long list of questions from a triplicate form.

Every nerve ending in Christy's body told her there was no time for that; whatever was taking shape around her—whatever Petrovsky's criminal scheme might be—it was happening now. And if it was to be stopped, Christy would have to take the initiative, act on her own. With two trembling hands she pressed the receiver back into its cradle. Then she stood away from the desk, struggling to master her panic and clear her mind.

She had to have a plan. Somehow Polly's murder must be bound up with her own midnight errand to the Andrews detention cells. But how? And why? Polly had been instructed to send the same message to Granger that Christy had carried to Mrs. Watkins. Was that why Polly had been murdered? Or had she stumbled across a sinister chain of events—as Christy had—and tried to pursue them to their objective only to meet her death?

What had Petrovsky said? *You are involving yourself in something beyond your understanding . . . and you may endanger your life.*

Then it must be true. Somewhere in the events of last night lay the motive for Polly's murder. And if there were evidence that identified the motive—and Polly's killer—it might at INI.

Christy had to get back to the office. She threw the door open and rushed out into the hallway and down the stairs.

At the sound of the door, the bay orderly looked up from her vacuuming and caught a glimpse of Christy disappearing down the stairs. That didn't concern her; what officers did generally didn't concern her. But the door to Sergeant Kulikov's room was open—and that did.

She shut off her vacuum, pulled her key ring out of her fatigues, and strolled down the hall.

Panting, gasping, Christy ran out the front door of the dorm and straight into Tod.

"Christ!" He caught her by the shoulders. "What happened in there?"

"It's Polly. She—"

Suddenly a casement window on the second floor slammed open and the bay orderly stuck her head out, screaming, "Help! Murder! Somebody! HELP!"

Christy and Tod looked up. So did a redheaded major walking his boxer dog on the far side of the darkened street.

"You there!" the major shouted at the orderly. "What's that racket, Airman?"

"There she is! She's the one! She murdered Sergeant Kulikov!"

They stood that way—the bay orderly, the red-headed major and his boxer, Christy and Tod—all frozen in a tableau of suspicion.

Then the major shouted, "You! Stay where you are!" He started across the street.

Christy grabbed Tod's arm. "Come on!"

The major shouted, "Sergeant! Detain that officer!"

Confused, Tod hesitated.

"Tod! We've got to get back to the office!"

"Sergeant—damn you! I'm giving you an order!" The major and his dog broke into a run.

"Tod! For god's sake!"

At last Tod turned and rushed Christy around the corner of the building.

They ran to the doors of his car.

"Get in!" she shouted.

They leapt into their seats.

"What the hell is—"

"Let's go! Go!"

Tod started the car, slammed it into gear, reached for the headlight switch.

"No! No lights!"

In darkness, he peeled backward out of the parking space. The dormitory fire alarm sounded as they roared away.

"Dammit, Chris, what happened in there?"

"Polly's dead. Murdered."

"My god! Who—" Before Tod could finish, the air was split by the sound of sirens.

Their eyes turned toward the windshield. Two air force security police cars were racing toward them, cherry-tops flashing and sirens screaming.

"Christ! What do we do?"

Christy grabbed the wheel. "Pull over! Stop and park. Don't draw attention to us."

"Chris, we're—"

"Do it!" she commanded. "Now!"

Tod swung the car to the curb.

Christy settled lower in her seat. "Now be quiet. Sit still."

The sirens wailed louder as the SP cars raced toward them down the darkened street.

Christy put her hand in the middle of Tod's chest and pushed him back into his seat. "Just . . . sit . . . still. . . ."

At the corner of Delaware and Constitution avenues, Lieutenant Colonel Richard Harding stood staring up at the United States Capitol. In the glare of the night lighting, the lofty marble columns were bone white against the solemn western sky. But at the apex of the dome, the first violet glow of dawn hazed the bronze statue of *Freedom*. Harding stared up at the heroic figure, girded as she was for battle, one hand resting on her sword's pommel, the other steadying her shield, the stiff cockade of her helmet flaunting the wind. There was such courage in her eye, such bearing. Harding wiped the terror sweat from his chin. When would he ever share her valor?

A mile and a half west of the Capitol, President Samuel Baker sat at his desk, hands before him on the blotter, fingers spread, steeling himself for the fight to save First Step.

Ted Harris stood at the window, waiting impatiently for morning.

Half a mile north of the White House—where Massachusetts and Rhode Island avenues crossed at Scott Circle—in the guttering, yellow flicker of a row of votive candles Colonel Tom O'Neill knelt at the altar of Saint Jude, his head bowed and his lips moving in whispered prayer.

"Most holy Apostle Saint Jude, faithful servant and friend of Jesus, the name of the . . . " But he could not say the next word; the word "traitor" stuck on his lips. He broke off, began again. "Patron saint of things despaired of . . . pray for me who am so miserable."

The door of the confessional beside him opened, an elderly woman emerged, and another took her place. O'Neill looked at his wristwatch—6:45 A.M.—1145 Zulu—12:45 P.M. in Geneva. It was almost time and he had not made his confession. He made the sign of the cross, but stopped abruptly when his fingertips touched the hardness of the detonator in his breast pocket.

Just over four thousand miles east at the American mission in Geneva, Ambassador Craig Mulholland sat at his desk. In the chair opposite, Jake sat stroking his beard as he studied the two columns of notations in the pad open on his knee. Major Sara Weatherby leaned back against the windows, her ash-blond hair gleaming in the sunlight, her gray, impassive eyes riveted on the bearded little man.

In his office at INI on Bolling Air Force Base, Colonel Steven Petrovsky folded a letter into an envelope, sealed it, and set it on his desk. The envelope bore a neatly typed address:

To the People of the United States

Wistfully—with a touch of sadness—Petrovsky looked around the office one last time. Then he opened his briefcase and placed the letter beside the pale bunch of lilies, the powerful plastic concussion grenade.

And in a car parked in the darkness a few streets away, Christy and Tod sat in desperate silence as two security police cars roared toward them.

Then something out the side window of the car caught Christy's eye, and she forgot the police cars, the death mask of Polly Kulikov, the screaming sirens, and the fear that stiffened her arms.

Above the wooded hills that flanked the eastern end of the base, a stiletto blade of light stabbed through the spiny maple branches.

Slowly, on the dull thunder of twin turbofans, a United States Navy Tomcat fighter climbed through the darkness twenty thousand feet above Long Island's Great South Bay. Suddenly a harsh yellow lit the uppermost tip of one tail fin, then the other, turning the aluminum to gold. Slowly, as the warplane climbed, the brilliant light—like an effusion of Saint Elmo's fire—slid down the fins until it washed the fuselage and canopy and the plane gleamed gilt against the violet sky.

Cholly Granger turned his face to the east and squinted into the rising light. Across the cold Atlantic, an angry ball of flame floated on the horizon.

Granger snapped his black plastic visor down. Reflected in it, the fireball burned blood red.

The sun was risen.

"My God," Christy whispered. "It's time."

ZULU TIME

It shall be the policy of this nation to regard
any nuclear missile launched from Cuba
against any nation in the Western Hemisphere
as an attack by the Soviet Union on the
United States requiring a full retaliatory
response.

PRESIDENT JOHN F. KENNEDY
OCTOBER 22, 1962

Washington	Zulu	Geneva
6:46 A.M.	1146	12:46 P.M.

A tiny object streaked across the face of the huge orange sun, drawing a thin scratch of vapor in its wake. As the sky brightened toward morning yellow, the object became clearly visible. It was a United States Navy F-14 Tomcat making Mach .88, aloft alone above Long Island's Great South Bay, its pylons and pallets hung with auxiliary fuel tanks, six massive white Phoenix missiles, and two slender Sidewinders. Its destination was 992 nautical miles and 113 minutes away.

On Bolling AFB, the quiet dawn was split by the sirens of two security police cars screaming down Defense Boulevard. For an instant, their headlights raked the black Ford parked in the shadows at the curb.

Tod flinched in the glare. "They're coming right at us!"

Christy's voice was firm, commanding. "Quiet . . . quiet now. . . ."

Then the SP cars flashed by, sirens trailing in the distance. The darkness fell again.

Christy looked after them. "All right. We're safe for now."

"What the hell happened back there?"

"Polly's dead. Shot through the forehead."

"Sweet Jesus. And they think you—"

"Don't worry about it."

"Don't worry? Chris, they saw you!"

"The bay orderly saw me. She never even looked at my nameplate. I don't live on base. She doesn't know who I am. Now, get us back to the office before someone reports us missing."

"And then what?"

"Then . . . we try to figure out what's going on."

★ ★ ★

In the New York Center air controllers' room, Tom Cuzzimano was trying to figure out what was going on. "Epstein! Get over here!"

His supervisor leaned in over his shoulder, pulling the wet end of his cigar from his mouth. "What's the problem?"

"Some sonofabitch just took off from Calverton without clearance. Flew right through the Kennedy TCA!"

"Goddammit! I told those nitwits no touch-and-goes in heavy traffic hours."

"I don't know, Packy. Looked like a single engine till he turned south. Then—zoom!"

Epstein squinted at the radar scope. "Where is he now?"

"Just blew out of my radar cap."

"Blew out? Or fell out?"

"Packy, he must have been doing five hundred knots when he crossed the Kennedy pattern."

Epstein grabbed the phone and punched a preset. "Calverton? Goddammit, this is Supervisor Epstein at New York Center. What the fuck—"

The tiny control tower of Calverton Field was jammed with crewmen and controllers. Against the rear wall, Lieutenant Dolman stood holding his cup of coffee close to his chest to still his shaking hands.

Brown, the crew chief, was shouting into the phone, "Some sonofabitch stole a jet fighter!"

Epstein coughed a lung of smoke. "What!"

Beside Brown, the senior Calverton controller was on another phone.

"This is Calverton Control. Who am I speaking to?"

At Oceana Naval Air Station, Chief Petty Officer Stuart Wayne sat before an air traffic radar screen. "Oceana Control. Chief Wayne."

"Chief, we had an unauthorized takeoff by one of your aircraft—a Fox-fourteen, designation Alpha-Delta-203. Departed Calverton Field at 1142 Zulu. Heading two four zero."

"Hold the line." Wayne squinted at the plotting display. Off the coast of Long Island, a lone dot of light was moving south at high speed. With the flat of his hand, Wayne rolled the ball that moved the computer's cursor to the dot and punched the IFF button. A data block appeared in the lower right hand corner of the screen. The dot was AD-203, climbing through flight level 220 at a speed of Mach .88.

"I got him. Now where the hell's he going?"

Aloft in the F-14, Granger half-turned back toward Logan; he couldn't see him past the ejection seat, but he knew he was there.

"How you been, Willie?"

"Fair. How's Julia?"

"Haven't heard from her in a couple of years."

"Sorry. Didn't know."

"Yeah. I'm sorry, too." Granger checked the fuel gauges; both feed lights were lit. That meant their external tanks were empty. They were already burning into the Tomcat's precious internal supply of 16,200 pounds of fuel. He leaned over and checked the open ocean below. "Jettison the external tanks, Willie."

Logan flipped up the two toggles, flicked the safety off, and pressed the red JETT button. Under the engine nacelles, the spring-loaded couplings tripped and the two empty fuel tanks tumbled back and downward. Logan watched them fall until they splashed into the sea.

"Okay, Cholly. What's the drill?"

"Climb to forty-one thousand and maintain five hundred twenty-five knots. Got a long ride ahead of us." Granger checked a pair of coordinates on a slip of paper, then stuffed it back into a pocket of his flight suit. "Set a course for twenty-two degrees thirty minutes north by eighty degrees west."

Logan keyed the data into the automatic flight control system. "What's down there?"

"Santa Clara, Cuba."

"Cute." The flight computer cycled. "Come left to heading two zero five."

Granger put the Tomcat into a slow bank. "Now, I had the kid run your missile check programs. They've changed a few things back there since we used to—" He glanced down at his weapons console and broke off.

The scope displays blinked in rapid sequence as Logan's skillful fingers reran the check programs and diagnostics.

Granger smiled. "Been doing your homework at that VA hospital."

"It's not true, you know—what they say about old dogs."

"No," Granger said softly. "No truth to it at all."

At NORAD Northeast Sector Operations Control Center at Griffiss AFB near Rome, New York, the hot line on the combat flight commander's console rang. Major Harry Johnson lifted the receiver. In the busy plotting room below him, TAC weapons directors manned twenty-four radar consoles. It was the Northeast SOCC's responsibility to track every aircraft entering an air defense identification zone that stretched from the Canadian border to Virginia.

"Northeast SOCC. Major Johnson."

"Chief Wayne at Oceana, sir. Do you have a bogey at forty degrees twenty minutes north by seventy-three degrees twenty minutes west?"

"Affirmative. We've been trying to contact him on TAC and emergency frequencies. Seems like he's got nav' and radio problems."

"He's one of our instructor pilots in a Fox-fourteen. No logical explanation for what he's doing."

"Don't worry, Chief. We'll scramble a national guard flight from Atlantic City. They'll show him the way home." Johnson hung up and hit the alert switch on his console. The intercept timer came on, clocking the response; it was 1148 Zulu and counting.

In the plotting room below, a red light began blinking on Weapons Director Lieutenant Andrew Maynard's console. Captain Pete Shortway, his weapons assignment officer, stepped up behind his chair and plugged his headset into Maynard's console to audit his instructions to the interceptors.

In the ready room beside the alert pad at the western end of Atlantic City International Airport, the klaxon sounded battle stations. Major Barney Merriman and Captain Rick Avila of the air national guard's 177th Fighter Interceptor Group dropped their paperwork and zipped up their G-suits. Outside, two crews of mechanics were running hell-for-leather through the wintry dawn to the twin revetments where two F-16 Falcons waited, fueled and armed with cannon and radar-guided Sparrow missiles. By the time the pilots burst out the door of the alert shack, the mechanics had external power flowing to the Falcons, and two crewmen were waiting atop the ladders, ready to strap the pilots in.

At 1153 Zulu—five minutes after the alert sounded—the tower had cleared the active runway and the Falcons thundered down the concrete and roared into the rising sun on target vectors from Lieutenant Maynard at the Northeast SOCC.

In the chilly orange light of dawn, Tod and Christy hustled up the walkway from the parking lot toward the entrance of INI.

"When we get in there I want you to pull the computer activity logs for the past two weeks. Check everything with Polly's access code. Bring me anything that has to do with transfers, reassignments, anything unusual that—" She broke off as Colonel Steven Petrovsky came out the front door, carrying his briefcase and taking the steps two at a time in his long, easy stride.

Christy and Tod braced, saluted.

Petrovsky stopped before them. He touched his fingers to his hat brim. "Report, Lieutenant."

"Sir, Sergeant Kulikov . . ."

"What about her?"

Christy took a breath. "Sergeant Kulikov has been murdered."

"Yes," Petrovsky said. "I'm sorry."

Christy blinked; beside her, Tod went rigid.

"What else, Lieutenant?" Petrovsky said.

"I—I believe Sergeant Kulikov may have been involved—"

It was the look in Petrovsky's eyes that made Christy hesitate. There was no guilt in them, no skulking shame, only the respect he'd always shown her as a fellow officer.

"Involved in what, Christy?"

"In . . . an illegal military conspiracy."

"I see. And what is the objective of this conspiracy?"

Christy shook her head.

Petrovsky raised one finger. "Framework, Christy. Find the framework. By eleven o'clock it will all be over." He stepped close to her; the long shadow he cast in the morning sun enveloped her and she was chilled. "This is the day you dreamed of and trained for. The day you lead while others follow." He stood looking down at her; the glow of sunrise hazed the gray in his hair and his face warmed with an inner satisfaction, as a father might look upon his daughter as a bride. "The sun is rising, Christy. Don't disappoint us."

Then he saluted her and walked away.

Christy stared after him. "All dead . . . or all heroes."

Beside her, Tod whispered, "You don't think he—"

She grabbed his sleeve. "Come on. We're wasting time."

Logan said, "Cholly, we got company." He stared at the two glowing symbols—2↑1 and 2↑2—entering the AWG-9's tactical information display from the west; each identified an unknown radar contact. The numbers left and right were the FONO—the firing order numeric. The 2 to the left of each icon was the bogey's altitude in tens of thousands of feet. The number to the right indicated the sequence in which the AWG-9 computer would attack the incoming aircraft if they proved hostile. Digital displays at the top of the screen indicated the ground speed and heading of the lead bogey. "I have two bogeys bearing two four zero. Range one fifteen miles and climbing through twenty-one thousand feet. Making five fifty knots. Looks like a couple of F-16s out of Atlantic City."

"What time is it?"

"1155 Zulu."

Granger sighed. Yes, the bogeys were air national guard interceptors from Atlantic City. The drama was beginning. "All right. Let's see what they want. Go to Guard."

Logan punched the radio to 243.0, the international emergency frequency, and a voice said, ". . . if you can respond. Over."

"This is Alpha-Delta-203," Granger said. "I read you loud and clear. Over."

In the lead Falcon, Major Barney Merriman was flying on vectors from the SOCC and staring at an empty radar screen when he heard Granger's voice; the Tomcat was still far out of range of the Falcon's onboard radar.

Merriman smiled. "Hey, AD-203. This is Checker-one—your good morning flight of two Fox-sixteens courtesy of the 177th FIG, don't you know. You got a nav' problem or what, friend? You're headed for open ocean. Over."

The voice in Merriman's headset said, "I have no navigation problem. What is your mission? Over."

"Mission? You kiddin', pal? That there's a real expensive piece of navy property you're joyriding."

And the voice in his headset said, "Do not approach this aircraft. If you continue to close, I will open fire."

Merriman looked out at his wingman; in the cockpit of the other Falcon, Avila was staring straight at him and his voice crackled through the radio. "Checker leader—did I hear right?"

Merriman tapped the talk button on his stick. "Alpha-Delta-203. Hey, good buddy—say again all after 'continue to close'." He pressed his hand against the side of his helmet, listening.

Granger's voice said, "I *will* open fire."

In the backseat of the Tomcat, Logan said, "Range one hundred."

"Checker-one," Granger said. "You are at one hundred miles. Turn back. At seventy-five miles, I will commence firing upon you."

"Now, just a second," Merriman's voice said. "Just a goddamn second—"

Granger held the radio switch open so Merriman could hear his order. "Lock 'em up, Willie."

With his joystick, Logan moved the cursor to the 2↑1 symbol that was the lead Falcon. Then he switched the AWG-9 system from long-range pulse-Doppler search to STT—single target track. The AWG-9 locked on the lead Falcon and began streaming guidance data to the Tomcat's Phoenix missiles. Instantly, the icon and FONO brightened; now the lead Falcon bore the symbol for a TMA—target under missile attack.

"I have a lock," Logan said. "Select Phoenix."

Granger thumbed the red WEAPONS SELECT button on the stick from SW for Sidewinder to PH for Phoenix. "Selected, Willie." The AWG-9 began updating the targeting data in the onboard computer of the Phoenix under the left wing pylon.

"Cholly, go master arm *on.*"

When Granger flicked the toggle switch, a single red light lit on Logan's weapons panel. "Good light," Logan said. "Hot trigger, Cholly."

In the cockpit of the F-16, Merriman's radar lock warning light flashed on and a low-pitched whine sounded in his earphone, alerting him he was targeted. "What the fuck?" He punched in on the radio. "Griffiss from Checker-one. Hey, man, this joker says he's going to fire. And I *do* believe he means it!"

At the Northeast SOCC, a group of officers had gathered behind Lieutenant Maynard's console, mesmerized by the radio chatter on the open speaker. "Say again, Checker leader?"

"The sonofabitch says he's gonna shoot!"

Maynard looked up at Captain Shortway. "Stand by, Checker leader," Shortway said. He picked up the phone to the combat flight commander.

In the elevated battle staff room, Major Johnson grabbed the receiver. "I heard. Stand by." He punched the button for the SOCC commander.

Colonel Jerry Higgins had been in a budget meeting with two TAC bean counters since 0515 and he was in a real shit-eating mood when the alert phone rang. " 'Scuse me, gentlemen," he said and went to his desk. "Colonel Higgins."

"Colonel, at 1153 Zulu we launched two alert ANG Fox-sixteens from Atlantic City to check out some navy clown joyriding in a Fox-fourteen. He's threatening to fire if our planes approach him."

"What is this—a fucking joke?"

"No, sir. Button seven."

Higgins punched in just in time to hear Granger say, ". . . You are at ninety miles. I repeat. At range seventy-five miles, I will commence firing upon you."

Higgins barked, "Have the interceptors stand off!" Then he hit the button for the CONUS/NORAD Regional Operations Control Center at Langley Air Force Base in Hampton, Virginia.

From his console in the SOCC, Lieutenant Maynard flashed the stand-off order to the Falcons.

"Checker-one copies," Merriman said. "And that's okay with us." He banked right and Avila's Falcon followed.

In the TAC underground battle staff room at Langley, Colonel Grant Summers sat amid computer arrays of the four NORAD regions. He picked up the receiver.

"Langley. Colonel Summers."

"Higgins at the Northeast SOCC. We've got two F-16s up to check out that runaway Tomcat. He's threatened to fire on our planes. We're standing off."

Summers punched the Northeast ADIZ into tight scale on his radar screen. Off the New Jersey coast, three blinking lights maneuvered against miles of open ocean. "Wait one, Colonel. Be back to you." He put the line on hold and hit another button on his telephone.

Deep beneath the granite flanks of Cheyenne Mountain west of Colorado Springs, a red light blinked in the battle staff room of the NORAD Command Center. Brigadier General Alton Burke lifted the receiver. "NORAD. Burke."

"Summers at Langley, sir."

"Yes, Grant?"

"The F-14 has threatened to fire if our interceptors continue to close him."

Burke weighed that. "Let's see if he means it. Order the interceptors to approach the F-14."

"I'll . . . need written confirmation, General."

Burke nodded to the sergeant at the comm console; he typed the code for Langley into his E-mail computer. "On the way."

The Falcons banked sharply left, swung back on their intercept course.

"They're coming," Logan said. "Range eighty miles."

Granger punched-in on the radio. "Checker leader—attention. You are approaching seventy-five miles. Turn back. I say again, turn back or I fire."

Merriman wiped the sweat from under his eyes with the fingers of his gloved hand. "Look, pardner, don't be a dope. We got orders to flag you down. Let's not do somethin' we're all gonna regret."

"Range seventy-five."

Grimly, Granger said, "Checker leader, I tell you for the last time—turn back or I fire."

"Goddammit! We have orders, you sonofabitch!"

Granger held the radio open. "Fire," he said.

Logan hit the red launch button. "Fox three."

For a moment there was nothing. The AWG-9 was streaming targeting data into the onboard computer in the first Phoenix—range to target, airspeed, rate of closure. Then, abruptly, two shotgun shells in the pylon fired, flinging the missile free. The huge, white Phoenix fell fifteen feet before its rocket engine ignited. There was a roar that shook the Tomcat, a burst of light like a blinding strobe, an enormous plume of white smoke as the missile thundered away, guided by telemetry from the AWG-9, steering itself into a collision course with the target seventy-two miles away. In Logan's tactical information display, the TMA changed from 2↑1 to 2↑84.

"Op away," Logan called. "Eighty-four seconds to impact." The right-hand numeric began counting down toward zero. "Come right to two two zero."

Granger rolled the Tomcat westward toward the Falcons, and Logan buttoned the AWG-9 antenna down to eighty degrees of sweep, sharpening its focus to monitor and guide the flight of the missile.

"Time check," Logan said.

"I make it"—Granger glanced at the clock—"1159 Zulu." He shook his head once in appreciation; the mission planning was impeccably precise. They had been airborne seventeen minutes and were locked in the initial combat.

They were right on schedule.

At each level of command, the plotting boards picked up the missile track. The officers surrounding Lieutenant Maynard gasped.

"My god!"

"Is that a missile?"

"Do you see that?"

"Is he crazy?"

Maynard shouted into his microphone, "I have a missile track!"

Merriman gaped at his empty radar screen; the SOCC radar had the power to discriminate the missile, the Falcon's onboard radar did not. "Jesus Christ—where?"

A mile ahead of the F-14, the Phoenix banked west, accelerating through one thousand miles an hour. Then its tailerons rotated and it nosed up, rocketing upward on a billowing rooster tail of smoke toward one hundred thousand feet.

At Langley, Colonel Summers muttered, "Sonofa—" and reached for the telephone to Cheyenne Mountain. Burke was already on the line.

"Terminate the mission. Tell them to take evasive action and get the hell out of there!" Burke hit another button on his phone. "Get me the White House air defense room."

High above the Atlantic, the two Falcons dived for the deck, pulled 6-G turns toward the coastline, and went to afterburner in desperation to escape.

Logan watched them on the AWG-9 radar. "Missile tracking true. Targets turning. They're backing off, Cholly."

"Okay. We made our point. Abort."

"Aborting." Logan snapped off the AWG-9's targeting radar, severing the data link with the Phoenix. "Come left to course two zero five."

For fourteen seconds, the radar in the Phoenix searched for its target. Then the missile went ballistic, and climbed until it flamed out at one hundred twenty-five thousand feet. When it crashed into the sea at 1202 Zulu, the fireball was two hundred feet across.

Just then, Bryant Gumbel was saying, "And we begin this Veterans Day edition of *Today* by talking with Senator Simon Whitworth, chairman of the Senate Armed Services Committee." The image of Simon Whitworth seated in the studio at NBC-owned station WRC in Washington keyed into the frame opposite Gumbel. "Good morning, Mr. Chairman."

In the Oval Office, Sam Baker sat in a wing chair before the television set; his press secretary Ron Fowler sat beside him. Ted Harris leaned against the mantelpiece.

"Hold on to your hats," Harris said. "Here's where the battle starts."

Gumbel said, "Senator, through two campaigns you've been one of

President Baker's most ardent supporters. Now you've taken the lead in opposition to First Step. Does this signal a major split among the party leadership?"

"Bryant, in 1941 this nation recognized the defense of Europe was indispensable to our own survival. That is why we became and have remained deeply committed to NATO. Our forces in Europe are the balance of power that has kept that continent at peace."

"But, Senator, hasn't the political reformation in Eastern Europe and the Soviet Union reduced the need for an American military presence in NATO?"

"Not yet. President Gorbachev's policies of *glasnost* and *perestroika* are in trouble at home. If conditions worsen and the Soviet system is threatened with collapse, the conservatives could seize power. They've already got the support of the army."

"Goddammit," Harris said. "What's the old fool trying to do—start a war bond drive?"

But Sam Baker sat silent. Simon Whitworth was not an old fool nor was he a militarist. He was a man who had stood his whole life against compromise. And he was a patriot whose opposition to First Step could not be ignored.

Gumbel said, "President Baker also proposed a zero-option on sea-launched nuclear cruise missiles. Even if you oppose further reductions in our conventional NATO forces, shouldn't we take the opportunity to eliminate this class of nuclear weapons?"

"Bryant, any zero-option requires verification. Without permanent on-site inspectors at every Soviet naval base and an agreement for no-notice boarding parties on the high seas, we can't verify Soviet compliance. Until the political turmoil in the Soviet Union ends, their generals can't be trusted. Even if the Politburo agrees to a zero-option, reactionaries in their military might contrive some scheme to circumvent the treaty."

Sam Baker glanced uneasily at Harris.

Harris growled, "Yeah, like our guys hiding missiles at Hakodate."

"Senator," Gumbel said, "some observers are already calling your opposition to First Step political suicide."

Whitworth smiled. "At my age, a better description would be retirement."

"Then why are you so dug in on this issue?"

Whitworth sat forward and, for all his years, there was still fire in his eye. "Because the nation must be told. As long as there is unrest in the Soviet Union—as long as there is any possibility that their military might destabilize their government—First Step is dangerous. It will seriously jeopardize our ability to defend our European allies and the United States."

Sam Baker grabbed the remote control from Fowler and zapped the television mute. "Ted, call Mike Marden at NBC News and demand he get Scowcroft on tomorrow to refute that!"

"Yes, sir. Right away."

Under the vaulted nave of St. Bridget's Church at the corner of Massachusetts and Rhode Island avenues, Colonel Tom O'Neill sat impatient in the last pew, whispering his rosary. At the front of the church, the slow legions of the elderly were beginning to find their places, and altar boys were preparing for the early mass. O'Neill remembered the distant mornings when he had served behind the communion rail, holding the silver salver beneath the chin of each communicant as the priest administered the Host. In his starched white surplice O'Neill had felt the holiness of God descend upon him like his mother's embracing arms. *When, O Lord, will I know again that state of grace?*

The door of the confessional beside him creaked open and an old woman stepped out; another took her place. O'Neill glanced at his wristwatch. It was 7:05 A.M.—1205 Zulu. He had a rendezvous; he could not be late.

"Get a load of this!" Tod carried the huge pile of green computer paper into Christy's office and kicked the door shut. "The printout of yesterday's computer activity log was missing."

"What?"

"Somebody either stole it or shredded it."

"Why would—"

He slapped the pile down on her desk and flipped back toward the final entries of the day. "I reprinted it. Here's why." He pointed to the bottom of a page. "Last night Polly accessed the air force MPC mainframe at Randolph. She erased four service records." Tod ticked off the names and serial numbers with his pencil. "This is Petrovsky. This is Harding. . . ."

Christy stared at the printout. First, Granger's service record and now the records of Petrovsky, Harding, O'Neill, and Watkins had been erased. It was another part of the puzzle—a puzzle without a framework. Whatever was happening around her was cryptic, enigmatic—a mystery she could feel but couldn't fathom, like fumbling for a slippery stone in oil.

Tod leaned across the desk. "Chris, for chrissake. What the hell is going on?"

Christy trembled at the answer. But it was inescapable now. "Petrovsky had Polly erase those service records. Then he murdered her to shut her up."

Tod's face went slack. "Jesus Christ. Why the hell would he—"

"I don't know. But—"

The door burst open. It was Dubinsky, bubbling with excitement. "Wanna hear a great one? A buddy from the Pentagon just called with the wildest bit you ever heard. Some navy jock named Granger stole an F-14. And he's fighting his way to Cuba!" He headed down the hall to spread the word.

Christy clutched Tod's arm. "My god. It's begun!"

By then, the phone they called the Nightmare Line had rung in the Oval Office. The president had excused his press secretary before he answered it. And when the commander of the White House air defense room asked to meet him in the situation room, Sam Baker had walked downstairs with Ted Harris. But it was only after Colonel Walsh had explained the circumstances of the stolen navy fighter, only after General Gaynor had laid out the options for an interception, only after Sam Baker had returned to the Oval Office that he had any inkling the hijacked F-14 might have something to do with First Step.

At NBC station WRC in Washington, Simon Whitworth stepped out through the soundproof door of studio A. Margaret was waiting for him in the corridor.

"Well, Peg," he said. "The battle lines are drawn."

"I saw." She took his hand in both of hers. "Simon, I've never told you this. All these years—you've not only been my husband. You've been my hero."

Rick Winters, the press aide, plucked at Whitworth's sleeve. " 'Scuse me, Senator. We're due in the Senate press room at eight."

Arm in arm like newlyweds, Whitworth and Margaret started up the hall.

Lieutenant Colonel Richard Harding stood before the front entrance of the Russell Senate Office Building. A few steps down Delaware Avenue, news crews and still cameramen were gathered, sipping coffee from paper cups, smoking, and yakking.

Harding waved to one of the reporters who hustled past him. "What's the excitement?"

"Whitworth's on his way. You know—the guy who just declared war on the president."

"What's down the street?"

"Back door. They all go in that way."

Christy sat at her desk, eyes closed, elbows before her, forehead resting lightly against her fingertips. *Service records erased. Polly murdered. A navy fighter hijacked.* What did it all mean? Where did the seemingly unrelated crimes intersect in an objective? Christy had stumbled into the middle of a mystery. She could sense it moving and slithering about her. Yet the more she plucked at the fragile web of clues, the more impenetrable the riddle became.

Tod leaned against the desk and shook his head. "All that just to hijack a fighter to Cuba? Doesn't make any sense."

"It makes sense. We just don't have enough Intel to see the frame—"

The computer beeped. Christy looked down. The legend MAIL began blinking on and off in the upper left-hand corner of the screen. Christy punched up the E-mail facility.

For an instant, the screen went blank; then a line of characters scrolled on:

```
Be bold, my love. And on the day, remember me.
                                        Bryan
```

Suddenly Christy went pale, as pale as if her heart had ceased to beat. Then a wave of desire boiled up inside her. Her hands shot forward and seized the monitor. Bryan was there. Somewhere in the vast global computer network of United States armed forces, Bryan was reaching out to her, challenging her.

"Chris, what is it?"

Taunting her.

Christy shouted, "No!" and slammed her fist down on the keyboard.

The message vanished.

Tod pulled her to her feet. "What was that all about? Dammit, Christy, what the hell is going on?"

But Christy didn't answer, didn't see him, didn't feel his hands on her. The shock of recognition jolted through her, shook her like a thunderclap. *Now* she understood why what was happening around her was so enigmatic—the strategy subtle and elusive, the framework invisible, the tactics daring, the objective masterfully obscured.

Whatever was happening wasn't Petrovsky's plan.

"My god. . . ."

It was Bryan's plan.

Tod shook her. "Chris, for chrissake—"

She caught two fistfuls of his shirt. "Tod, we've got to get back to the detention cells at Andrews!"

"What? Why?"

"To find out what Petrovsky said to Watkins."

She tried to push past him; he held her fast. "Wait a second! Dammit, we're in enough trouble already! It's not our—"

The door of the office slammed open. It was Harding's secretary, Sergeant Dana Pavlov, in tears. "Christy. Polly's dead! Some woman officer murdered her!"

She flung herself into Christy's startled arms, weeping against her shoulder.

"What the hell took so long?" Harris said. General Gaynor and his exec, Colonel Walsh, stood before the president's desk in the Oval Office.

"Commander Granger's personnel records were erased last night," Walsh said.

"Erased? By whom?"

"We're trying to determine that, Mr. Harris. This information had to come by fax from the Federal Personnel Records Center in St. Louis."

"All right, Colonel," the president said. "Just give us your report."

Walsh flipped open the steel cover of his clipboard. "Commander Charles Louis Granger. Forty-five. Divorced, no children. Commissioned January 1968. Two cruises in the Tonkin Gulf aboard the *Enterprise.* Shot down March 1970. Three years in a VC prison. Repatriated February 1973." Walsh turned the page. "After that, he bounced from one squadron to another until he got himself assigned to weapons systems training at Oceana in 1988."

"That doesn't tell us a goddamn thing."

"Ted, please," the president said. "What else, Colonel?"

Walsh ran his finger down the page. "He's overage and overgrade for flying. Turns down every desk job he's offered. Fights like hell to keep his job in weapons training. Other than that, a model officer."

"Not entirely," Harris grumbled.

There was a knock and the door opened. The president's secretary, Katherine, entered carrying two sheets of teletype paper.

"Colonel Walsh, this just arrived from the Naval Investigative Service in New York." She handed him the telex and went out.

Walsh scanned it, and brightened. "This is promising. The NIS has arrested a VA physical therapy nurse named Margery Kessler. She brought Granger's accomplice to Calverton Field." He flipped to the second page. "He's retired Navy Lieutenant William Logan and he—" Walsh broke off, but his eye continued down the telex.

"What, Colonel?"

"Apparently, he's a double amputee. And—" Again, Walsh hesitated. "Excuse me, sir." He handed the telex to Gaynor and turned away.

Gaynor read it out. "Lieutenant Logan was Granger's radar intercept officer in Vietnam. On March 16, 1970, their Phantom aircraft was struck by a missile over Ban Don, Vietnam. The force of the blast collapsed the fuselage, trapping Logan's legs under his control panel. Firing the ejection seats would have severed his legs. Lieutenant Granger in command of the aircraft refused to eject. They fell six miles together in flames."

"And?" Sam Baker said. "How did they survive?"

"Logan pulled the ejection handle himself."

Sam Baker's breath caught.

"They were awarded Silver Stars." Gaynor laid the telex on the president's desk.

"Perfect!" Harris snapped. "Two war heroes. One who cut his legs off to save his buddy's life. Reunited to hijack a twenty-eight million-dollar warplane to Cuba. The network news will have a circus with this!"

The president turned to Gaynor. "General, what options do we have?"

"He's not responding to radio calls. We've dispatched a flight of F-15 Eagles from Tyndall to Homestead Air Force Base near Miami in case you decide we should intercept him."

"What about those rockets he's carrying?"

"As I explained, sir. He has five Phoenix missiles. We send six planes. If he doesn't surrender, they engage him."

"Out of the question! Dammit, I'm not going to kill five men to stop a couple of lunatics from . . ." But Sam Baker's voice trailed off. Something was nagging at him—some second sense that there was more to the hijacked fighter than two malcontents defecting to Cuba.

About him the men stood waiting.

"General . . . when will this decision have to be made?"

"Within the next half hour, sir. The Eagle flight is fueled and armed, awaiting your order."

Sam Baker nodded. "Thank you, General. You seem to have thought of everything. Now, would you and Colonel Walsh please excuse me?"

When the door closed, the president beckoned Harris to his side. "Ted, you don't think this business with the fighter could be some form of protest against First Step?"

"Maybe."

They stared at each other; both saw the paradox.

"If we let them go to Cuba, they make their point. If we shoot them down—"

"We make it for them," Harris said.

Sam Baker turned, went to the windows, and held the curtain back. The rising November sun was burning off the fog; through the tangled branches of the Presidential Grove the sky was brightening to a steely blue. Soon, the fence beyond the south lawn would be lined with families and children clutching little paper flags, walking the great monuments of the city, celebrating Veterans Day.

"Doesn't make sense, Ted. Two war heroes—former POWs. If anyone wanted to reduce the risk of war, you'd think it would be them. Why the devil would they—"

"Sam," Harris said darkly. "Maybe you should ask Zack Littman."

Granger looked down at the fuel gauges. They were off the North Carolina coast now, thirty-eight minutes into the mission and already down to less than eleven thousand pounds. Westward through the canopy, beyond the fragile clouds scattered along the horizon, the coastal towns of Cape Hatteras were drowsing into Monday morning. "Anything out there, Willie?"

Logan's radar scope was empty. "Negative. Guess NORAD's giving it a think."

"What do you figure?"

"Long as they think we're going to Cuba, we're okay."

"And once they catch on?"

"Interceptors out of Homestead."

Granger smiled; after all the years of flying with trainees, he had a real RIO behind him. "Glad you're back there, Willie."

"Where else would I be?"

In the rising light of the November morning, Lieutenant Colonel Richard Harding stood just inside the back door of the Russell Senate Office Building, his sweating hands driven down into the pockets of his trousers to hide their tremors. Behind him, guards were checking visitors' IDs, screening parcels and briefcases through the X-ray and metal detectors.

Outside the door, a few steps down the stairs, a gaggle of news crews and still cameramen stood gabbing and smoking at the curb. Abruptly they tossed away their cigarettes, raised their cameras, and switched on their sunguns as a black Oldsmobile swung in at the curb. Inside the doorway of the building, Harding stepped back out of the light.

Rick Winters, the press aide, climbed out of the car and held the door for Whitworth and his wife. Reporters and cameramen swarmed about them, shouting questions over the pop of strobes, the whir of cameras.

"What about it, Senator?"

"Can you stop First Step?"

"Has the president called you?"

"Can you rally the votes to block it?"

Whitworth did his best to shield his wife and push through the mob. "Please. Excuse us. Let us through. Not now. . . ."

Winters waved his arms and shouted, "Come on, fellas! The senator will have a statement in the press room."

But the reporters wouldn't take no for an answer. They pressed in, surrounding Whitworth, barring his way. Finally Whitworth nodded to Winters.

"All right! All right!" Winters shouted. "Ten minutes."

Whitworth turned to face the microphones.

Harding watched; perspiration beaded on his forehead.

Tod's car ground to a stop in the parking lot before the Andrews security police HQ. Christy clambered out and started for the front door. Tod caught her arm.

"Chris, wait. I've been thinking . . . the SPs are looking for us. Sooner or later, they're going to figure out who we are. As long as we're going in there, let's ask to see their commander. Tell him the whole story."

"You mean, give ourselves up?"

"Yeah. Let the SPs take it from here."

"Tod, there's no time. Whatever Petrovsky's involved in, it's already happening."

"I don't care. Dammit, I don't want to go to jail!"

"Neither do I. But they didn't erase their records and murder Polly just to hijack a plane. Watkins might know what it's about."

And before he could respond, she said, "Tod, this may be a conspiracy against the government of the United States." She turned and pushed through the door into the building. He stood, frozen to the spot.

Sergeant Jeeter stepped up to meet Christy at the counter. Behind him, a security policeman was peeling the morning's alert bulletins out of the fax machine.

"Yes'm?"

"That prisoner—Terry Watkins. I want to see him," Christy said.

"Y'all missed him. He's gone."

Christy blanched. "He was released?"

"Din't give us no selection—up and died."

Christy looked at Tod coming in the door, then back to Jeeter. ". . . Died?"

"Kilt hisself. Lil' pack of poison chewing gum. Don't that beat all?" Jeeter leaned across the counter, grinning. "D.C. cops out lookin' for the wife. Figger she slipped it to him."

"What are you talking about? Colonel Petrovsky gave him—"

"Colonel who?"

"Petrovsky. He was in the cell when you—"

"No, ma'am. Ain't no colonel been in that cell. Not never."

"That's a damn lie! He was in there and you—"

"Ma'am, think y'all a little bit confused." Behind Jeeter, the SP tore a sheet from the fax machine and pinned it to the bulletin board.

Christy was losing her temper. "Now you listen to me, Sergeant—"

Tod grabbed her arm. She glanced back, then followed Tod's eye to the bulletin board. The security alert notice carried a sketch of a sloe-eyed, dark-haired female lieutenant and the legend:

WANTED FOR QUESTIONING
MURDER

Jeeter shot a sneering glance at the nameplate on Christy's jacket. "Lookie here, L'tenant *Roo-soff*. Y'all got some kinda orders I could see? 'Cause if you don't—"

Christy slammed her fist down on the counter. "Dammit! I was here last night and—"

Jeeter turned to the security policeman. "Harry, show this lady to the door." Then he walked away.

Tod grabbed Christy's elbow. "Come on. Let's—"

But she pulled free and strode down the counter after Jeeter. "Just a damn minute. . . ." And when he ignored her, she shouted, "Sergeant! I'm talking to you!"

But Jeeter had turned his back to her and stood staring up at the bulletin board.

Tod whispered, "Chris, let's go."

Reluctantly she let him drag her toward the door. As Tod reached for the knob, Jeeter turned and shouted, "Arrest that officer! Arrest her!"

"Come on!" Tod pushed through the door to the parking lot and yanked Christy after him.

The SP shouted, "Halt! HALT!" He vaulted the counter, burst through the door and tackled Tod from behind. Tod wheeled and threw a hard overhand right that sent the SP sprawling.

The alarm klaxon sounded as Tod and Christy ran toward their car.

"Get in! Hurry!"

They leapt into their seats. Tod started the engine and threw the car into gear. With a screech of tires they skidded toward the gate.

The SP scrambled to his feet, drew his sidearm and leveled it at the fleeing car. Behind him, Jeeter shouted, "Shoot her! Goddammit— shoot that little cunt!"

The SP opened fire.

Tod shoved Christy to the floor as the first bullet crashed through the rear windscreen and smashed out the window on the passenger side. Before the SPs at the gate could draw their sidearms, the Ford screeched through the exit archway and out of the line of fire.

Tod jammed the accelerator to the floor. As they roared toward the Beltway, he reached down and helped Christy to her seat.

"Are you all right?"

"I'm okay."

"Christ, he saw your nameplate! They know who you are! What the hell do we do now?"

"The wife . . ."

"Who?"

"Watkins's wife. Maybe he told her something."

"Chris, the police are looking for her!"

"Yes. But they don't know where to find her. We do."

Tod shot a desperate glance at her.

But she sat staring straight ahead, jaw set, eyes narrowed and determined.

"I've got the Myrtle Beach VORTAC off the starboard beam," Logan said. "We're crossing the South Carolina border. Say, Cholly—how are we on gas?"

Granger looked down at the fuel gauges. They were fifty-six minutes into the mission and down to less than eighty-six hundred pounds. "Better if you don't ask."

The president's intercom sounded. "Yes, Katherine?"

"I have the Secretary of Defense, sir."

Sam Baker lifted the receiver. "Zack, have they filled you in?" Ted Harris leaned against the far wall of the Oval Office and folded his arms.

Secretary of Defense Zack Littman stood alone in the stateroom of the *Odalisque*. "Yes, sir."

"What's your recommendation?"

"Six interceptors out of Homestead."

Sam Baker took a breath; there was no time for niceties. "Zack, I know you conspired to pass information to the Soviets about those nuclear cruise missiles at Hakodate." There was silence on the line. "Zack, did you do that?

"Yes, Sam. I did."

The president lowered his head; his Secretary of Defense had just confessed to treason. "Zack—this plane. Is flying it to Cuba part of your—"

"No."

"If we have to intercept the fighter there could be shooting. Men may die."

"Mr. President, I know nothing of this plane."

"Are you asking me to believe the hijacking is a coincidence?"

"Sam," Littman said quietly. "I'm not the only man who opposes First Step."

The president hesitated; the morning's events had already proved that true. His hand tightened on the receiver. "Zack, you know if we engage the F-14, the Soviets will spot it with their satellites—"

"Sam, I told you—"

Then Sam Baker's patience ran out. "Dammit, Zack, I know you and everyone else in the Defense Department is dead set against First Step! But if there's a dogfight—if men kill one another over this—the press will scream the house down. The Soviets will think they've got more leverage in Geneva. And First Step will be a dead letter!"

Littman said, "Mr. President, you have my recommendation." He hung up.

Sam Baker set the receiver in its cradle. Then he shut his eyes and slowly massaged them with his fingertips.

"Well?" Harris said. "Did he admit to—"

"Ted, call our ambassador in Moscow."

"Jack Matlock?"

"Fill him in on Hakodate and the F-14. Have him make an appointment at the Soviet foreign ministry to brief Bessmertnykh. I don't want this madness to wreck any chance we've got to save First Step."

"Right away." Harris went to the door. But he stopped there and looked back at the president. "Sam . . . I'm sorry about Littman."

Sam Baker didn't raise his head. "So am I."

Twenty-five miles south of Miami—in a low cinder-block building a few steps from the alert pad at the western end of Homestead Air Force Base—Lieutenant Julie Kerner, a trim blond Intel officer, stood behind the desk at the front of the briefing room. In the two rows of chairs that faced her, the six pilots of Bravo flight sat in their G-suits, chewing gum, chewing tobacco, taking notes.

"Five remaining Phoenix and two Sidewinders," Kerner said. "Plus twenty-millimeter cannon. That's about it."

"That's enough," Captain Bret Foster said from the back row.

"What about ECM?" Colonel Harvey Miller said. He was wing commander of the 325th TFW, but he was leading this intercept personally.

Kerner checked her notes. "Unfortunately, this Tomcat is a high-class trainer. It's got the latest and greatest jamming gear: barrage, deception, noise, scan-rate, track-breaker, spot, group simulation. He's going to throw everything under the sun at you."

Foster said, "What is this, a loyalty test? Boss, we really going after a Phoenix-shooter with Sparrows?"

The other pilots stirred uneasily. Sparrow was the air force's long-range missile; it could be fired from thirty miles against a fighter-sized target, well beyond visual range but fifty miles short of the deadly reach of the Phoenix.

"Let's hope not," Miller said.

Captain Billy Crowder raised his hand. He was a good ol' boy from Tuscaloosa and the best flier in the wing.

"Yes, Captain?" Kerner said.

"L'tenant, y'all know *why* this motherfucker is going to Cuba?"

Tod's car skidded to a stop at the curb before the row of old clapboard shanties. Christy leaped out, rushed up the steps and pounded at the door. The burly white man in coveralls and undershirt opened it a crack. "Whaddya want?"

"Please! I have to speak to Mrs. Watkins!"

"She ain't here." He started to shut the door.

Christy leaned against it. "Listen to me! There's an emergency! Her husband—" She broke off.

In the shabby, cluttered parlor Mrs. Watkins stood, a handkerchief pressed against her mouth, her face streaked with tears. Christy threw her shoulder against the door and shoved her way inside.

"Hold it, you!" The man grabbed Christy's arm.

Then, softly, Mrs. Watkins said, "Leave her be, Ned."

He released Christy; quickly she crossed the room. "Mrs. Watkins . . ."

"Ain't you done enough? He's dead. You can't hurt him no more." The woman sat down on the faded, threadbare sofa.

Christy's voice dropped. "Oh. You heard. . . ."

"Cops busted into my place. My neighbor, Fay, she wouldn't tell 'em nothin'." Mrs. Watkins turned on her, eyes fiery red from crying. "He's free now. They can't punish him no more."

Christy eased down on the couch beside her. "Mrs. Watkins, please . . . I have to ask you. Last night—the three officers. What did they want your husband to do?"

"Terry wouldn't do nothin' for your colonel!"

"But what did they want? What did they ask him to do?"

"He never said." Mrs. Watkins turned away.

Christy sat back—checked. The trail was broken, her options spent. Her training, wit and instinct could take her no further. Bryan's strategy, Bryan's plan, Bryan's objective remained an impenetrable enigma.

Slowly Christy rose and started for the door.

Behind her, Mrs. Watkins sniffled against her tears. "You . . . gonna tell the police where I am?"

Christy shook her head. "No. Goodbye. And . . . I'm sorry."

Ned held the door open. But as Christy was about to step through it, Mrs. Watkins said, "They wanted Terry to murder Senator Whitworth. When Terry said no, they murdered Terry instead."

Rick Winters waved his arms and stepped between Senator Whitworth and the reporters. "All right. All right! Thank you, ladies and gentlemen. The senator will have a further statement in the press room."

Whitworth took Margaret on his arm; together, they began the short flight of steps to the rear entrance of the Russell Building. The news crews and reporters pursued them, shouting.

"One last question, Senator!"

"Just one more!"

Lieutenant Colonel Richard Harding wiped the perspiration from his eyes. With his trembling right hand he drew the 9-mm automatic pistol from inside his jacket. Then he pushed the door open and stepped out, blinking in the harsh morning light. The checkered handle of the gun was slippery in his sweaty palm. He stood at the center of the top step, struggling to level the pistol at Whitworth and his party.

There was a moment when Whitworth, Margaret, Winters, and the reporters looked up and saw Harding looming over them. All went silent. All stared.

Then Harding's hand holding the pistol stopped trembling. His eyes opened wide and clear. He was a man again, a soldier.

Margaret screamed, "NO!" and threw herself before her husband.

Harding fired. The detonation broke like thunder over the crowd. Margaret was flung backward as though hit by an automobile, went careening down the steps, aortal blood spurting across the clothes and faces of reporters. At the bottom she fell headlong to the pavement in convulsions. The reporters screamed, gagged, scattered, ran.

Whitworth looked down in horror at his wife, then up at Harding.

"Colonel, are you mad?"

"God bless the United States of America," Harding said. His second bullet struck Whitworth in the eye.

Harding pumped six more deliberate shots into Whitworth's fallen body. Up and down the street, reporters and passersby screamed and ran for shelter.

Then Harding flung away the empty pistol, dashed down the steps and through the melee. Capitol guards rushed out the door of the Russell Building, drawing their sidearms. A young black sergeant stood behind them, his automatic pistol raised. He shouted, "Halt!"

Harding ran out across Constitution Avenue, dodging the screeching traffic toward the north lawn of the Capitol.

The sergeant shouted, "Halt—or we fire!"

But Harding ran on toward the safety of the trees.

"Fire!"

A savage burst of gunfire struck Harding from behind. The front of his uniform exploded outward, scattering his service ribbons on the grass. His body slammed into the ground, convulsed once, and lay still. In the silence that followed, there were only the whimperings of the terrified and the soft snap of the flag above the steps of the Capitol.

Slowly, Christy walked down the rickety steps from the shanty. She opened the car door and slid in beside Tod.

"Chris, what is it? What did she say?"

But Christy sat silent. *Active duty files erased. Polly murdered. A warplane stolen. An attempt to suborn the murder of a senator.* What did it all mean? Somewhere in the riddle of events was Bryan's dazzling intellect, spinning out a web so fine the focus of its strands defied detection. Softly she said, "I need to get to a telephone, please."

"Sure. Okay." Tod put the car in gear.

Granger's eyes flicked to the fuel gauges. They were eighty-eight minutes into the mission and down to thirty-three hundred pounds. "Willie, where are we now?"

"Off Daytona Beach. How are we on gas?"

"Lousy." Granger looked out through the cockpit canopy. The glittering disk of the morning sun spread a blanket of silver across the gently rolling sea. Westward toward the Florida coast, puffy cumuli hung motionless, suspended in the warm, blue void. The sight reminded him of the first time he had flown into the stratosphere and seen God's grandeur with his own eyes. "Pretty day for a fight."

Logan followed his gaze toward the horizon. "Best day I ever lived."

Security police with drawn sidearms stormed into the ground-floor bull pen of INI. Lieutenant Nicky Dubinsky scrambled out of the way. "Hey, Sarge! What's going on?"

The SP stopped before him, his 9-mm automatic cocked and pointed at the ceiling. "Lieutenant Russoff! Is she here?"

"N—no."

"Where the hell's her office?"

"In . . . in the back." Dubinsky stepped into his own office and shut the door.

It took only a moment for the SPs to swarm over Christy's desk, only another moment for them to find the .25 automatic pistol with the silencer hidden in her bottom drawer.

★ ★ ★

Tod braked hard and pulled the car sharply to the curb beside a bus stop shelter. Christy jumped out, hurried to the pay phone, inserted a coin, and punched the number for the Pentagon. As the ringing began, she turned. In the window of the appliance store behind her, a display of television sets were tuned to NBC. The same news bulletin was visible on every screen.

Dumbfounded, Christy gaped at the shaky, hand-held images as Harding shot Senator Whitworth, fled, was cut down by Capitol guards' gunfire.

Mechanically—the phone call forgotten—Christy hung the receiver back in place. Gripped by the mesmerizing images of death, she moved slowly toward the shop window and rested both hands against the glass. Transfixed, she watched the assassination replay in slow motion, watched the shuddering camera focus on Harding's body on the bloody grass.

Then the conversation with Colonel Petrovsky in the billiard room came back to her, blew through her like a freezing wind. *You and I know First Step will put the nation in jeopardy. You're an Intel officer. What must be done?* She remembered the way Harding and Petrovsky had embraced—like comrades preparing for a last stand, men who realized they would meet again only in death.

Christy whispered, "The errand."

And in that moment she knew the objective of Bryan's plan.

"My god . . . First Step."

She turned, ran to the car, yanked her door open, leapt inside. "We've got to get back to the base! Hurry!"

She slammed the door shut as Tod slapped the accelerator down. The car screeched away from the curb.

"Melbourne VORTAC bearing two seven zero," Logan said.

"Okay, Willie. It's time." Granger reached into the breast pocket of his flight suit and unfolded a slip of paper. "Set a new course for twenty-five degrees ten minutes north by seventy-six degrees fifty minutes west."

Logan began keying the coordinates into the automatic flight control system; the system cycled and responded with course, range, and flight time. "Hey, Cholly, I make that over two hundred miles. You sure we got enough gas?"

"We've got fuel to target and a couple of minutes on afterburner . . . if we're lucky."

"Then not to worry. Today, I'm the luckiest man alive." Logan tapped the computer. "Come left to heading one four zero."

The last elderly woman stepped out of the confessional and went silently toward the side chapel to say her penance. Colonel Tom O'Neill opened the door, slipped inside the small, camphor-smelling stall, and crossed himself.

The priest on the other side of the screen began murmuring the ritual of confession. "In the name of the Father, the Son, and the Holy Spirit, amen."

O'Neill began, "Bless me, Father—" Then the words caught in his throat. He lowered his head and shut his eyes. "For I have sinned."

"How long has it been since your last confession?"

"Easter, Father."

"Do you trust in God?"

"Yes. I do."

"May God, who has enlightened every heart, help you to know your sins and trust in his mercy."

"Amen," O'Neill whispered fervently. "Father Bill?"

"Yes?"

"It's Colonel Tom."

On the other side of the delicate screen, Father Bill Voss smiled. He was a young man, barely thirty, with short-cropped black hair and a strong chin for which the old women of the parish adored him.

"Hullo, Tom," he said. "And how is Sister Mary Patrick?"

"Father, I may have to kill again."

Father Bill sat silent. Then he said, "Tom, we each have our calling, our own way of serving God. Yours is to protect your country from foreign enemies."

"This enemy, Father—he isn't a foreigner. He's an American. An evil man."

Father Bill heard the anxiety in O'Neill's voice. "Have you tried to turn him from evil? Have you tried to reason with him?"

"I can't do that, Father."

"Why not?"

"Because . . . he's the president of the United States."

The red light flashed above the elevator doors at the rear of the White House air defense room and a bell sounded. A marine guard braced and shouted, "Ten-*hut!*" Then the elevator doors opened and the president and Ted Harris stepped out. They went up the three steps into the small glass-enclosed room where the battle staff waited. A marine guard shut and locked the door.

"Carry on," Sam Baker said. "What is it now, General?"

"Mr. President, something very peculiar has turned up." Gaynor nodded to Colonel Walsh.

"Three minutes ago, the runaway F-14 made a course correction. If you'll please watch the plotting screen. . . ." A radar image of the coastline from Georgia to Cuba and the Caribbean was projected at the front of the ADR. The delicate green tracery showed a single blinking diamond—a solitary aircraft—off the coast of southeastern Florida.

Walsh pressed a button on the console. "Here's the course the Tomcat took after leaving Calverton Field." A thin yellow line appeared, connecting the F-14 with Cuba. "This is the correction." Walsh pressed another button; a white line appeared, veering sharply eastward toward the Caribbean.

"I don't understand," Sam Baker said. "Is that significant?"

"Mr. President," Gaynor said, "this was no random change of heart."

He reached past Walsh and hit another button on the console. All eyes turned to the plotting screen.

In Exuma Sound off the west coast of Eleuthera, a bright red dot appeared at the end of the new course line.

"What's that?" Sam Baker said.

"The motor yacht *Odalisque.*"

"The boat Zack Littman's on?"

"How the hell can he do that?" Harris said. "How would he know the yacht's location?"

"There's only one explanation," Gaynor said. He nodded toward the plotting room. "Someone down there in the ADR gave it to him."

". . . *What?*"

The president turned, stepped to the observation window, and looked down. Below him, the ADR was busy with air force officers and NCOs at their workstations; men and women in crisp blue uniforms, sworn defenders of the flag and Constitution. A chill swept through Sam Baker. *What if the defenders of the flag became its enemies? Who then would defend the state?* He brushed the disturbing thought away; American armed forces could never turn on the nation they had sworn to defend. Never.

"General . . . do you really believe the runaway fighter is going to attack the yacht?"

"We feel that's a ninety percent reliable assumption, sir. We've alerted the *Odalisque* and dispatched a rescue helicopter from our embassy in Nassau. And we've relieved our ADR holiday staff and called in the regular weekday contingent. I'd suggest you have the White House communications center do the same."

The president looked to Harris.

"I think Secretary Littman better get his ass out of there," Harris said.

Sam Baker drew himself erect. Every instinct told him events were going too far, were careening out of his control. He had to take command. "General Gaynor, you are to order the air force to intercept the hijacked fighter."

Gaynor braced. "With what rules of engagement, sir?"

"If he will not surrender . . . they are to shoot him down!"

The klaxon sounded in the alert briefing room at Homestead AFB. Then the PA crackled and a voice barked, "Battle stations. Bravo flight. Battle stations." The scramble timing light blinked 1307 Zulu and counting.

The six pilots sprinted out the door, out across the tarmac to the waiting line of F-15 Eagle air superiority fighters. At the top of each cockpit ladder, a crewman waited to strap the pilot in.

"Last one back to the barn buys the beer," Foster shouted.

Grimly, the others ran in silence.

Tod was speeding, weaving, fighting the Ford through the commuter traffic on the Anacostia Bridge.

Christy shouted, "There! Pass him! Pass him!"

Tod swung the wheel hard right, cut in front of a semi. "You're going to get me court-martialed *and* killed! What the hell happened?"

"You wouldn't believe it."

"Try me." He slalomed the Ford wildly through the rows of cars.

Christy was thrown left and right. She clung to the dashboard as they skidded into the fast lane. "Harding murdered Senator Whitworth."

"What?"

"I saw it! On television! It's a conspiracy to stop First Step—and it's happening now!" She grabbed hold of the door handle to steady herself. "Hurry, Tod! Hurry!"

The car shot across three lanes of traffic and down the off-ramp to the Anacostia Freeway, leaving a cacophony of screaming horns behind.

The battle staff had assembled in the small elevated room that overlooked the White House ADR. The door was locked. An armed marine guard stood outside to prevent intrusion; a second stood inside, against any disturbance within. The Zulu clock read 1312 and counting.

Side by side at the counter that ran the length of the window over the ADR, six specialist field grade officers sat, each with a gray encryption phone before him. From left to right they sat in the same order that the battle staffs were now seated at the Southeast SOCC at Tyndall, at Griffiss, at NORAD's Cheyenne Mountain: air defense, intelligence, missile warning, space defense, command-and-control systems, and commander's exec. Behind them at a radar console, General Gaynor sat in the commander's chair.

Beside him, Sam Baker stood, holding a telephone. "That's the lay of it, Zack. We're only guessing. But I'm afraid we may be right."

On the fantail of the *Odalisque,* Littman stood holding a portable phone. Clara sat sunning in a chaise beside him, thumbing a copy of *Vogue.* Beside her, Louise sat on the deck, coloring with crayons.

"All right, Sam," Littman said, and did his best to conceal the quaver in his voice. "When will the helicopter from Nassau get here?"

"Approximately eleven minutes. The flight from Homestead will intercept the navy fighter twenty miles north of your position. That's the best we can do."

"We'll be ready."

"Zack."

"Yes, sir?"

"God be with you."

"And with you, Sam." Littman switched off the phone.

Clara lowered her magazine, took off her reading glasses.

"Sweetheart," Littman said. "Can I speak to you a moment in our stateroom?"

The six F-15 Eagles of Bravo flight rocketed through the clear air above Biscayne Bay at 550 knots, climbing through sixteen thousand feet, steering east on heading zero eight zero. Colonel Harvey Miller looked out through the canopy at the formation. "Bravo flight, go tactical." The planes left and right of him banked away, opening up fifteen hundred feet of airspace between each leader and wingman. "Bravo five and six. Trail fifteen miles, flight level two one zero."

Captain Bret Foster eased the throttles back; he and his wingman were the designated backup team. "Say, Colonel—we really gonna shoot this cuckoo down?"

"Quiet, Frosty. Bravo two through four to afterburners—now."

The four lead Eagles soared upward through the speed of sound and climbed away.

The ringing telephone caught Tom Brokaw at the door of his apartment. He lifted the receiver.

Mike Marden's voice said, "You saw it?"

"I'm on my way." Brokaw hung up, went out the door, and slammed it.

Sam Baker stood among the officers in the battle staff room. On the plotting screen, the coastlines of Florida and the Bahamas were projected in tight scale. The six dots that were the Eagles moved slowly eastward on an intercept course for the Tomcat. Southward in the Caribbean, the sliver of Eleuthera hung suspended in the electronic darkness like a crescent moon; within the arc of its arms, the red dot of the *Odalisque* blinked in Exuma Sound.

Walsh put down the phone. "The embassy helicopter is sixteen miles east. ETA five minutes."

"When's the F-14 due over the yacht?"

"He's cruising at Mach .88. At that speed—fourteen minutes. The F-15 flight from Homestead is airborne. They'll intercept the F-14 in twelve minutes. We may be all right."

Colonel Tom O'Neill walked slowly down Executive Avenue to the awning that marked the entrance to the West Wing of the White House. An air force colonel waited impatiently at the door.

"Hurry up, O'Neill! The holiday staff's already out of the ADR."

O'Neill increased his pace.

Suddenly a voice from the street shouted, "Tom! Tom, in God's name! Stop!"

O'Neill froze, looked back.

At the Pennsylvania Avenue fence Father Bill Voss was struggling to push past the White House security guards. "Tom! On your immortal soul—"

"Dammit, O'Neill!" the colonel shouted. "This is an emergency! Stop wasting time!"

"Yes, sir." O'Neill went inside and down the hall to the elevator to the ADR.

"NO!" Voss shouted. "Let me go! I have to see the president!"

The security guards were trying not to hurt him. "Come on, Father," the old guard said. "You know the president's a busy man."

"Please! It's a matter of life and death!"

"It always is, Father." The guard nodded to his partner.

Gruffly, they hammerlocked the priest and dragged him away.

Walsh said, "Mr. President, the interceptors have orders to challenge the F-14 once they're airborne. We can listen in, if you like."

Sam Baker nodded.

Walsh turned to the sergeant at the comm console. "Guard frequency on speaker one."

The sergeant flicked a switch and the cool, authoritative voice of Colonel Miller cut through the static. "Calling Alpha-Delta-203. Do you copy? Over." There was a beat of silence; then Miller repeated the challenge. "Bravo flight from Homestead calling Alpha-Delta-203. Do you read me? Over."

In the battle staff room the men sat forward, listening. Outside, a marine sergeant tapped on the glass door. He held up a slip of paper and waved it toward Ted Harris.

A guard unlocked the door and brought the note inside. Harris scanned it, and the color drained from his face.

Without a word he passed the slip of paper to the president. Abruptly, Sam Baker rose. "That remarkable old man. . . ."

Gaynor and Walsh stood. "Sir?"

"Senator Whitworth is dead. Assassinated"—the president turned on the officers—"by an air force lieutenant colonel." He crushed the paper in his hand and raked the roomful of uniformed men with bitter eyes.

At the rear of the ADR, Tom O'Neill stepped off the elevator and pushed through the side door into the deserted locker room. He dialed the combination on his locker and swung its door ajar. Gently he lifted out his briefcase, carried it into the men's room, went into a stall, and bolted the door behind him.

"Question."

"Yes, Mr. Harris?" Gaynor said.

"If Phoenix missiles are accurate at almost a hundred miles, why don't our interceptors open fire as soon as they have the F-14 in range?"

"They will, if he won't surrender. But—" He hesitated.

"What is it, General?" Sam Baker said.

"Mr. President, the interceptors are air force F-15 Eagles. They don't carry the Phoenix. They carry the Sparrow and the Sidewinder."

"I don't see—"

"The Sparrow has a range of only thirty miles."

The men were silent. The implications were obvious and deadly.

"General," Sam Baker said softly. "How long will our interceptors be vulnerable to the F-14's missiles before they can fire?"

"About two minutes. He's probably picking them up on radar now."

Logan looked up from his radar screen. "Here comes the reception committee."

"Whatcha got, Willie?"

Six radar blips glimmered against the green screen of the tactical information display. Each was bracketed and numbered in order of threat from 4↑1 to 2↑6. "I have six bogeys spread from twenty-one thousand to forty-one thousand feet. Four leading, two trailing fifteen miles. Bearing zero six five. Range one twenty miles and haulin' ass. Looks like twelve hundred knots ground speed."

"F-15s from Homestead. What's their ETA?"

"If we stay on this heading, maybe eight minutes."

"All right. Let's get ready." Granger touched the toggles on his weapons panel. "Master arm is on. Phoenix selected."

On the backseat weapons panel, the arming light burned red. "I show hot trigger, Phoenix selected. Those kids are buying some tough tickets."

"Let's see if they're calling. Punch up GUARD."

The voice of Colonel Miller crackled in Granger's headset. ". . . do you copy? Over."

"This is Alpha-Delta-203," Granger said. "Do you read me? Over."

In the cockpit of the lead F-15, Colonel Miller glanced up to the empty horizon. "AD-203, this is Bravo leader with the recon flight out of Homestead. I read you loud and clear."

Granger's voice said, "Bravo leader, I'm in a hurry. What's your mission?"

"Alpha-Delta-203, I order you to lower your wheels and allow this flight to escort you to Homestead Air Force Base. Will you comply?"

"Negative. Bravo leader, I have you at one hundred twenty miles. If you close within seventy-five miles, I will open fire. Do you understand?"

"Affirmative. If you do not lower your wheels and follow us, I have orders to engage you." Then, slowly and deliberately, Miller said, "Commander Granger . . . do you understand me?"

★ ★ ★

In the elevated battle staff room, Sam Baker stood among the tense and silent officers. Beside him, Harris was squinting at the plotting screen, his great, hard hands clutching the back of the chair before him.

The speaker crackled with Granger's voice. "Affirmative. I understand you, Bravo leader. We will not comply."

Harris's hands released the chair back. He turned, and met the president's stare. All hope of avoiding air-to-air combat was lost.

Colonel Miller thumbed his radio. "Bravo flight—precombat checklists. Now."

Fifteen miles behind the lead formation, Captain Bret Foster flicked the master arm toggle on his weapons panel up from SAFE to ARM; in the single-seat Eagle, the lone occupant was both pilot and weapons operator. A tiny + winked on in the glass of the heads-up display above the central console, indicating the boresight line of the F-15's M61A-1 Vulcan 20-mm electric cannon. After the aircraft's thirty-mile Sparrow missiles were launched, after its five-mile Sidewinders were expended, the high-explosive-firing Vulcan was the Eagle's last-ditch weapon; it had an effective range measured in thousands of feet against an enemy that might be closing at thousands of miles an hour.

Sam Baker turned to Walsh. "Where is that helicopter now?"
Walsh checked the clock—1320 Zulu. "Three minutes away."

Above the warm blue waters of Exuma Sound, the MH-60G jet rescue helicopter was flying at full speed—170 knots—skimming low across empty ocean toward the *Odalisque* invisible beyond the horizon.

On the prow of the yacht Zack Littman and the two aerospace executives stood at the rail, silently staring west across the empty sea toward Nassau. Through the open cabin door behind them their three wives waited. Clara clutched Louise in her arms.

Vander Pool leaned in beside Littman. "Suppose we took the dinghy?"

Together they looked back at the motor lifeboat hanging off the stern.

Littman shook his head. "We wouldn't get a mile. And if he caught us in open water, it would be a turkey shoot."

In his office at the American mission in Geneva Jake was holding the telephone receiver to his ear. Sara sat in a chair opposite the desk, a computer printout in her lap, her pale eyes fixed on him.

"I see," Jake said softly. "Thank you." He hung up and sat unmoving, deep in thought.

"What is it, Doctor?"

"An air force lieutenant colonel just shot Senator Whitworth to death on the steps of the Russell Building."

"I'm very sorry to hear that, sir."

"Yes," Jake murmured. "Tragic news." He stroked his beard, pondering. Within an hour of announcing his opposition to First Step, Simon Whitworth had been assassinated by an American serving officer. An odd coincidence . . . if a coincidence. "Weatherby . . ."

"Yes, sir?"

Then Jake caught himself. "Nothing." He smiled stiffly. "Perhaps a coffee in the Winter Garden . . . ?"

Tod's car came skidding down the freeway off-ramp and almost plowed into the double row of vans and trucks lined up for clearance at the Bolling gates.

Christy shouted, "Through the exit! Go around!"

Tod cut the wheel sharply left, swung the car into the empty exit lane, narrowly missed a heavy truck, and fishtailed through into the base. Two startled security policemen rushed out of the sentry booth and ran after the car, reaching for their sidearms.

"The O-club!" Christy shouted. "Take me to the O-club!"

Logan said, "How's our gas?"

Granger tapped his finger on the glass plate of the gauge. The F-14 was down to two thousand pounds of fuel—fourteen minutes' flying time at cruising speed in its present configuration—a fraction of that if they had to go to afterburner. "Not good. How are those bogeys?"

Logan checked his radar screen. "Coming hard."

"Any sign of the boat?"

Logan cranked the scan plane of the radar down to sea level. The sea was empty. "Nothing."

Granger's fist tightened on the stick; like their fuel, their luck was running out.

Sergeant Dave Wang stood in the blustering wind that screamed through the open cabin door of the MH-60G helicopter. Behind him, a marine lieutenant and a corporal with a Stinger anti-aircraft missile launcher slung over his shoulder waited in the winch harnesses. Forty feet below, on the glassy water of Exuma Sound, the fantail of the *Odalisque* slid into view.

Wang shouted, "In the door!"

The two marines stepped to the threshold. Wang hit the winch controls and the marines swung out and downward toward the fantail of the yacht.

"Daddy!" Louise cried over the roar and whistle of the propwash. "Lookit the soldiers climbing!"

The marines dropped onto the deck beside her.

The lieutenant shrugged off his harness. "Secretary Littman?"

"I'm Littman."

"Lieutenant Wunderleigh." He saluted. "We'll have your party up and out of here in five minutes."

The marines began strapping the women into the slings.

In the ADR, Walsh was on the phone. He covered the mouthpiece and shouted, "The helicopter's overhead! They'll have them aboard any moment!"

"Thank god!" Sam Baker said.

The Ford slammed to a stop at the curb before the O-club. Christy and Tod jumped out, ran up the path to the door and pushed their way inside. Officers quietly chatting in the foyer looked up from their newspapers and conversations.

The manager stepped out from behind the reception desk. "Hey, Sarge, this is the Officers'—"

Christy shouted, "This is an emergency! Have you seen Colonel Petrovsky?"

"Not since 0600."

"Come on!" Christy ran down the hall. Tod followed.

"Hey, just a minute there!" The manager rushed after them.

Christy and Tod ran down the long hallway toward the billiard room. Behind them, the manager was shouting, "Lieutenant! Look here! You can't bring enlisted personnel into—"

At full speed, Christy ran into Nicky Dubinsky coming out of the lounge. Startled—then delighted—he caught her in his arms.

"Hey, girlfriend. Did you hear the awful news about Polly?"

"Nicky! Have you seen Petrovsky?"

"Went to Arlington this morning. Said he had to run an errand." Then he saw the manager rushing toward them. "What's going on?"

"Nothing. Nicky, let me go!"

But he held her as the manager stormed up, steaming. "Dammit, Lieutenant—"

Tod grabbed Dubinsky, flung him at the manager. The two went sprawling on the floor.

"Come on!" Christy pulled Tod through the archway into the billiard room, slammed the heavy oak door and bolted it.

Breathless, panting, Christy stood at the end of the deserted room, her eyes sweeping down the walls. Through the door behind her she could hear the men yelling, pounding with their fists.

"What's in here?" Tod said.

"The key."

Willie Logan peered at his scope. "Cholly, lead bogey is at one hundred miles."

"How long before they can fire?"

"Four minutes."

"Range to target?"

"Maybe a hundred twenty miles."

Grimly, Granger said, "We've got no choice. We've got to go to afterburners."

"Roger."

"We'll be tapped out, Willie. There's no way home."

"Cholly—I am home."

For a moment Granger shut his eyes. Then he slammed the throttles forward.

Within the tailpipe extensions of the twin F110-400 General Electric turbofans, concentric rings of tiny nozzles bubbled at the tips, then sprayed JP-5 fuel into the superheated air that roared out of the two-stage high-pressure compressors. Two twenty-foot bolts of blue flame shot out the tail at 1,800°F. The F-14 bucked once, then screamed through the sound barrier.

Christy reached up and lifted the framed *Pravda* clipping down from the billiard room wall and turned it to the light. In the faded, yellowed photograph, seven tattered American POWs stood surrounded by a ring of grinning Vietcong guerrillas. What had Petrovsky said? *Seven good men—or women—could stop First Step.*

"Hold this." She thrust the clipping into Tod's hands and grabbed the wall phone. "Operator! Operator, this is Lieutenant Russoff. I need air force security at the Pentagon. This is an emergency. Hurry!"

★ ★ ★

Logan looked up from the radar screen. "Cholly, the lead F-15s are at ninety miles."

Granger punched-in on the radio. "Bravo leader, do you read me? Over."

And Miller's cool voice came back, "Commander, I read you loud and clear."

"Bravo leader, you are at ninety miles. Turn back. At seventy-five miles, I will commence firing upon you."

In the lead Eagle, Colonel Miller stared at his blank radar screen. The Eagle's APG-63 combat system did not have the range of the Tomcat's AWG-9; his flight was still on vectors from the Southeast SOCC. A glowing symbol on the tactical electronic warfare system display and a low beeping in his headset told Miller the F-14 was already tracking them. Calmly he thumbed the microphone switch. "Commander, I have my orders."

In the battle staff room of the ADR, the Pentagon line rang on the command console. General Gaynor lifted the receiver. "ADR. Gaynor."

"Luke? Deke Goodwin at Pentagon security. You won't believe this. SPs have been looking for an Intel lieutenant who's wanted for murder—"

"Deke—can't talk. We're—"

"Now she calls in with some crazy story about a group of officers who hatched a plot to steal a navy fighter and—"

"Patch her through!" Gaynor commanded. "Now!" The line crackled. "This is General Gaynor in the ADR."

Christy said, "General, I believe I have the names of the officers who planned the assassination of Senator Whitworth and the theft of the F-14."

"Who is this speaking?"

"Lieutenant Russoff. INI." She took the *Pravda* article from Tod. Banging and muffled shouting came through the billiard room door. "Their objective is to stop First Step and—"

"Say again your name, Lieutenant?" Gaynor flipped open a yellow pad.

"First Lieutenant M. C. Russoff."

"And the conspirators?"

"Yes, sir." Christy held the article into the light and began to scan the Cyrillic text. She looked up suddenly at the *crash!* of splintering wood as the lock on the billiard room door shattered and security policemen charged down the length of the room, their sidearms drawn and cocked. "Hands up! You're under arrest! If you resist, we'll shoot to kill!"

"No! Wait! I'm talking to the White House!"

Two SPs slammed Tod back against the wall; one tore the *Pravda* article and telephone from Christy's hands. The SP lieutenant roared, "Handcuff 'em and get 'em out of here!"

"No!" Christy shouted. "I have the names of the conspirators!"

But the SPs yanked Christy's arms behind her back, slapped the handcuffs on her wrists, and dragged her toward the door.

She struggled, tried to pull away from them. "Wait! You've got to let me—" Then she saw Nicky Dubinsky among the gaping onlookers.

"Nicky! The *Pravda* article! Give the White House the names!"

But he only stared at her in dread.

Frantic, Christy screamed, "Nicky! For god's sake! Please! The phone—"

But the SPs dragged her out the door and down the hall.

Logan said, "Cholly, range eighty."

Granger sat up against his harness. The moment was coming.

Now for the first time Granger's voice rose. It rang in the headsets of Bravo flight, rang from the speakers in the White House ADR, rang in the Tyndall SOCC and in the battle staff room in Cheyenne Mountain—rang through the whole NORAD system, a call to battle, clear, intrepid, bold.

"Bravo leader—hear me now. Turn back! Turn back or I fire."

Softly, Miller said, "Listen to me, Granger. I've got five real nice kids up here behind me. There isn't one of them you wouldn't be proud to call your own. Think what you'll be doing if you—"

Logan said, "Range seventy-five."

"Granger! You took an oath!"

"Yes, Bravo leader. And I intend to keep it." Cholly Granger snapped off the radio. Then he gave the order.

"Shoot."

In his headset Logan's voice said, "Fox three."

There was silence while the AWG-9 computer streamed final targeting data to the Phoenix on the starboard wing pylon. Then the shotgun shells fired and the missile fell away. The Phoenix roared ahead of the Tomcat, accelerating skyward on a huge cone of white smoke.

"*Op* away," Logan said. "Forty-three seconds to impact." In his detail data panel display, an X marked the target as the Phoenix and the AWG-9 opened the electronic dialogue that would guide the missile to within ten miles of the Eagles. "Missile's targeting the wingman to the south."

"Force a firing order change," Granger said.

"Target?"

Granger stared out into the distance. Somewhere beyond the delicate veil of stratus clouds at the horizon, six fine young men in gleaming air force Eagles were streaking toward him, closing at half a mile a second.

"Target?" Logan said again.

"Kill the leader."

Logan engaged the target acquisition lock on his stick and moved the cursor from the wingman to the leader. Instantly, the AWG-9 flashed the digital command to the Phoenix already three miles away, updating the onboard computer to the new target. Instantly, the Phoenix streamed back an affirmative and the FONO icon for the leader brightened.

In the cockpit of the lead F-15, the low beep in Colonel Miller's headset kicked up in pitch and frequency—became an intermittent chirping sound. He looked down at the TEWS display; a missile was in the air, and he was targeted. Miller turned the volume of the warning system down.

The Zulu clock flashed 1324. Suddenly Walsh pointed at the plotting screen. "Missile track!"

Sam Baker clenched his fists. "Goddamn him!"

Walsh punched in on the PA system. "Fight's on. I say again—fight's on!"

In the Southeast SOCC plotting room at Tyndall, a dark-haired twenty-eight-year-old weapons director, Lieutenant Leanne Madison, sat hunched over her radar screen. Captain Leo Marx, the senior director, stood behind her, headset plugged into her console to audit her instructions to Bravo flight. On the raised platform at the rear of the plotting room the battle staff sat ready.

Leanne racked the computer's cursor to the fast-moving dot of light speeding westward from the F-14. In an instant the computer cycled and a long data list popped up in the lower right-hand corner of the screen. The object was unknown. Not air-breathing. Traveling at Mach 2.7. Accelerating. Climbing through 520—52,000 feet.

"Bravo flight, I have a missile track," Leanne said softly. She was a Louisiana girl and her voice had a gentle southern roll.

Colonel Miller came back, "Where away, Tyndall?"

"Bearing three three zero at fifty-six miles. Angels fifty-two and climbing. Mach 2.7." The computer cycled. "Check that. Angels fifty-five. Mach 2.9."

Like all the pilots in the interceptor flight, Captain Bret Foster listened to her voice and stared at his own onboard radar screen. The screen was blank. Foster flicked on his radio. "Hey, boss. Is there a Phoenix on the way?"

"Get off the air, Frosty. Everybody—ECM to radar-guided, phase four."

Each of the F-15 pilots hit the last switch on his ECM panel, switching on his Eagle's ALQ-135 jammer. Now the flight was bombarding the Tomcat's AWG-9 receptors with a snowstorm of false signals. That was the Eagles' first line of defense. If the RIO in the F-14 could guide the Phoenix through that maze of electronic ghosts, the Eagles would fire chaff—bundled tiny strips of aluminum foil that would produce another array of false targets. And if the Phoenix homed through those, the Eagles' last-ditch defense was to turn ninety degrees to the Phoenix, trying to pick their way through the electronic gate in the missile's pulse-Doppler radar and vanish against the background.

If that failed, they would have to outfly the monster to survive. Their only hope was to lure the Phoenix into a steep dive, then pull up sharply and pray the missile overshot its mark.

The radar screens in both cockpits of the F-14 lit like a snowstorm as the AWG-9 picked up the Eagles' jamming.

"Lot of junk out there," Granger said.

Logan flicked on the ECCM panel—electronic countermeasures for the jamming. Quickly, his hand on the stick guided the cursor back and forth across the radar scope from dot to dot. As he did, the AWG-9 analyzed each dot, comparing its apparent movement against its own prodigious digitized memory of fighter behavior, discarding every dot that didn't match a profile, performing thousands of analyses each second.

"Good target track?" Granger said.

"Still got the leader. But I'm dropping track on the wingmen."

"Range to the yacht?"

"A hundred miles—if it's there."

The helicopter hovered above the *Odalisque,* winching Clara and Louise aboard. On the deck below, Zack Littman, the two executives, and the yacht's crew clustered, shading their eyes against the prop-wash. Behind them on the fantail, two teams of marines were readying shoulder-launched Stinger anti-aircraft missiles.

In the bathroom stall off the locker room behind the ADR, Colonel Tom O'Neill finished screwing the slender, cylindrical detonator into place. When it was tightened, he teased the two protruding wires into the contacts of the timer and locked the thumbscrews down. It had taken three months to carry the packets of Semtex explosive, the connecting cables, and timing mechanism into the White House bit by bit, wire by wire to avoid detection. Now the question was—would the device perform? He drew a breath and flicked the toggle switch; a red light in the detonator circuit began blinking. It would.

He bent to set the timer.

In the lead F-15 Colonel Miller stared at his radar screen. What he saw made his eyes widen in surprise. At a range of fifty nautical miles—the far limit of the APG-63 radar to discriminate a fighter-sized target—a single dot of light glowed against the green. The dot was the Tomcat. And the dot burned steady and true. There was no interference, no clutter, no false images—nothing except a target every onboard computer in the Eagle flight could see and hit.

Like Miller, Captain Billy Crowder saw the same clear target on his radar. "Leader, where's his jamming? Is he askin' us to shoot him down?"

At the Bolling O-club a group of shocked officers stood gaping and whispering in the billiard room doorway. At the far end of the room, Lieutenant Nicky Dubinsky picked up the dangling receiver of the telephone. "Hello?"

A commanding voice roared, "This is General Gaynor! What the hell is going on!"

Dubinsky's spine snapped straight. "Uh . . . General . . . Lieutenant Russoff's been arrested and—"

"The names!" Gaynor shouted. "Do you have the names?"

Dubinsky picked up the framed *Pravda* clipping from the billiard table. "Sir, I don't . . ." Then his eye found them in the text. "Yes, sir!"

"Well, dammit! Give them to me!"

The seven were listed in alphabetical order, beginning with

Командир Даниил Петр Браян

which Dubinsky translated as Captain Daniel Peter Bryan.

Logan leaned forward, peering into his radar scope. Despite the successive waves of jamming from the F-15s, the symbols for the lead interceptors burned clear and steady at a range of forty-five miles. "They'll open up with Sparrows any time now."

"Range to target?"

"Eighty miles."

"You getting anywhere with that ECM?"

"I'm through the ECM, Cholly. I got them on ice." An orange light began flashing in the corner of the screen. "Cholly, Phoenix one just went active."

At Mach 5.5 and one hundred thousand feet, the soaring Phoenix missile was coming into range of the F-15s; its computer switched on the missile's onboard look-down, shoot-down radar. Its ECCM system shrugged off the interference from the interceptors and saw the same array of symbols Logan saw. Now the missile was polling Logan for a final target. With his joystick Logan slid the cursor of the AWG-9 to the symbol for the lead Eagle and pressed the lock button. The orange light turned red.

Like a falcon towering in its pride of place, the Phoenix soared on majestically for a moment. Then the guidance system locked on the lead Eagle. Instantly the missile's tailerons flexed and the Phoenix nosed over into a thirty-five-degree dive and rocketed downward at forty-one hundred miles an hour. The onboard computer shut down its transceiver circuit to the Tomcat, cutting the cord; now the Phoenix was beyond recall; the beast was hunting on its own. A pulse from its computer armed its fuses: a proximity radar target detector mounted behind its avionics package and two magnetic proximity fuses at its waist. Any one of them could detonate the 130-pound continuous-rod warhead. The computer calculated the Phoenix's rate of closure with the lead Eagle at 5,163 miles an hour, calculated the intercept path and terminal homing time over the thirteen miles that separated the two. The Eagle had 9.2 seconds to break the radar lock or die. The Phoenix dropped from the sky like God's vengeance.

In the Tyndall SOCC Lieutenant Leanne Madison took hold of the edge of the radar console before her. "Missile track descending. Angels ninety. Mach 5.5."

Through the open speaker, the men in the battle staff room of the ADR heard the tension in her voice.

The radar lock light burned steadily in the cockpit of Colonel Miller's F-15. His voice was steady, calm. "Where, Tyndall?"

"Bearing three four zero." Leanne's voice rose. "Angels eighty. Harvey—"

"Easy, honey," Miller said.

The SPs hustled Christy and Tod down the steps of the O-club toward the open doors of a blue air force security police van.

"Wait!" she shouted. "It's a plot against First Step! I have to talk to—"

They shoved her into the van and slammed the doors behind her.

Leanne's voice said, "Angels seventy."

Miller shouted, "Bravo flight! Break turns! Missile!"

The six Eagles scattered into 5-G turns left and right, abandoning their intercept course toward the Tomcat, banking perpendicular to the incoming missile, trying to slip through the range gate of its pulse-Doppler targeting system and disappear among the radar signals bouncing off the surface of the ocean.

Leanne tightened her grip on the console. "Angels sixty."

The Eagle pilots hunched and groaned against the hard bladders of their inflating G-suits, tensing their bowels to drive their blood upward against a blackout.

"Angels fifty!"

Colonel Miller yanked his fighter into a hard right bank and shot a glance up through the canopy. Dimly, he could see a vapor trail high in the stratosphere. Otherwise the sky was clear, the Phoenix invisible. The missile warning in the TEWS display burned steadily and he could hear the chirping growing louder in his earphones.

Leanne shouted, "Angels forty!"

"Chaff! Chaff!"

Each Eagle pilot squeezed the switch on the throttles under the fourth finger of his left hand. The AN/ALE-40 chaff dispensers on the underside of the planes' fuselage fired a barrage of four-inch plastic canisters into the airstream, each filled with thousands of delicate strips of aluminum foil cut to match the wavelength of the aggressor's radar signal. Instantly, each packet bloomed into a cloud the size of a fighter, resonated in the missile's radar and bounced back a deceptive image.

The planar radar array in the Phoenix read those images. As the missile screamed toward its target, the onboard computer worked at the speed of light, picking through the chaff, comparing those false targets with its digitized memory of fighter behavior, discarding those that didn't match a profile.

"Angels thirty!" Leanne scrambled to her feet. "Harvey—"

Suddenly the intermittent chirping in Colonel Miller's headset became the raspy warning of a rattlesnake.

Its eerie rattle echoed in the headset of Weapons Director Leanne Madison at Tyndall.

It grated through the open speaker at Cheyenne Mountain, through the speakers in the White House ADR.

Sam Baker turned to Walsh. "What's that dreadful noise?"

Then Leanne screamed, "HARVEY! LOOK OUT!"

Like a white streak of flame, the Phoenix roared into the midst of the careening Eagles.

Miller slammed the stick hard right and down, slammed the nose of the F-15 toward the sea at thirteen hundred miles an hour. At the last possible instant, he pulled back hard on the stick to force the Phoenix to overshoot.

When the missile struck, the fireball of the disintegrating F-15 was four hundred feet across.

From his place at the railing on the fantail of the *Odalisque,* Zack Littman was the first to see the blast. It was as if a magnesium flare had exploded high up in the western sky. Involuntarily he raised his hand to shield his face.

Above him in the helicopter, Louise screamed in her mother's arms.

General Gaynor released the disconnect button on his phone and looked up from the list of conspirators. "Operator. Get me—" He broke off.

On the plotting screen at the front of the ADR, a tiny, silent flash appeared among the maneuvering interceptors. The image struck Gaynor dumb.

"What's that?" Sam Baker said. "That flash? What was that?"

The battle staff room sat in silence. Gaynor lowered the receiver to its cradle; like a man distracted, he rose and made his way to the window.

"General? Was that a hit?"

Softly Gaynor said, "Yes, sir. God forgive us. Yes."

★ ★ ★

Frosty screamed, "Goddammit! They got Miller!"

"Jesus Christ!"

"Did you see that? My god!"

Then a voice commanded, "Get off the air!" It was Major Kelly Ross, Miller's wingman. "Bravo flight, go tactical. We've got a job to do!" The formation turned toward their prey.

"One gone," Logan said. "That slowed them down."

Granger sat silent.

"Cholly? The other five are coming. We've got to keep them busy."

"All right." Even so, Granger hesitated.

"Cholly, we've got no choice."

"I know. Fire two."

Logan thumbed the launch button. "Two fired."

With a clunk and burst of flame the second Phoenix fell, ignited and roared away.

"Fire three."

"Op away."

Again, the dull, explosive thud.

"Fire four."

Granger sat silent, listening to the sequence as the Phoenix roared into the clear, cold sunlight, carrying its one hundred thirty pounds of death.

"Op away. One Phoenix left."

Granger wiped his gloved hand across his eyes.

Behind him Logan said, "One more, Cholly."

"Go ahead."

"Fox three. Op away."

"God help them," Granger said.

O'Neill pushed through the locker room door into the ADR. He carried his briefcase at his side. Beyond the elevated glass partition at the rear of the room, he could see his old friend, Colonel Walsh, standing among the president and the battle staff. O'Neill nodded to Walsh; he winked back a quick hello. Then, abruptly, Walsh's eyes snapped up to the plotting screen at the front of the ADR. O'Neill followed his glance.

Four new missile tracks from the F-14 appeared on the plotting screen, spreading toward the interceptors like the deadly tines of a pitchfork.

Walsh shouted, "They've salvoed their missiles!"

"My god, it's a maelstrom!" Sam Baker said. "General, can our boys fly through that?"

Gaynor hesitated.

"Can they?"

"Mr. President . . . I don't know."

Harris pushed through the group of men and pointed at the bottom of the plotting screen. "General, what are those lights down there?"

All along the northern coast of Cuba, dots of lights were turning east and north in flights of six and eight.

The air defense officer punched in on the PA. "Attention. The Cuban air force has scrambled. I say again, the Cuban air—"

A sharp, metallic ringing sounded through the speakers overhead. General Gaynor turned to the command console and grabbed the blue line from NORAD. "ADR. Gaynor."

"Summers at Langley. Havana Center has been calling for fifteen minutes. They've canceled their civilian operations and rerouted all westbound traffic to Haiti."

"Tell them it's an exercise."

"We did, Luke. Now they've seen a kill. They've just scrambled every base from Baraco to Pinar del Rio."

"What do they think it is? A one-man invasion?"

Abruptly, a loud klaxon sounded through the battle staff room. The president looked to Gaynor.

There was a loud beeping in Gaynor's phone, and a voice said, "This is General Kutyna at Cheyenne Mountain. We have seized this phone line."

Another voice broke in. "This is General Powell at the Joint Chiefs of Staff. Do you confirm the Cuban scramble?"

From Langley, Colonel Summers said, "Affirmative."

"Wait a second, Colin," Gaynor said quickly. "It's the runaway F-14 that's got them spooked. When we splash the F-14, they'll settle down."

Powell's tone remained unchanged. "Luke, one more time—do you confirm the Cuban alert?"

"Yes, dammit."

"DEFCON3," Powell said and hung up.

A siren sounded throughout NORAD headquarters under Cheyenne Mountain. The emergency action cell director at the console behind General Kutyna pressed one button and at Griffiss, Tyndall, Langley, and every installation throughout the four NORAD regions—at every major air force installation worldwide—the same panel on every status board lighted preliminary to the transmission of combat readiness instructions:

SECRET WHEN LIT

Gaynor turned to the president. "JCS has ordered DEFCON3."

The men in the battle staff room stiffened as though hit by a bolt of electricity.

"In the name of God," Sam Baker said. "Why?"

"Standing presidential orders since the Cuban missile crisis," Harris said. "Remember what Jack Kennedy said? Any attack launched from Cuba against the United States will be considered an attack by the Soviet Union."

At the front of the ADR—under the Zulu clock—under the bright red lozenge with the legend SECRET WHEN LIT—one-by-one the panels on the NORAD status board began to light. Younger officers slowly got to their feet; none had ever seen the panels lighted except during an exercise. The first read:

AIR DEFENSE WARNING

At thirty TAC and air national guard bases on the borders of the United States, on Hawaii and Alaska—at USAFE installations in Bitburg, Germany, and Zaragosa, Spain, and Soesterberg in the Netherlands, at every interceptor station in the system that stretched to Misawa, Japan, and Osan, Korea—pairs of alert pilots scrambled toward waiting F-15s, F-16s, and F-4s.

Momentarily, the status board at the front of the ADR gleamed the code words for the routine minimum alert status known as DEFCON4:

BEACH DAY

Then the panel winked, and the legend changed to the code words for DEFCON3:

MORNING STAR

In the underground command center below the rolling front lawn of Strategic Air Command headquarters in Omaha, Nebraska, Colonel Neil Jaeger flipped up the Lucite cover and thumbed the red ALERT button. Behind him, the contoured seats of the four-tiered war theater were already filling as the battle staff hurried to their places, some pulling on their jackets, some still tying their neckties. One-by-one, the eight huge video panels that dominated the front of the theater began to light with the status of SAC aircraft and missiles worldwide, and with real-time satellite projections of Europe, the Pacific, the Arctic, and both coasts of the United States. In the vast communications center behind the war room, every light on the comm panel burned red and a sergeant began reciting the DEFCON3 order over the primary alerting system. At every SAC installation around the globe—from RAF Mildenhall thirty miles northeast of Cambridge to Andersen AFB on Guam—a klaxon sounded and air crews ran toward alert bombers and tankers angle-parked within the barbed-wire enclosure at the edge of the runway.

From the Mediterranean to the Sea of Japan, shipboard klaxons sounded general quarters and six deployed navy carrier battle groups began turning into the wind. On supercarrier CVN-69 *Dwight D. Eisenhower* one hundred miles west of Messina in the Ionian Sea, loudspeakers roared, "Pilots, man your planes!" Belowdeck, weapons handlers in flameproof coveralls charged up the gangways toward the thick steel doors of the missile vaults.

Sam Baker stood at the window of the battle staff room, feeling all about him the awesome power of the war machine beginning to turn on its mammoth gears. His instinct was to intervene—to countermand the order. But he hesitated. What if the assassination of Simon Whitworth and the flight of the hijacked F-14 were preludes to some greater act of terrorism? What if the Cuban scramble were part of some sinister collusion between the men in the Tomcat and fanatics in the Castro government? No, the best course was to take every precaution, follow procedures and rely on standing orders.

On the status board at the front of the ADR, the ROE panel blinked on, indicating the rules of engagement for American combat forces worldwide. The panel flashed:

PEACETIME

Then it went black. When it lit again, it read:

TRANSITIONAL

In the Sea of Japan west of Sado-shima Island, guided missile cruiser CG-50 *Valley Forge* went to flank speed—thirty-six knots—steering northwest through rolling five-foot seas toward the Asian mainland and the Soviet missile complexes at Sovobodonyy and Olovyannaya.

At his official residence on the grounds of Georgetown's Naval Observatory, Vice President Charlie O'Donnell looked up from his newspaper at the sound of knocking on his study door. It was Jeff Blackmon, chief of his executive protection detachment.

"Mr. Vice President, JCS has called a DEFCON3 alert. A chopper's on the way to ferry you to Andrews."

O'Donnell just stared.

Sixty feet beneath the snowbound flatlands northeast of Cheyenne, Wyoming, the alert light burned in Launch Control Center T of the Ninetieth Strategic Missile Wing. Captain Dallas Thompson and Lieutenant Steve Kranz swung into chairs at opposite ends of the launch console. In silos buried within a thirty-mile radius of their command post, ten LGM-118A Peacekeeper intercontinental ballistic missiles waited, engines fueled and ready, one hundred nuclear warheads targeted and prearmed. Thompson barked, "On my command—isolate. Now."

Kranz began flipping through a set of toggles, double-bolting the blast doors and isolating the control center from the outside world.

At Andrews Air Force Base, the white-and-blue Boeing E-4B that was the National Emergency Airborne Command Post—the plane with the peculiar acronym of *Kneecap*—swung to the end of the active runway, its four jet engines idling. The plane was a 747 reengineered and reconfigured to make it one of the most powerful communications centers in the world. The main deck was divided into a National Command Authority suite, conference and briefing rooms, a battle staff room, and a huge communications center served by radios with ultra-high-speed data links, and supported by massive Hughes computers that occupied the entire lower deck. With inflight refueling, the aircraft and its complement of fifty-two civilian and military personnel could remain aloft for five days. The plane's enormous capacity to receive and process data from ground installations and satellites gave the battle staff of Kneecap the capacity to monitor and fight a global nuclear war. The plane also carried two other devices indispensable to its mission. Stored in a portable computer harddisk was the recorded message from the president that would command the nation's strategic forces to implement SIOP-91—the Single Integrated Operational Plan for an all-out nuclear attack against the Soviet Union—and would issue the eight-digit code that released the final interlock and armed America's land-based and airborne strategic nuclear weapons. Kneecap also carried an airborne launch control system that could bypass every level of command, retarget, and fire America's entire arsenal of one thousand Minuteman and Peacekeeper intercontinental ballistic missiles. Even if the chain of command were broken, even if every landline and data link to the buried missile launch control facilities were disrupted by the devastating electromagnetic impulses that accompanied thermonuclear detonation, even if the launch officers mutinied and refused to enable their missiles—even then, the president or his representative aloft in Kneecap could single-handedly strike the Soviet Union a blow from which mankind itself might never recover. In that way, Kneecap was not merely an airplane, but the most powerful weapon on the face of the earth.

The front passenger door of the plane swung open; the mobile stairway vehicle pulled alongside to await Vice President O'Donnell's helicopter.

At Andersen AFB on Guam, Major Marvin Cutler steered the lead B-52H of Charlie flight of SAC's Forty-third Bomb Wing through the pelting rain, following the trail of blue taxiway lights that steamed in the equatorial night. At the foot of the active runway, he shut the engines down to idle, locked the brakes, and slouched back in his seat and yawned.

"Time is it?"

Beside him, copilot Captain Eddie Foyle punched the Zulu clock to local time. "Almost ten-thirty."

"Picked a great night for a drill."

Through the blowing sheets of rain—by the flashing of the bomber's navigation strobes—six AGM-86B air-launched nuclear cruise missiles were dimly visible on the tandem pylons under each wing. In the bomb bay behind the flight deck, eight more were mounted on two rotary launchers in the bomb bay. The three B-52Hs of Charlie flight carried more destructive force than all the armies that had fought on both sides in World War II. At Strategic Air Command bases throughout the United States, 217 similarly armed B-52s and B-1s sat idling at the end of runways.

★ ★ ★

Three hundred feet below the glassy surface of the Adriatic, the electronic gong pulsed through the corridors of SSBN-726 *Ohio.* "General quarters, missile operations. General quarters, missile operations." In the missile operations center, officers and enlisted men scrambled to their places at the launch console. Rear Admiral Henry Beame stepped through the hatch. A seaman slammed and battened it. The exec handed Beame a clipboard.

"Yes, Mr. Wellesley?"

"There's a Cuban scramble. We're ordered to DEFCON3."

Beame nodded. "Prearm Tridents one through twenty-four." The launch officer began opening the safeties, switching the first line of red toggles down. One by one, the needles in the pressure gauges trembled as the missile launch tubes began to fill with live steam.

At RAF Mildenhall the first KC-135 Stratotanker thundered down the runway and lifted off for its refueling station in the Greenland Sea, 650 miles northwest of Tromso, Norway. At RAF Lakenheath the first FB-111A rolled to the end of the runway and locked its brakes, just as it had before the raid on Libya in 1986. But this time its wing pylons mounted four AGM-69A nuclear short-range attack missiles. Two more nestled in its bomb bay.

Ted Harris pointed at the tracks of the four Phoenix missiles closing on the F-15s. "You mean we're going to DEFCON3 over *that?*"

In the Tyndall SOCC, Weapons Director Leanne Madison shouted, "INCOMING!"

The three remaining lead Eagles rolled and dived, spewing bursts of chaff as the salvo of Phoenix missiles came screaming out of the stratosphere.

Sam Baker stood at the window over the ADR, both hands pressed against the glass. A tiny flash of light appeared on the plotting screen. Then another. And another. Silently, the three lights sparkled and went out; three lives consumed in bursts of lethal heat and blast.

Behind him Walsh said, "Sweet Jesus . . . four of them."

Gaynor pointed at the board. Two dots that were interceptors and one streaking missile remained. "There! That's the last Phoenix!"

Fifteen miles behind the battle, Captain Bret Foster could hear the radar lock of the last Phoenix rattling in his headset over the roar of his own panting. He glanced up through the canopy; twenty thousand feet above him, a tiny scratch of white light marked the diving missile.

Foster slapped the stick hard right, firewalled the throttles and stood on the rudder pedal. The F-15 spiraled downward toward the ocean at eleven hundred miles an hour. The Phoenix jinked, followed unerring, seared downward through the humid air at four thousand miles an hour. Then, suddenly, Foster slammed the stick left, hurling the Eagle to the side. With a shock wave that tossed the fighter like a playing card, the Phoenix rocketed past the canopy, plummeted the last two thousand feet, and exploded on the surface of the sea. The rattle in Foster's headset went dead.

On the plotting screen in the ADR, the last missile track faded into nothingness. Two F-15s remained.

"Mr. President," Gaynor said. "They're our last chance."

Foster pulled the Eagle into a stiff climb through ten thousand feet and scanned the empty sky. There were no parachutes. Below him on the sea, scattered wreckage burned in floating clumps, indistinguishable as the remains of Bravo flight. He thumbed his radio and his voice crackled through the speakers of the ADR. "Creeper? Wildman? Breaker? Anybody? Anybody still alive?"

Sam Baker pressed his fingertips to his forehead and shut his eyes against the lonely, desperate calls.

"Jesus Christ, guys. . . ." Foster's voice quavered. "Isn't anybody alive?"

Then another voice whimpered, "Frosty . . . they got Wildman. And Creeper. And . . ."

Ted Harris reached out and gently laid his hand on the president's shoulder.

Then Foster shouted through the overhead speakers, "Goddammit! Goddamn that sonofabitch! Stretch, get on my wing and let's kill that bastard!"

The two dots of light closed and turned toward the F-14.

Gaynor lifted the receiver of the red telephone. "Dispatch air/sea rescue," he said softly. The battle staff room sat silent as death.

Logan cranked the scan plane of the AWG-9 radar down to sea level and peered at the screen; suddenly his eyes widened. "Hey, Cholly, I've got a slow mover. I've got a helicopter down there!"

Granger sat up against his harness. "Where?"

"Southeast. About fifty miles. Looks like it's hovering."

"How 'bout a steer?"

"Come left to heading one four five."

The F-14 banked eastward on the mission's final leg.

In the back of the air force security police van, Christy sat struggling against her handcuffs. Beside her, Tod sat staring blankly at the floor. Two security policemen sat opposite, their dull eyes glaring.

She was pleading. "Listen to me! Please! They're trying to stop First Step!"

The van's radio crackled. "Attention all officers and enlisted personnel. Attention. United States forces to DEFCON3. I repeat. United States forces to DEFCON3."

Christy gasped. The two young security policemen eyed each other in alarm. One of them turned up the radio volume.

"This is not a drill. All leaves and furloughs are canceled. All officers and enlisted personnel report to their DEFCON alert stations immediately."

Softly in her throat, Christy said, "My god, they're taking the bait." Then she stood and shouted, "Stop the car! For god's sake, get me to a phone!"

"Shut up!" One of the SPs lashed out with the back of his hand, struck her hard across the face.

The force of the blow flung Christy back against the steel wall of the van; she crumpled to the bare floor, writhing in pain.

Tod lurched at the SP, shouting, "Fucking coward! I'll—"

The other policeman pounded his fist into Tod's stomach, doubling him over.

"Time to target?" Granger said. The Tomcat was making Mach 2.0—thirteen hundred miles an hour.

"Just over two minutes. Fuel?"

Granger tapped the gauges. They registered eleven hundred pounds. With afterburners lit, the Tomcat burned eight hundred pounds a minute. "What fuel?"

He peered out the cockpit window. Thirty thousand feet below, the dark green ocean rolled to the horizon.

In the glass-roofed Winter Garden behind the American mission, Jake and Sara sat over linzertorte and coffee in the bright November sun. Suddenly the lobby door burst open and Jake's secretary, Miss Green, rushed in.

"Doctor Handlesman, forgive me. It's—"

Lieutenant Colonel Robert Wilding came in behind her, following a marine guard who clutched the struggling Mikhail Lermontov by the arm. "Doctor Handlesman, this man insists—"

"I must speak with you!" Lermontov shouted.

Jake stood abruptly. "It's all right, Colonel. Misha, what's the matter?"

Lermontov's hands were shaking so badly he could barely read from the ragged scrap of telex. "American fighter planes engaged in aerial combat off Eleuthera. Four planes destroyed. U.S. strategic forces moving to alert."

"Let me see that!" Jake snatched the telex from his hands and scanned the text. His eyes fixed on the Russian characters that spelled "Eleuthera." Zack Littman was on a yacht somewhere near that island. Abruptly, Jake turned to Sara. "Get confirmation."

"Yes, sir." She went out the door to the mission's communications center.

"What does this mean?" Lermontov gasped.

"It means"—Jake stared at the dispatch, pondering—"that you are just in time for chess."

"They'll open up with Sparrows any time now," Logan said.

"How many left?"

"Just two."

Granger sighed. "Ready with the ECM?"

"I was born ready."

Zack Littman stood in the pitching cabin of the helicopter as Sergeant Wang unhitched the rescue sling. Behind him, marines were helping the aerospace executives, their wives, and the crew of the yacht to buckle their seat belts. In the corner of the cabin Clara held the weeping Louise to her breast.

Wang barked into his headset, "They're aboard! Haul ass!"

Littman looked down one last time at the fantail of the *Odalisque*. Lieutenant Wunderleigh stood below him, shading his eyes against the propwash. Littman touched his brow in a grateful salute. Smartly, Wunderleigh saluted back. The helicopter banked sharply west and the *Odalisque* swung from Littman's view.

Colonel Walsh covered the phone and shouted, "They're aboard the chopper!"

A cheer went up through the battle staff room.

★ ★ ★

At the end of the active runway of Andrews Air Force Base, Vice President Charles O'Donnell stepped through the doorway of Kneecap. Major General Clayton Burns saluted. "Welcome aboard, Mr. Vice President. If you'll follow me. . . ."

He led the way to the National Command Authority suite aft of the cockpit. Behind them a marine guard slammed and locked the door. The pilot released the brakes and the 747 began its takeoff roll.

Foster squinted at the heads-up display above his console. There in the center of the computer projection a tiny rectangle of light marked the dot that was the F-14. The rangefinder ticked to thirty miles.

"He's in range!" Foster shouted through the radio. "Go radar-guided." He moved the cursor to the target; the dull drone in his headset became a shrill electronic whine. "Fox one! Fox one!"

Two white Sparrow missiles dropped from the fuselage of each Eagle. The missiles' motors fired and they roared into the sky ahead.

Abruptly Logan looked up from his scope. "I have three . . . no, four missile tracks."

"What's our time to target?"

"Eighty seconds."

"How long before those missiles get here?"

"I make it . . ." Logan punched his computer; then his voice fell. "They'll be all over us in fifty seconds. Cholly, we're not gonna make it."

The Eagle's missile tracks flashed on the plotting screen in the ADR.

Walsh shouted, "They've fired!"

"At last!" Sam Baker wrung his hands.

"We've got them. By god, we've got them!"

Through the speakers overhead, Foster's voice was breathy with excitement. "Missiles tracking true! We've got 'em, Stretch!"

Logan said, "Four missiles locked on us. ETA forty seconds."

"Time to target?"

"Seventy seconds."

"Listen, Willie," Granger said. "We're tapped out of fuel. We've got four Sparrows on our tail." He half-turned in the seat. "You want out? Or you want to go for it?"

"I can handle the Sparrows, Cholly."

"Willie—"

"I can handle 'em."

Granger hesitated. Then he smiled. "You know, I bet my life you can."

Kneecap climbed through two thousand feet and turned southeast over Chesapeake Bay. Its secret flight plan would take it far out over the Atlantic—far enough from the landmass of the United States to avoid nuclear blast contamination in the event of war.

Behind the flight deck, the National Command Authority briefing room was small and thickly carpeted in beige, the walls a soft sky blue. It might have been a doctor's waiting room, except for the dull drone of the jet engines and the glowing status board and plotting screen.

At the comm console, Sergeant Larry Grimes nodded to General Burns. "JCS on the line, sir."

Burns swiveled his seat to face Vice President O'Donnell. "We can begin the briefing any time you're ready, sir."

O'Donnell shifted uneasily in his chair. In February of 1985—a month after being sworn in as vice president—he had spent a day in Pentagon briefings and taken an orientation flight in Kneecap. Even so, he was not prepared for this flight today; this was the journey he prayed he'd never have to make.

O'Donnell nodded and Grimes punched the button for the overhead speakers.

"This is General Powell at the JCS."

"Colin, what's the situation?" O'Donnell said.

Powell's voice was coolly analytical. "Soviet strategic forces are still on peacetime status. But the NSA is monitoring unusually heavy microwave traffic between Moscow and their National Technical Assessment Center in Tyuratam. Apparently they've begun to pick up signs of our alert and they're trying to figure out what's going on."

O'Donnell looked up at the polar projection of the Northern Hemisphere on the plotting screen at the front of the room. Within the borders of the United States and at military installations in Europe and the Pacific, dozens of white lights were winking on as America's strategic weapons systems moved to alert. Within the borders of the Soviet Union, scattered dots of reddish light began appearing. Off the east and west coasts of the United States tiny asterisks that indicated Soviet ballistic missile submarines glowed deep scarlet.

O'Donnell stared in silence at the plotting screen; on it, he saw the curtain rising on the last act of human history.

The four Sparrows were tiny, speeding points of light on Logan's radar screen. "Twenty seconds to impact."

"Time to target?"

"Fifty seconds."

Sam Baker stood at the window overlooking the ADR, eyes fixed on the plotting screen.

"Yes, sir," Walsh said beside him. "We're gonna get them!"

Logan called, "Fifteen seconds . . ."

Granger's pulse beat in his temples; his hand tightened on the stick.

On the fantail of the *Odalisque*, Lieutenant Wunderleigh turned to the Stinger missile crews. "Prepare to fire!"

Logan said, "Ten seconds to impact. . . ."

Granger raised his head; through the thin, frigid air of the stratosphere, his hunter's ear caught the shrieking frenzy of the missiles' flight.

He sat up against the belts of his harness. "Willie, ECM to radar-guided! Now!"

Logan threw the toggle that switched on the Tomcat's ALQ-165 jamming transmitters. The Eagles were only ten miles aft, guiding the Sparrows by bouncing radar signals off the F-14; at such close quarters, the power of the Tomcat's jammers was immense.

In Foster's cockpit the radar screen of the APG-63 went white. "Jesus Christ! I'm blanking! Stretch? Do you still have him?"

"Frosty! I'm blind!"

The Sparrows broke through the wispy clouds and thundered down on the Tomcat.

Suddenly Granger felt death's talons seize him by the shoulders.

Logan shouted, "Break starboard! Missiles!"

Granger slammed the stick hard right, turned perpendicular to the Sparrows. He shot a glance through the canopy; four white dots were searing straight at them.

Logan shouted, "Chaff!" But Granger had already thumbed the white button on the stick, ejecting eight chaff bundles from the boxes located on the bottom of the Tomcat's tail. Then suddenly he slammed the stick forward and dived.

Gaynor pointed at the plotting screen. "They're on them!"

A sonic shock wave smashed the diving Tomcat downward as the blinded Sparrows thundered past overhead. The proximity fuse of one missile detonated; a foot-long shrapnel rod slammed through the

F-14's port tail fin. The Tomcat skidded as though struck by a gigantic roundhouse blow, spun like a pinwheel. Granger fought the controls.

"Was that a hit?" Sam Baker said.

Foster's voice thundered through the speaker overhead. "Sonofabitch! He's still got power!"

Granger whipped the stick; the Tomcat found itself, rolled out, and leveled. "Need a steer, Willie!"

"Ship bearing zero five five. The chopper's zero seven five—hightailing west. We gotta move!"

"Time to target?"

"Thirty seconds."

"Watch for Sidewinders."

"Wilco." Logan looked back; the Eagles were five miles behind and closing hard.

"Come on, Stretch!" Foster shouted. "Let's finish him with Heaters." He thumbed the launch button twice; two slim white Sidewinders rocketed down the rails, accelerating toward Mach 2.5.

Logan wrenched around in his seat and shouted, "Winders in the air! Five o'clock long."

Granger leaned forward, peered over the heads-up display at the ocean. The fuel gauges were bouncing on empty. They had only seconds of flight time left. Eight miles ahead, he could see the low, white shape of the *Odalisque* and—moving west—the black pinpoint that was the rescue helicopter. "Down to our last out, Willie."

"I'm with you, Cholly."

Granger's voice was crisp, precise. "Keep an eye on those Winders. On your call, I'll pull a loop into their teeth. And lights out. If we get through, we'll take the chopper with RIO rapid lockon. I'll use guns for the yacht." Granger toggled the AWG-9 from PH to SW. "Sidewinders selected." The Tomcat began pumping liquid nitrogen through the rail umbilicals to the seeker heads of the two Sidewinder missiles, supercooling them to hunt the helicopter engines' heat against the sky; even the best infrared missile could only find and hit a jet engine that was burning hard and out of aspect with the sun.

"Testing guns." Granger pulled the trigger on the joystick. Beneath his left foot, the M61A-1 Vulcan six-barrel rotary cannon spun up to speed. Its high-explosive incendiary ammunition chattered through the feedway underneath the console behind Granger's left elbow, and a stream of flame shot from below the left side of the Tomcat's radome.

"Gun's live," Granger said. He squared his oxygen mask against his jaw. Their fuel was almost gone; their time, their lives were running out. "We'll only get one pass, Willie."

"Only used to take one." Logan snapped the AWG-9 to NRL—the mode that slaved the Sidewinders' seeker heads and AWG-9 radar to his joystick. In rapid lockon, the RIO aimed the radar and the missiles' seekers at the target and the pilot pulled the trigger; the two men had to act in perfect unison. There was no room for error. None.

"Winders closing!" Logan said. "Stand by!"

Foster could see the flames of the Sidewinders ahead of him, bearing down on the Tomcat. "Go low, Stretch!" The Eagles slowed and split—one high, one low—to finish the Tomcat off with cannon fire.

On the fantail of the *Odalisque,* the marine crews crouched in readiness. In their helmets, both gunners heard the electronic whine as the Stingers' infrared detectors caught their first scent of the F-14. Beside them, Lieutenant Wunderleigh drew his automatic pistol and chambered a cartridge.

Half a mile behind the Tomcat, the four Sidewinder missiles thundered through the clouds, broke clear and steered screaming toward the heat of the F-14's exhausts.

Logan shouted, "Cholly! Break turn! Port!"

"Hang on!"

Granger slapped the stick hard left, stabbed the Tomcat's nose directly at the sun. Then he pulled back hard—pulled the plane over on its back in a 9-G loop. The force drove him down into the ejection seat; the G-suit around his legs and torso swelled until he couldn't breathe. Through the tremendous G-force, Granger groped forward until he caught the red-and-white striped levers of the twin fuel cutoffs. He yanked them hard. Instantly, the F-14's twin turbofans flamed out, went dark.

The Tomcat seemed to hang in silence, as though time itself had stopped.

Then the four Sidewinders thundered past with a sonic boom that shook the Tomcat to its rivets, screamed past and jinked hard toward the heat of the sun.

Logan shouted, "Jesus Christ! Cholly! You did it!"

"Goddamn him!" Foster screamed through the overhead speakers in the ADR. "The sonofabitch flew right through the salvo!"

Walsh shouted, "God in heaven. NO!"

Quickly—before the Tomcat lost all hydraulic pressure—Granger hit the air start for the port engine, snapped the stick hard left. The turbofan coughed and lit; the F-14 surged downward, tumbling wildly through the air, over and over like a leaf in a whirlwind.

Foster threw his Eagle into a dive, pinned the helpless Tomcat under the reticle of his cannon sight. "I got him, Stretch! I got him!"

Suddenly the other Eagle shot through his field of vision. "He's mine, Frosty!"

"Stretch! Look out!"

Foster slammed his stick right, jinked hard as his wingman dived left to avoid a midair collision. At eleven hundred miles an hour, the Eagles careened past the plunging Tomcat before they could fire.

"Goddammit, Stretch! He's getting away!" Foster swung into a desperate 9-G turn, but at Mach 1.6 the Eagles' turn radius was almost four miles.

In the battle staff room of the White House, men stood rigid at their places.

In the cockpit of the tumbling F-14, Granger toggled the air start compressor to the starboard engine. Beyond the canopy, the world was spinning madly end-over-end; sky and sea whirling together in a blur of blue and green. It was as though the Tomcat had flown beyond the bounds of earth, had broken through existence into pandemonium. Cholly Granger looked into the whirling chaos, and he recognized the place.

He had returned for one last moment to that battlefield where there was neither up nor down nor earth nor sky, to the field of glory of his childhood's dreams, to the place where he and his Tomcat were supreme—the eternal jungle of the hunter's heart.

He wrenched the stick back and shouted, "The chopper, Willie! Get the chopper!"

The sea and sky and sun whirled past the canopy in one long streak of blue and white. But Willie Logan saw only the AWG-9 screen before him. He nailed his joystick to the blip that was the helicopter and shouted, "Cholly! Shoot!"

Granger pulled the trigger twice. The slim Sidewinders' engines fired, slamming the missiles off their launch rails; they heeled hard to starboard and rocketed after their prey, their seeker heads already locked on the heat of the helicopter's turbines.

Logan shouted, "Op away! Cholly! The boat!"

"I don't believe it!" Foster shouted through the speakers in the ADR. "He rolled through the salvo! Pulled an Immelmann out of a spin! And shot two Winders at the chopper on his back!"

Then he screamed, "WHO ARE THESE FUCKING GUYS!"
Sam Baker gasped in terror.

On the fantail of the *Odalisque* Lieutenant Wunderleigh tensed as
the F-14 came screaming down out of the sky. Then his hand holding
the pistol shot forward. "There he is! Fire! Fire!" He pulled the trigger
until the pistol's magazine was empty.

On blasts of flame that seared the lacquer of the fantail decking, the
Stinger missiles roared away.

Granger saw the flash of their launch through the glass of the
heads-up display. He could see the *Odalisque* rushing toward the
aiming reticle of the Vulcan cannon as the Tomcat bore down, accelerating toward six hundred miles an hour. Somewhere behind him,
he knew the Eagles were swinging back onto his tail, searching desperately for him in their gunsights.

Granger's eyes narrowed; his finger tightened on the trigger. The
black dots of the Stingers wobbled toward the Tomcat against the
open sky. His only chance to avoid the missiles was to break off the
attack, dive past them toward the sea.

But he held the Tomcat steady in her dive, held the *Odalisque* under
the Vulcan's reticle and squeezed the trigger hard. A hot stream of
high explosive shells and tracers spewed from the cannon, chopping
huge plumes of water across the ocean surface. When they intersected
the yacht, the explosions shattered wood and glass and bodies, disintegrating everything before them.

The Stingers jinked one last time and closed. Behind the Tomcat,
the Eagles opened fire with their cannon.

"Incoming! Willie—"

"I'm with you, Cholly!"

The Tomcat disintegrated in a searing ball of gas and shrapnel as
the two Stingers detonated.

The *Odalisque* erupted in an enormous fireball as the high explosive
shells ripped through her diesel fuel tanks.

The flash of that explosion caught Zack Littman's eye; he glanced
out the side window of the helicopter in time to see the Sidewinders
screaming in at seventeen hundred miles an hour. He shouted,
"The—" Then two Sidewinder hits enveloped the helicopter in a globe
of flame that vaporized his throat and lungs with superheated air.

A huge burst of orange light lit the plotting screen in the ADR. Sam
Baker and the battle staff fell back as though slapped. In the half-light
that followed, the men cowered in their chairs.

The Zulu clock winked to 1330. It was 8:30 A.M. in Washington, 2:30 P.M. in Geneva.

The Tomcat's mission was accomplished.

"In five . . . four . . ."

Tom Brokaw pushed his tie knot tight, straightened his blazer jacket, and settled himself in his chair; the NBC News flash desk hid his blue jeans and sneakers.

"Three . . . two . . ." The TelePrompTer began to roll.

> BROKAW
> This is Tom Brokaw with an NBC News Special
> Report. A few moments ago, a Pentagon spokes-
> man confirmed that interceptors had scrambled
> from Homestead Air Force Base in Florida to turn
> back a navy defector attempting to fly a stolen
> fighter plane to Cuba.

In the National Command Authority briefing room aboard Knee-cap, General Powell's voice crackled through the overhead speaker. "Mr. Vice President, NSA intercepts and satellite projections indicate Soviet strategic forces are now moving to alert status. Under standing orders, we're required to move to DEFCON2."

O'Donnell's hands tightened on the arms of his chair. He turned to General Burns. "Get me the president."

> Some analysts suggest the theft of the navy fighter
> may be linked to the assassination of Senator
> Simon Whitworth and that both crimes are the
> actions of a military conspiracy determined to un-
> dermine President Baker's First Step disarma-
> ment initiative.

Slowly, the men in the ADR straightened in their chairs. Sam Baker said, "May I have an assessment, please."

General Gaynor stepped to the comm console and picked up the microphone. "This is General Gaynor calling the leader of the Homestead interceptor flight."

A voice crackled through the speakers overhead. "Captain Bret Foster, sir."

"Report, Captain."

There was silence. Then, softly, Foster's voice said, "Target destroyed. Four of ours down."

"The helicopter?"

Foster banked his Eagle right. A small, floating gasoline fire and steaming debris were all that marked the place where the helicopter had gone down. "Two missile hits. Disintegrated."

"And the yacht?"

"Cannon fire. Blown up. Nothing left but toothpicks."

Gaynor took a breath. "Survivors?"

Foster wiped his eyes; there were tears in them. "Negative."

Gaynor snapped off the radio. The battle staff room sat in silence.

Beside the command console, Sam Baker slouched in his chair and let the sense of loss envelop him; Zack Littman was dead, as were his wife, his child, his friends. Simon Whitworth and Margaret were dead as well. The nation would be a long time mourning those it had lost today.

Then beyond Sam Baker's sadness, a darker apprehension stirred. Whitworth and Littman were statesmen—seasoned, sober, and pragmatic. And they *were* patriots. Yet Whitworth was prepared to lay down his political life to oppose First Step, and Zack Littman had thrown his career, his future, even his honor to the wind by the treason of Hakodate. Clearly, these were desperate acts of last resort.

And what of the suicidal missions of Whitworth's lone assassin and the men in the stolen fighter plane? What motive lay behind them? A veteran air force lieutenant colonel and two navy war heroes—men of proven loyalty and valor—who went to their deaths without a word of explanation, apology, or protest as if their sacrifice were some sort of duty.

But duty toward what?

The red phone rang; Sam Baker shrugged off the reverie and lifted the receiver. "This is the president."

"Sam, it's Charlie. I'm in Kneecap. The Soviets are moving to alert. Our standing orders call for DEFCON2."

"NO!" Sam Baker roared. "This insanity has gone far enough! Charlie, you telex Soviet Supreme Command on the hotline. Right now! Tell them exactly what's happening. Then stand by." He hung up and turned to Gaynor. "General, make telephone contact with President Gorbachev in Moscow." Gaynor signaled to the sergeant at the comm console.

A marine guard knocked at the battle staff room door. "Mr. President, Press Secretary Fowler called. NBC News is reporting that these attacks are the actions of a military conspiracy."

Sam Baker looked to Walsh. "Can we see that down here?"

A sergeant at the video display console punched NBC up on one of the monitors. Tom Brokaw sat at the flash news desk.

> . . . but why the military conspiracy should have begun with the murder of Simon Whitworth, a staunch opponent of First Step, remains an unexplained mystery.

"Sonofabitch!" Harris grabbed the phone. "Get me Mike Marden at NBC News in New York. Tell his secretary I want him on this phone this goddamn minute!"

Gaynor stepped around Harris's back for a better view of the monitor; as he did, he bumped the command console. He looked down.

His yellow pad lay where he had left it beside the phone.

He snatched it up. "Mr. President, we believe we have the names of the conspirators."

All heads turned to Gaynor.

"We've got one of their accomplices in custody now. Her name is Lieutenant M. C. Russoff. She says their objective is to stop First Step."

Sam Baker looked to Harris; it was as they had feared.

Two security policemen dragged Christy up the narrow path toward the Andrews detention facility. Her right eye was swollen and closing where the SP had struck her. Behind her, two SPs dragged Tod, handcuffed and doubled over.

Sam Baker handed the list of conspirators back to Gaynor. "All right, General. Follow procedure." He turned to the sergeant at the comm console. "Where's that call to Moscow?"

"Sir, President Gorbachev has left the city. Soviet Stavka Command is trying to patch us through."

"Tell them to hurry, dammit!"

Gaynor handed the list of conspirators to Walsh. "Call the OSI. Tell them—"

"My god!" Walsh stabbed his finger at a name on the yellow page. "That's Tom O'Neill!"

"Who?"

"The communications officer! For god's sake—he's down there in the ADR!"

"*What?* Call the guard! Arrest him! Do it now!"

Walsh rushed from the room.

Harris growled into the phone, "Mike? That you?"

Mike Marden stood at his desk on the third floor of 30 Rockefeller Center, holding a sheaf of faxes. At the conference table near the windows, the editorial board of NBC News was assembled, sifting through sheaves of wire service bulletins. Staffers from the telex room dashed in and out with fresh dispatches.

"Yeah, it's me. What the hell is going on?"

"Never mind what's going on! Dammit, Brokaw's going to scare the shit out of the country with that crap about a military conspiracy! Get him off the air! And keep him off until I call you again!"

"Like hell I will! We've got sources that say two Vietnam veterans stole a fighter. And they're trying to kill the Secretary of Defense."

Harris snapped, "No comment."

"They're telling me these military maneuvers are no drill." A staffer thrust a slip of paper into Marden's hand. He scanned it and gasped. "U.S. forces ordered to Defense Condition 3 . . . armed SAC bombers in runway roll out . . . Peacekeeper missile bases sealed . . . ?" Then he shouted, "Ted, for chrissake! Are we going to war?"

Harris slammed the phone down.

Abruptly the door to the battle staff room opened. Lieutenant General Hawley Taylor, an army three-star, entered, went directly to the president, and braced. "Mr. President, our military forces are at DEF-CON3. Under emergency war orders, you are required to accompany me to the National Military Command Center without delay."

Sam Baker turned to the comm console. "Not until I get that call to Moscow!"

Outside the battle staff room, Walsh and a squad of marine guards with drawn sidearms hustled down the steps to the ADR. They moved quickly into the communications center and surrounded O'Neill.

"Colonel O'Neill," Walsh said sharply. "You are under arrest. The charge is treason."

Slowly O'Neill rose to face them.

"Tom?" Behind the anger, there was pain in Walsh's eyes. "Tom, are you part of it?"

O'Neill hesitated.

"We've got all the names, Tom. Will you just tell me why?"

O'Neill glanced at the Zulu clock; it was just coming up on 1335— 8:35 A.M. "For the same reason we both put on these uniforms." Then he crossed himself.

The sergeant at the comm console called out, "Mr. President, ready with your call to President Gorbachev."

Sam Baker grabbed the receiver. "Mikhail. Thank god! Something terrible has—"

The president broke off and raised his eyes. The room was filled with a bright golden glare. Then the windows of the battle staff room seemed to flex inward, bent like bubbles toward him. Beyond them in the ADR, a globe of light expanded like a newborn sun.

Sam Baker thought, *Curious . . .*

Then the force of the explosion smashed him headlong back against the wall.

On the comm panel in the National Command Authority briefing room aboard Kneecap, the red light for the voice/data link to the White House air defense room winked out. Sergeant Grimes toggled in the backup circuit; the light remained dark. He punched the intercom to the specialist in the communications center aft. "I have no light for the ADR. I say again—no light for the ADR."

And the specialist crackled back, "They're off the air!" Grimes looked to Burns.

"Mr. Vice President," General Burns said—and he understood the significance of his words—"we've lost contact with the White House Air Defense Room."

In that moment, Charlie O'Donnell had become Commander in Chief of the armed forces of the United States.

The picture of Tom Brokaw cut to a live shot of the rear steps of the Russell Building. Behind the yellow police barricades, stunned bystanders and eager news crews jostled for a better view of the coroner's men closing body bags.

> In Washington, officials of both parties have expressed shock and outrage at the brutal assassination of Senator Simon Whitworth and his wife. . . .

West across the Capitol Mall, a gardener hosed blood off the grass where Lieutenant Colonel Harding had fallen.

> And speculation is mounting that these bizarre attacks may be a coordinated offensive by dissident officers. . . .

At the Bolling officers' club, a janitor finished sweeping the wood chips from the shattered billiard room door. Before he put his broom away, he picked up the framed *Pravda* clipping and hung it back in its place on the wall.

> And, despite denials from Pentagon sources, NBC News has learned that the ringleaders of this conspiracy may be a group of embittered Vietnam veterans.

The soft morning light through the billiard room windows glazed the yellowed photograph. The seven ragged prisoners were barely recognizable as American servicemen: Petrovsky, Harding, O'Neill, and Watkins bore the litter on which Logan lay. Granger stood beside him.

Behind them stood a seventh man—tall and fair—with haunted, vacant eyes. He had once been a strong man; his hands were still large. But his flesh hung from his bones. He had a look of death about him. He looked like a man capable of passion—and revenge.

> In a related incident, NBC News has learned that an air force lieutenant and master sergeant have been arrested and charged with the murder of an intelligence analyst found dead this morning in her quarters at Washington's Bolling Air Force Base. The two alleged killers are being held without bail under military law, firing speculation that they may be the first of many conspirators to be arrested.

As the guards dragged Tod and Christy toward the Andrews detention cells, she struggled, shouted, "For god's sake, listen to me! It's a conspiracy! They're trying to—" She broke off, went rigid.

At the entrance to the cell block, Sergeant Jeeter stood gloating.

"Him!" Christy screamed. "He's part of it!"

Jeeter laughed and nodded to two waiting policewomen; they seized Christy's arms. Then Jeeter waved the SPs hauling Tod to the right and Christy realized they were being separated. "Wait! He's innocent! Leave him alone! Tod!"

The policewomen turned Christy toward an open cell. She looked around in panic. "Stop! Where are you taking me?"

They dragged her through the door and out of the light.

> Secretary of Defense Zack Littman, on a "working vacation" off Eleuthera, remained unavailable for comment.

Captain Bret Foster banked his Eagle and stared down through the canopy at the smoky gasoline fires burning on the softly rolling Caribbean. There was no sign of life; only death and an unsounded sea.

> And Vice President O'Donnell's office will not confirm reports that he left the Capitol aboard a military helicopter for a secret destination.

"JCS on the line," Grimes said.

General Powell's voice crackled through the overhead speakers in Kneecap's National Command Authority briefing room. "Mr. Vice President, White House security reports a high-explosive detonation in the air defense room. Marine rescue teams are on their way down to seek survivors."

O'Donnell stiffened. He looked at General Burns, but Burns's eyes showed no emotion. *Are they all like this?* O'Donnell wondered. *Professional stoics? Was that the mark of the thermonuclear warrior?*

"All right, Colin," O'Donnell said. "What's your recommendation?"

"Until we know if the president—" Powell broke off and his tone changed. "Until we reestablish contact with the president, the Joint Chiefs recommend United States strategic forces move to DEFCON2 as a precaution."

O'Donnell hesitated. Beyond DEFCON2, there was only one higher level of alert.

At DEFCON1, they would be in a shooting war.

"Mr. Vice President," Powell said. "Only you can give the order."

Charlie O'Donnell slouched in his chair. "DEFCON2," he said.

> Pentagon sources have told NBC News that the so-called military conspiracy—if it exists—poses no threat whatsoever to national security.

In the devastation of the White House ADR, the only sound in the darkness was the dull crackle of flickering fires and the sizzle of electric circuits shorting out. On the front wall of the room, beyond the debris of overturned desks, shattered computer consoles, and fallen bodies, the status board glowed through the pall of swirling dust. Silently, unseen by men, the DEFCON panel momentarily went dark and then gleamed the code words for DEFCON2:

SUN RISE

On Guam, the voice of Andersen base radio crackled through the night. "Charlie flight, you are cleared for takeoff at 1336 Zulu. I say again—Charlie flight, you are cleared for takeoff. This is not a drill."

In the lead B-52H, copilot Captain Eddie Foyle took the chewing gum out of his mouth and turned to Major Marvin Cutler. "Did I hear right? Not a drill?"

"You heard." Cutler put his gloved hand on the throttles. Foyle covered it with his own. "Let's go to Russia, Eddie."

Together, they pressed the bomber's eight jet engines forward to one hundred percent power. Cutler slipped the brakes; like rolling thunder, the flight of bombers began its deadly journey north.

> Meanwhile, there are unconfirmed reports that U.S. strategic forces are involved in massive maneuvers.

On CVN-69 *Eisenhower,* 110 miles west of Messina in the Ionian Sea, a red light began flashing above the weapons vault door. The electronic screws whined, drawing the heavy bolts, and the blast doors swung slowly open. A wave of freezing air washed over the weapons crews outside. Inside, bright fluorescent lights blinked on, bathing the thermonuclear cruise missiles in an unearthly glow.

At Launch Control Center T sixty feet beneath the frozen Wyoming plains, Captain Thompson barked, "On my command . . . enable. Now." Simultaneously, she and Lieutenant Kranz toggled down the switches that armed the chemical packets in the baseplates under the engines of the Peacekeeper missiles—the cold-launch devices that would pop the missiles from their silos before their engines fired.

On the foredeck of CG-50 *Valley Forge* in the Sea of Japan west of Sado-shima Island, two steel flaps dropped with a deafening clang, and the armored box launcher amidships pivoted to starboard. Computers in the battle room began streaming the data that would vector the first four TLAM-N nuclear cruise missiles to their targets in Amur Oblast on the Soviet mainland.

> A Pentagon spokesman has characterized the maneuvers as "a routine exercise in preparedness—"

Just then, the lead FB-111A from RAF Lakenheath crossed the North Sea coastline at Sheringham. Captain Jerry Simon tapped the intercom. "Descending to three hundred feet. On my command, begin arming sequence for eight AGM-69A SRAM nuclear missiles."

Beside him, weapons systems officer Lieutenant Brian Park flipped to the first page of his checklist.

> —but independent sources have told NBC News these exercises are "global and total—a maximum effort."

In the quiet, sequestered Winter Garden of the American mission, Jake and Mikhail Lermontov sat across a chessboard. Major Sara Weatherby entered; Jake waved her to their corner. "Well, Major? What's the report?"

Sara looked at Lermontov and hesitated.

"Out with it, Major! What's happened?"

"Sir, Secretary Littman is dead. Killed in a rocket attack by a United States Navy fighter plane."

"What?" Jake scrambled to his feet. The chessboard tipped; the chessmen clattered to the marble floor and lay about his feet, two armies in disarray—two strategies shattered.

Tom Brokaw looked up as the stage manager stepped on to the set and handed him a sheet of telex paper. Brokaw began to read the text aloud, then stumbled over the words.

> This just handed me. Radio Cuba . . . excuse me . . . Radio Cuba reports that . . . American fighter planes . . . have . . . have been shot down in combat off the Caribbean island of Eleuthera.

In the missile operations center of SSBN-726 *Ohio,* Rear Admiral Harry Beame and Captain Wellesley stood, each with his key in the lock mechanism that enabled the submarine's twenty-four Trident missiles. In the gangway outside the bolted hatch, Chaplain Lieutenant Mark Klastorin knelt, murmuring the Lord's Prayer.

Sergeant Jeeter looked on, leering, as Christy struggled with the policewomen. "Hold still, squint-eyes. They're gonna give ya a medal."

"Please!" Christy shouted. "He's one of them! He was here last night! He—"

One of the women began unbuttoning Christy's jacket; the other began slipping on a pair of rubber surgical gloves, and Christy realized she was going to be strip-searched. "No! Take your hands off me! Don't touch me!"

The woman tore her jacket open.

"NO!"

But the more Christy struggled, the more fiercely the two policewomen tore away her clothes. She screamed, "God! GOD!"

When they were done violating her, she dropped to her knees on the concrete floor, her underwear in tatters.

Colonel Steven Petrovsky stood holding a handful of lilies. About him lay a peaceful, sunlit grove. His face was calm and thoughtful. Above him, a gentle breeze whispered among the bare branches. He bent and tenderly laid the lilies on the browned grass that covered the grave. It might have been any grave in a row that was one of many, many rows rolling softly down the wintry hills of Arlington National Cemetery. Petrovsky drew himself up, stood to attention. He raised his hand to the brim of his hat, saluting the dead of wars that were, of battle joined, of desperate hours yet to come.

Naked and bruised, her face streaked with tears, Christy huddled on the concrete floor at Sergeant Jeeter's feet. He flung a dirty prison smock at her and turned for the door. Christy clutched it to her bosom. "Please . . . listen to me. . . ." She gasped through the pain. "They're all in on it: Bryan . . . Petrovsky . . . Harding . . . O'Neill. . . ." Christy stiffened. "O'Neill?"

Then the realization rolled over her like the cold, green sea.

"NO!" She scrambled to her feet as Jeeter slammed the door. She rushed to the bars, grabbed them, and screamed, "They're going to kill the president!"

★ ★ ★

In a cell at the far end of the detention block, Tod sat on an unmade bunk, hands cuffed behind him. Two security police stood over him.
"Look, guys, I haven't done anything. I'm innocent. I—"
They moved toward him.

On the warm waters of Exuma Sound, the debris of the Tomcat, the helicopter, and the *Odalisque* drifted together on the soft swells—a life preserver, a Raggedy Ann, a military cap. Two F-15 Eagles swept low over the water, dragging their flaps as airbrakes—two mournful birds searching for their lost young.

Three thousand feet above Guam's Tumon Bay, the three B-52Hs of Charlie flight from Andersen Air Force Base climbed northwest over the endless dark Pacific. The bombers were eighty-six minutes from their rendezvous with the KC-135 Stratotankers from Kadena Air Force Base on Okinawa.
They were 143 minutes from fail-safe.
And their AGM-86B nuclear cruise missiles were two hundred minutes from their targets at Vladivostok and the headquarters of the Soviet Pacific Fleet.

In the National Command Authority briefing room aboard Knee-cap, Vice President Charlie O'Donnell sat in silence as the 747 turned southeast over the open Atlantic; sliding shafts of sunlight through the windows played across his haggard face.

In Arlington National Cemetery—among the endless rows of silent crosses—a handful of lilies lay upon a single grave. They were pale flowers—delicate and sad—not even a dozen. Only seven.

The United Express twin-engined turboprop rumbled down the runway of Dulles Airport and nosed gently upward into the chilly morning air. Colonel Steven Petrovsky looked out the window and watched the cold, brown landscape of Virginia fall away until the trees and streets and houses became a toy world of infinitesimal beings like some animated picture in a vast computer game. Then the plane banked south and the winter sun raked his gentle blue eyes shut.

Christy sat huddled in a corner of the detention cell. A bright pattern of sunlight through the prison bars lay soft across her shoulders. Slowly, she extended her hands palms upward into the rectangle of light. Then she looked toward the window—stared straight into the sun. Her arms and legs were battered, skinned to bleeding; her right eye was blackened, swollen closed. But her left eye gleamed defiance.

She was captured.

But she was not defeated.

A breeze stirred the lilies. They scattered before the wind.

PRISONERS OF WAR

Executive Order 10631
Every member of the armed forces of the
United States is expected to measure up to the
standards embodied in this Code of Conduct
while he is in captivity. To ensure achievement
of these standards, each member of the armed
forces liable to capture shall be provided with
specific training and instruction designed to
better equip him to counter and withstand all
enemy efforts against him.

DWIGHT D. EISENHOWER
THE WHITE HOUSE,
AUGUST 17, 1955

CODE OF CONDUCT FOR MEMBERS OF THE UNITED STATES ARMED FORCES

I

I am an American fighting man. I serve in the forces which guard my country and our way of life. I am prepared to give my life in their defense.

II

I will never surrender of my own free will. If in command I will never surrender my men while they still have the means to resist.

III

If I am captured I will continue to resist by all means available. I will make every effort to escape and aid others to escape. I will accept neither parole nor special favors from the enemy.

IV

If I become a prisoner of war, I will keep faith with my fellow prisoners. I will give no information or take part in any action which might be harmful to my comrades. If I am senior, I will take command. If not, I will obey the lawful orders of those appointed over me and will back them up in every way.

V

When questioned, should I become a prisoner of war, I am required to give my name, rank, service number, and date of birth. I will evade answering further questions to the utmost of my ability. I will make no oral or written statements disloyal to my country and its allies or harmful to their cause.

VI

I will never forget that I am an American fighting man, responsible for my actions, and dedicated to the principles which made my country free. I will trust in my God and in the United States of America.

ANDREWS AFB, CAMP SPRINGS, MD

8:38 A.M. The scream of turbofans was deafening. The taxiways were jammed. One by one, at twenty-second intervals, the transport planes and interceptors of the Andrews squadrons roared down the runways, fleeing to their emergency dispersal points. With each take-off, the cinder-block walls of the detention facility trembled. But in cell #6 Christy didn't hear the roar or feel the tremors; she sat on the bare mattress of the prison cot, knees drawn up and clutched against her bosom, eyes fixed on the concrete floor.

A single shaft of sunlight descended through the barred window in the door; Christy stared at the trapezoidal pattern it threw beside the bed. It was an intricate pattern crosscut by the shadows of bars and wire. It was a framework.

Her body ached. Her right cheek throbbed, her knees and elbows stung; she burned inside where the policewomen had invaded her. But she ignored her injuries. Her consciousness was groping through four dimensions of strategic thought, hunting the framework of Bryan's plan. Bryan had taught her the disciplines and Christy clung to them against the pain.

What did she know in fact? A navy fighter had been hijacked— apparently to Cuba. Senator Whitworth was dead—perhaps the president as well. The radio in the SP van had announced United States strategic forces were ordered to DEFCON3; by now, the Soviets must also be on alert. And Colonel Petrovsky had told her it would be over by eleven o'clock—two hours and twenty-two minutes from now.

That was all she knew, but it was not all the information she had.

What was it safe to surmise? That Bryan's objective was to stop First Step seemed clear enough; if there was a plot to kill the president and if it succeeded, First Step might die with him. But . . .

Then why kill a senator who opposed the initiative?

And what was the mission of the hijacked F-14?

Those were questions she couldn't answer.

Any strategy can be defeated. But, to be defeated, it had to be known. Christy knew she had two pegs of the framework—Whitworth and the president. But without at least one more she could not triangulate the whole, could not discern the master plan, and Bryan's strategy remained enigmatic, cloaked in stealth and cunning.

Know your enemy; know how he will react. That was the key to tactical victory, and Bryan knew Christy well. Now she understood that last night's dangled mystery had been a trap, irresistible to an Intel officer, elegant and titillating, almost a seduction: O'Neill's visit, Petrovsky's order, the midnight errand, the coded password and compartmented information, the hints, the whispers of sedition. All the while Christy thought she was tearing through a web of camouflage, Bryan had been leading her. And from the moment Christy discovered the body of Polly Kulikov, the more she tried to help the air force, the more her superiors suspected her. Bryan had contrived to snare Christy between her sense of duty and the innate suspicion of the military mind.

But why? How could the arrest and detention of a female first lieutenant—a lowly intelligence clerk—figure in Bryan's awesome strategy?

And why had Bryan sent the E-mail message and revealed the identity of the master criminal behind the conspiracy? To taunt Christy?

Or—perhaps—to challenge her?

Know your place in battle. That was every soldier's obligation. But how could Christy find her own? She was imprisoned—suspected of murder and treason. While she languished in an eight-by-twelve-foot cell, the conspiracy drove relentlessly toward its objective. Somewhere in the world Bryan was methodically turning up one card after another, a single player in a showdown against the government of the United States.

It was inconceivable—one officer challenging the most prodigious military power in the world. It was impossible.

But it was happening.

And who but Bryan would dare defy such an adversary?

Christy remembered the day Bryan had handed back her thesis on the Cuban missile crisis of 1962—"Disinformation as Deterrent: A Case Study in Fear"—with the word "Outstanding" printed across the cover page.

"You're good, Christy."

"I want to be as good as you."

A wry smile had bent Bryan's mouth. "A student who does not surpass her master fails her master."

Now as Christy sat shivering in the drafty detention cell, her heartbeat quickened. *That* was why Bryan had sent the E-mail message; so Christy would know who had imprisoned her, isolated her, stripped her of every weapon but her intelligence; so she would understand her place in battle was here—in this detention cell—in the place where all armed struggles were won and lost before they were fought.

In the infinite theater of war that was the human mind.

The E-mail message had been a battle cry—a call to combat in the greatest war game of them all. Christy felt her face flush, felt her skin begin to tingle.

It was *not* Bryan against the United States of America.

It was Bryan against *her.* Mind against mind.

30 ROCKEFELLER PLAZA, NEW YORK CITY

8:39 A.M.   Mike Marden stood atop a desk in the center of the third-floor news room; he was in a fury. About him, the NBC News staff—producers, researchers, clerks—clustered, tense and silent; men and women sniffled, dabbed their eyes with handkerchiefs.

"The murders of Whitworth and Littman are part of some monstrous conspiracy!" Marden shouted. "The government's hiding something so big it's shut down every source we've got." He raised an angry finger, jabbed out his orders. "Call in every marker. Squeeze every source. Pay any price—but get it! GET IT! This could be the biggest story ever."

John Chancellor sighed. "Or the last story ever. . . ."

The hall door burst open and a messenger from communications rushed in, waving a sheet of telex paper and screaming, "They've bombed the White House!"

Chaos.

WHITE HOUSE AIR DEFENSE ROOM, WASHINGTON

8:40 A.M.   Sam Baker was the last to realize he was alive.

Under the pall of swirling smoke—by the sputtering flashes of electrical fires—the ADR was a black nightmare of rubble and bodies, an image out of primal chaos. At the front of the room, unseen by men, the charred status board glowed with the code words for DEF-CON2—

—and the awesome strategic might of the United States took shape on the scorched canvas of the plotting screen.

In the elevated battle staff room, chairs and desks lay overturned, consoles upended, radar screens imploded. A smooth blanket of gray ash covered men and machines; they looked like castings of the dead from the buried city of Pompeii. Then the silence was cut by the shriek of smoke detectors and the thud of emergency ventilators kicking in. The backup lighting circuits switched on, bathing the room in dusky orange light.

At the end of the elevator hallway the fire alarm sounded. The overhead sprinklers hissed to life, tapping fingerprints in the dust. One of the bodies twitched and moaned; slowly, painfully, others began to shift, roused by the falling water. The men groaned softly, coughed against the taste of grit in their mouths. General Hawley Taylor, the army three-star, shivered and groped for his right knee; the broken bone of his femur poked a red gash through his trousers and the trickle of black blood slid down his dusty pant leg like a snake.

Coughing and hacking, General Gaynor struggled to his hands and knees. Then he realized what had happened and his duty came back to him and he wheezed, "Mr. President . . . ?"

The sound of his voice roused Ted Harris. He rolled over, spitting phlegm. Dust coated his lashes and crew-cut hair; his eyes burned with the harsh rasp of concrete. He pushed himself into a sitting position against the wall, let the falling water from the sprinklers stream down his face, wiped his eyes, and blinked them open. "Was that . . . a bomb?" Then he remembered the president. "Sam? Sam! Where are you?" He scrabbled through the damp debris ignoring the splinters that cut his knees and palms, and picked among the fallen bodies, searching for the president.

Gaynor staggered to his feet and leaned back against the wall for balance.

"You see him?"

"No." Then Harris did. "Dear god—"

Under the dust and shards of broken glass, Sam Baker lay face down, his knees pulled up against his chest, his body curled like a sleeping child's. Harris crouched beside him, laid his hand on the president's head, and gently brushed his hair.

"Wait! Don't turn him over." Gaynor stooped, knelt at the president's side. "Is he . . . breathing?"

Harris leaned an ear close to the president's face. "I think . . . yes!" Then he whispered, "Sam? Sam, can you hear me?"

No. Sam Baker could not hear him. He was far out of earshot of the battle staff room of the White House ADR.

He was standing in a shady grove where the wintry sunshine descended through a ring of maples to form a yellow oval on the grass. He was staring out across soft rolling hills, listening to the November breezes moving in the treetops. Six men were standing at attention before him. Sam Baker did not recognize them, could not make out the names stenciled above the right breast of their flight suits. They had grave faces—the severe and fearless faces troops always wore at a presidential review. Sam Baker was surprised the men had dared appear so unkempt before the Commander in Chief.

There were jagged rents in the fabric of their flight suits, as though the cloth had been punctured by shrapnel. Beneath the gashes were purple flowing stains, as though their blood had run and dried. Sam Baker stared at the stigmata and wondered why he—the president of the United States—was standing in that meadow. There was no Ted Harris at his elbow, no rostrum, no clique of dignitaries, no Secret Service men, no color guard, no band, no crowd, no television crews— none of the honors due him as head of state. It wasn't seemly. It wasn't suitable. He was *the president;* why should he review six disheveled servicemen without the ceremony proper to his office? He snorted and turned to walk away.

Then somewhere in the distance a single drumbeat fell.

Sam Baker stopped and listened. But there was only silence—not even the song of birds. He took another step.

The drumbeat tolled again.

He turned and glared. It was some kind of trick and he had grown impatient. "What's the meaning of this?" he demanded.

The six stood silent.

"I have no time for nonsense." Again he turned to walk away.

It was then he heard the muffled sound, the slow beat dead-march cadence of the drums.

He stopped and raised his eyes. And then the banners broke the line of hills above him. He could see the withered flags, the tattered battle ribbons. He could hear the soft thud of ten thousand feet in lockstep coming down.

He squinted. One by one, he recognized them: the Second Pennsylvania, Fourth Georgia, Seventy-seventh New York Volunteers and First Virginia—their muskets clattering and sabers gleaming. Down they came from four horizons—musketeers and fusilleers, dragoons and skirmishers and scouts in buckskin. Down they marched into the valley where he stood, the thousands stretching to the limits of his sight, phalanxes of blue and gray, the officers bolt upright in their saddles, the caissons draped in black.

Then Sam Baker remembered: it was Veterans Day.

Without command or sign or signal, they gathered, found their places, stood to attention in corps upon corps, in column rows and ranks. Sam Baker straightened, prepared to greet them.

And then he realized they had not come to honor him, but to welcome six new arrivals. It had been 125 years since American soldiers had died in combat against their own.

It had been 125 years since an American president had ordered fratricide.

The dead march ceased.

All was still.

Then, softly, it began to rain. The tattoo of droplets trickled down Sam Baker's face. It trickled down the battle pennants, glistened on the bayonets and on the young men's beards. The beat of raindrops seemed to whisper Shiloh. And Antietam. Gettysburg and Chancellorsville.

Sam Baker blinked against the falling droplets, squinted at the multitude. Before him stretched two armies who had faced each other across battlefields of hate and blood—who had inflicted on the nation more slaughter than all its other wars combined. It struck him strange to see the Blue and Gray assembled in one grand parade of death. Yet they stood together now as brothers.

He looked at the six men standing before him. Four were young air force officers; two were older and their insignia were navy. Surely they should not stand together. But they did, as if some unseen bond united them.

The dead stood waiting. And Sam Baker realized it was time for him to speak the invocation. But he was not prepared . . . he had no script before him . . . he could not think of what to say.

He thought of Lincoln and he wished to cry out, "I'm no Lincoln!"

But before he could, a commanding voice thundered, "Pre-sent h'arms!"

The legions braced, their muskets held before their bodies. The six men in flight suits saluted.

Sam Baker let his eyes wander across the armies of the dead and understood. So this was why they had summoned him; this was their message: death settled all debate.

All patriots were one beyond the grave.

Then how the weight of office bore upon him. How the heritage of the republic seemed to rest its crushing mass upon Sam Baker's back.

And he understood what a dread thing it was to have the power to order men to die.

He wished to weep. But he could not; he was *the president* and he must play his part in this parade as he had done in others. At last he put his hand to his heart to honor the glorious dead.

Then he realized his heart was beating and he did not belong among them.

And when Harris and Gaynor dragged him to his feet and his eyes opened, Sam Baker looked down and saw the carnage in the ADR, the bodies of Walsh and O'Neill and the others, and saw that he himself was sullied with the ashes of the dead.

At the upstairs elevator lobby, Secret Service men were waiting. They formed a human ring around the president, hustled him across the South Lawn toward the waiting helicopter. Behind them, firemen were hacking through the walls and windows of the Oval Office, trampling down the dormant bushes in the Rose Garden, playing hoses through the smoke that belched from the basement ventilators. The wash of the helicopter's rotors swirled the smoke into a whirlwind.

As the helicopter climbed into the morning sky, Sam Baker looked down in despair at the great monuments of the District: the Lincoln Memorial, the Washington monolith, the Capitol. Strange—the streets were all but deserted. It was Monday morning—Veterans Day—but the city lay silent, the sidewalks lifeless, the great Mall desolate. Where had all the people gone?

Then the helicopter banked north, and he could see the Anacostia Freeway and John Hanson Highway choked with fleeing cars. And then his eyes were blinded by the sun.

AFOSI HQ, BOLLING AFB, WASHINGTON

8:44 A.M. Major Dan Tweed dropped the file on his commander's desk, dropped himself into the chair opposite Colonel Hernandez. Tweed was a stumpy, short-necked block of a man with a whisk broom mustache; he wore an ill-fitting brown civilian suit. He had been an NYPD beat cop for four years before he took the colors, and he still looked like a fat cop who stole apples.

"Sir, you could read that," Tweed said and nodded at the pile of papers. "But considering we're at DEFCON2, maybe I'd better save you the time."

Colonel John Hernandez said, "Thanks." But he picked up the arrest report and began reading anyhow. "If the alert is called off, we've got plenty of time. If it isn't . . ." He smiled. "Then this won't matter, will it?"

Tweed sat back and laced his hands behind his head. He liked working for Hernandez; the man *was* logical. The tall, dark-eyed Hispanic was thirty-eight, not much older than Tweed. But Hernandez was a fast-tracking blue-flamer who had made bird colonel at thirty-six with three below-the-zone promotions. He was one of those officers who believed that to articulate a problem was to begin solving it, and he had the investigator's instinct for asking the right questions. Now he was the number-two man at the air force Office of Special Investigations—the elite investigative unit founded in 1948 by a group of FBI retreads.

Most of the OSI's six thousand annual cases were burglaries, drugs, rape, and fraud; but Tweed knew why he'd been instructed to hand deliver that particular file to Hernandez. A military conspiracy against the government of the United States was the OSI's worst nightmare; it was everyone in Washington's worst nightmare.

"Okay. Bring me up to date," Hernandez said, and flipped a page and went on reading.

"Got a Lieutenant M. C. Russoff in the lockup at Andrews. She's the one who tried to call the Pentagon with the names."

That made Hernandez look up. *"She?"*

"Yep."

Hernandez made a clicking sound with his tongue. "Figure she's in on it?"

"How else would she know there was a plot to kill the president? We're also holding her accomplice—a master sergeant named Browning. He's her lover."

Hernandez curled his lip in distaste. "Charming." He tapped the arrest report. "If Russoff's part of the conspiracy, why would she try to turn the others in?"

"SPs found an automatic pistol in her desk. Looks like she shot the Kulikov dame, then got cold feet and blew the whistle."

"Real little sweetheart, isn't she?"

"Regular Mata Hari. Gun's down in ballistics now."

"Have Russoff and Browning been charged?"

"The lawyers are wrapping the paperwork as we speak."

"Tell them to fax it to Andrews—on the double. And get an SP officer to read it to her. We can't question her until she's been charged."

"Wilco."

Hernandez set the arrest report aside and paged into Christy's service record. "What else?"

"In other news, seven Vietnam veterans are running all over creation, shooting senators and chopping up cabinet secretaries with F-14s. Five are dead. Watkins—"

"Who?"

"Some *gunny* doing thirty to life for murder. They flew him in from Leavenworth, then poisoned him."

"Why?"

"Maybe he didn't get the joke."

Hernandez picked up the list of conspirators; as Tweed ticked off the men, he drew a single pencil line through the names of the dead.

"Granger and Logan in the fighter. Harding—the one who shot Whitworth and his wife. And O'Neill. The guy who blew up the ADR."

Hernandez put a check mark beside the next name on the list. "Captain Daniel Peter Bryan—what do we know about him?"

"No longer on active duty. Getting his records from the Federal Personnel Center in St. Louis. Be here any time."

He put a check beside the last name. "What about this Colonel Steven Petrovsky?"

"Number-one candidate for ringleader. SPs are on the way to his office right now."

"Lot of Russian surnames bouncing around this thing." Hernandez looked at Tweed.

"Yeah. That kinda caught my eye, too."

Hernandez flipped to the next page. "This VA therapy nurse— Marge Kessler. NIS get anything out of her?"

"She asked the shore patrol for a pack of chewing gum in her handbag. It was flavored with strychnine."

"Well . . ." Hernandez sighed. "We know they're not afraid to die." He, too, had taken the soldier's oath, had sworn to defend his country and give his life in its defense if necessary. But the notion of dying for a cause was alien to John Hernandez. He'd been first in undergraduate pre-law at Oberlin and Law Review at Emory. When he'd graduated, he'd found the doors of exclusive law firms shuttered tight against a black-eyed boy named Julio Jésus Hernandez. The air force had offered him an equal opportunity that private practice didn't. That was why he was wearing air force blue; not for love of a country that treated him as an orphan, but for a chance.

He tapped the covers of the personnel files. "This is just Russoff and Browning. What about the records of the others?"

"Erased," Tweed said. "Getting backups from the microfiche vaults now."

"If they were coming out into the open, why erase their records? Seven Vietnam veterans staging a mutiny against the government of the United States. Isn't the whole point their war records?"

"You'd think." Tweed pulled his mustache; he did that whenever he was stumped. "So why erase 'em?"

"Obviously, some form of protest."

"Obviously."

"Or . . ."

"Or what?"

"Something they were trying to hide."

"Such as?"

Hernandez shook his head. "Dunno." He held up Christy's file. "If Russoff's part of it, why didn't they erase her service record?"

"Search me."

"Doesn't add up," Hernandez said. He set the file aside. "Has she made a statement?"

"Nope—'cept for screaming her head off that this is a plot to stop First Step."

"If that's true, why kill Whitworth and Littman? They opposed First Step."

Tweed pulled his mustache again. "I give up. Why?"

"That," Hernandez said, "is today's bonus question." He closed the folder. "All right. Let me think a bit."

Tweed rose and went to the door. "By the way, General Williams went to brief the president. Says he wants you to handle this personally. And he wants results—now."

"Naturally." Hernandez stared at the list of names before him. After ten years with the OSI, he was a journeyman in crimes of passion, crimes for gain; he understood the selfish, brutish, even psychotic motives that drove criminals to steal, to rape, and to murder. But now he was confronted with seven veterans who had committed themselves to a suicidal conspiracy against the government of the United States. What could tempt men who had spent their lives in faithful service to the state to sudden, ignominious rebellion? What calling could compel a handful of aging veterans to rise against a power so mighty that all the nations of the earth trembled before it? What conviction could bind men together in a trust so perfect that they freely gave their lives for common cause?

Hernandez rocked back in his chair. Even now, he could see these riddles would be the greatest mysteries of his career.

AMERICAN MISSION, 11 ROUTE DE PREGNY, GENEVA

2:47 P.M.   In the basement of the American Mission, the doors to the bubble were locked and bolted. Two marine sentries stood before them, M-16 rifles loaded with live ammunition, bayonets fixed and gleaming. Inside the bare-walled, chilly concrete room General Fuchs sat at the head of the table, chairing the briefing for the START team leaders; Sara and the other aides sat in chairs against the walls.

Colonel Gunderson, the military attaché, was summing up from the telexes in his blue file. "And overall alert performance has been considerably better than projection. We've got eighty-one percent nominal on the Peacekeeper. Just under eighty percent on the Minuteman. And ninety-one percent of our alert bombers are airborne. That exceeds expectation by—well, give or take a fraction—four percent."

Whittaker, the Edwardian watercolor expert and State Department specialist, raised his hand. "Anything from the navy on the Tridents?"

"The 'silent service'?" Gunderson snorted. "You know how they are. But I think it's safe to assume they've met the same criteria. Otherwise they'd already be banging on the door of the Appropriations Committee."

The men chuckled.

At the far end of the table, Jake sat stroking his beard. He, himself, had nothing to fear; the bomb already held a lien upon his life. He was a condemned man who had lived so long with death that it held no terror. But what of the others at the table? The strategic forces of East and West might be on a collision course to Armageddon, yet the START men kept their perspective, their sense of pride and purpose, even their sense of humor. Was it because they had worked so long under the shadow of the nuclear cloud? Or was it because—even at this moment—the extinction of the human race still seemed improbable? Only Mulholland showed any effect of the strain; he sat beside Jake, ashen, ceaselessly rolling a yellow pencil in his beefy hands.

"Anything on the Soviet estimate?" Drysdale said.

Gunderson opened his red file. "NSA Rhyolite satellite intercepts detected their Supreme Command's order to alert almost eight minutes after our step up to DEFCON2. That puts their Stavka about three minutes behind NBC News."

Some of the men at the table sniggered; others shook their heads. The Soviet Union was decades behind the United States in electronic intelligence gathering; the standing joke was that during a strategic confrontation with the United States, the Soviets' principal intelligence source would be CNN.

Drysdale elbowed Whittaker. "So much for launch-on-warning."

Whittaker shrugged. "Guess so."

Jake smiled at the exchange; if the alert did not annihilate mankind, it would prove a useful laboratory for the strategic planners. For years the United States military had debated whether the Soviet war-fighting plan still called for launch-on-warning—Khrushchev's threat to unleash Soviet strategic rocket forces at the first sign of an American attack that dated from the Cuban missile crisis. For twenty-three years launch-on-warning had remained the pronounced policy of Soviet strategic rocket forces while the Politburo spent billions of rubles on an antiballistic missile defense and civilian fallout shelters. As late as 1985, the Soviet Union remained the only nation on earth that believed a nuclear war could be fought and won.

Judging from the fact that the world was still intact this afternoon, more enlightened minds prevailed under Gorbachev.

Gunderson flipped a page. "Reconsat data is sketchy so far. But projections off our KH-11 imaging of selected Soviet SS-18 complexes indicates an enabled level of over seventy percent. More than two hundred road-mobile SS-25s have been confirmed in Irkutskaya Oblast, and rail-mobile SS-24s are on the move on the Novosibirsk-Tomsk line. And, of course, we show heavy Bear and Blackjack activity at every airfield from Murmansk to Komsomolsk."

By the time Gunderson had finished, the men at the table were no longer smiling. In the silence that followed, Whittaker said, "I think it would be constructive if we had a detailed Soviet capabilities analysis when the alert is terminated."

"I'll see that's done."

Fuchs said, "Anything else, Colonel?"

Gunderson checked his notes. "Only that the National Command Authority is still with Vice President O'Donnell in Kneecap. And the Joint Chiefs have recommended our strategic forces remain at DEFCON2 until we assess the extent of the conspiracy at home. We're working to reestablish contact with the president. And awaiting further orders."

Fuchs turned to the room. "Questions, gentlemen?"

"General. . . ." Mulholland's voice quavered. "How could this happen?"

"Jason, maybe you'd run that down from a foreign policy point of view?"

Whittaker shrugged. "Entangling alliances. Kennedy told Khrushchev *If your pal, Castro, misbehaves, there'll be hell to pay.* That threat's still on the books. The Cubans scrambled—"

"And the shit hit the fan."

"Yes," Whittaker said with obvious distaste. "You could put it that way, Ruf."

"The point, Mr. Ambassador," Gunderson said, "is that this is—how shall I say—only a technical alert. There's no real threat scenario out there. What we're really looking at is"—he hunted for the words—"well, a kind of full-system drill on both sides. Nobody's going to start shooting. As soon as we reestablish contact with the president and get him on the hot line—"

"Yes, of course," Mulholland said. "*We* know that. But do the Soviets?"

Gunderson looked to Fuchs.

"Well," Fuchs said with a tight smile, "if they don't I'm sure they soon will. Thank you, Colonel." Gunderson took his place at the table, and Fuchs turned to the other men in the room. "That's the situation. I hardly need remind you this briefing is top secret and you are not to discuss it outside this room or with any member of your staff. . . ."

Fuchs droned on, reciting the routine national security caution. Jake sat back, fingers absently curling the ends of his beard. Three acts of violence had tipped the armed forces of the United States and Soviet Union down a slide that might tumble the whole world headlong into thermonuclear war. Yet the dialogue around the table concerned only the statistics of the impending confrontation. None of the men in the bubble seemed the least bit curious about the motives of the conspirators. None seemed the least intrigued by the fragility of their planet's lethal balance the morning's events had so dramatically underscored. The bombing of the White House and the assassinations of Whitworth and Littman were brutal savageries. But set against the global scale of existence they were little more than pinpricks. Since the sun had risen over Lake Geneva that morning, thousands of human beings had been born and died without altering the arc of humanity by one millionth of a degree. Yet three infinitesimal acts by a handful of uniformed men now threatened the whole of mankind with extinction. Jake pondered that; clearly, the great questions of the moment were not about the reliability ratios of the missiles. They were questions about the conspirators themselves. Silently, his mind set off in pursuit of the villains, like an old bloodhound snuffling after their fading tracks; if there were a hidden strategy behind their reprehensible acts—as there must be—somewhere in the labyrinthian maze of thermonuclear logic he must find the lurking men.

What was their motive? Were the attacks a vicious expression of the military's dissent against First Step or was their timing merely coincidental? Jake weighed that. If the military supported First Step, they could simply keep silent and let the necessary legislation pass as it surely would in a post–Cold War Congress. No, the military *must* oppose First Step. Of that much, he was sure. The president's initiative would deprive America's armed forces of enormous resources of violence; the military must dispute any covenant that threatened their capacity to make war.

Jake thought of his friend, Zack Littman. He mourned Littman; he would say Kaddish for him when there was time. Together, they had planned the Hakodate gambit to derail First Step; they had at least succeeded in delaying it. Did the attack on the president prove there were other enemies of First Step, others more daring—men who were willing to risk death as well as disgrace for their convictions? Perhaps. But if the conspirators opposed First Step, why murder Littman and Whitworth, both sworn opponents of the initiative? On the face of it, that made no sense. Jake's trail of logic ended in a paradox; for the moment, the motive behind the violence remained a mystery—elusive and obscure.

But his mind shuffled down another line of reasoning. *What was the extent of the conspirators' capabilities?* Were two murders and a bombing an end to their terrorism, or did they possess the capacity for even more heinous brutality? That was a simpler question to answer. Three provocative acts had prodded the strategic forces of the United States and Soviet Union to nuclear war-fighting readiness. But now, left to themselves, the armies would simply remain at alert until the politicians parlayed and recalled them. Without further impetus, the two nations' strategic forces would eventually be ordered back to peacetime status. Jake mulled that. Could the conspirators' crimes have been intended to cause only a momentary strategic glitch?

No. The ferocity of their violence pointed to some greater goal.

Then there *must* be more shocks to come. Jake twisted the ends of his beard.

The fascinating riddle was—where?

General Fuchs began to review the intricacies of the Kneecap command-and-control systems. But Jake's mind rambled on after the fleeting shadows of the conspirators. *What sort of men were they?* Clearly, the perpetrators knew where the tripwires lay in the underbrush of the nuclear jungle. Their attacks had been meticulously planned, ruthlessly executed. But to what purpose? If the conspirators' objective was to nullify First Step what other atrocities would they dare to achieve their goal? How far toward Armageddon would they goad the government of the United States? And where in the enormous worldwide deployment of America's strategic forces could they find the pressure point to force the politicians to capitulate?

There was only one place. Jake checked his watch. Only one.

General Fuchs leaned forward and rested his elbows on the table. "A final word. I know many of you have families in the United States and you're concerned for their safety. But, as we've indicated there's no cause for alarm. Both the Soviet and American strategic systems have a long list of built-in safeguards. Take my word for it, we're a long way from doomsday."

"About two hours and ten minutes," Jake said.

Every head in the room turned his way.

"What are you talking about, Jake?" Fuchs said. "Hell, this whole thing's an accident. Few words over the hotline, we'll stand down and so will they."

"Perhaps. But has it occurred to you that some of our bombers are"—Jake scratched a calculation on the pad before him—"less than fourteen hundred miles from fail-safe at this moment?"

"So what?" Drysdale said. "For chrissake, the bombers are the least of our problems. Our missiles went enable ninety seconds after the JCS declared DEFCON2. The Soviets were on a hot trigger ten minutes after that. Even if our bombers fly as far as fail-safe, they just circle until they get the recall code."

"But, Rufus, our bombers and their refueling aircraft fly to fail-safe at forty thousand feet. The Soviets can track them on radar. Suppose our bombers reach fail-safe and begin descending under five hundred feet? If our bombers begin dropping off the Soviets' radar screens, don't they have to assume an attack is under way?"

Fuchs was growing irritable. "What do you mean drop off their radar screens? The Soviets have the same kinds of AWACS warning planes we have. They can track our bombers all the way to their targets. That's why we built the stand-off cruise missiles. So our planes don't have to penetrate Soviet air space."

"Yes, the Soviets have the planes. But have they perfected the electronics? If it takes them eight minutes to detect a massive DEF-CON2 alert, what makes you think they can track a single bomber flying fifty feet above the Barents Sea?"

Fuchs started to answer, then he couldn't.

Gunderson said, "Dr. Handlesman, surely you're aware our missiles and airborne nuclear weapons can't be armed without National Command Authority? They need an eight-digit code from Kneecap or the president before they can be fired."

"He knows that," Drysdale sneered. "And so do the Soviets."

"Yes," Jake said. "But suppose one of our bomber crews should turn toward the Soviet mainland, descend to firing altitude, and open their bomb bay doors? Would the Soviets gamble their national survival on an eight-digit number? Would we?"

Fuchs snorted. "Cut it out, Jake. Why the hell would one of our crews do a crazy thing like that?"

"Indeed," Jake said softly. "Why would two navy veterans murder the Secretary of Defense?" He looked about the room. "Eh?"

He did not expect an answer. Nor did he get one from the tense and silent men.

Forty thousand feet above the nightbound Pacific, the three B-52Hs of Charlie flight from Guam droned northwest through the blackness of the stratosphere. They were 72 minutes from rendezvous with their tankers, 129 minutes from fail-safe.

In the navigation bay, Lieutenant Arnold Boyce finished decoding the satellite weather report on sea level conditions at their nuclear cruise missile launch point southeast of Vladivostok in the Sea of Japan. He toggled the intercom. "Major, heavy squalls moving eastward through the Sea of J. Ceiling zero. Winds forty knots."

On the flight deck, copilot Eddie Foyle leaned in beside Major Cutler. "Gonna be one helluva bumpy ride if we get ordered down into that."

Cutler stared straight out through the canopy. "You don't know how bumpy. . . ."

INI, BOLLING AFB, WASHINGTON

8:51 A.M.   The door of Colonel Petrovsky's office slammed open and a squad of SPs burst through it, automatic pistols and M-16 rifles at the ready. Petrovsky's tough sergeant-secretary, Lulu, jumped up in fright.

"We're here to arrest Colonel Petrovsky!" the lieutenant shouted. "The charge is treason. If you interfere, we'll shoot to kill."

The SPs trained their rifles on Lulu. She opened her mouth to speak but words wouldn't come.

The lieutenant kicked open the door to Petrovsky's office and the SPs burst through it; in a moment, one came back to the threshold, shaking his head.

The lieutenant caught Lulu's arm. "Where is he?"

"I don't—"

"Did he say anything when he went out? Did he do anything?"

"He—he—"

"Dammit, Sergeant! Spit it out!"

"He called United Air Lines. But I couldn't—"

Abruptly, the lieutenant shoved her aside and grabbed her desk phone. "Operator! Get me OSI headquarters! On the double!"

"Hey," Lulu whimpered. "I gotta pee."

DETENTION CELL #6, ANDREWS AFB, CAMP SPRINGS, MD

8:52 A.M.   The cell door slammed open and a gust of frigid winter morning cut through the tattered fabric of Christy's smock. And when she saw it was the two policewomen who had strip-searched her, she scrambled to her feet and shouted, "Stay away from me!" and backed against the wall and clenched her fists.

But one of the policewomen was carrying a steaming bowl of water and a sponge, the other a fresh blue smock and underwear. The younger woman—the one who was black and not much older than Christy—said, "We ain't gonna hurt ya, honey." But the older one said, "You look like shit. You don't want us to wash you, the guards can do it." She nodded toward the cell door; through the barred window a man's sullen eye stared.

At last, Christy turned her back to the window and let them undress her, standing naked and shivering in the center of the cell while they sponged her down, feeling that man's eyes on her body, sensing the ugly way they explored her.

This, too, was part of Bryan's plan. Christy understood the humiliation was designed to strip her dignity as they had stripped her body. The isolation, the cold, the vicious epithets, the brutal body search, the blows. All their tactics had a single purpose: to break her spirit and, with it, her will.

She knew their motive; she would resist; she would not fall into the trap of self-pity. If she did, Bryan had won. Christy's body was defenseless, but her mind was not. She gritted her teeth and endured the grating of the sponge between her buttocks. And she resolved herself. They would not prevail.

Gruffly, the policewomen wiped her breasts and belly. The cold air stung Christy's dampened flesh and made her tremble. She struggled to control her shaking hands; she must not let them think she trembled out of fear. The harsh disinfectant soap stung her eyes and wounds but she didn't wince, would not give them the satisfaction of knowing she was in pain.

When they were done, they watched her step into the cotton underpants, the polyester smock, and the rubber clogs. Then they handcuffed her and tied her hair back with a rubber band.

"Tell your commander I must talk to the Pentagon," Christy said. "It's an emergency."

"Yeah. Sure," the black policewoman said. "We'll do that. Right."

"And I demand to see a doctor."

The older woman shoved her in the back of the head. "You ain't hurt—yet." Then they went out. The guard slammed the door and there was silence.

NATIONAL MILITARY COMMAND CENTER, FORT RICHIE, MD

9:01 A.M.   Sam Baker changed to slacks and a cardigan sweater, chased away the fretful doctors, and pushed through the door of the bunker sick bay into the presidential command post. His back ached and the fingers of his right hand were sore and stiffening. But his mind was clear and that was what mattered.

Ted Harris was waiting for him. "All the comforts of home," he said.

The National Military Command Center was a hardened star-shaped complex of concrete and steel bunkers buried four hundred feet under the Appalachian Mountains on the Pennsylvania-Maryland border, fifty-eight miles and eighteen helicopter-minutes from the White House. At the axis of the star sat the presidential command post—a miniature of the White House ADR with computer consoles, plotting screens and a NORAD status board; a large soundproofed plate glass window overlooked a busy communications center. Down the hallways left and right were secure conference rooms, a television and radio broadcast control room, and a mock-up of the Oval Office—complete with painted scenery behind the empty window frames—for use in the event the president had to address the nation. In the tunnels that radiated from the command post, more than two hundred air force officers and enlisted personnel operated elaborate command-and-control facilities that allowed the president to audit military activities around the world and fight a global war.

Sam Baker looked up at the status board. The DEFCON panel was illuminated with the code words:

SUN RISE

"What the hell . . . ?"

"Charlie O'Donnell," Harris said. "When Kneecap lost contact with the White House ADR. As a precaution, he kicked the alert to DEFCON2."

"My god! What about the Soviets?"

General Gaynor stepped out from behind the command console. "Soviet Stavka Command telexed the Joint Chiefs on the hot line when the alert B-52s out of Griffiss crossed the Canadian border. JCS told them it was a drill."

"Dammit! Since that Shevardnadze deal in '89, you know we have to give them seven days' notice of a strategic exercise. They must have gone berserk!"

"Soviet strategic forces are at full alert. Missiles. Bombers. Everything. The Joint Chiefs have recommended we remain at DEFCON2 until we've determined the scope of the conspiracy."

"Perfect," Harris snapped. "The Soviets won't stand down until we do. And we can't stand down until we know what the hell is going on."

"Mr. President," Gaynor said. "The vice president has been calling to—"

Sam Baker waved him silent and stared up at the plotting screen; a chill rolled through him. Once again he had the ominous feeling of a man who hears the earth begin to rumble beneath his feet, who senses he is standing on a volcano. Around the globe millions of men and women in the uniforms of a score of nations were moving under standing orders, stepping to their battle stations, glaring at each other through radar screens, preparing to loose the dogs of war. Sam Baker stared at the polar projection of the Northern Hemisphere, at the thousand gleaming symbols that identified the positions of strategic force elements—white for U.S. forces, blue for NATO, red for the Soviets—and the image seared him.

Yes, he had attended the secret briefings, had studied the charts and diagrams, listened to the experts' theories of the thrust-and-parry game of escalation. But, until this moment he had never touched the beating heart of terror. Now it throbbed inside him. This was the moment when the sleeping war plans roused, when standing orders and computer programs seized control and drove the complex, deadly mechanism of men and weapons headlong toward destruction.

Now—at the very moment when the president had to act decisively to break the spiral into madness—he was trapped within the tyrannical logic of deterrence.

He was a prisoner of war.

Sam Baker reached out and caught Harris by the sleeve. "Ted, we've got to crack this conspiracy and recall our forces. The Soviet ambassador—"

"Volokin."

"Have the State Department call his embassy and arrange to bring him here by helicopter. Right away."

Harris reached for the phone.

The president turned to Gaynor. "I want a briefing on the conspiracy. Everything we know. Everything we don't."

"General Williams of the OSI is in the waiting room."

"Get him. Now."

Gaynor pressed a button on the desk. The rear door opened and Brigadier General Warren Williams entered and braced. He was a dark-haired, introspective man—serious and competent.

The president nodded at a chair. "No formality, General. Just talk."

"Yes, sir." Williams sat, opened his briefcase and found a yellow file. "Colonel John Hernandez will be conducting the investigation. He has a list of the conspirators supplied by one of their accomplices—a Lieutenant Russoff. Five of the perpetrators are dead. The two survivors are a Colonel Steven Petrovsky and a Captain Daniel Peter Bryan. Petrovsky appears to be the ringleader. He's Russoff's supervisor at—"

Sam Baker started at the Russian names. "Petrovsky?"

"Yes, sir. He's director of INI."

"Of what?"

"The air force directorate of Research and Soviet Studies. A minor intelligence unit whose mission is to assess Soviet readiness through analysis of Red Army publications and NSA intercepts."

"Who staffs this INI?"

"Principally officers of Russian descent. Native speakers. Second generation—"

"Excuse me, General," Sam Baker said. "Are you telling me there's an intelligence unit in the United States Air Force staffed by *Russians*?"

"Well, yes, sir. On the theory that ethnic Russians can better understand the Russian military mind. It's accepted standard practice in modern armies."

Sam Baker's eyes narrowed. *Curious. Ominous.* "All right, General. These conspirators—what do we know about them?"

Williams closed his file. "Their service records were erased. We're getting backups from—"

"Why the hell would they have erased their service records?" Harris said.

"Colonel Hernandez believes it was intended as a form of protest," Williams said. "Or because there's something in those records they want to keep secret as long as possible."

"What?"

"We don't know."

"Any idea what else they might be planning?"

"No, sir. Obviously, they are desperate. Their lives mean nothing to them. Whoever planned this will dare anything."

Harris growled, "Obviously, you don't know a lot."

Before Williams could respond, Gaynor said, "Excuse me, Mr. Harris. I don't understand that remark."

"You heard me." Harris jammed his fists down into the pockets of his jacket. "You've got a million guys in uniform running all over the place. The most sophisticated computers in the world. A security system that is supposedly impenetrable. Yet an officer waltzes into the White House with a bomb. And seven lunatics have the world on the brink of a shooting war."

"Mr. Harris, what are you implying?"

"I'm just wondering how high up the chain of command this damned conspiracy goes."

Suddenly Gaynor lunged at Harris and grabbed the collars of his jacket. "Listen, you—"

The president stood. "Gentlemen!"

Gaynor hesitated. Then he threw Harris's lapels back at him. Shaken, he turned to the president. "I beg your pardon, sir. It's . . . been a trying day."

"All right, General." Sam Baker understood; the tension was getting to all of them. He had to act. "General Williams, what can I do to help you prosecute this investigation?"

"Well, sir . . ."

"Please, General. There's no time."

"Declare martial law."

Sam Baker stiffened.

"Sir, the Constitution specifically recognizes that the writ of *habeas corpus* may be suspended by the president in time of rebellion. The military police must have the right to detain and question suspects without interference from the civilian courts until the present emergency is past."

Time of rebellion. The words stung Sam Baker like a slap in the face. In more than two hundred years of the republic, only one president—Abraham Lincoln—had ever declared martial law within the continental United States. Was the nation for the second time in its history facing a military rebellion? And had Sam Baker now no choice but to abolish freedom to preserve the state?

The direct line from the State Department rang; Harris grabbed it. "Harris." He listened and his eyes widened. "Goddammit. Don't they know there's a war going on?"

Sam Baker's breath caught at the word.

Harris slammed the phone down. "The Soviet embassy. Volokin's away for the weekend. They won't say where."

"What? Soviet strategic forces are on alert—and their ambassador isn't at his embassy? I don't believe it."

"They're beeping him. They'll call us back." Harris muttered, "Goddamn bunch of—"

The red phone rang. Gaynor answered it. "NMCC—Gaynor." Then he handed the receiver to the president. "Vice President O'Donnell from Kneecap."

"Charlie? Hello?"

Charlie O'Donnell sat alone in the private conference room of the plane's National Command Authority suite. "Sam! Are you all right?"

"I'm fine. Few cuts and bruises—that's all."

"Thank god! We'll make those bastards pay for this."

"When we find them."

"Hell, Sam, they're telling me a couple of Russian officers planned this thing! The Soviets are behind it. That's plain as the nose on your face!"

"Charlie, listen to me. The Cold War's over. No assumptions until we have the facts. Have you talked to Gorbachev?"

"I tried. The bastards severed all phone contact when they saw us move to DEFCON2. JCS thinks they're afraid we've got some way of tracing the call and finding Gorbachev's hideout. Everything's got to go by telex through their Supreme Command in Moscow."

"Dammit. Why are they always so suspicious?" Sam Baker knew why; today, he couldn't blame them. "What's the status of the alert?"

"NATO and the Soviets have everything they've got in the air. The French are screaming their heads off. Japan's demanding an emergency meeting of the United Nations Security Council."

"All right. We're trying to reach Ambassador Volokin. When he gets here, we'll agree a time to stand down. I'll telex Moscow—you let our allies know." He started to hang up, then he caught himself. "Charlie, can you get word to Mulholland? I don't want this insanity to wreck any chance we've got of salvaging First Step."

"Leave it to me."

Sam Baker hung up. He had to act; the weapons moved so quickly they outran diplomacy. He turned to Williams. "General, I am placing the District of Columbia and other areas you deem necessary under martial law for the duration of the emergency. Now, gentlemen, would you excuse me?"

"Yes, sir." Gaynor and Williams nodded their way out.

When the door closed behind them, the president walked to the plate-glass window that overlooked the communications center. Beyond the window, a score of air force officers and NCOs sat intently at computer consoles. He beckoned Harris to his side.

"What is it, Sam?"

"I was just thinking. . . . You and I are probably the only two civilians in this whole complex."

"So?"

Sam Baker shrugged. "I don't know. I guess I never realized the president could be so isolated from . . ."

"From what, Sam?"

"From the world. From people." He looked at Harris. "Right now, we're totally dependent on our military. For protection. For information and advice. For the air we're breathing. We're completely at their mercy."

Harris cocked his head. "Sam, what are you getting at?"

The president leaned close to him. Then he whispered, "What do you really think?"

"About the alert?"

"About the conspiracy."

"You mean—suppose it *does* go higher in our military?"

"Suppose it does?"

Harris blew a breath. "I'm worried, Sam."

"So am I." The president took Harris by the arm. "Ted, take a helicopter back to Washington. See this Colonel Hernandez. Size him up. See if he's loyal."

"Loyal to the Constitution . . . or loyal to the air force?"

AMERICAN MISSION, 11 ROUTE DE PREGNY, GENEVA

3:05 P.M. "Queen to king's rook five." Jake stood before the sliding glass doors at the far corner of his office, squinting down at the street through the orange sunlight of the fleeting November afternoon. On the plains of two continents, beneath the waters of two oceans, Soviet and American ballistic missile forces stood at alert; above the Pacific, above the icy wasteland of the Arctic, hundreds of strategic bombers hurtled toward fail-safe. Somewhere in the nuclear labyrinth, a group of ruthless conspirators was preparing yet another escalation while the diplomatic channels of the world sizzled with bitter messages of protest, and billions of terrified civilians sought safety where there was none. Jake looked down through the window and couldn't help but smile; on the deserted sidewalk of the Route de Pregny a middle-aged woman in a knit hat and loden coat was leading a dog along the curb.

"Remarkable. Eighty thousand megatons of destruction on a hair trigger. And a Swiss *hausfrau* goes out to walk her schnauzer." He turned. Behind him, Sara sat at the coffee table, studying the chessboard before her. "What do you make of that, Weatherby?"

"Of the schnauzer, sir?"

"Of the alert."

Sara didn't look up. "Saber rattling. Empty posturing. Pawn to queen's bishop four. Are the Soviets behind the conspiracy?"

"What motive could they have? Queen takes bishop." Neither reached to move their chessmen. The board was bare; they were playing blindfold.

"Gorbachev's in trouble," Sara said. "He's riding the whirlwind. Nothing like a national emergency to rally the motherland behind him." She glanced at Jake. "It worked for Stalin in 1940. Rook takes queen."

"An intriguing possibility. But I think not. The emergency may pass. The problems of *perestroika* will not. Knight takes rook. Checkmate."

Sara stared at the empty squares. Then she sat back, disgusted.

Jake folded the board and set it aside. "Don't be so hard on yourself, Major. How long have you been playing now?"

"Three months."

He went to the bar and uncapped a bottle of Power's Irish. "You don't become a grand master in three months, no matter how determined you are. Whiskey?"

"No, thank you, Doctor. I don't drink on duty."

"Noble," Jake said with a droll grin. "Considering the alert, perhaps even heroic." He poured for himself. "You're taking all this very calmly."

"What can we do if Washington and Moscow decide to blow the world away?"

"Tell me."

"Nothing. Except walk our dogs."

Jake toasted her. "Precisely." He drank. Then he turned a chair to her and sat.

The moments Jake spent talking with Major Sara Weatherby were one of the delightful perquisites of his job. The woman was ineffably beautiful. But it was her eyes that lent her face its singular and riveting quality; emotion never flickered in their paleness—not even when she smiled. That gave her a coldness, a hauteur; for the male in Jake that aloofness was an ever-present challenge, a lascivious provocation that excited him even more than the quickness of her mind. "Tell me,

Weatherby, how do men and women in uniform feel about all the talk of cuts in our defense spending?"

"I don't know, sir. I rarely discuss my work with others."

"How do you suppose they feel?"

"Ambivalent."

"Yes," Jake said. He sipped his whiskey, rolled it on his tongue. "Soldiers have two contradictory instincts. They're men and women who want normal lives. But they're also warriors; their work is the management of violence—the destruction of normal lives. How do you cope with that?"

Sara shrugged. "It's a calling."

"Indeed." Jake lowered his voice and sat forward. "But suppose our soldiers' darker feelings got the upper hand one day. Suppose the warrior strain became dominant. What might happen then?"

"I'm sorry, Doctor. I don't understand."

"Suppose our government decided to cut military spending and the Pentagon rejected the decision."

"That's not possible, Doctor. Soldiers must obey."

"Humor me, Weatherby." Jake set his glass down, rose from the chair, and paced. "Consider this—the Baker administration proposes massive new reductions of our conventional forces in Europe and the elimination of all nuclear *slick-ems.* Those actions would dramatically reduce the war-fighting capacity of our armies. Wouldn't they?"

"They will."

"But what if a small group of zealots decided the Pentagon shouldn't accept the reductions? What if they staged a rebellion to demonstrate their antagonism toward First Step?" He stopped pacing and looked back at her. "Wouldn't that explain what happened this morning?"

"Yes, sir. But . . ."

"But what?"

"Unless there's another incident, the politicians will order a stand-down and things will be exactly as they were—including First Step."

Jake chuckled with delight. "Weatherby, you are my touchstone." He came back to his chair and sat. "So we come to the bombers." He leaned toward her and rested his elbows on his knees. "What if one of our bombers should fly past fail-safe toward its target? What would happen then?"

Sara stared at him. "Excuse me, Doctor. We're not allowed to discuss details of the alert outside the bubble."

"Speculate," Jake prodded. "Just between us."

"I'm sorry, Doctor. It's not permitted."

Jake sighed and picked up his glass. "Ah, Weatherby, what a pity you are such a model soldier." He sipped his whiskey and wiped his beard with the back of his hand. "Tell me—what are your plans after the army? I mean—provided we survive today's alert."

"I have none, sir."

"You should have. You know, I taught at Harvard forty years off and on. I had them all. The Kennedy boys . . . Elliot Richardson . . . Bobby McNamara. I've only had one student with your potential. A little Russian girl."

"Russian, sir?"

He stared into his glass, remembering. "Outside, she was as American as apple pie—everything but her eyes." Jake touched the corner of one eyelid. "Little Russian eyes. Exotic. Fetching, in a way." He stroked his beard. "Inside, she was so typically Russian. Never took anything at face value. Never really trusted anyone. Always deduced for herself. After you, she had the finest mind I've ever trained."

"Thank you, sir."

"All she ever wanted was to be a soldier and—"

The phone rang. Jake lifted the receiver. It was Mulholland. "Jake? Karpov just called. He's on his way over to deliver the Soviets' formal letter of protest. Can you come to my office?"

"Right away." Jake hung up, rose, and went to the door. "I'll be with the ambassador"—he raised his eyebrows and flashed a puckish grin—"to hear the Soviet assessment." He went out.

DETENTION CELL #6, ANDREWS AFB, CAMP SPRINGS, MD

9:07 A.M. Christy stood at attention in the corner of the cell, clutching the tattered prison smock closed across her bosom. Before her, a steely little SP major named Carraway stood holding a clipboard. Behind him, two security police waited at parade rest.

"Lieutenant Marina Christina Russoff, number 208569210, I am required under the Uniform Code of Military Justice to advise you that you have been arrested and detained under certain articles, and have been formally charged with certain offenses as follows." Carraway flipped the cover page. "Article one: That you did conspire with certain fellow officers to make a treasonous mutiny against the United States of America." He looked at Christy over the top of his glasses. She stood, rigid, straight-backed, staring into his eyes.

"Article two: That you did join with these same fellow officers in perpetrating a mutiny. Article three: That in the course of perpetrating this mutiny, officers and enlisted personnel of the United States Air Force, United States Army, and United States Marine Corps, along with certain civilian personnel, were murdered with premeditation and malice aforethought." He flipped a page. "Article four: That you did influence and suborn enlisted personnel to mutiny against the United States of America." He looked up; the rest he knew by heart. "For which crimes, the Chief of Staff has ordered a court-martial to be convened with all deliberate speed, and you to be thereto summoned to answer these articles and charges, the penalty for which, should you be found guilty, is death."

Christy stood at attention, her expression blank, emotionless. The scratches on her arms and legs were black and stiffening. Her right eye was swollen shut, her cheek distended with edema from the blow the SP had struck her. But she stood erect, unmoving. Bryan had planned her internment with infinite care.

It was useless to demand to speak to the Pentagon. To her captors she was an enemy and a criminal—a suspected murderess and collaborator in a conspiracy that threatened not only the order of the state, but the military's allegiance to the Constitution. Christy knew what to expect. In their brutal, military zeal they would threaten, harass, and persecute her, use every means at their disposal to intimidate her. Even now they were testing her, probing for a weakness. She would show them none.

"Article five . . ."

At the opposite end of the detention block Tod stood leaning against the wall of his cell, arms tightly folded across his chest. An SP captain named Berry was reading from a clipboard.

"That in concert with certain officers of the United States Air Force you did conspire to murder Technical Sergeant Polly Kulikov, number 118577904. Article six—"

"I didn't do it."

Berry glanced at Tod—a searing, caustic glance. His voice toughened. "Article six: That you did perpetrate the murder of Sergeant Kulikov with premeditation and malice aforethought. For which crimes, the Chief of Staff has ordered a court-martial to be convened with all deliberate speed, and you to be thereto summoned to answer these articles and charges, the penalty for which, should you be found guilty, is death."

Tod started at the word.

Berry paused, waiting.

Tod shook his head. "Nothing."

"Article seven . . ."

"That in violation of Article 134 of the Uniform Code of Military Justice, you did fraternize in a lewd—"

Christy stood at attention, but hearing this made her cheeks burn.

"—and lascivious manner with enlisted personnel, making a threat to good order and discipline, and in disgrace of your oath-in-commission as an officer in the United States Air Force." Carraway shot her a withering look. "The penalty for which is dishonorable discharge with forfeiture of pay and benefits."

Christy felt her mouth go dry. In a way, the threat of dishonorable discharge was more real and more terrifying than the specter of capital punishment—because her guilt was real. Then she saw Carraway's eyes on her, watching, measuring. She stiffened her spine.

"Do you understand these articles and charges?" he said.

Crisply, Christy answered, "Yes, sir."

"Will you sign this to indicate you have heard and do understand these articles and charges?" He handed her a ballpoint pen; without hesitating, Christy signed her name, rank, and service number.

Berry said, "Answer the question, dammit! Do you understand the charges?"

Again Tod nodded slowly.

"You answer *Yes, sir,* you sonofabitch!"

"Yes, sir, I understand the goddamn things. They're just not true."

Christy stood at attention as Carraway and the SPs turned to leave.

"Sir, I request a lawyer be appointed to represent me."

Carraway looked back at her. "What lawyer would want to?"

1422 K STREET SE, WASHINGTON

9:08 A.M.   Mrs. Mary Watkins brought the glass coffeepot from the stove. "Warm-up?"

Her lover Ned sat at the table in his grimy overalls, thumbing the racing form. "Nah."

Suddenly the kitchen door smashed open. Air force security policemen flooded the room, pistols drawn and leveled. The lieutenant shouted, "Nobody move! The city is under martial law! You're under arrest for treason!"

Ned scrambled to his feet. "Get outta my house. You got no right to—"

"Shut up!" The lieutenant cocked his pistol and pushed it against Ned's chest.

Mrs. Watkins cried out and dropped the coffeepot; it shattered on the floor.

HELICOPTER MARINE THREE, OVER NORBECK, MD

9:09 A.M.   The roar of the helicopter's engines was so loud the marine sergeant had to shout. Even then, Ted Harris didn't understand he had a call until the sergeant held up the receiver of the airphone.

Harris put the receiver to one ear and pressed a palm against his other. "Harris. Go."

Mike Marden sat alone in the cabin of the General Electric Gulfstream-4. "I land at National in fifteen minutes. I want answers."

"Press briefing at the Pentagon this afternoon," Harris said. "Be there."

"We're hearing rumors the president is dead."

"Bullshit."

"And the girl you're holding is Russian."

Angrily Harris stared at the receiver in his hand. Then he put it to his ear. "No comment."

But Marden wasn't backing down. "Ted, either you give me some answers, or we're going on the air with the Russian connection story.

And if America believes Moscow is behind this conspiracy, you can kiss your precious First Step goodbye."

"Goddammit—that's blackmail!"

Marden shouted, too. "Listen, you sonofabitch. They've already killed fifty people! And damn-near murdered one of my news crews in front of the Russell Building!"

Harris set his jaw. "In front of the Jefferson Memorial."

"When?"

"When I get there." He slammed the receiver down.

AMERICAN MISSION, 11 ROUTE DE PREGNY, GENEVA

3:10 P.M.   Surreal—that's what it was. Mikhail Lermontov could not shake the feeling that the scene before him was surreal. He and Soviet Ambassador Viktor Karpov sat side by side on the sofa in the American ambassador's office. Across from them, Mulholland and Jake Handlesman sipped cups of coffee while the Soviet interpreter droned through the text of the formal protest against the American alert. Meanwhile, in the deep cold of the oceans, in hardened silos scattered across Wyoming and on the permafrost of Irkutskaya Oblast, American and Soviet strategic missile forces waited at battle stations while hundreds of nuclear bombers flew toward fail-safe, unit commanders listening for the terse instructions that would write the period to human history.

When the interpreter had finished, Karpov handed a copy of the letter to Mulholland.

"Thank you," Mulholland said stiffly. "I will communicate this to my government."

"*Spasibo.*" Karpov nodded to the interpreter; the man rose and went out. Now the meeting had become informal—no interpreters, no stenographers. The men spoke quietly in English. The important dialogue had begun.

"According to your media, this is some form of military insurrection," Karpov said.

"Yes," Mulholland said. "I'm ashamed to say it is. But our security people have identified the conspirators. Most of them are dead. The remaining fugitives will soon be in custody."

Karpov sighed. "In our great country we, too, have such zealots.

A constant danger. Regrettable. Tell me"—he stirred his coffee—"are you still planning to hold your Armistice Day gala at four o'clock?"

The question took Mulholland by surprise. "Well . . . no. I hadn't thought of it. Under the circumstances—"

"If I may suggest . . ." Karpov picked another *tuile* from the platter. "Cancellation might further panic the diplomatic community. On instructions of my government"—he made a tiny, nodding bow—"in the interests of normalcy, the Soviet delegation will be pleased to attend your Armistice Day celebration as planned."

Mulholland hesitated, astonished.

Jake's eyes never left Karpov's face. For the sake of normalcy the Soviets were prepared to be entertained at the American mission while the human race trembled on the brink of annihilation? *On instructions of my government*? So the Soviets were prepared to wait out the alert while American strategic bombers thundered toward fail-safe? *Astounding. Remarkable.*

The intercom sounded; Mulholland pressed a button on his telephone.

His secretary's voice said, "Mr. Ambassador, the vice president is on the secure phone."

"Dorothy, say I'm in conference with the chief of the Soviet delegation."

"I have, Mr. Ambassador. He says it's most urgent."

"Excuse me, gentlemen." Mulholland rose and went to his desk. His hand trembled as he lifted the receiver and turned the key that activated his secure line. "Mulholland."

Vice President Charlie O'Donnell sat in the commander's chair in the battle staff room of Kneecap. "Craig? Now listen carefully—"

"Charlie, I've got Ambassador Karpov with me—"

"I don't give a shit if Gorbachev's in there and you've got me on the speaker phone! Washington's under martial law. We have one of the bastards in custody. She's Russian, and it's beginning to look like Moscow's behind this. But until we get anything out of her, we're just guessing."

Mulholland leaned against the desk to steady himself. "What . . . what can I do?"

"Keep your lines of communication with the Soviets open. We've got to save First Step if we can."

"I'll try."

"But tell that sonofabitch Karpov for me that if anything happens to Sam Baker, I'll push the fucking button myself!" He hung up.

Slowly Mulholland lowered the receiver to its cradle. He stared at Karpov; the Russian smiled back unawares.

"Viktor, I'll—" Mulholland's voice quavered "—I'll inform the Swiss foreign ministry we'll proceed with the gala as planned. Cocktails and hors d'oeuvres at four, to be followed by a buffet and dancing."

"And the toasts to be brief," Lermontov said sarcastically. "Just in case."

"Yes," Mulholland said, and missed the gallows humor. "Of course."

Jake sipped his coffee. *Astonishing. Electrifying.*

Downstairs in the ground-floor commissary, mission staffers huddled around the television set, watching CNN *International.* Some whimpered, some wept openly as the litany of shocks rolled over them: the murders of Whitworth and Littman, the Cuban scramble, the bombing of the White House, the global strategic alert, the city of Washington under martial law.

Lieutenant Colonel Robert Wilding, the commander of Marine Security Detachments/Europe, tapped Sara's empty coffee cup. "Time for one more?"

"I have to get back upstairs."

He gave her his best smile.

She shrugged. "Sure."

Wilding looked for a waitress; there were none. As reports of the alert had begun to trickle out over Swiss radio and television, the mission's domestic staff had evaporated. One by one, the waitresses and janitors had silently slipped out the door and headed home.

"Got to fetch our own today," he said.

Sara rose and walked with him toward the steam tables and coffee urns. "Picked a fine day for your inspection visit."

"Didn't I?"

"Why do people do that?" Sara said. "Go home?"

"Where else is there to hide?"

Sara pressed the cock and poured her coffee. "There is no place to hide."

"Tell you what. If the world scrapes through this . . . whatsay I bunk at your place tonight?"

"I told you, Bob. I'm busy."

Wilding followed her back to the table and sat down. "Busy with anyone I know?"

She sighed. "Why do you do that? Make yourself jealous?"

Wilding reached across the table, set his hand on hers. "Sara, you're the most fascinating woman I've ever met. And the most difficult."

"Thanks." She took her hand away.

"You're the toughest, smartest, most capable, the best lover and . . ." He paused.

"And *what*?"

"And the loneliest, most unhappy woman I've ever known."

Impatient, she tossed her hair. "Bob, make your point."

He put his spoon down, turned it over, then turned it up again. That took her by surprise; it was a shy gesture, like the downcast eyes and shuffling feet of a little boy.

"I just wish you'd give me a chance to make you happy," he said.

Sara reached out and touched Wilding's cheek—not to comfort him, but to make certain he listened closely; beneath his skin, she could feel the old wounds of his imprisonment, the scar tissue of the reconstructive surgery that had given him the appearance of a man again. "Would you believe me if I told you I *am* happy?"

"No, Sara."

She stared at him with those gray, impassive eyes. "Then you will never be able to make me happy."

MAGNOLIA HOUSE, RIVER ROAD, HIGHLAND SPRINGS, VA

9:13 A.M. To the slow tick of a dignified Seth Thomas long-case clock, Colonel Steven Petrovsky sat in a balding red plush wing chair, his arms resting on its yellowed lace antimacassars. A linen napkin the smoky color of old ivory was spread across his lap; on it, he balanced a Meissen saucer and mismatched teacup.

The sitting room of the dreary antebellum mansion was cold; no crackling oak logs bowed the massive fire dogs. In the south corner of the room the fringes of the faded moiré curtains trembled in drafts that whistled through the splintered saddles of the old french doors. Beyond the buckled planks of the veranda, Petrovsky could see the cherry walk down to the Chickahominy River was overgrown, its slate steps lost in matted creepers and a scrub of desiccated vines.

His mother, Roslyn Dant Petrovsky, sat opposite on the threadbare red plush love seat. Her silver hair was swept up, held in place by two blue-lacquered chinoiserie clips; she wore an old blue organdy dress that buttoned to the throat, and a Victorian pendant watch hung with its hazy crystal inverted above her breast.

She stirred her tea. "Is it . . . dangerous?"

Petrovsky smiled; his mother had a tiny, high-pitched voice, had never lost the chirpy drawl of Savannah and Oglethorpe Square. "Yes, Mother."

She studied him, and he admired her eyes; even at seventy-one, they were clear sapphire, very near the color of her dress.

"Is it . . . indispensable?" she said.

"The people must be told."

"I see." She picked up the Meissen teapot; once, its painted orioles had wheeled in orange-breasted splendor; now, chipped and bleached by the decades, they seemed weary of their flight to nowhere. "More tea, Steven?"

"No. I have a plane to catch. I'm sorry."

She set the teapot down. "Seven years ago, when we went to Normandy for the fortieth observance, I stared at those old men and wondered what your father would have looked like if he'd come home and grown old." She slipped the hankie from her cuff and touched her lips. "Silly daydreams of a soldier's wife. . . ."

Petrovsky checked his watch. He set his teacup and his napkin on the table.

"So soon?" she said.

"Yes, Mother." He rose.

She looked up at him, her blue eyes steady on his own. "So, you've come for a blessing."

"Yes."

"And to say goodbye."

"Yes."

"And you're never coming back."

Softly he said, "No."

"Well." She drew herself up straight so that her back was not touching the settee. "For five generations this family has carried the flag." Her eyes locked his. "Don't shame us. Do what you have to."

Then she picked up the pot and poured herself another cup of tea. And as though he had already left the room, she said, "Chilly for this time of year. . . ."

Dismissed, Petrovsky turned, took his briefcase, and went out.

DULLES AIRPORT, HERNDON, VA

9:18 A.M. "Are the snipers set?"

"Yes, sir." Lieutenant Robert Gleason turned, looked upward.

Colonel Hallas followed his eyeline; he was fifty—a tough, runty Greek with a taut black mustache. He was boss of security police for the Air Force District of Washington and he wasn't going to let this snatch go sour.

"One in the manager's office." Gleason pointed to the second-floor balcony; an SP with a sniper's rifle crouched behind a column. "And one in the Voyager's Club." At the far end of the terminal, an overhead window was open; crouched behind it, another SP marksman waited.

"All right," Hallas said. His eye swept the empty arrivals area. The terminal was strangely silent—deserted except for security policemen who stood along the perimeter walls, helmeted and wearing flak jackets, their M-16 rifles at the ready. The president's declaration of martial law had empowered the air force to close Dulles Airport and reroute all flights but one through Baltimore. Beyond the airside windows the runways lay empty and still.

But from the driveway at the front of the terminal Hallas could hear a rumble of angry voices. As reports of the alert had hit the network news, Washington's visitors and temporary residents had rushed to telephones, booked reservations, dashed to trains and airports in rented cars and cabs. Now the travelers found the airport doors were locked against them. They jostled and sparred with Virginia state police.

"If possible, I want to take him without incident," Hallas said. "Hopefully, without any shooting. And we must take him alive."

"Yes, sir."

Hallas looked at Gleason. "Lieutenant, how old are you?"

"How old, sir?"

"Yeah. Your age."

"Twenty-five."

"Ever shot anybody?"

"N—no."

"Don't start today. All right. Get your men ready."

Gleason turned to the SPs. "Flight! Ten-*hut!*" The twelve men braced.

AFOSI HQ, BOLLING AFB, WASHINGTON

9:22 A.M. "I'm asking you point-blank," Harris said. "Why don't you have Petrovsky and Bryan in custody right now?" He sat before the desk of Colonel Hernandez. Major Tweed stood aside.

"Mr. Harris, you don't seem to want to understand," Hernandez said. "The service records of the conspirators were erased yesterday. Until we get copies from the vaults in St. Louis we're chasing shadows."

Harris ran his eye down the list of names before him. "This sergeant who erased the air force files—"

"Polly Kulikov."

"Have you picked her up?"

"She's dead," Tweed said. "Shot by Russoff and her boyfriend."

"What about this Russoff? What's your plan?"

"She's heard the charges, asked for a lawyer. We can't question her until she's had a chance to meet with one."

"Dammit, Colonel! This is a national emergency. You have the powers of martial law. Use them!"

"We *are* using them, Mr. Harris." Hernandez could not hide his distaste; under martial law civilians could be arrested by military police, held without bail, tried in military courts. The whole order of the state that made the military the servant of the people had been turned upside down. While the president's proclamation was in force, freedom was a prisoner in the District of Columbia.

"We're detaining every witness," Tweed said. "Petrovsky's secretary, Watkins's wife. We've—"

"The hell with witnesses!" Harris snapped. "Russoff's one of *them*!"

"Mr. Harris," Hernandez said and he was measuring his words, "even martial law is law. According to the Supreme Court decision of—"

"Goddammit, Colonel"— Harris got to his feet— "by lunchtime, there may not be a Supreme Court!"

Warily, Hernandez eyed him. "Exactly what are you suggesting?"

"Use your imagination. Offer Russoff immunity to tell what she knows. If the little bitch plays hardball, sweat her. Break her! Bug her cell. Do whatever you have to do to find Petrovsky and Bryan!"

"Mr. Harris, this is a capital case. Lieutenant Russoff faces the death penalty on five counts of—"

"Colonel!" Then Harris caught himself and lowered his voice. "Colonel . . . let's not put too fine a point on the matter."

"Mr. Harris, are you suggesting we break the laws we're sworn to defend?"

Harris put his fists on the desk and leaned across it. "I'm not suggesting you do that, Colonel. I'm ordering you to do it."

CHAPEL OF ST. MARY-IN-THE-WOODS, ARLINGTON, VA

9:25 A.M. After she had rung the bell for morning prayer, Sister Mary Patrick O'Neill had gone to the Mother Superior and asked for a dispensation to hold a vigil. Then she had made her way in silence to the tiny chapel of Saint Jude and knelt there, praying with the very music of her soul for the guidance of her father.

> Saint Jude, glorious Apostle, faithful servant and friend of Jesus, the name of the traitor has caused you to be forgotten by many, but the true Church invokes you universally as the patron saint of things despaired of; pray for me, who am so miserable.

Softly, behind her, the door of the chapel opened. Two by two a squad of air force security police entered, rifles raised and ready. They were trying to be quiet, but the hard stone floor and hollow chapel rang with the shuffling of their boots, the clatter of arms.

Sister Mary Patrick heard that noise. She broke off her prayer, opened her eyes, and listened. But she did not look back. Instead she stared up at the painting of Saint Jude that soared above the altar, the tormented man's neck hung with a cruciform icon of the glory he had followed.

A young black lieutenant came cautiously down the aisle and stopped, his automatic pistol leveled at her back. When she heard the heavy footsteps pause behind her, Sister Mary Patrick crossed herself, clasped her rosary in both her hands, and shut her eyes.

She whispered, "If you are going to kill me, do it quickly."

Abashed, the lieutenant lowered his pistol.

In the lead B-52H of Charlie flight from Guam Major Marvin Cutler tapped in on the intercom. "How long till we rendezvous with the tankers, Arnie?"

In the navigation bay, Lieutenant Arnold Boyce punched the dead reckoning computer. "I make it thirty-seven minutes, Major."

Copilot Eddie Foyle leaned in beside Cutler. "Surprised they let us go this far. Probably get the recall any time now."

"Yeah," Cutler said. "Probably."

67 CHANDLER ROAD, SPRINGFIELD, VA

9:26 A.M.   Fat Beth Harding had started on the Budweiser at 7:45 A.M., right after Bryant Gumbel came on with the first flash bulletin of the murder of Senator Simon Whitworth and the death of his assassin, Lieutenant Colonel Richard Harding. By the time Fat Beth had padded into the kitchen, opened the refrigerator, and pulled the tab on the first can, her phone had begun to ring. Five minutes later her neighbor, Angelique, started pounding on the side door and hollering her name. Beth put the phone off the hook, let down the blinds, and turned the television up to drown the knocking.

Now she slouched in her Barcalounger, holding an ice bag against the bruises on her throat, watching *The Dating Game* and wondering if the beer in the refrigerator would hold out until she could slip down to the 7-Eleven after dark. And it had just occurred to her she could call Domino's for a cheese and bacon breakfast pizza and two more six-packs when something went *crash!* in the front hallway.

By the time Beth twisted around in her chair, three air force security policemen were standing in the archway with their sidearms leveled at her.

She flashed a beery smile, pushed herself up in the chair, and put a hand back through her hair. "Well, don't just stand there, boys. Come on in."

JEFFERSON MEMORIAL, WASHINGTON

9:31 A.M.   Mike Marden stood in the shadows between the soaring concentric rings of Ionic columns, chewing his pipe, waiting. It was Veterans Day; the Memorial should have been crowded; it was not. It was deserted.

Instead, a stream of honking cars rushed past across the Fourteenth Street Bridge—cars packed with families, bulging trunks tied closed with rope—escaping from the nuclear bull's-eye that was Washington. But escaping to where? To where does one escape when there is no escape?

Marden stepped back into the shadows of the dome and squinted up at the colossal twenty-foot statue of Jefferson that stood beneath the cupola. It occurred to him that, sometime before noon, Jefferson's statue and his monument—all of federal Washington—might be ashes. On the wall beyond the statue's shoulder, bronze letters embedded in the granite spelled out an excerpt from the Declaration of Independence.

We hold these truths to be self-evident: that all men are created equal. . . .

Mike Marden stared at those words. Most men lived out their lives without ever conceiving one genuinely original idea. Jefferson had been a fountainhead. Imagine being the first to write all men are created equal. . . . Was all this majesty—the crowning achievement of three million years of human evolution—to be lost in a wink of primal fire? Had God chosen this day to revoke the miracle of His creation? Marden's eye ran down to the end of the quotation.

And for support of this declaration, with a firm reliance on the protection of divine providence, we mutually pledge our lives, our fortunes and our sacred honor.

"Amen," he whispered.

The thudding sound of rotors caught Marden's ear. He turned his eyes upward, shading them against the sun as the marine helicopter flared to a landing in the empty parking lot. The door swung open, the steps swung out, and two marine riflemen clambered down. Ted Harris followed.

"Let's walk," Harris said, and set off briskly down the quay along the Tidal Basin. Marden tapped the ashes from his pipe and fell in beside him.

"Seven men," Harris said. "No evidence of a Moscow connection."

"Seven men did all this damage?"

"Seven men with modern weapons."

"What about the girl in custody?"

"Grandparents born in Russia. Otherwise, she's American as you are."

"Some kind of mole?"

"No proof of that."

Marden caught the sleeve of Harris's jacket and stopped him. "Is it possible?"

"Today anything's possible."

"And DEFCON2?"

"We tried to intercept the lunatics who murdered Littman. The Cubans scrambled when they saw the dogfight. NORAD bumped it to the Joint Chiefs."

"But the Cold War's over. How the hell can this happen?"

"Standing orders; if the Cubans go up in an emergency, so do we."

"And the Soviets? NATO?"

"Everybody's in the air."

Marden took the pipe out of his mouth. "Jesus Christ. What is Baker going to do?"

"Call it off."

But Marden understood the paradox. Both sides were at high levels of alert; whoever backed away first would be dropping his guard, perhaps inviting a devastating blow. "Who does that first? Them or us."

"Got to be coordinated."

"Has Baker talked to Gorbachev?"

"No comment." Harris started walking again.

But Marden didn't follow. "Ted, the seven men who staged this—is one of them a colonel named Petrovsky?"

Harris stopped dead. His eyes swung back to Marden. "Where the hell did you get that name?"

"Sources."

Harris grabbed Marden's arm. "Don't give me that shit!"

"Petrovsky's one of them. Isn't he?"

"Listen to me, Mike," Harris said, and his voice thickened with menace. "This is a national emergency. The city's under martial law. Friendship doesn't count. The First Amendment doesn't count. Now, you answer me"—he nodded toward the helicopter—"or I'll have those marines question you. And they won't be fussy about your civil rights!"

"Don't threaten me, Ted," Marden said softly. "I've been threatened by experts." He pulled his arm free. "Half an hour ago Petrovsky called every network with a Washington news bureau. Said he wants a press conference at eleven o'clock to deliver a message to the American people."

"Press conference? That crazy sonofabitch! Where?"

Marden put a match to the bowl of his pipe. "Where else? The Vietnam War Memorial."

DETENTION CELL #6, ANDREWS AFB, CAMP SPRINGS, MD

9:34 A.M.   The air force captain stood just inside the cell while the guard shut and bolted the steel door behind him.

Christy stared at the man; the nameplate on his uniform read SHAPIRO. He was in his thirties—squat, short necked, and dark—with a body like a barroom bouncer and a frazzled black mustache. Behind the lenses of his glasses, his eyes were close-set but sharp. He said, "You okay?"

"Yes, sir." Christy held up her manacled wrists. "Excuse me not saluting."

"Forget it. What happened to your face?"

"An SP hit me."

"He have provocation?"

"He was frightened."

"Stand at ease." He set his briefcase on the table and walked slowly around her, eyeing the blackened latticework of scratches on her arms and legs. "What's all this?"

"The policewomen. I resisted when they tried to search me."

"Body cavity search?"

Christy gritted her teeth. "Yes, sir."

"They find anything?"

"Of course not. The desk sergeant—Jeeter. He had them do it to humiliate me. He's an accomplice."

"He is, huh? Can you prove that?"

"Well . . . no."

He stopped in front of her. "Jeeter, huh?"

"Yes, sir."

"Okay. I'll check it out." He dropped into one of the chairs beside the table, opened a pad, and made a note. While he was writing, he said, "Name's Lewis Shapiro. Penn State and Georgetown Law. Last three years, I been stuck in a closet at the Pentagon, drafting procurement contracts. Twenty minutes ago, they handed me your paperwork, ordered me to defend you, and stuck me on a chopper." He looked at her. "Tell you the truth, I'd rather have hemorrhoids."

She felt his eyes on her—contemptuous, pitiless. "I understand."

Shapiro leaned back in his chair. "How come you're so calm? They said you were screaming somebody was gonna kill the president."

"It's too late for that."

"How do you know? You been in solitary."

"This is a guerrilla action. In Mao Tse-tung's handbook, he says strike everywhere at once, like rain."

"Real poetic."

"Did they succeed?"

"Succeed at what?"

She eyed him; he was dull, but he was no fool. "Is the president dead?"

"What do you care?"

"Because I do."

Shapiro opened his briefcase. "The president survived. The Secretary of Defense wasn't so lucky." He drew out a yellow file folder and flipped it open on the table. "They read you the charges?"

But Christy didn't answer. The Secretary of Defense was dead. She remembered last night's televised press conference, the reporter's sneering question about Secretary Littman being on one of his fishing trips to Eleuthera. She imagined the map of the Atlantic and the Caribbean—the tip of southern Florida and, to the east, Eleuthera and Exuma Sound. Her thoughts flashed to the runaway F-14.

"Captain, the hijacked navy fighter—it didn't go to Cuba. It attacked the yacht Secretary Littman was on, didn't it?"

Shapiro straightened. He stared at her.

But Christy's mind was already tracking the Tomcat's flight path. "The Southeast SOCC picked up the fighter—" In her imagination she could see interceptors screaming off the runway, tilting bright wings toward the rising sun. "TAC scrambled interceptors—" She could see the planes against the Caribbean sky, the plumes of flame that drove them into battle, the wispy contrails of the rockets, the fireballs of kills. "There was a fight—" Then her mind's eye slid down the conjured map, past Exuma Sound and the Bahamas to the humpbacked mass of Cuba. On its northern coast, burned into her memory like glowing cinders, lay the MiG-25 bases at Nuevitas and Morón. "The Cubans scrambled and—that's why we're at DEFCON3!"

"What the hell are you raving about?"

Christy stepped forward. "Captain, you've got to find a way for me to talk to the Pentagon! This whole plot was designed to stop First Step and—"

"At ease!" Shapiro slapped the file shut; Christy flinched, fell silent. "I'm sure the Pentagon understands the objective of this mutiny." He glared at her. "You're one of them, aren't you?"

"No."

"Look, lieutenant. If you're part of this, just tell me now. Save us both a lot of grief."

"I told you, I'm not."

"Then how the hell did you know the plane attacked the yacht?"

Christy lowered her head. Bryan had isolated her in a prison *and* a paradox; every time Christy tried to help the air force unravel the mystery, she only affirmed her own complicity and guilt. If she were to crack Bryan's riddle, she would have to do it alone.

She turned away. "I said I'm not involved."

For a moment Shapiro sat glaring; then he muttered, "Have it your way." He opened the file and irritably shuffled through his papers. "Like I said—you heard the charges?"

But Christy stood silent, manacled hands pressed against her belly. The fighter had been hijacked to kill the Secretary of Defense; that much was certain. But was the DEFCON alert intended or coincidental?

"Dammit!" Shapiro waved the indictment under her chin. "Is this your signature?"

Christy glanced at it. "Yes."

"Well, here's the bottom line: five counts of treason and murder, any one of which will get you hanged."

"I'm innocent."

"And one count of fraternization with an enlisted man. That'll cost you the leniency vote on any court-martial." He took his glasses off and set them on his briefcase. "And I may as well tell you up front, I hate what these guys did. And you fucking an enlisted man makes me want to puke. Understand?"

She stared straight ahead. "Yes, sir."

"So. Do you want me to try to save your life?"

That made her look at him. "Can you?"

"Dunno."

"Would you take yourself as your lawyer if you were me?"

"I'd want John Hernandez of the OSI."

"I want him."

"He's putting together the case against you."

"Then who picked you?"

Shapiro grumbled, "My CO volunteered me. Doesn't like guys who go to church on Saturday." He turned the empty chair to her. "Okay. Sit down, lieutenant."

She did.

"And answer me one question. If you're innocent, how the hell did you get into this mess?"

"Following orders."

"What does that mean?"

"Last night Colonel Petrovsky ordered me to pick up a woman named Mrs. Mary Watkins, tell her *the sun will come up tomorrow,* and bring her to these detention cells to see her husband."

"Why?"

"Petrovsky wanted him to murder Senator Whitworth."

"Come on . . . Petrovsky said that? You actually heard him say that?"

"No. When we got here they slammed the door in my face. On the way home, she warned me it won't be over until they're all dead—or all heroes. That's all I knew."

"Yeah? Then how'd you know the names of the conspirators?"

"Petrovsky showed me their picture."

"Gimme a break. Petrovsky showed you a picture and told you he was planning a mutiny against the government of the United States?"

"Petrovsky didn't plan this."

"Then who did?"

"Bryan."

"Bryan? How do you know?"

"Petrovsky's an analyst, not a strategist. Bryan—" Suddenly, Christy broke off. "Captain, what DEFCON level are we at?"

"What do you care?"

"When I was in the SP van the alert was at DEFCON3."

"So?"

"Are we still at DEFCON3?"

Shapiro hesitated.

"Answer me!"

"Okay, okay, we're at DEFCON2."

Christy reached out and caught hold of the edge of the table. How could she have been so stupid?

She remembered Bryan's class at the naval school in Monterey. Dimly through the haze of memory, Christy could see the series of circular lantern slides Bryan had used to explain DEFCON deployments. Each image was an artist's rendering of a polar projection of the Northern Hemisphere as it might appear to an American surveillance satellite—the North Pole at the center, Canada and the United States below, Europe and the Soviet Union hanging upside down at the top. Colored dots on the continents and in the seas identified the strategic forces of the adversaries: American in white, NATO in blue, Soviet in red. Now, at this very moment—in the Pentagon, at NORAD Cheyenne Mountain, at the National Military Command Center in the Adirondacks and aloft on Kneecap—the same image was glowing on real-time plotting screens with the code words for DEFCON2:

SUN RISE

Christy's hand went to her throat. *The sun will come up tomorrow.* The alert was not an accident—it was intended. Bryan had planned to bring United States strategic forces to DEFCON2.

But why? Surely not to trigger a nuclear exchange between the superpowers; that could only have one possible outcome—the extinction of the human race. But if not . . . what was Bryan's purpose in raising the alert?

And why such a transparent password? The coded message could have been anything: My dog has fleas, Fish swim in water. Why would Bryan risk revealing the design of the conspiracy to Christy through the password?

There was only one possible explanation. Bryan was leading her, challenging her again. Then, quite suddenly, Christy understood; she was meant to solve the riddle.

"Dammit, pay attention!" Shapiro growled. "I said what about the gun?"

Christy blinked and looked at him. "Which gun?"

"The gun that killed Kulikov. The SPs found it in your desk."

"In my—" Christy broke off. Good god, how insidious Bryan was, how treacherous, how sly. The gambit was not merely an entrapment, it was a pincer. Now nothing she could say would convince her captors of her innocence. "I didn't kill her."

"Then how'd the gun get in your desk?"

"I don't know." And then she did. "Petrovsky. He must have put it there."

"Why the hell would he do that? What's he got against you?"

It was another question Christy couldn't answer. She looked at Shapiro; she could see suspicion in his eyes. "You don't believe me. You think I'm guilty."

Shapiro sighed. "Lieutenant, the important thing isn't whether I believe you but whether you live 'til Christmas."

EGLISE RUSSE, RUE CHARLES STURM, GENEVA

3:37 P.M.   The cobbled, narrow streets of the old district they called St. Léger were strangely silent and deserted for a Monday afternoon. But inside Saint Basil's church the nave was lit by a thousand candles of devotion, thronged with worshipers and priests, thick with the incantation of desperate prayers. Hat in hand, Jake pushed through the multitude: mothers pressing infants to their bosoms, elderly couples clutching hands, tall young men with tear-swollen eyes. He studied the pale Slavic faces. Nothing like the fear of death to raise the fear of God.

At the front of the nave before the gaudy maroon-and-gilt iconostasis, a line of hooded priests bowed their long white beards to the images of black-eyed saints. Jake picked his way among the faithful, murmuring, *"Prastee'te . . . prastee'te. . . ."* The believers had more to fear than they knew; in eighty-three minutes American bombers would begin reaching fail-safe.

On the other hand, at least the congregation had time to shrive themselves. Ten years ago the American alert might have already precipitated a wholesale launch of Soviet strategic missiles; by now the world might have been at war. That there had been no launch-on-warning today did not surprise Jake; Nobel laureate Gorbachev was no great humanist, but he was no fanatic either.

What *had* startled Jake was Ambassador Karpov's tone at the meeting in Mulholland's office. The Soviet delegation had been ordered to attend the Veterans Day gala at the American mission because canceling the gala would only further panic the diplomatic community. Did that mean the Soviets believed there was no real cause for panic? Apparently, yes. Even though the B-52s were less than nine hundred miles from fail-safe, the Soviets understood the bombers could not be recalled nor the Peacekeeper and Trident missiles disabled until the Pentagon had assessed the extent of the conspiracy.

Then there had been Karpov's uncanny reference to the conspirators themselves. *In our great country we, too, have such zealots. A constant danger. Regrettable.* Yes, the Politburo could empathize with President Baker's predicament. Soviet civilian governments had a long history of mistrust of their armed forces. In 1919, Lenin had used his *Cheka* to infiltrate his own general staff. Stalin had murdered most of his field marshals and admirals during the Great Purges. Even now, the brooding Stavka generals were the iron fist behind Kremlin conservatives' efforts to muzzle Gorbachev and reverse his *perestroika* reforms.

Did Karpov's words mean the Soviets interpreted the conspiracy as a series of isolated protest attacks against First Step? Or had the innate suspicion of the Russian mind painted the morning's events with some darker significance? That was a question Jake could not answer on his own. But it was a question that held the promise of a glittering opportunity for all mankind.

In the farthest corner of the church, Jake stopped at the threshold of the chapel of Archangel Mikhail. The tiny vault was deserted but for a single worshiper. Beneath the icon of the archangel a gray-haired figure in an old cloth coat knelt alone in whispered prayer. He was the man Jake was looking for—the man who might hold the answer.

Jake waited respectfully at the doorway until Lermontov crossed himself; then he walked up the aisle between the columns and stopped beside him. "You're coming to our Veterans Day reception, I hope."

The old Russian shook his head. "It is too bizarre."

"To cap a day of bizarre events. In a way, it seems appropriate."

Lermontov muttered, "The White House bombed . . . distinguished leaders assassinated . . . brave men killed. . . ." He crossed himself again.

"You've done worse in Afghanistan and Ethiopia. Destabilizing acts, I think you call them."

"We've both done worse."

"Yes," Jake said softly. "I suppose we have."

He looked up at the ornate columns, the arched ceiling frescoed with ancient images of saints, each head pillowed on a flaking, gold-leaf halo. Above him arced the pantheon of Russian Orthodoxy—the Father, Son, and Holy Spirit, and ranks of angels bearing books and swords—the glory, the word, and the power.

Lermontov followed his gaze. "Lovely, is it not?"

"Yes. An age when only God knew the mystery that lights the stars."

"Will you kneel with me and pray?"

"My soul will kneel even if I stand."

"And do you believe?"

"Like those frightened worshipers outside," Jake said. "I believe in God—and in the power of the bomb." He looked down at his old friend. "Your government is showing remarkable restraint today."

"Does that surprise you?"

"Frankly, yes."

"Did you think we were savages who would destroy our world to save it?" Lermontov prepared to rise.

Jake took him under the elbow, helped him to his feet. "No launch-on-warning?"

"No."

"Perhaps you'll launch at fail-safe?"

Lermontov brushed the dust from the knees of his trousers. "My friend, your question is improper."

"Perhaps . . . you will not launch at all."

Lermontov stared at Jake with an odd cast to his eyes.

Then Jake realized Lermontov was not looking at him, but past him into the nave of the chapel to make certain they were alone. "Misha? What is it?"

Lermontov took hold of Jake's sleeve and drew him closer. His voice was whispered, tense. "Some of my comrades believe your Pentagon ordered the murders of Secretary Littman and Senator Whitworth to silence opposition to First Step. They suspect your military wants this accord."

"What? Why?"

"Because they have some new weapon that will give you superiority. There are rumors of a new generation of hypersonic bombers."

"That's preposterous." Jake tried to pull free.

But Lermontov held him fast. "Many of our people want to break off the talks and go home."

"Misha, you're talking nonsense. They set off a bomb in the White House. If these madmen support First Step, why would they have tried to kill the president? First Step was his idea."

The old Russian eyed him shrewdly. "How do we know they tried to kill the president? We have only your word for it."

"*What?* For god's sake. You've seen the televised reports!"

"And did you not see 'televised reports' of how America was winning the Vietnam War? Perhaps the truth is . . ." Lermontov hesitated.

"Is what?"

Still he didn't answer.

"What, Mikhail? What do your comrades think is the truth?"

"That your armies are out of control."

Jake stared at the Russian. So *that* was the Soviet assessment. In spite of all the treaties and accords, in spite of both superpowers' declarations that the Cold War was over, in spite of every indication the American government was committed to massive reductions in defense spending, the Soviets still believed America's *military* was determined to achieve war-fighting superiority—even if by treason. The old demons of fear and suspicion of the Red Army still bedeviled the minds of the Politburo. Poor, sad descendants of the Bolsheviks; the paranoia of Stalin—and of Lenin before him—was a legacy that tormented the men who governed the Soviet Union to the present day. Jake sighed in despair; all nations were prisoners of their histories.

"Misha," he said. "You don't really believe American armed forces are in open rebellion against the government of the United States?"

For a moment, Lermontov studied him. Then he shook his head. "I'm too old for fairy tales."

"Then what do you believe?"

The old Russian turned from Jake to the altar and stared up into the eyes of his patron, Archangel Mikhail. "I believe every age has a beginning, a middle, and an end. The age of faith. The age of nuclear terror."

"And what follows the nuclear age?"

Lermontov sighed. "The stone age."

Together, their hands embracing, the old men bowed their heads. And Jake trembled with the realization that whatever the conspirators' motive might be, their acts of terrorism had placed his dream within his grasp.

AFOSI HQ, BOLLING AFB, WASHINGTON

9:39 A.M.   The projector winked and another slide lit the screen. In the gray reflected light, Colonel John Hernandez sat at the head of the table; his investigative assistant, Lieutenant Bruce Wheeler, sat beside him taking notes. Down both sides of the long conference table, the OSI investigating team stared in uncomfortable silence at the images of American prisoners of war in Vietcong custody: ragged men hunched in bamboo tiger cages; groups of tattered, barefoot officers covering their heads against the pelting stones of villagers; rows of haggard POWs posed stiff as mannequins for banks of Soviet-bloc photographers. The droning, unemotional voice from the darkness only added to the horror.

"We have no pictures of Chu My itself. Like other jungle prisons, Chu My wasn't built as a permanent internment camp—only as a holding area. But bombing made it dangerous for Charlie to move his POWs. So the stockade remained active from 1966 to 1973."

Momentarily the narrator leaned into the light of the projector; he was a civilian—a man in his late forties, white-faced, bald, without so much as eyebrows. He wore the Bronze Star rosette in his lapel.

"During all that time Chu My had no proper medical facilities or kitchens. Prisoners were fed a gruel of thin soup and half-cooked manioc or rice. The gruel was cold in the morning, sometimes hot at the evening meal. Occasionally there was a piece of potato in the gruel. Usually not."

The projector cycled *click-click.* Another image of inhumanity appeared.

"There was no regular exercise. There were no regular latrine periods. Many of the men had diarrhea for months. Many died of dehydration. Any man who showed resistance to authority was beaten with bamboo poles and locked in a tiger cage in his own filth."

Click-click. They were disturbing images: American fighting men— but unarmed, unmade, unmanned. Their uniforms were spattered with dirt and feces, bodies ravaged with dysentery, eyes staring through the bamboo bars in terror or despair.

"Talking was a serious offense. Anyone overheard talking was beaten and hung in a tiger cage. No respect was given to rank. All officers were subjected to endless, repetitive interrogation. Any officer considered uncooperative was beaten and hung in a tiger cage."

Click-click.

"There were no blankets or bedding—only dirt and planks. During the winter rains the captives were continuously cold and wet for up to ninety days. Each week the prisoners were marched into nearby villages to be humiliated. The villagers threw garbage and their own waste at them. Prisoners were coerced into making anti-war statements and confessing to war crimes. Soviet bloc photographers filmed these outrages."

Click-click. A slide of the *Pravda* article about the seven conspirators appeared on the screen.

"In 1971, Charlie started an intense campaign of re-education on the Chu My prisoners. The objective was to extract war crimes confessions from them. Five hours of VC propaganda and rote recitations every day. Long tirades about the growing peace movement in the United States, the demonstrations and draft card burnings. Every kind of psychological brutality to make the prisoners feel isolated and abandoned by their government and the American people. Any prisoner who refused to participate was severely beaten and deprived of food and medical attention. Any prisoner who lagged behind the group in memorizing slogans was locked overnight in a tiger cage. These seven men spent an aggregate of twenty-three years at Chu My before repatriation. Most made confessions. As a rule, POWs who didn't make confessions didn't come home."

The narrator's voice droned on. But Hernandez was no longer watching the slides.

His policeman's mind had stepped through the screen into the stinking, vermin-crawling darkness of the prison. In the echoing blackness—by the slow *drip-drip* of fetid water—he could hear the labored breathing of the internees on the splintered planks beside him. He could feel the dampness of the mud reaching for him through the soggy wood. Night in Chu My. In the abyss of the jungle beyond the bamboo stockade, monkeys screamed and tigers grunted. Within the compound, in the narrow hooch, the men moaned in their sleep and Hernandez could sense their dreams—dim images of home and family and softball in the park on Sunday morning and . . ."

No. Those were *his* dreams, not the dreams of the prisoners of Chu My. What *did* warriors dream? Or did they dream at all?

Then, softly in the prison darkness, Hernandez felt a hand on his. And then another. And another. He tried to wrench away, to flee—but they held him. He tried to cry out but they silenced him. He could not escape; none of them could. They were bound together by their jailers, their suffering, their fate. But bound in what?

In what?

The screen went black. The room lights snapped on. Young officers around the table shifted uncomfortably in their chairs.

"Questions?" the narrator said.

Lieutenant Wheeler raised his hand; he was twenty-four, a round-faced, soft-eyed boy, an Idaho Mormon with a slow smile and a scrupulous, orderly mind. "Colonel Masters, what was the mortality rate?"

The civilian turned to him; one of his sleeves was empty, pinned up to where his armpit used to be. "In Chu My—thirty percent the first year, another thirty percent the second. After that, it was a matter of hanging on to life one hour at a time."

Wheeler's voice dropped. "What . . . kind of man would have the best chance of survival?"

"Hard to say. A determined man. A private man. A man who could eat centipedes and roaches. A man with an enormous capacity to endure inhuman cruelty. A man who could rise above his pain."

"Excuse me, Colonel," Hernandez said. "Rise above his pain to what?"

Masters shrugged. "Dunno. I didn't have it so bad. I was in the Hanoi Hilton—not Chu My."

DETENTION CELL #6, ANDREWS AFB, CAMP SPRINGS, MD

9:41 A.M. "This is getting us nowhere!" Shapiro slapped his pencil down, stood up and paced to the end of the narrow cell. The indictment, a copy of Christy's service record, notes on balls of foolscap cluttered the table, lay scattered on the floor.

Christy slouched in her chair. "I don't know what you want from me."

"Dammit, they found the gun that killed Kulikov in your desk! You've got to give me something to convince them you're not guilty!"

"I'm not. I'm innocent." She leaned forward, rested her elbow on the table, and lowered her forehead into the palm of her hand. She was exhausted, drained. She'd had less than two hours' sleep; it was a struggle to keep her eyes open. The wounds on her arms and legs were burning, stiffening; her swollen cheek throbbed relentlessly with pain. And she could not ignore the tingling sense of panic in her gut. The planted murder weapon had sealed her guilt. The air force had already tried and convicted her of treason to the state and to her uniform. The bluff monolith of the military mind was a door that opened only from within.

And no one knew the military mind better than Bryan. No one better understood its rules, its tyrannous rigidity. Bryan had taught her: in battle, there are no coincidences.

Once the Cubans detected American fighter planes in combat over the Caribbean, they had no option but to sound their own alert. When the Cubans moved in force, the Kennedy Doctrine demanded escalation. From then on—in a litany as rigidly prescribed as the Order of the Mass—the two greatest military powers in history rose toward violence.

In the same way, Christy's path to imprisonment was preordained from the moment she picked up the first clue that led her to Polly's body. Once Christy had been identified with the conspiracy, the Uniform Code of Military Justice demanded her arrest. In the military's desperation over the alert, martial law and brutal imprisonment had followed, as they must have.

All that had happened had to happen, except for one detail: why had Bryan instructed Petrovsky to plant the murder weapon and mark Christy a murderess?

There had to be a purpose to it.

But what if there were no purpose? What if it were an act of naked malice—or worse, revenge?

A shudder ran through Christy, a deeper, inner cold than she had ever known. Could three years apart somehow have deformed Bryan's love for her to hate? Could this be Bryan's retaliation for some unintended love-wound that had festered to malignance?

Christy remembered the October afternoon she and Bryan had followed 17 Mile Drive to the Pacific shore and walked the empty, windswept beaches. The autumn rains had routed and dispatched the summer tourists. The gabled houses of the rich stood empty, curtains drawn, windows frosted blind by salty ocean spray. The two were alone; they might as well have been invisible.

"You never told me why you joined the air force," Bryan said.

Christy had her reasons, but they were private. "AFROTC gave me a scholarship to Harvard."

"You could have had other scholarships."

"I suppose."

"Then why the air force?"

"My father was in the air force."

"You never told me that."

"He died. A long time ago. In Vietnam."

At the tideline, a starfish lay half-buried in the sand. Christy knelt, and picked it up; it was a bat star—ruddy colored, stiff and prickly—with a tiny webbing between its arms like a military emblem. She turned the bat star over; its thousand tiny tube feet recoiled as if in fear. Poor creature—the retreating sea had left it to its fate; by night-fall, it would be dry and dead.

Gently Bryan said, "How did your father die?"

"His plane was hit by a Soviet-made missile over Hanoi."

"So you joined the air force for revenge?"

Christy tossed the dying red star on the sand, rose, and clapped her hands clean. "You could say that."

"Then you'll never be a real soldier."

"Why not?"

"Because your hate will blind you when the crisis comes. You're an intelligence officer. Your job is to *prevent* combat. Two armies with perfect intelligence will maneuver, but they won't engage." Bryan bent, picked up the starfish, flung the creature far into the surf, back into the safety of the sea. "No one hates war more than the warrior."

Christy remembered that lesson in compassion; the instinct to pre-serve that tiny life could not have been a lie. Bryan could not have planted the murder weapon to make her appear a murderess out of vengeance or malice—any more than Bryan could have raised the DEFCON2 alert to plunge the world into a nuclear holocaust. Like the alert, the planted murder weapon must have a larger purpose.

But what purpose?

Shapiro came back to the table. "Look, Christy, I can't help you if you don't help me. You can't hide behind name-rank-and-serial-number. You're not a prisoner of war."

Christy bristled. "Then why are they treating me like one?"

"Because they're the fucking air force—that's why!" Shapiro tossed his eyeglasses on the table in disgust. "I keep telling you—"

"What time is it?"

"What's the difference?"

"Please, what time is it?"

"Twenty to ten. Now, listen, the only way you're going to get any leniency . . ."

Christy turned away. Shapiro might be the most well-intentioned man in the world, but his questions were a nagging distraction. She had to put any thought of her own salvation aside. All that mattered was cracking Bryan's riddle.

But time was running out. In less than eighty minutes the conspiracy would have run its course.

Shapiro put one foot up on the chair beside her and leaned his elbow on his knee. "Christy, I'm not getting through to you. The air force has a massive circumstantial case. You worked for two of the conspirators. O'Neill came to your house last night. You brought Mrs. Watkins to the prison. The gun that murdered Kulikov—"

"Dammit. I told you. I was following orders!"

"Oh, yeah? Well, they picked up Mrs. Watkins. She says you went to see her this morning."

Christy hesitated, trapped.

"That true? You go to see her again this morning?"

"Yes."

"Why?"

"I knew Colonel Petrovsky was doing something illegal. I was trying to find out what it was."

"Why? What the hell was it to you?"

Christy shook her head. What was it to her after all? At any moment last night or this morning she could have walked away. She could have turned her back, ignored the clues, let the whispers of sedition go unheard. She could have let the conspiracy become someone else's problem. How could Bryan have been so sure she would take up the challenge and make the struggle her own?

Christy remembered standing over the footlocker in Polly's bedroom, staring at the streaky bloodstains on her fingers and knowing—knowing in that moment—that her next step would be a life-choice.

And at the same time realizing she had no choice.

The whole world could come crashing down around you and you'd still do your duty, wouldn't you?

"Hey!" Shapiro said. "I asked you a question. What was it to you? Huh?"

"It was my duty."

"Duty?" He leaned down, stuck his face in hers, and spat the word. *"Duty?* You think a court-martial's going to believe—" He shut his eyes and ran his hand back through his hair. "For chrissake, you're hanging yourself every time you open your mouth!"

Christy put her elbows on the table, lowered her head, and covered her ears with her hands. But even that did not dull the sound of Bryan's laughter ringing in her ears.

In the moonless darkness of the stratosphere, the three B52-Hs of Charlie flight bore northward above the black abyss of the Pacific.

In the navigation bay behind and below the cockpit, Lieutenant Arnold Boyce fine-tuned the shortwave band until the sound of Buddy Holly singing "Peggy Sue" cut through the static. He tapped the intercom. "Coming up on the Tropic of Cancer, Major. Radio Iwo Jima on the shortwave. Want me to feed it through?"

In the cockpit, Major Cutler tapped in on the intercom. "Maybe not tonight, Arnie."

"Yeah. Right. Sorry, Major." Boyce snapped the music off. They were twenty minutes from rendezvous with their tanker, seventy-seven minutes from fail-safe.

AFOSI HQ, BOLLING AFB, WASHINGTON

9:43 A.M. The Security Policeman held the door and Fat Beth Harding plowed into Colonel John Hernandez's office, the long dirty skirts of her muumuu hanging out beneath the hem of a military raincoat.

Lieutenant Wheeler, the investigative aide, turned a chair to her. "Mrs. Harding, won't you please sit here?"

But she stood glaring. "The hell you want with me?"

"A few questions about your husband," Hernandez said. "That's all. Please."

Fat Beth dropped into the chair before the desk. "He's dead. What else is there to know?"

"Well, for one thing," Wheeler said, "why he assassinated Senator Whitworth."

She stared at the fresh-faced young lieutenant. "That's the dumbest fuckin' question I ever heard."

Wheeler winced.

"Mrs. Harding," Hernandez said, "did your husband ever express opposition to the president's First Step—"

"Aw, cut the crap, Colonel. He shot the bastard because Petrovsky told him to."

"How do you know that?"

"He always did what Petrovsky told him. Ever since Chu My."

Hernandez sat forward. *That* was the heart of the mystery. "Yes,

I'm sure that's true, Mrs. Harding. But why? What hold did Colonel Petrovsky have on your husband?"

"Hold on him?" Fat Beth cackled bitterly; she eyed the officers with contempt. "Brotherly love, asshole."

DETENTION CELL #6, ANDREWS AFB, CAMP SPRINGS, MD

9:44 A.M. Shapiro signed for the envelope, then stood staring at it until the SP guard closed and bolted the cell door.

From her place at the table Christy watched him, uneasy. "What's that?"

"Not the room service menu." Shapiro slit the seal with a yellow pencil and scanned the official notice. "I'll be a—they've arrested your grandmother!"

Christy scrambled to her feet. "What? Why?"

Quickly Shapiro ran his eye down the bill of particulars. "Did your grandmother become an American citizen?"

"She . . . she never even learned to speak English."

"They're calling her an illegal alien." He flipped to the second page "And they're going to deport her to the Soviet Union!"

"NO!"

Christy snatched the letter from his hand; the stationery bore the seal of the United States Immigration and Naturalization Service. She tried to read the words, but her eyes couldn't focus, couldn't frame them into sentences. Her voice broke. "They can't—"

"Christy." Shapiro plucked the letter from her trembling fingers. "They can."

"But why would they do that? She's an old woman. She doesn't—"

He took her by the shoulders. "Christy, listen to me. They don't give a damn about your grandmother. They're trying to squeeze you. They think if they squeeze you hard enough, you'll talk."

Christy stiffened; Shapiro was right. It was another of her captors' maneuvers to harass and degrade her. Last night and this morning, she had done her duty as she saw it, as Bryan had known she would; because she had, she was imprisoned and accused of capital crimes. Now her tormentors were escalating their brutality. Christy thought of her grandmother clutching her shawl about her, surrounded by armed men in uniform, understanding neither their conversation nor their purpose nor why they had dragged her from her home. Christy could feel her grandmother's fear and confusion; she burned with rage and indignation.

Why was Bryan torturing her this way?

Christy reached out and caught Shapiro's arm. "Captain, you've got to do something!"

"Like what?"

"Call the Pentagon. Talk to the chief of staff. She has nothing to do with this. She must be terrified."

"All right. All right." Shapiro peeled her fingers from his wrist. "Lemme go. I'll see what I can do." He rapped once on the door for the guard.

Dazed and drained, Christy sank into a chair. "I can't believe the air force would do this."

"Hey—remember the My Lai massacre? In war desperate men do desperate things." The guard unbolted the door and Shapiro hurried out.

AFOSI HQ, BOLLING AFB, WASHINGTON

9:46 A.M. Major Madeline Follett, the OSI psychiatrist, was summing up. "Intense feelings of loyalty to the group. High levels of personal bonding. A belief in the infallibility of their leader. And, as we've seen, an obvious indifference to the value of human lives, including their own."

Lieutenant Wheeler leaned in beside Hernandez. "All of which would make a man a pretty good soldier."

"Tell me about it," Hernandez said.

The conference table was strewn with papers, notes, and files; Wheeler and the other junior officers had hung their jackets over the backs of the chairs. Only Colonel Hernandez sat stiffly in uniform. A blow-up of the *Pravda* photograph of the seven Chu My prisoners was pinned to the corkboard behind the table. An angry red X had been drawn through five of the faces. The faces of Petrovsky and Bryan—the two men still unaccounted for—remained untouched.

Major Follett closed her notebook. "That's about it. Except for a predictable bitterness toward the government for turning its back on them during the Vietnam War. And deep feelings of guilt among those who made political statements for their captors."

Hernandez stared at the warriors' faces in the photograph. His mind fingered their features, struggled to feel their pain, their sense of alienation, the resentment they must have felt toward a government that had mired them in a senseless war and then repudiated them. But the distant eyes confessed no secrets.

The door opened; an airman entered. "Pardon me, Colonel. Sergeant Tuttle has arrived."

Hernandez didn't recognize the name. Wheeler said, "The man who was in Chu My prison with our friends."

"Good." Hernandez got to his feet. "Show him in, Airman. Thank you, Major."

But as Follett started for the door, Tuttle rolled in and blocked her way. He was a burly man in a wheelchair; he had a knotty black beard and shaggy hair tied behind his neck in a red bandanna. He wore the boots and leathers of a Hell's Angel, and he wasn't happy to be there.

"What the fuck is goin' on? SPs hustle my ass out of bed like the house was on fire. Who the hell—"

Quietly Hernandez said, "Mr. Tuttle, I'm Colonel Hernandez. What we have here is a national emergency. We think you can help us."

"Me? Why should I?"

"Mr. Tuttle, the country's in danger. You've heard reports of the alert."

"So? What the hell has this country done for me?"

"Please, Mr. Tuttle," Hernandez said. He nodded to Wheeler.

Wheeler pointed to the photograph pinned to the corkboard. "Mr. Tuttle, do you recognize these men?"

Tuttle gave it hardly a glance. "Bunch of clowns like that? Fuck, no!"

"They were in Chu My prison with you."

Tuttle looked back over his shoulder. "Say what?" Then he turned his chair, rolled closer to the wall, stared up at the photograph, and began to chuckle. "Well, lookie here. That's whatshisface—Petrovsky. And Harding, his android."

"His what?"

"His gofer. His errand boy." Slowly Tuttle rolled his chair, passing the prisoners one by one. "That's Watkins—snooty black bastard. And O'Neill—always mumbling over his beads. That one on the stretcher is Stump Logan. Sonofabitch cut his own legs off when he ejected. And that one's Granger. Nursed Logan like his fucking baby. And—" He broke off and stopped before the image of the last prisoner.

"Do you recognize that man?" Wheeler said.

"And that's the Ice Man." There was an odd cast to Tuttle's eyes. "He was the boss coolie."

"No, Mr. Tuttle," Wheeler said. "Captain Petrovsky was the senior officer in the prison."

Tuttle didn't look back. "Yeah. Petrovsky was the brass. But Bryan, he was the strength."

"How do you mean?"

"The more they beat him, the more he wouldn't bend." Through the black tangle of Tuttle's beard a crooked smile bent his lips. "Poor bastard would just sit out all night in that cage in his own shit, promising the moon he'd make it home and tell people the truth about the fuckin' war."

Hernandez stepped past Wheeler. "Mr. Tuttle, why did Charlie beat Captain Bryan more than anyone else?"

" 'Cause he wouldn't make no statement for 'em. Wouldn't confess to no war crimes. Just kept repeating his name, rank, number and his birthday."

Wheeler snorted. "That's all any prisoner of war has to tell his captors."

Abruptly Tuttle pivoted his chair. Then he rolled to Wheeler and shouted, "After what they did to us we said anything they wanted us to say! And so would you—you motherfucker!"

Hernandez stepped between them. "Yes, Mr. Tuttle—I'm sure we would." He turned a chair from the table, sat down face-to-face with the man. "But if Captain Bryan didn't believe in the war, why was he the only one who wouldn't make a statement?"

Tuttle wiped his nose with the back of his hand, and Hernandez could see there were tears in his eyes. "Because he loved this shit-eating country more than he loved his life."

Hernandez stared at Tuttle in silence. It was the one motive he had not considered.

Wheeler leaned in beside Hernandez. "Sir, if that's what we're up against . . ."

"Yes. We're in trouble."

AMERICAN MISSION, 11 ROUTE DE PREGNY, GENEVA

3:50 P.M.   Jake pushed through the door to his office, flung his overcoat across a chair, and punched a button on his intercom. "Weatherby, I need you."

"On my way, sir."

On eager, bouncing steps Jake hurried to the windows and looked out. The afternoon sun was already settling toward the western hills. November in Switzerland. The days were short. His time was short. He looked at his watch. The B-52s from Guam were seventy minutes from fail-safe, and this opportunity might never come again. Whatever the objective of the conspirators, whatever other atrocities they might be planning, they had blundered onto a stratagem that might impel mankind to renounce forty-five years of thermonuclear insanity.

There was a tapping at the door and Sara entered. "Yes, sir?"

Eagerly, Jake drew her into the room, shut and locked the door. "Listen to me, Weatherby. Something's happened. Something enormous."

"What, Doctor?"

"Nothing."

"I beg your pardon?"

"Nothing's happened. Don't you see?" Jake paced excitedly. "For years, Soviet war plans called for launch-on-warning. That gangster, Brezhnev, even bragged about it. Now, this morning we discover they're prepared to sit out a DEFCON2 alert and see what happens. What does that tell you?"

"Perhaps . . ."

"Yes?"

"Perhaps they've seen the light."

Jake clapped his hands together. "Exactly! My god, Weatherby. This alert has given us a chance to break these talks wide open!" He went to the door, unlocked it, and stuck his head out. "Miss Green! Call the ambassador. Tell him we must convene the START team in the bubble immediately!" He turned to Sara. "Come on, Weatherby. There's no time to lose. A new world is waiting to be born!"

DETENTION CELL #6, ANDREWS AFB, CAMP SPRINGS, MD

9:51 A.M.   In the chilly silence, Christy lay on the bare mattress of the cot, her arms clutched to her breast against the November cold, her eyes shut, her breathing soft and measured. But she was not sleeping. Sentimental images of her grandmother flooded over her: summer afternoons in the rose-scented garden behind the matchstick house in Trenton; the dusky, reassuring breast she'd run to when the other children called her Piggy Eyes and Squinty; the Russian *matrioshka* doll at Christmas—shaped like a bowling pin and heavy for a child—with one figurine inside another down to a miniature baby doll that fit like a blessing in her hand.

Christy shook her head, shook off those thoughts. She already knew what the Pentagon would say when Shapiro protested her grandmother's arrest. *Put it in writing. The chief of staff will take it under consideration. You will be advised.* She could not help her grandmother. She could not help herself. She was isolated and alone, deprived of friendship and freedom, under indictment for capital crimes and already condemned by her captors. What had Petrovsky said about his imprisonment? *It's a strangely liberating feeling, the moment you realize you've been abandoned and doomed to die. It lets you see things as they really are.* There was nothing to be gained by wallowing in self-pity now. She had to fight back with the weapons that she had—her discipline, her sense of duty, her courage, her intelligence.

She forced herself to think again of that recurring, hazy image—the circular lantern slide of the DEFCON2 deployment she had studied in Bryan's class. That polar projection of the alert was shining now on plotting screens throughout America's strategic command. At DEFCON2, the American and Soviet land- and sea-based missile platforms had become tiny, static pinpricks of light. The nuclear teeter-totter had yawed and gimbaled, only to recover its equilibrium and lumber onward toward the moment of ultimate terror Bryan called *Point Paradox.*

Christy squeezed her eyelids tight, peered with her mind's eye at the ghostly vision. It remained cloudy, indistinct. Even so, she could see the deadly game was drawn.

Or was it?

Softly in the dark recess of her imagination she heard a rumbling like distant thunder. Christy cocked an inner ear. Slowly—by degrees—the reverberation rose around her. Christy felt her muscles tighten; her arms and legs went cold. The roar grew louder, swelled and deepened until it seemed to shake the very bed she lay on, boomed against the walls of the detention cell. The air in her lungs thinned, went frigid, turned crystalline. The thunder rose to deafening. Her heart began to pound. She panted, gasped, opened her mouth to breathe—

And then her mind's eye saw the flights of B-52 bombers breaking from the clouds, climbing into the brilliant light and frigid stratosphere, thundering toward fail-safe.

Christy sat bolt upright on the cot, her face and body drenched in perspiration; only when the bombers began reaching fail-safe would the alert achieve *Point Paradox*. She jumped from the bed, rushed to the cell door, pounded on its cold steel.

"Guard! GUARD!"

A laconic voice outside muttered, "The hell you want?"

"What time is it?"

"Whadda you care?"

"Please, what time is it?"

"Ten to ten. Now shut up!"

Christy leaned against the door. It was 9:50 A.M.—1450 Zulu. Her mind spun through the calculation. Sunrise: about 6:45 A.M. Flying time to Cuba at Mach .9—perhaps a hundred minutes. That put the DEFCON2 order near 8:30 A.M. By now, the Strategic Air Command's alert bombers had been aloft for an hour and twenty minutes. Her memory clicked through the list of SAC alert bases: Loring, Griffiss, Minot, Ellsworth, Fairchild. Bombers based along the northern tier of the United States—in New York State, North and South Dakota and the state of Washington—were still thousands of air miles from fail-safe; bombers based in Arkansas, Louisiana, and Texas were even farther.

Christy slouched against the door. For the moment there was no cause for panic. There was time to . . .

Then she remembered.

Guam.

SAC bombers conducted regular training exercises out of Andersen Air Force Base on Guam—twenty-four hundred air miles from Vladivostok. Christy raised her head; the bomb wing from Guam would be at fail-safe in just over an hour.

1600 Zulu.

11:00 A.M. Washington time.

The time of the veterans.

Christy went rigid. There are no coincidences.

The bolt slammed back, the cell door swung open. It was Shapiro—grim. Christy's mind flashed to her grandmother.

"Well? What did they say?"

Shapiro pushed past Christy, threw his briefcase on the desk. "Sergeant Jeeter went off duty at 0900. SPs are looking for him now."

"I mean about my grandmother! Captain?"

"Yeah. Your grandmother." He turned on her; his eyes were angry. "Was your grandmother awake when O'Neill came to see you last night?"

"What?"

"Was she awake? Yes or no?"

"Well . . . yes. She let O'Neill in and—"

"Did she overhear your conversation?"

"I don't—"

"Dammit! Did she overhear your conversation with O'Neill?"

"I suppose so. What's the difference? She barely speaks English."

"You said she *didn't* speak English. You said that this morning!"

"Doesn't . . . barely . . . what's the—"

Then something in Shapiro seemed to snap. "You lied to me about your grandmother! You lied to me about Mrs. Watkins!"

"No. I just—"

"Goddammit! If you knew where Mrs. Watkins was hiding, why didn't you report it to the police? Answer the question!"

"Because I didn't want the police to know where to find her."

"Jesus H. Christ! Why not?"

Christy shut her eyes. What was happening could not be real. It couldn't happen in an American military prison. But it *was* happening. By some alchemy, Bryan had plunged her through a crack in reason, had flung her headlong into a perverse, inhuman world where sadistic brutes in uniform mocked the laws of war. Bryan had incarcerated her in a place of nightmares where every honorable act was rewarded with contempt. A place where every duty was repaid in cruelty.

"Dammit!" Shapiro shouted. "Why not?"

Dully, distantly, Christy murmured, "My god . . ." and recognized where she was.

In a place exactly like the jungle prison called Chu My.

AMERICAN MISSION, 11 ROUTE DE PREGNY, GENEVA

3:54 P.M. "Shut the goddamn door!" Mulholland snapped. The marine sentry yanked the door of the bubble closed with a resounding *clang!* Grumbling, the START team leaders took their places at the table; Sara sat against the wall behind Jake's chair. "Now, what's so damned important, Jake? The Soviet delegation is due here any minute."

Jake was breathless with excitement. "Mr. Ambassador, has it occurred to you that we're alive?"

"What?"

"Oh, Jesus," Drysdale said. "Here we go again. What is it this time, Jake? More launch-at-fail-safe bullshit? Or some wacko bomber crew single-handedly attacking the Soviet Union?"

Whittaker guffawed.

Jake ignored their ridicule. He looked up at the clock above the door; the first B-52s were sixty-six minutes from fail-safe. "Mr. Ambassador, an hour ago the Soviet ambassador came to your office to deliver their formal protest—but asked us not to cancel this afternoon's gala. Didn't that strike you odd?"

"No. Karpov felt a cancellation might—"

"But do you remember what he said? In our country, too, we have such zealots."

"Now what the hell does that mean?" General Fuchs said. "That they've got a conspiracy going on over there, too?"

"No, Arnold, that they understand we have no franchise on fanatics."

Lazily, Drysdale tipped his chair back and cocked the sole of one shoe against the table. "Jacob, my friend. You better tell me something I *don't* know in about the next ten seconds, or I'm going up to my office and take a dump—y'hear?"

"Rufus, are you aware that if this alert had happened, say, in 1982, the world might already be a cinder?"

Drysdale snapped his fingers. "That reminds me—I gotta write Gorby a thank-you note."

The men around the table chuckled.

But Jake pressed on. "This afternoon the Soviet ambassador told us they've ordered their Strategic Rocket Forces to wait out a DEF-CON2 alert."

"For Pete's sake," Whittaker snapped. "What the hell do you expect them to do?"

"No, Jason. Until this morning, what did we *all* expect them to do?"

Sara watched the faces of the men; their smiles faded as they began to sense the logic.

Jake said, "If we had war-gamed this yesterday . . . if we had postulated the Soviet Stavka would come back from lunch to find United States strategic forces moving to DEFCON2 . . . every one of us would have bet his life we'd be at war right now."

The men looked back and forth among themselves; there was no denying it.

"Well . . . what do you make of that?" Mulholland said.

"They know," Jake said.

"They know?" Drysdale muttered irritably. "They know *what?*"

"They know we aren't preparing to attack them."

Drysdale blinked; then he turned nasty. "Now, Jake, that is *fucking brilliant.* For chrissake, all they have to do is turn on CNN to see this alert was triggered by a bunch of—"

"You're missing my point." Jake got to his feet. "Gentlemen, you're thinking about this as Americans. That's a mistake. You've got to try to see what's happened today through Russian eyes." He paced the length of the table. "Television news reports can be faked. Treason can be suborned. As far as the Soviets know, this whole conspiracy could have been devised by the Pentagon as a pretext for launching an all-out first strike. Those are the kinds of possibilities that have been running through the minds of the Politburo and Stavka this afternoon. Remember, their general staff are the same officers who sent provocateurs into Afghanistan to foment unrest and then sent troops to pacify the country." He stopped at the end of the table. "Do you really think the Soviet leadership would stake the survival of their homeland on a CNN report that the conspiracy is real? There's only one way—only one—they could be certain we're not going to attack them."

"Yeah? What's that?"

"They know we can't fire our missiles."

General Fuchs snorted. "What the hell would give them a dumb idea like that?"

"Because this afternoon as they prepared to respond to our alert, they finally realized they cannot fire theirs."

For a moment, the room sat silent.

"Jake," Whittaker said gently. "I think your imagination is—"

"Just a minute," Mulholland said. "Jake, what are you getting at?"

Jake stood at the end of the table; behind the gray of his beard, his face was flushed. "Since the Second World War, one Soviet government after another has clung to the absurd belief that a nuclear war could be fought and won. Now, today, they finally realized that's impossible. Mr. Ambassador, we must recall our bombers. Before they reach fail-safe. And we must—"

"Forget that!" Fuchs snapped. "We've got to coordinate the recall with the Soviets. Otherwise they could catch us with our pants down."

"And do what, Arnold?" Jake demanded. "Do *what*?" He scanned the table. "Don't you see what's happened? Dawn is breaking, gentlemen. The Soviets have finally realized the weapons are useless."

"Oh, for chrissake—"

"They *are* useless! If anyone should know that—we should!"

"Goddammit, Jake—"

Mulholland slapped his open palm down on the tabletop. "General, that's enough!"

Fuchs slouched back in his chair.

"All right, Jake," Mulholland said; his voice was pinched and tense. "Assuming you're right—what then? After we've recalled the planes?"

"Get Karpov back here. This afternoon. Begin negotiations to eliminate all offensive strategic nuclear weapons—beginning with the multi-warhead intercontinental missiles. Now, while they still have the taste of fear in their mouths. While the will to live is stronger than the will to conquer."

Mulholland hesitated, vacillating.

Jake stood before him, eyes desperate. "Mr. Ambassador, we've waited for a chance like this since 1948! We may never have another chance like this again."

Mulholland looked down the table. "Jason?"

Whittaker smiled gently. "A lovely notion, Jake. But politically impractical."

"General?"

Fuchs crossed his arms. "I won't dignify this nonsense with an answer."

"Rufus?"

Drysdale pushed his chair back from the table and stood. "Gentlemen, I'll be in the john." He opened the door of the bubble and Jake's dream walked out with him.

NATIONAL MILITARY COMMAND CENTER, FORT RICHIE, MD

9:56 A.M.   General Gaynor put down the telephone and turned to the president. "Ambassador Volokin is at the Soviet embassy. We've dispatched a helicopter from the Pentagon. He'll be here in twenty minutes."

"At last!" Sam Baker said. "Thank you, General." He turned to his press secretary, Ron Fowler. "All right, Ron. What is it you wanted me to see?"

Fowler hit the remote control; the videocassette recorder whirred and the image on the television monitor rolled and locked. It was NBC correspondent John Cochran standing before the smoke-blackened West Wing of the White House. Behind him, firemen carried hoses and axes back to their trucks as Secret Service men stood by, automatic weapons cradled in their arms.

> COCHRAN
> Tom, the fire in the White House ADR is out. But even as the cleanup begins, the extraordinary violence of these coordinated attacks, which have left more than fifty dead, has stunned even anti-terrorist professionals. Pentagon spokesmen refuse to characterize this as a "military conspiracy," even though all the known perpetrators are navy and air force active duty personnel or veterans. Presently, five of the conspirators are known dead, two accomplices are in custody. And a massive manhunt is under way to locate and apprehend two remaining fugitives who are believed to be . . .

Sam Baker sighed; the violence had stunned him as well. He glanced at Gaynor. Was it—as they assured him—only seven men? Modern weapons had given individuals the power to change history. Three million had died to transform the government of Russia in the revolution and civil war of 1917–20; ten million were dead before Mao finally communized China in 1949. But fewer than six thousand died when Ceaușescu fell in 1989. And it had cost only 150 American lives to drive Saddam Hussein from Kuwait and destroy his army. The more highly trained and technically equipped the soldiers, the fewer required to topple a government. And if seven men could do this much damage, what could 700 or 700,000 do?

It beggared the imagination.

That was why the massive standing armies had to be reduced. Yes, the money was important—reductions in the Pentagon budget would diminish the federal deficit and ease the nation's simmering economic crisis. But that was only the proximate cause, not the underlying reason. Soldiers who had been trained and equipped to kill *were* dangerous. In Europe, in Asia, and the Middle East—wherever men with tanks and guns faced each other across ideological barricades—there was jeopardy.

And yet . . .

That was *not* where the danger lay this morning. It was 1456 Zulu by the clock—almost an hour and a half into the alert—but, in Europe, the conventional forces of NATO and the Soviets had only begun to mobilize. In Germany, the first M-1 Abrams tanks were just rolling out of their garages in Lübeck and Kassel. At Fort Bragg and Ord in the United States, the paratroops of Special Operations Command were still packing their gear.

Sam Baker turned away from the chatter on the television set and walked to the plotting screen. He stared at the tiny circles of light that were the Peacekeeper and Minuteman missile complexes in the northern United States, at the glowing asterisks in the Atlantic and Pacific that were America's Trident submarines. Those were the danger this morning: the land- and sea-based intercontinental missiles.

To be a convincing deterrent, those missiles had to be ready to fire at a moment's notice. This morning, sixteen hundred missiles bearing six thousand nuclear warheads were poised to rain a fury of destruction on the Soviet Union in a war that would be won and lost before NATO's tankmen came within miles of an enemy. In a curious way, First Step—like twenty years of SALT and START negotiations before it—had ratified and legitimized the deterrent. Rather than seeking by every means possible to *eliminate* strategic nuclear weapons, three decades of superpower dialogue had only sought to *control* them. Now, this morning, it was the weapons that were in control. Whether the opposing sides had fifty thousand warheads or had reduced their stockpiles to twenty-five thousand was immaterial to the point of absurdity. Sam Baker looked up at the plotting screen abashed; he had understood that paradox, but he had never stared it in the eye. Before him on the plotting screen the world's deterrent forces had unmasked themselves.

They were not a shield.

They were themselves the jaws of Armageddon.

Behind him, Fowler said, "Mr. President, you'd better see this."

On the television monitor an image of Tom Brokaw appeared, sharing the screen with John Cochran.

BROKAW

John, have there been any further reports on the whereabouts of President Baker or his condition?

COCHRAN

Tom, White House officials insist that President Baker is safe and unharmed. But NBC News has received unconfirmed reports the president may have been seriously or even fatally injured by the explosion in the underground air defense room. Until the president appears in public, we have no way of knowing—

Fowler zapped the television mute. "Mr. President—"

"All right, Ron, I understand."

"There's a mock-up of the Oval Office in this complex. You could address the nation from—"

Sam Baker shook his head. "No. The country knows the Oval Office was destroyed. The president speaking from an underground military command center would only terrify the public even more. As soon as Volokin and I agree on a time for a stand-down of forces, we'll move back to the East Wing of the White House and—"

The door slammed open. It was Ted Harris, in a lather. "That sonofabitch Petrovsky called a press conference!"

"*What?*"

Harris panted the words. "Eleven o'clock. The Vietnam Memorial. Camera crews are already setting up. All the American networks, the BBC, the CBC—the whole damn world will be there!"

"We can't let that madman have an international forum to—"

"Don't worry. I've taken care of it." Harris mopped the perspiration from his neck. "Military police are waiting for Petrovsky at Dulles Airport. The FBI and park police have the Mall sealed off. He won't get within a mile of—" He broke off. "What the hell?" He snatched the remote control from Fowler and zapped the television sound on.

The image on the monitor was Mike Marden, seated at the NBC News Washington flash desk. "Senator Whitworth and Secretary of

Defense Littman were heroes to all men and women who love liberty. We at NBC News will pursue the conspirators who murdered them"—Marden paused for emphasis—"even if the trail leads to Moscow and the KGB."

Harris growled, "That sonofabitch. . . ."

The image slowly zoomed to a close-up of Marden. "And if President Baker is still alive, we demand he answer two questions: If there is no threat of Soviet military action, why are America's strategic nuclear forces at full alert? And if this is *not* a military conspiracy . . . why has a senior air force officer called a press conference to explain why seven war heroes attempted to assassinate the president of the United States?"

Harris glared at the image of Marden and gritted his teeth. "Where's that crazy navy pilot now that we really need him?"

DULLES AIRPORT, HERNDON, VA

9:58 A.M. Through the bronze solar glass windows Lieutenant Robert Gleason could see the lone people-mover making its slow, wobbling journey toward the arrival gate. Behind him the flight of security police stood at parade rest, their rifles with fixed bayonets beside them. At the far side of the deserted waiting area Colonel Hallas stood behind a column, half out of view.

The public address chimed and a voice crackled, "United Express announces the arrival of flight 1267 from Greenville, Norfolk, and Richmond."

Gleason turned to his troops. "Take your positions!" With a clatter of arms, the men ringed the jetway door, their weapons ready before them.

The people-mover reached the jetway; passengers began to disembark. Some were military who exchanged nods with Gleason. Most were civilians who stopped to stare at the armed SPs. But a sergeant and two airmen hustled them through the security barriers, into the arms of waiting state police who rushed them down the escalator to the baggage claim and out of the line of fire.

An air force colonel in a trench coat came through the door. Abruptly Gleason stepped into his path. "Colonel Petrovsky, you are under arrest!"

The colonel stared at Gleason in astonishment. Then he opened the front of his coat; the nameplate on his uniform jacket read HOPKINS. "What's the meaning of this, Lieutenant?"

Gleason flushed. "Excuse me, Colonel." Embarrassed, he hurried toward the jetway.

"Now just a damn minute!" Hopkins stomped after him.

Colonel Steven Petrovsky stepped through the doorway; he carried his briefcase in one hand, a raincoat over his other arm. He saw the line of armed SPs and stopped. Gleason confronted him.

"Colonel Petrovsky?"

"What can I do for you, Lieutenant?"

"Colonel, I have orders to place you under arrest."

Hopkins barreled up between them. "See here, Lieutenant! You can't insult a superior officer like that and—"

Quietly Petrovsky said, "Lieutenant, would you and this fool and your troops please get out of my way."

Hopkins glared. "Who are you calling a fool?"

Petrovsky laid his raincoat on a railing. In his hand he held a plastic concussion grenade. The pin had been pulled; Petrovsky's thumb held the spring-loaded safety lever closed.

Without hesitating, Gleason drew his automatic pistol, cocked it, and aimed it at Petrovsky's chest.

Hopkins looked back and forth between them. "Hey, listen . . . no offense meant—none taken . . . right?" He drifted aside, then hurried away.

Slowly, measuring his words, Gleason said, "Colonel Petrovsky, where is the pin for that grenade?"

"In my pocket. And if you don't clear this area, you're going to have a lot of bodies to bag."

"Colonel, I demand you give me the pin so I can immobilize that grenade."

Petrovsky smiled at the young man. "Lieutenant, are you prepared to die for your country?"

Gleason blinked. "Yes, sir. That is . . . if my duty requires it."

"Well, I'm one of those old-timers who doesn't think of it as a duty but as a privilege. Do I make myself clear?"

Colonel Hallas stepped out of the shadows. "That will be all, Lieutenant. Thank you."

"Yes, sir." As Gleason backed away, Hallas said, "Hello, Steve."

"Vinnie. Still pulling every lousy detail."

"Yeah. Rotten habit." Hallas shrugged. "It's over, Steve. Five are dead. There's only you and Bryan."

"Then it's not over."

"Where's Bryan, Steve?"

Petrovsky looked at his watch. "Vinnie, I don't have much time. What do you want?"

"Answers."

Petrovsky held up his briefcase. "They're in here. I'm on my way to deliver them to the American people."

"Can't let you do that, Steve. Country's on a hair trigger. Too much has happened."

Petrovsky let his eyes wander over the line of troops marshaled in the arrivals area. "So we have a standoff. You won't let me pass. And you can't kill me or you lose your last link to Bryan."

" 'Bout sums it up."

They stood a moment, measuring each other.

Then Petrovsky said, "Here," and held the briefcase out to Hallas. "Take it. Don't worry, it's not loaded."

Hallas took the case. "Okay, Steve, now shove the pin back into that grenade. Lot of people want to talk to you."

"Vinnie, do an old soldier a favor. Pull your troops back. Give me a minute to think."

"All the exits are covered."

"You were always thorough."

Hallas turned to Gleason. "Lieutenant, run this case through X-ray and get it on a chopper to OSI HQ. And move the men behind the security barricade."

Gleason took the case, called, "Flight—fall back!" and led the SPs to new positions beyond the tall glass barrier. Now the boarding area was cleared; the two men stood alone.

Hallas raised a finger. "One minute."

"Thanks." Petrovsky watched Hallas follow the SPs out. Then he scanned the deserted terminal.

Without people, there was an eerie strangeness about the huge building with the upward-sweeping roof. There were no announcements, no families with crying babies, no jabbered foreign tongues, no tearful greetings or farewells—only silence. Driving through the Richmond suburbs in the taxicab that morning, Petrovsky had been struck by the desolate streets, the shuttered stores, the empty sidewalks. Where were the people? At home? At church? Perhaps they were somewhere considering man's fate or pondering for the first time the nuclear cat's cradle their world had become. Petrovsky sighed. He had done his best to help them understand. He had done his duty. He could do no more.

At the far end of the gate area a large American flag hung suspended from the ceiling. Slowly at first, then in long, graceful strides, Petrovsky walked to the flag and stopped beneath it. He craned his neck, stared up at the great stripes of red and white that soared to the starfield.

Then he pulled himself to attention and snapped his right hand to the brim of his hat in a salute.

Hallas stepped out in front of the security barrier. "What the hell . . . ?"

There was a soft *ping* when Petrovsky released the safety lever of the grenade, a tinkle when the metal hit the marble floor.

Hallas shouted, "YOU SON OF A BITCH!"

The force of the explosion flung him backward through the tempered glass.

AMERICAN MISSION, 11 ROUTE DE PREGNY, GENEVA

4:00 P.M.   The Swiss were nothing if not punctual. On the dot of four, the first junior foreign ministry boys in navy suits and smart silk ties were already stepping out of their black Mercedes 190s, coming up the red carpet to the conference complex in the west wing of the American mission, queuing to shake hands and exchange taut bows with Ambassador Mulholland. Mission secretaries had been pressed into service to replace the missing Swiss housekeeping staff; they shuttled back and forth, carrying coats to the checkroom, passing trays of the obligatory California champagne.

In the conference wing of the mission, the large reception room was decorated with Soviet and American flags, dotted with cocktail tables surrounding a portable dance floor. A marine guard in civilian clothes sat at the piano, struggling through a fake book of golden oldies. But there was no gaiety in the room, no laughter—only soft solemnity and whispered conversation.

Jake and Lermontov stood at the makeshift bar, sipping champagne and watching the uneasy scene.

"My compliments," Lermontov said. "Under the circumstances . . . a lovely party."

"You mean a lovely paradox." Jake couldn't hide his rancor; while Mulholland, Drysdale and the diplomats munched hors d'oeuvres, a priceless opportunity to break the nuclear stalemate was slipping through their doughy fingers. "The bombers are sixty minutes from fail-safe. The Peacekeepers and SS-18s are enabled. The Typhoon and Trident submarines are ready to fire. Eighty thousand megatons of nuclear destruction prepared for launch." Jake looked about the room and sneered. "And we're gathering for champagne and caviar."

Lermontov took a miniature quiche from a passing platter. "Everyone's carrying it off very well, don't you think?"

"Considering the danger—brilliantly."

Lermontov leaned close to Jake and whispered, "Does it not frighten you?"

A sudden *crash!* turned their heads and shocked the room to silence. Women gasped. Men went rigid. The music stopped.

"Sorry, sorry," the secretary murmured and bent for the fallen tray. Others hurried to sweep up the broken glass, brought paper towels to sop the spilled champagne.

"On the contrary," Jake muttered with contempt. "It proves how truly civilized we are."

DETENTION CELL #1, ANDREWS AFB, CAMP SPRINGS, MD

10:01 A.M. Tod lay on his bunk, staring at the ceiling. The cell door vibrated with the grating sound of steel on steel. Then a sharp white light cut through the gloom and flashed into his face. He turned to it, squinting.

A guard's voice barked, "Back against the wall there, Browning."

Slowly Tod rose from the bunk.

The guard said, "Sure you wanna go in there, Cap'n?"

Captain Lewis Shapiro stood at the threshold. "I'll be all right. Thank you, Airman." He stepped inside and waited while the guard locked the door and his heavy footsteps faded in the distance.

"Well, Sarge, you've gotten yourself into one hell of a mess," Shapiro said.

"Guess so, sir."

"Stand at ease."

Tod did. "You my lawyer?"

"Christy's lawyer. You'll get a lawyer if the air force decides to go to trial."

"If?"

"Sit down, Tod." And when they were seated on the bunk, Shapiro said, "Your case depends on Christy's. If she's innocent, you'll go free."

"She's innocent. So am I."

"And if she isn't, you're going to hang beside her."

That silenced Tod.

"Now listen, Sarge. We don't have much time. What we say is protected by client-lawyer privilege. Nothing we say in here can be used against either of you in a court-martial. Do you understand?"

Tod nodded.

"Right now, the air force doesn't believe in 'innocent until proven guilty,' " Shapiro said. "The only way Christy can save herself—and save you—is by proving she's not involved in this conspiracy. And the way the case is stacking up against her, that's going to be damned hard to do."

"What do you mean, stacking up?"

"Tod, think about it. Christy worked for two of the conspirators. She led you to the dormitory where Sergeant Kulikov was murdered. They found the murder weapon in her desk." Before Tod could speak, Shapiro held up his hand. "I know. All circumstantial. But taken together, it looks like Christy had prior knowledge of—"

"She didn't. She didn't know any more than I did."

"Then how did she—"

"She just figured it out."

"Figured it out?"

"From the errands and the files that were erased and . . ."

But the words stopped coming. And Tod sat silent, pondering what he'd said.

Shapiro sighed. "See what I mean?"

Slowly, Tod raised a hand to his brow; his fingers were trembling. "Jesus Christ. . . ."

Shapiro laid a hand on Tod's shoulder. "Look. I may be able to arrange for you to be alone with Christy. Out in the exercise yard where you can't be overheard. If you love her, talk to her. Reason with her. You've been around. She hasn't. You know what the air force is like. Help her."

Shapiro leaned closer. "If she's innocent, I'll do everything I can to save her. But if she's involved—even in the smallest way—you've got to convince her to tell them everything she knows. Now. While it might be worth something to them." He rose and went to the door. "Get me something and I might be able to buy her life. Both your lives."

NATIONAL MILITARY COMMAND CENTER, FORT RICHIE, MD

10:03 A.M. "Mr. President, Colonel Petrovsky is dead," Hernandez said.

In the presidential command post, Sam Baker's hand tightened on the telephone receiver.

Ted Harris was listening on the extension. "Dammit!" he snarled. "You were supposed to take him alive!"

Hernandez sat in his office at OSI headquarters; Petrovsky's briefcase lay open on his desk. "The colonel's death was unavoidable, Mr. Harris. He took his own life . . . with a hand grenade." Hernandez set aside the envelope addressed to the American people, handed the typewritten press statement it contained to Lieutenant Wheeler, and waved him out the door. "He was carrying a message addressed to the American people. It's being faxed to you now."

Sam Baker looked to Harris. "Well. Maybe we'll finally get some answers. What else, Colonel?"

"We have the backup personnel files on all the conspirators except Bryan." Hernandez leafed the pile of dossiers. "All of them served in Vietnam. All were captured by the VC between 1968 and 1971 and interned together in a jungle prison called Chu My. Except for Granger and Logan, there is no indication they knew each other before their imprisonment. Six of the seven confessed to war crimes under duress. They were repatriated together in February of 1973."

"I see," the president said. "Anything else?"

"Yes, sir. Apparently the coded message Lieutenant Russoff carried to Mrs. Watkins was 'The sun will come up tomorrow.' "

"What does that mean?"

"We don't know, sir."

Harris covered the mouthpiece of his receiver. "I'll tell you what it means. It means we're dealing with a bunch of madmen."

"Colonel, what about the seventh man?" the president said. "What about Bryan?"

"He's no longer on active duty. We'll have his records any time now. Lieutenant Russoff says he's the ringleader—the mastermind behind the conspiracy."

"Figures," Harris said. "Any other leads?"

"We've picked up Mrs. Watkins. She says Petrovsky asked her

husband to kill Whitworth. When he refused, Petrovsky apparently poisoned him." He flipped a page. "We've picked up O'Neill's daughter, and we're looking for a Sergeant Jeeter. Russoff says he's an accomplice. And we've questioned Harding's wife."

"Does she know anything?"

"No, sir."

"Well, did she speculate? Did she give you any reason why—"

"She said it had something to do with . . . brotherly love."

Harris covered his mouthpiece again. "Jesus Christ. Sam, I'm telling you. They're all crazy."

Sam Baker looked up at the plotting screen—at the DEFCON2 deployment arrayed across the polar projection of the Northern Hemisphere. The conspirators had planned well; the president was trapped, hamstrung, caught in a double paradox. He could not order American strategic forces back to peacetime status until the Soviets agreed to a concurrent stand-down of their forces. And while he waited for the marine helicopter to bring Ambassador Volokin to the Presidential Command Post, global tensions ratcheted toward hysteria.

"Madmen perhaps," the president said. "But not crazy. All right, Colonel. Keep me informed."

He hung up and turned to Harris. "All of them in the same Vietcong prison. You don't suppose they were . . . brainwashed?"

Harris just stared; it was an ominous possibility.

Sam Baker rose, went to the plotting screen, and stood before it. At DEFCON2 the strategic forces of the Soviet Union and United States stood immobilized at their highest level of alert. Before him on the plotting screen, the superpowers' deterrent missiles had turned the world into a tinderbox. One tiny spark struck now—one glancing blow to either nation's strategic system—and civilization would be a smoking ruin.

Sam Baker shook the morbid thoughts away. Even at DEFCON2 the missile systems were secure. They had built-in safety measures, complex arming controls, fail-safe mechanisms that precluded any risk of—

A flickering movement on the plotting screen caught the president's eye.

Slowly, by tiny increments, a spider's web of filaments was stretching northward from the bases of the Strategic Air Command, marking the slow flight of the nation's nuclear bombers toward fail-safe. Sam Baker squinted at the screen. The deterrent missiles had gone enable ninety seconds after the DEFCON2 order; in the furor and hubbub that had followed, he had neglected to consider the bombers. No matter; the manned bombers were still far from fail-safe. In an age when computers and ballistic missiles could fight a world war to conclusion in forty minutes, manned bombers had become an anachronism.

Sam Baker thought wistfully of the big, slow planes—the graceful B-1Bs and the ungainly old B-52s that had sheltered the nation under their mighty wings for decades. They were a weapon a man could relate to, a reminder of simpler times when men followed their ideals and not economics into battle, when soldiers fought to protect civilian populations, not to exterminate them. The planes were not steered by mindless microprocessors; they had men aboard, and men had souls. Once the bombers reached fail-safe they would not fly on blindly to their targets. They would circle harmlessly while their crews awaited orders to—

Sam Baker broke his line of thought. What had Hernandez said the password was? The sun will come up tomorrow? A sinister whisper swept through Sam Baker. "Ted, the men flying our bombers—could any of them be Vietnam veterans?"

"No chance. SAC flying officers average thirty-three years old. Most of them are younger than the planes."

"Suppose they were *sons*?"

"Sons? What are you talking about?"

"Suppose they were the sons of veterans—their children."

Harris missed the point. "Sam, we're all veterans' sons."

In the darkness 350 air miles east of Daito Island, Major Marvin Cutler struggled to maneuver the lead B-52H of Charlie flight under the beacons of the KC-135's refueling boom. Above him, the huge tanker was barely visible by the pale glow of the crescent moon and ping of navigation strobes. In the strong westerly wind, the two mammoth planes yawed and pitched in a clumsy *pas de deux*.

In the navigation bay, Lieutenant Arnold Boyce tapped the intercom. "Got to lock up ASAP, Major. We're two minutes behind flight plan."

Cutler struggled with the steering yoke. "We'll make it up, Arnie."

Boyce shook his head. "Not in these headwinds, sir."

DETENTION COMPOUND, ANDREWS AFB, CAMP SPRINGS, MD

10:05 A.M.   The steel door rolled open and a policewoman shoved Christy through it. She stood, blinking and shivering in the strong November sun. Between the high fences topped with barbed wire the narrow concrete courtyard seemed empty.

"What am I supposed to—"

But the steel door slammed shut behind her.

Surprised to be left alone, Christy stood staring at the door. Then a familiar voice behind her called her name. She turned. Tod was coming toward her.

"Chris, are you all right?"

Her heart leapt; here was one man who loved her and would not abandon her. "Tod! Thank god you're . . ." Then she caught herself and looked around. "Wait a second. How did you—"

"Your lawyer."

"Captain Shapiro?"

"Yeah. He arranged it."

Warily, Christy scanned the compound; they were alone. And yet it was strange they should be permitted to meet this way.

Tod took her arm and led her to a corner near the fence. "Shapiro says my case depends on yours. If you're innocent, so am I."

"Then you're safe. They can't prove we're guilty if we're not."

"Christy, Shapiro's worried because of the way you seemed to figure it all out. It's all so whadyacallit . . ."

"Circumstantial?"

"Makes it look like—"

"I was part of it?"

He nodded silently.

She caught his hand. "Tod. You were with me. You know I wasn't—"

"Christy." Then his voice broke. "They're going to hang us. Please."

"Please *what*?"

Suddenly, he clutched her by the shoulders. "If you know anything about this damn conspiracy, tell them!"

She stared at him in disbelief.

"Christy, please! I don't want to . . ."

Her steely eyes silenced him. She tried to step back; he held her.
"Let go of me, Tod."

"Chris—"

"Sergeant! Let go of me *now*!"

He did, and stood, arms hanging limply at his sides. She turned to walk away.

"Chris, wait." He stared at her in awe. "Aren't you . . . afraid?"

"Afraid of what?"

"Of them, for chrissake! Of the air force!"

She raised her chin. She knew she was seeing him for the last time. "I love the air force."

She banged on the door for her jailer.

AFOSI HQ, BOLLING AFB, WASHINGTON

10:08 A.M.   John Hernandez sat at his desk; a copy of Colonel Petrovsky's prepared statement for the press lay before him. But Hernandez was not reading. He was staring at the clock on the wall, listening to its dim, incessant tick. Six of the conspirators were dead, but he still had more questions than answers. Where was Captain Bryan? What was he planning? Who—or what—would be the target of the next attack? And beyond those mysteries lay the greatest unanswered question of all: Why?

There was a knock at his office door; Lieutenant Wheeler pushed inside, waving a folder. "Colonel, it's here! Bryan's service record from St. Louis. We've found the seventh man!"

"Thank god!" Hernandez grabbed the file and slapped it open. "Do we know where he went after he was discharged?"

Wheeler leaned in over his shoulder and rifled through the faxes. "We should have that in the—" He broke off, eyes frozen on a document. "Oh, no."

Hernandez reached out, and yanked the page from Wheeler's hand. But he didn't have to read it; the legend across the top told him everything there was to know.

DETENTION CELL #6, ANDREWS AFB, CAMP SPRINGS, MD

10:09 A.M. The guard slammed and locked the cell door behind Christy. Shapiro stood waiting for her. "You talked to Tod?"

"Yes."

"Did he—"

Abruptly Christy pushed past him, went to the table, and sat down. "I want to see my grandmother."

Shapiro stared at her. Then he said, "I tried. No way."

"What about Sergeant Jeeter?"

"Nothing. Until the SPs find him—"

"Dammit—"

"Christy, I'm doing everything I can."

She slapped her hand down on the table. "I want to talk to the chief of staff! I want to see him myself!"

"Maybe we can make a deal."

That made her look up.

"I said maybe. It's a long shot, but it's worth a gamble."

"What kind of deal?"

Shapiro drew in the other chair and sat down beside her. "Tell them what else the conspiracy is planning. Maybe they'll let your grandmother go."

"Don't you think I would if I—" She broke off. "You still think I'm part of it!"

He seized her hand. "Christy, I'm trying to save your life."

She pulled free and scrambled to her feet. Her chair tumbled to the floor. She shouted, "You think I'm guilty!"

"I'm a soldier! I'm not paid to think!"

They glared at each other.

Then Shapiro muttered, "Sorry. I lost my temper. Sorry." He bent for Christy's chair and stood it beside the table. Then he picked up his yellow pad and flicked back to the beginning of his notes. "All right"—he yanked his tie knot down and snapped his collar open— "let's go over this from the beginning." He turned to her service record. "Your first interview with Petrovsky—you remember what was said?"

"No."

"What did he ask about?"

Sullen, she muttered, "Nothing important."

"Christy, come on."

"The usual thing. My family. My education. Why I wanted to be an air force officer."

"Why did you?"

"Because I love my country." Then she boiled over. "Dammit! Why don't you find Petrovsky and ask him?"

"They found Petrovsky."

Christy's head snapped around. "What? When?"

"Ten minutes ago. I got word while you were with Tod."

"Why didn't you tell me? My god, did he say anything? Did he—"

"Nope. Just blew himself up with a hand grenade."

A black wave of nausea swirled up out of Christy's gut. She clapped her hand over her mouth, choked down the spume of vomit that seared her throat, turned her face to the cold concrete wall, and rested her forehead against it, gasping for breath.

Shapiro tipped back in his chair. "You gonna be sick?"

She struggled to control her breathing. "No . . . no!"

"You sure? You don't look so good."

"I'm all right!" She swallowed the bitter, burning taste and shook her head clear. "I'm all right. What were we—"

"You were saying why you joined up."

She steadied herself against the wall and fought the rising dizziness. "My father. He was in the air force. He was shot down. Over North Vietnam. By a Soviet-made missile."

Shapiro stopped making notes and put his pencil down. "Well. Now we're getting somewhere. So you got into the air force to fight the Soviets."

She nodded, and pressed her arms against her sides to still the tremors that shook her shoulders.

"Only you woke up one morning and the Cold War was over."

"Yes."

"Then your buddies Petrovsky and Bryan came along and offered you a little chance for adventure and the next thing you knew you're part of a conspiracy that's got the United States and Soviet Union—"

Christy pushed herself away from the wall. "NO! Dammit! I told you, I'm not guilty!"

"Okay. Okay. Tough little cookie, aren't you?" Shapiro's mouth bent in grudging admiration. "Funny. You're Russian yourself but you—"

"I'm not Russian. I'm American."

"Come on—your name's Russian. Your grandmother's an old woman from the Crimea who hardly speaks English. And what about this? Huh?" He pulled at the corner of one eyelid. "You know the old saying. If it walks like a duck and quacks like a duck . . ."

Shapiro rattled on. But Christy's mind flashed: the Soviets.

Why hadn't she thought of *them*?

The Soviets also had plotting screens—in Moscow, Tyuratam, Olenegorsk, Pechora, Mukachevo—in all their strategic command-and-control centers from Lyaki to Petropavlosk. Dimly the familiar, murky image of the DEFCON2 deployment began forming in her mind. But this time the Soviet Union was at the bottom and the image of the United States and Canada hung from the top—inverted, upside down—as though seen from the other side of the world. Whenever Bryan had discussed DEFCON alerts in class there had been two slides: one, the American point of view; the other, the same image seen from the opposite side of the world through Russian eyes.

Bryan was not a fanatic, but a teacher; this morning Bryan had projected those paired images again. But this time they were not pictures in a lecture hall in Monterey. This time the world was Bryan's classroom and the images were burned into the very soul of mankind. What lesson was Bryan trying to communicate?

Shapiro growled. "Pay attention. I said—"

"Captain, what time is it?"

"The hell's the difference?"

"Dammit. . . ."

"Ten after ten."

Christy turned away from him, went to the tiny, barred-and-wired window, and drew deep breaths of the sharp November air to clear her head. The SAC bombers from Guam were fifty minutes from fail-safe. She was running out of patience, running out of time. She couldn't master Bryan's lesson and she could feel herself beginning to lose control.

Dammit—what did the paired images mean?

Behind her, Shapiro put on his glasses and flipped back to his notes. "Okay. Your interview with Petrovsky—anything else you remember?"

"No." Christy took hold of the bars in the window. The enigma defied her; Bryan's lesson was beyond her grasp.

"Christy, don't give up now. If we can figure out why Bryan and Petrovsky dragged you into this maybe we can—"

"All right, all right. . . ." She shut her eyes and groped after the recollection. She could remember sitting in the ROTC office at MIT, sitting straight up in a straight-backed chair while Petrovsky questioned her. She had expected him to be a hard-nosed officer in iron pants; instead, behind the uniform and chest of campaign ribbons, she had sensed a gentle man. By the time their interview became a chat about her studies she had begun to like him. Now he was dead, and she felt strangely as though a light that had led her way was dimmed.

Then a curious thought occurred to Christy. With Petrovsky and Harding dead, *she* was the senior surviving officer of INI. She was imprisoned. But she was in command. It was up to her to assess the Soviets' intentions. Bryan's words whispered through her consciousness like prophecy. *You will lead men into battle.*

Christy's eyes opened.

"Well?" Shapiro said.

"Well, what?"

"Your interview with Petrovsky. What else did you talk about?"

"Just my classes."

"What about them?"

"Nothing important. He was impressed I'd been accepted to do a master's in Russian studies at Harvard. And that I was going to study with Doctor Handlesman."

"Who?"

"A great teacher. A man who understands the world."

It had been a long time since Christy had thought of Jake Handlesman; she smiled at the memory of the pipe smoke curling above his balding head, the way he jabbed the air to make his points, the way little showers of cinders singed his beard. He had often talked to his classes about his fitful career in arms control, the paradox of deterrence, the ludicrous, pig-headed SALT and START negotiations that ground on for decades under the looming shadow of intercontinental ballistic missiles. In Jake Handlesman's classes Christy had come to understand what two generations of wise men in government somehow could not: before the world could hope for lasting peace, strategic nuclear missiles must be banned. Of all men, Jake Handlesman would have been in the front rank of those ready to oppose First Step, as he would oppose any treaty that made the world permanently dependent on nuclear deterrent missiles to keep the peace.

Shapiro pulled at his mustache but wrote the name down anyhow. "Maybe we could call Handlesman as a character witness. He still at Harvard?"

"No. He's working in arms control again. On the START negotiating team in—" She broke off at the sound of a scuffle outside.

Beyond the cell door a man was shouting, "Can't you read? I've got authorization to see the prisoner!" Shapiro rose and went to the door.

But Christy didn't hear the shouting, didn't see Shapiro leave the table.

With the sudden impact of a hammer stroke, the last corner of Bryan's framework came crashing into place. And in that moment of revelation—in a burst of illumination like a magnesium flare that lit the entire landscape of the conspiracy—Christy saw the genius of Bryan's plan.

Sometimes to achieve an objective, you have to be oblique, play the angles, do the opposite of what your enemy expects.

It was a bank shot.

It was *inversion*.

Her mind whirled. Suddenly . . . suddenly . . . yes! It all made sense—the hijacked fighter, the murders of Whitworth and Littman, the eerie echoes of the Cuban missile crisis, the attempt to kill the president. Seen through American eyes those could only be the irrational acts of a handful of madmen. But through the eyes of a Soviet Politburo which had feared and mistrusted its own Red Army for seventy-five years, the morning's violence made terrifying sense.

To Russian eyes, it might be the prelude to a full-scale military insurrection.

Suddenly the hazy lantern slides that had vexed and confounded Christy snapped into crystal, multileveled focus.

They were not two reciprocal views of the morning's alert.

They were the revealed image of the nuclear deterrent paradox itself—so clear-cut and unambiguous that even the dullest minds in government and the military must recognize the absurdity and unspeakable danger.

Christy's fists snapped shut.

Bryan's objective was not to alarm the Americans but to terrify the Russians. And its goal was not merely to stop First Step.

"My god," she whispered, "START."

In the walkway between the barbed-wire fencing, a young redheaded air force captain was trying to push past the guard and shouting in a squeaky voice, "What's the meaning of this? I've got a pass to see the prisoner! Let me by! This is a capital crime!"

Shapiro rapped on the door and shouted to the guard. "Okay, Airman! Let him through!"

"Wait!" Christy shouted. "Captain! I know what—"

"Not now!" Shapiro elbowed her aside and rushed to gather up his papers.

"Captain, listen to me! It's not just First Step! They're trying to destroy the START talks!"

"Christy—" He shoved past her. "I've got to check some things. I'll see you later!"

The guard opened the door and Shapiro slid out as the other captain forced his way inside. The door slammed shut.

Christy stepped back against the wall. "Who the hell are you?"

The little red-haired man adjusted his glasses. He was flushed and flustered, gasping for breath. "I'm Lewis Shapiro, your defense counsel." He thumbed at the figure fleeing down the walkway. "Who on earth was that?"

NATIONAL MILITARY COMMAND CENTER, FORT RICHIE, MD

10:13 A.M.   In the tiny, silent conference room behind the presidential command post, Sam Baker sat alone at the table. He was staring at the fax of the typewritten text of Colonel Petrovsky's message to the American people, but his mind was on Geneva.

The Soviet-American dialogue in Geneva was—in microcosm—the relationship the rival nations *must* accept if they were to coexist on earth. Now, less than an hour and forty minutes into the alert, the START talks were the one strand of contact between the two governments that had survived intact. The talks had to be preserved.

But as Sam Baker fingered the fax of Colonel Petrovsky's statement, he realized that last fragile link of trust between the superpowers was targeted for destruction.

The conference room door opened; it was Ted Harris. "They're ready with your call to Mulholland."

"Ambassador Volokin?"

"Helicopter's on final. Be here in five minutes." Harris nodded at the phone. "Line three."

Sam Baker lifted the receiver. "Craig?"

"Yes, Mr. President?"

"Craig, has your Veterans Day reception started?"

"Yes, sir."

"And the Soviets?"

"Karpov and the others just arrived."

"Good." Sam Baker sat forward. "Craig, listen to me, and listen carefully. We've just learned that one of the conspirators called a press conference to announce First Step had been abandoned and the START talks broken off."

"... *What?*"

"Listen." Sam Baker slipped on his reading glasses, raised the type-written sheet into the light, ran his eye down to the last paragraph.

> We few who have known war—who have felt on
> our own bodies the inhumanity of which men are
> capable—have given our lives to prevent our na-
> tion from taking a path to madness. First Step has
> been rescinded. The START talks in Geneva have
> broken off. God bless America.

"But . . . that's crazy," Mulholland said. "The talks haven't broken off."

Sam Baker looked up at the row of time zone clocks on the wall; it was 10:14 A.M.—1514 Zulu—4:14 P.M. in Geneva. "Craig, this announcement was scheduled for 11:00 A.M. our time. That's 5:00 P.M. in Geneva."

"I . . . I don't understand."

"There's one more conspirator at large—a Captain Daniel Peter Bryan. He's the ringleader. Our people think he may be planning one more attack somewhere within our strategic force system in the next forty-five minutes." The president took his glasses off and set them down on the fax. "Craig, we cannot let these madmen wreck the talks. If anything happens, you *must* assure Karpov it's the work of a small group of dissident Vietnam veterans, not the policy of the government of the United States. You must keep the Soviets' confidence until we crush this conspiracy."

"I'll do my best, sir."

"All right, Craig. And good luck."

Sam Baker started to hang up, but Mulholland said, "Mr. Presi-dent, one of our negotiators had an interesting hypothesis about the Soviets waiting out the DEFCON2 alert. He believes—"

"Craig. Can't it keep till tomorrow?"

"Well . . . yes, sir. I suppose so."

They hung up.

Mulholland checked his watch; beads of perspiration were forming on his forehead. He pressed a button on his intercom. "Dorothy, find that Colonel Whatshisname—you know, the visiting marine security chief."

"Lieutenant Colonel Wilding?"

"Yes. And tell Jake Handlesman I need him. Now."

In the National Military Command Center, Ted Harris stood in the doorway of the tiny conference room.

At the table, Sam Baker sat staring at the fax of Colonel Petrovsky's message.

"Patriots . . ." he said. And the word was an expectoration.

AMERICAN MISSION, 11 ROUTE DE PREGNY, GENEVA

4:15 P.M.   Alone in the basement ward room of the American mission, Marine Lieutenant Colonel Robert Wilding finished hooking the tight round collar of his dark blue Dress A jacket at his throat and cinched the belt snug at his waist. Then he bent to the light blue slacks, brushed the lint from the broad crimson stripe that ran down the side of each pant leg. On the bench beside him lay his white hat and gloves and his dress sword.

Wilding turned and looked at himself in the mirror. The jacket fitted him well; his insignia and campaign ribbons glistened. Each snippet of colored cloth told a tale—of war, of pain, of pride. He had grown used to the craggy face that stared back at him; it was not his own, but it was not a stranger's anymore. Sometimes, when his mother opened her scrapbook, he looked over her shoulder at the boy he used to be—fair haired, light eyed, lighthearted—and wondered what had become of him.

Wilding knew. The boy had become a soldier. He had gone to war. He had been taken prisoner and had returned a man. He stared at the soldier in the mirror. The few. The proud.

He bent and took his saber by the handle, drew the gleaming steel from its scabbard. It was an elegant weapon, a weapon of a more honorable time. He turned back to the mirror, swept the saber up, held it erect before his face with the handle just below his chin—a crisp salute.

The concave blood-gutter of the blade caught the glint of lamplight. And the cold steel bisected his face into a warrior and his double.

"Excuse me, Colonel . . ."

A corporal in dress uniform stood in the ward room doorway. Wilding lowered the saber. "What is it, Corporal?"

"The ambassador's compliments, Colonel. Can you come to his office, please?"

Upstairs, on the ground floor of the mission, the Winter Garden bustled with secretaries and junior employees struggling to set the buffet tables, pour hot water into the chafing dishes and light the tins of Sterno that would warm the chicken à la king and seafood Newburg. The sound of tinkling piano music and laughter drifted through the open doorway, mingled with the banging of the stainless steel, the muttered curses of the secretaries. Sara sat in a quiet corner, bathed in the gentle glow of early twilight through the windows, thumbing an old edition of Beaudelaire.

"So a chance to free the human race from nuclear bondage has been lost," Jake said behind her. "What do you make of that, Weatherby?"

Sara didn't look up from her reading. "Did you really expect them to listen, Doctor?"

Softly, Jake sighed.

That made her raise her head. "I'm sorry, Doctor."

"So am I." He took the white wicker chair beside her. "The sad thing is the Soviets might have been willing."

"Do you think so?"

"We'll never know." Jake sat back in the chair, stroking the ends of his beard. "Tell me, Weatherby, do you think the conspirators' objective might have been the Soviets all along?"

"You mean inversion?"

"It would stop First Step. It makes the pieces fit."

"All but one," she said.

"Oh? Which one?"

"If the conspirators' objective is to stop First Step, why would they do something so obviously self-defeating? Aren't their attacks bound to cause a backlash in Congress? And encourage even greater cuts in military spending?"

Jake stared at Sara; she was canny, and she was wise. A backlash against the military must follow hard on the heels of the conspirators' crimes. The outraged calls for new congressional controls over the Pentagon would begin ringing through the Capitol tomorrow. "So you don't believe their objective is to stop First Step?"

"I can't say, sir."

"But what do you think?"

Sara rose and returned the old book to the shelf. "I think if Ambassador Mulholland and the others had listened to you, we'd be opening discussions about the elimination of intercontinental ballistic missiles, not celebrating the end of some forgotten war."

"Yes," Jake said sadly. He glanced at his wristwatch. It was 4:16 P.M. America's strategic bombers would begin reaching fail-safe in forty-four minutes. "Even now—even when mankind might be less than an hour from nuclear war—they cannot think beyond superiority." He looked at her, his eyes weary, his shoulders bowed with disappointment. "Why is that, Weatherby?"

"You know why, Doctor. Because men are fools."

A marine guard entered. "The ambassador's compliments, Doctor. Will you join him in his office, please?"

"Of course." Jake rose; he beckoned to Sara. "Come, Major. Let's see what new absurdities they have in store for us."

Lieutenant Colonel Wilding was already seated before Mulholland's desk, his scabbard resting across his knees. Jake sat beside him; Sara shut the door and stood against it. Together, the three watched Mulholland pace the room.

"Doesn't make sense . . ." Mulholland muttered. "If this Captain Daniel Peter Bryan and his gang *oppose* First Step, why murder a senator and Secretary of Defense who agree with them?"

Wilding shook his head. "I don't know, sir."

Jake raised one finger. "Gentlemen, if I may . . . ?" He took his pipe and tobacco pouch from his pockets. "Actually, it could be a simple inversion gambit."

"Inversion?"

Jake plucked a pinch of tobacco from his pouch and gently prodded it into the bowl. Without looking back at Sara, he said, "Major Weatherby?"

Sara said, "The president proposes a radical reduction of our NATO forces. A small group of officers opposes his plan. Problem: how can they prevent the plan's implementation if they can't influence the president, the Congress, or American public opinion?"

Mulholland shrugged. "Obviously, they can't."

Jake raised his pipe stem. "Mr. Ambassador, you forget—the president linked the NATO reduction to a zero-option on cruise missiles that requires action by the Soviets. If the conspirators fail in their attempt to kill the president, they can still stop First Step by convincing the Politburo to reject the zero-option."

"Seven Americans influence a Soviet strategic arms decision? That's absurd."

"Precisely," Jake said. "And, therefore, we come to inversion. Major?"

"If the conspirators can make it appear our military is systematically murdering the opponents of First Step to silence them, the Soviets must deduce our military *favors* the plan."

Mulholland snorted. "That's ridiculous. Why would our military favor First Step when it means emasculating NATO and decommissioning our *slick-ems*?"

"Any number of reasons," Jake said. "Perhaps Star Wars works. Perhaps because we have some new superweapon—say, a hypersonic bomber—some monstrosity that will give us an invincible advantage."

"Nonsense."

Jake smiled. "Of course it's nonsense. But, Mr. Ambassador, remember—we're looking at this through Russian eyes. Hiroshima came as a nasty surprise to the Soviets as well as the Japanese."

Mulholland started to answer; then he couldn't.

Jake said, "And this is where the Russian character, the Russian psyche becomes decisive. Major?"

"If the Soviets are nothing else, they're suspicious," Sara said. "Suspicious of us, of NATO, of each other. It's their Achilles' heel. Play on that suspicion, and you can get them to do anything you want. If the Soviets suspect our military is killing the opponents of First Step to silence them, the Soviets won't accept its terms. And First Step doesn't happen." She smiled. "Of course, that's only theory, gentlemen."

"Thank you, Major," Jake said. Yes, it was only theory. But it made perfect sense; clearly, the conspirators' path through the thermonuclear labyrinth led to quashing First Step by inversion.

Yet Weatherby's question nagged. Why *would* the conspirators do something so obviously self-defeating?

Mulholland shook his head. "I don't believe it. People aren't that crafty, that subtle."

Jake smiled. "Mr. Ambassador, you're a gentleman. You do not understand the power of disinformation." He dug through his pockets until he found a pack of matches. "In the winter of 1943 Berlin was snowbound and isolated, short of food and fuel. Popular opinion was turning against the war. Something had to be done. So Goebbels called upon all German civilians to donate their winter coats to their freezing boys on the Russian front. That sacrifice made the civilian population realize their sons were worse off than they were. Goebbels collected three hundred thousand coats. And created a wave of patriotism that kept Germany in the war another year."

"Well," Mulholland said. "At least those civilians were doing something for their boys."

Sara began to laugh.

"What's so damn funny, Major?"

Jake struck a match, put it to the bowl of his pipe. "Tell him, Weatherby."

"Goebbels knew he didn't have enough fuel to transport the coats to Leningrad. He had barely enough to take them out beyond Templehof and burn them."

Mulholland looked at Sara, then at Jake. Then his lip curled in disgust. "There are times you people make me sick."

NATIONAL MILITARY COMMAND CENTER, FORT RICHIE, MD

10:19 A.M.   Ted Harris pushed through the door into the mock-up of the Oval Office. "Volokin's here!"

"At last!" Sam Baker got to his feet. "Show him—no. Wait. Give me a second." He scanned the desktop for any papers that might be classified and began to close the cover of his leather correspondence folder over the fax of Petrovsky's press statement.

Then Sam Baker caught himself.

Today, wasn't the habit of secrecy absurd? Wasn't the whole point of his meeting with Volokin that both governments understood the dimensions and danger of the alert? Hadn't the Cold War legacy of secrecy and suspicion helped create this crisis? Weren't secrecy and suspicion as much to be feared as the weapons themselves?

But Sam Baker let the cover of the correspondence folder drop shut; old habits died hard. "All right, Ted. Show the ambassador in."

Harris opened the door and Soviet Ambassador Vassily Volokin entered. He was a dashing, silver-haired and charismatic man in a natty blue English suit—one of the new breed of *perestroika* diplomats that Gorbachev had installed at Soviet embassies around the globe. He was a far cry from the saturnine Molotov and dour Dobrynin of the Cold War era. But, like all Soviet diplomats, he was honed in subtlety, ruthless in negotiation. He also spoke English like a native; his burly, vestigial interpreter, Gregor Malkin, came in behind him and took a seat on the sofa. Harris leaned against the door.

Quickly Sam Baker crossed the room and took Volokin's hand. "Mr. Ambassador, thank you very much for coming. I hope the helicopter ride wasn't too uncomfortable."

"Not at all," Volokin said. "It is a difficult time." He looked around approvingly. "Very clever. Just like your office at the White House."

"Yes. They built a bunch of these. So you won't be able to find me in case of war."

Volokin smiled. "In case of war I won't have to find you, Mr. President. We'll all embrace that night in hell."

They sat. Harris leaned against the door.

Volokin said, "Is this military insurrection under control?"

"Is it under *your* control?" Sam Baker said.

The two men eyed each other; they were well matched and they knew it.

Then Volokin smiled and sat back. "President Gorbachev anticipated you might ask that, Mr. President. He instructed me to remind you of your private luncheon conversation during the Moscow summit. And, in that spirit, to assure you we bear no responsibility for these acts."

Sam Baker remembered that frank discussion at Gorbachev's rustic dacha in the Moscow suburbs; both men were riding political and economic whirlwinds. By the time their conversation ended, Sam Baker understood that he and Mikhail Gorbachev *must* succeed where generations of peace makers had failed, because they had no choice.

"All right," the president said. "The violence this morning is not an insurrection. It's a few dissident officers, that's all. Now as to—"

"Are you certain, Mr. President?"

That stopped Sam Baker. "Of course I'm certain. Why shouldn't I be?"

"If you'll forgive me, Mr. President. First, your military tries to silence the opponents of First Step. Then they make an attempt on your own life. Frankly, we are beginning to wonder if your military is out of control."

Sam Baker sighed with impatience; why was the Russian talking rubbish? "Vassily, let me assure you. The American military is and always will be under civilian control. Now can we get on with—"

But Volokin broke in on him again. "If your own Secretary of

Defense places nuclear missiles at Hakodate, how can we be certain your Pentagon will respect the terms of First Step . . . or any treaty?"

"We've always respected our treaties with you. Secretary Littman is dead. There's only one more conspirator at large. We know his identity and we'll have him in custody at any moment." Sam Baker was becoming irritable; why was the man wasting precious time in spurious, irrelevant speculation?

"I hope so," Volokin said. "And you understand we must respect-fully request a full briefing on this matter when you have resolved it."

"Yes, yes. Soon as we have the facts. Now, the important thing is to coordinate the stand-down of American and Soviet strategic forces. Is your government prepared to cooperate?"

"By all means. But will your air force?"

". . . What?"

"If you recall your planes, will they, in fact, turn back?"

"Of course they will."

"But if your military is out of control—"

"I've told you, it's a handful of dissident veterans. The boys flying those planes are—"

"Yes," the Russian said softly. "Quite young. I understand."

Sam Baker eyed Volokin; the crafty diplomat was harping on this theme for a reason; he was maneuvering toward some objective.

"In any case, Mr. President," Volokin said in his most courtly manner, "since your military created this alert, we ask one small concession before we agree to a coordinated stand-down."

Sam Baker sighed; so that was it. The Soviets never missed an opportunity to advance their interests. "What small concession?"

"A certain Dr. Jacob Handlesman."

Sam Baker shot a look at Harris.

"The *starik,*" Volokin said with disdain. "The old intellectual who fantasizes himself a strategist. We insist Dr. Handlesman be removed from the American delegation to the talks."

Sam Baker rocked back in his chair; two could play at this game. "Why him?"

"He's a saboteur, a wrecker. He opposes First Step. He gave us the information on your missiles at Hakodate." Volokin smiled shrewdly. "No doubt you are aware of that and already planning his dismissal."

The president cocked his head. "Even if we were, why would *you* want him dismissed? You used that information to suspend the negotiations."

"No, no." Volokin chuckled. "We can break off the talks any time we wish. We were merely using Hakodate as leverage to secure better terms on verification."

The words hit Sam Baker like a kick in the gut.

For a moment he sat staring. Then he rose from his chair and turned to the window. But he stopped short. There was no glass in the window panes. And beyond the empty frames the Presidential Grove was a painted canvas. Then he remembered: this was not the Oval Office. It was a fortified bunker four hundred feet beneath a granite ridge in the Appalachian Mountains, a television stage set designed to assure the American people that, whatever happened, the president was still in control. The room was a remarkable replication, down to the copy of Charles Wilson Peale's portrait of General Washington above the mantel. But it was a copy, a sham.

He glanced back at the sleek-suited, smiling Russian. How much of what Volokin said was real—how much a sham? Then Sam Baker thought of the missiles at Hakodate; he himself had instructed Mulholland to tell the Soviets the missiles weren't nuclear.

How much of what they *both* said was a lie?

Sam Baker put a hand on the desk to steady himself. "Vassily, when I tried to reach you earlier . . . you weren't away for the weekend, were you? You were at your embassy, conferring with Moscow, preparing for this meeting. That's why your formal protest came through Geneva."

Volokin sat as he was. Then he gave a tiny shrug.

Sam Baker felt his stomach churn. Since the age of the bow and arrow, men had controlled weapons. But, somehow these nuclear deterrent monsters overmastered the men who had devised and deployed them. The missiles' warheads not only radiated neutrons, they radiated fear. For thirty years, they had spread that sickness in ever-widening rings of mistrust and deceit, as fear begot lie and lie begot lie and falsehood, falsehood, until the missiles had made liars of them all.

The truth was that through twenty-two years of SALT and START negotiations, neither superpower's pursuit of nuclear superiority had wavered. As long as there were thousands of strategic nuclear missiles in the world, it never could.

And in that numbing, heartbreaking moment, Sam Baker understood.

First Step was a mistake.

Softly he said, "All right, Vassily. When the Soviet strategic systems come down from full alert, Dr. Handlesman will be dismissed and prosecuted."

Volokin made a little nodding bow. *"Spasibo,"* he said. Then he checked his watch. "Now, as to the alert. . . . By the time I get back to my embassy and send the necessary cable . . ." He looked up and smiled. "Shall we say stand-down at eleven o'clock?"

The phone rang; Ted Harris lifted the receiver. "Mr. President, it's Colonel Hernandez. He says it's urgent."

Quickly Sam Baker went to his desk. "Excuse me, Vassily, this may be the break in the conspiracy we've been waiting for." He grabbed the receiver. "Yes, Colonel?"

"Mr. President," Hernandez said. "We've found Captain Bryan."

Sam Baker's breath caught; he covered the mouthpiece. "They've found the seventh man!" He clutched the receiver in both hands. "Where? Where is he?"

A small ring of air force security police stood together in a leafless wintry grove. Within the circle of their heavy boots, a stumpy granite headstone stood white against the dormant grass. The stone was one of countless thousands that followed the rolling hills of Arlington National Cemetery. One of the SPs kicked aside the scattered husks of lilies browning in the cold. Another dug the first shovelful of earth from the grave of Captain Daniel Peter Bryan.

"Mr. President," Hernandez said, "Captain Bryan died in 1973 and was buried in Arlington Cemetery. It's apparent Lieutenant Russoff lied when she said he was the mastermind behind—"

Slowly Sam Baker lowered the receiver to its cradle. Then he sat staring into space.

The three B-52Hs of Charlie flight thundered northward through the stratosphere toward their fail-safe point south of Japan's Yaku Island. In the cockpit of the lead bomber Major Marvin Cutler tapped the intercom. "Time to fail-safe, Arnie?"

In the navigation bay Lieutenant Arnold Boyce punched the dead reckoning computer. "I make it forty minutes, Major."

"How are we against flight plan?"

"Still two minutes behind schedule."

Cutler eased back in his seat. He had never flown to fail-safe, never flown this close to fail-safe in an exercise. No nuclear-armed American bomber had. He'd always wondered how it would feel, and how he would react if the battle order came.

Copilot Eddie Foyle leaned in beside him. "What do you think?"

"I think we'd better not be late." Cutler slid the throttles forward.

AMERICAN MISSION, 11 ROUTE DE PREGNY, GENEVA

4:22 P.M. "Ladies and gentlemen! May I have your attention!" Ambassador Mulholland stood in the center of the dance floor, holding a sheet of telex paper above his head and waving for quiet. The pianist broke off his tinkling; the roomful of diplomats burbled into silence. "I have just received word that an agreement has been reached between the Soviet and American governments to end the present emergency. At 5:00 P.M. Geneva local time, United States and Soviet strategic forces will simultaneously receive orders to stand down from alert and return to peacetime status."

The room rocked with cheering, handshakes, embraces.

Mulholland raised his hands for quiet. "Ladies and gentlemen. May I ask you to join me in a moment of silence to thank God for our deliverance." He bowed his head and shut his eyes.

From the Winter Garden doorway Jake looked on. The Americans and Swiss bowed in silent prayer; the atheist Russians stood uneasy, shifting from foot to foot. Beside him, Lermontov made the sign of the cross.

Jake shook his head. All of them were so eager to believe the danger had passed; none was willing to believe there might yet be one blow to fall. Like their blind faith in deterrence, within the hour their penchant for denial might prove a lethal vice.

When the pianist had resumed, when the secretaries began scurrying about refilling champagne glasses and the predictable round of toasts began, Jake took Lermontov by the arm and steered him into a quiet corner near the south windows. Outside, the November sun lay low on the western hills; its golden light gilded the branches of the birches in the woods beyond the compound walls.

"And whom do your atheist comrades thank for their deliverance?" Jake said.

"They thank your manned bombers for not flying beyond fail-safe."

"So it's true. Your airborne warning system is imperfect. And your war plan calls for—"

"I didn't say that. But," Lermontov shrugged, "*if* your bombers began disappearing from our radar screens, what choice would we have but to assume the worst?"

"What choice indeed?"

Jake sighed. After decades of clinging to the idea that a nuclear war could be fought and won, the Soviets had finally realized their missiles could not be fired. Mulholland and the START team had refused to believe that; because of American arrogance and stupidity, another precious opportunity to stifle the nuclear menace had been lost, as it had been at the United Nations in 1948.

And this time, perhaps, it had been lost forever.

"Misha . . . what if our bombers do not obey the recall order? What if even one bomber flies beyond fail-safe toward its target?"

"Why should they do such a barbaric thing? The men flying your bombers are not fanatics—are they?"

"No. But perhaps they are patriots."

Lermontov's eyes narrowed. "I do not understand. . . ."

"An Arab who places a bomb aboard a civilian airliner or drives a truckload of explosives into a marine barracks in Beirut—is he a fanatic? Or a patriot? There's a fine line between the two, wouldn't you say?"

Lermontov chuckled. "My friend, you are too morbid. Rejoice. We have survived."

Jake squinted into the sunset. Ten thousand miles away, the moon would soon be rising over the Sea of Japan, glinting on the bombers' wings. "Have we? Have we indeed?"

NATIONAL MILITARY COMMAND CENTER, FORT RICHIE, MD

10:23 A.M.   Sam Baker sat holding the telephone and staring at the time zone clocks on the wall. Harris sat opposite, listening in on an extension.

"Handlesman?" the president said. "What possible connection could Petrovsky have with Handlesman?"

In his office at OSI headquarters on Bolling Air Force Base, Colonel John Hernandez sat at his desk. Major Tweed sat across from him, still wearing the uniform with captain's bars and the impostor's nameplate that read SHAPIRO.

"Lieutenant Russoff was a student of Handlesman's at Harvard," Hernandez said. "She told our undercover agent that the objective of the conspiracy is to disrupt the START talks."

Sam Baker's hand tightened on the receiver. "Colonel, you are to order the security guards at our Geneva mission to arrest Dr. Handlesman. Now."

"On what charge, sir?"

"Why . . . treason, of course."

"Mr. President, I don't think that's a good idea."

"Dammit, why not? Handlesman's the seventh man and that's an end to it! He passed classified information to the Soviets this morning. Volokin just confirmed that."

"Sir, if we arrest Handleman now, we may drive the rest of the conspiracy underground."

"What *rest of the conspiracy*?"

"Mr. President," Hernandez said softly, "what makes you so sure it's only seven men?"

Sam Baker hesitated. What if there *were* more conspirators? He thought of the bombers flying toward fail-safe; his instinct was to recall them immediately. But that might be dangerous. He thought of Volokin's question. What if the bombers did not obey the recall command? What if the defenders of the state *had* become its deadly enemies? If the president could not rely on the loyalty of the men who controlled the weapons of annihilation—in god's name, who could he rely on?

Sam Baker lowered his voice. "What . . . do you recommend?"

"Brief Ambassador Mulholland," Hernandez said. "Keep that army intelligence operative close to Handlesman. If he makes a move, we arrest him and throw the book at him."

Sam Baker looked to Harris; he nodded.

"All right, Colonel," the president said. "Please brief Ambassador Mulholland."

"Yes, sir. Right away."

Hernandez hung up. Then he punched his intercom. "Andrea, get me Ambassador Mulholland at our Geneva mission."

"By the way," Tweed said, "SPs found that Sergeant Jeeter at his apartment in Rosemont. Crazy bastard wrapped his head in the flag. Then put a .45 to his ear and pulled the trigger."

Hernandez looked at Tweed—at the name SHAPIRO on the impostor's uniform, then bitterly away. "Major, get out of this office and take off that uniform!"

"Yes, sir." Tweed rose and shuffled toward the door.

In the quiet of the NMCC conference room, Sam Baker turned to Harris. "Russoff studied with Handlesman."

"He taught her more than history."

"He's the seventh man, but Hernandez won't arrest him."

"Sam, I don't like it."

Sam Baker could feel suspicion gnawing at him, wheedling at his confidence; he had never understood suspicion was such a virulent disease. "Ted, are you certain we can trust Hernandez?"

"Right now I don't trust anyone in uniform."

Abruptly the president stood. "Order the helicopter."

Harris got to his feet. "Where are we going?"

"Back to the White House. Alert the Secret Service. Get Hernandez and his staff over there. And that Lieutenant Russoff. Everyone else in uniform out of the building—marine guards, National Security Council staff—everyone in uniform—out!"

DETENTION CELL #6, ANDREWS AFB, CAMP SPRINGS, MD

10:25 A.M.   "I don't get it . . ." Captain Shapiro muttered. He sat at the table, holding the indictment at arm's length, studying the text through the lower lenses of his bifocals. "Five charges that could get you the death penalty on nothing but circumstantial evidence? And ordering a court-martial without an Article 32 proceeding? Doesn't make sense."

Christy leaned against the far wall of the cell, watching, wary. This Shapiro was an effete and fragile little man with freckled skin that suited his red hair. Behind the thick lenses of his glasses his eyes were prim sky blue. He looked like he belonged in a Boy Scout uniform, not the sharp-shouldered air force captain's jacket that seemed too big for his body. Was he another impostor, another spy sent to insinuate himself into her confidence? Or was he really the simpleton he appeared to be—the Pentagon's perverse idea of a joke? And was there no end to her captors' inhumanity? She burned inside with frustrated rage and indignation.

"And what the heck is this?" Shapiro said. He held up the letter from the Immigration Service. "Why the devil would INS arrest your grandmother? No judge in his right mind would send her back to Russia. They must know that."

Christy sighed with exasperation; was this naïve boy *really* all that stood between her and the hangman? "Captain, I keep telling you. The air force has been persecuting me. Someone at the Pentagon probably asked the INS to arrest her."

Shapiro sniffed at the idea. "Our air force doesn't persecute prisoners. Not even in wartime. Besides, the Pentagon is Department of Defense. INS is Department of Justice." Shapiro dropped the letter back into a file. "Either it's a coincidence—"

"There are no coincidences."

"—or you've got to believe somebody higher up is out to get you."

"Higher up?"

"You know—cabinet level. Or higher." Before she could reply he raised his hand. "Hold it. Don't go paranoid on me. Like I said—it's a coincidence." He picked up the arrest report and began paging through it.

But Christy stood staring. Was it possible? Could her brutal treatment be the policy of the government of the United States? No. That was beyond belief, incredible, unimaginable.

Shapiro flicked the arrest report with his fingernail. "Well. Their whole case comes down to one piece of hard evidence."

"What hard evidence?"

"The murder weapon they found in your desk."

"It was planted."

"Could your fingerprints be on it?"

"No."

"Good."

"Good?"

"Christy, evidence cuts both ways. If the gun doesn't prove you guilty, maybe it'll prove you innocent." He rocked back in his chair and looped his thumbs under his belt. "Anyway, they blew their case against you by using that impostor. I can almost guarantee the indictment will be thrown out."

"What do you mean—almost?"

He grinned and shrugged. "Well, you know what they say. Military justice is to justice as military music is to music."

Suddenly the door bolt slammed back. A sergeant and two SPs stamped into the cell. The sergeant slapped an envelope into Shapiro's hand; the two SPs checked Christy's handcuffs, took her by the arms, and turned her toward the door.

She struggled, tried to pull away from them. "What is it? What's happening?"

Shapiro scanned the message and scrambled to his feet. "Colonel Hernandez's order. We're moving out."

"To where?"

"It doesn't say." Shapiro turned to the sergeant. "I demand to know where we're being taken."

"How the hell would I know? Come on, Captain. Chopper's waiting on the pad."

Shapiro clamped his pudgy fists against his hips. "Sergeant, we're not leaving this cell until I know our destination. And when the alert's called off, I'll have you know I'll be seeing the Inspector General about this."

The sergeant leaned against the door. "Where you been, Captain? Stand-down's ordered for eleven o'clock. The war's over."

Eleven o'clock. Christy's mind flashed to the bombers; at the very moment the B-52s from Guam reached fail-safe—at the instant the paired images of the alert became *Point Paradox*—the bombers would be ordered home. But for the next half hour, the bombers would drone onward toward their battle stations while political and military leaders on two sides of the world followed their flight on plotting screens. Christy saw those screens. And—for the first time—she saw the frightened men seated before them.

By raising the DEFCON2 alert and sending the bombers on their fateful journeys, Bryan had sounded a note of dread no government, no band of politicians, no generation could forget.

Beyond the brilliant strategy of provocation, Bryan's lesson was becoming clear at last. It was not a lesson about the nature of the bomb.

It was the same lesson Christy had learned as a prisoner of war: a lesson in the cruel and unpredictable nature of men.

It was a lesson for the nuclear age that mankind must learn—or die.

The sergeant folded his arms across his chest. "Look, Captain. My orders are to put you and the prisoner on that chopper. Whether you want to get on or not."

"Come on, Captain," Christy said and started for the door. Between her escort of security policemen, she stepped out of the detention cell, out into the brilliant November sunshine.

The freezing downwash from the helicopter's rotors tossed her hair and galvanized her skin.

Bryan was about to turn the final card. And a world balanced on the turn.

AMERICAN MISSION, 11 ROUTE DE PREGNY, GENEVA

4:27 P.M.   "Jake? Jake Handlesman? I don't believe it!" Ambassador Craig Mulholland stood behind his desk on the second floor of the American mission, holding the receiver of the secure telephone. The tinkling sound of cocktail music rose from the reception below.

"He's our prime suspect," Hernandez said.

"But he's worked on arms control for forty years! Why should he wreck his life's work now?"

"We don't know. But we're certain he passed classified information to the Soviets this morning."

"What?"

"The Soviet ambassador just confirmed that to the president."

Limply, Mulholland sagged into his chair.

"Army intelligence has had Dr. Handlesman under surveillance for more than two years," Hernandez said. "Their operative is waiting in your anteroom. I've spoken to Lieutenant Colonel Wilding. His marine security detachment is at full alert. If Handlesman tries anything, they'll scoop him up."

"All right, Colonel," Mulholland said softly. "You'll have my complete cooperation."

"Thank you, sir."

They hung up.

Mulholland sat silently in his chair. Through the windows overlooking the driveway, he could hear the chatter of arriving dignitaries. As word of the stand-down of strategic forces spread through diplomatic Geneva, the American mission had become the place to be, the place to celebrate deliverance. At last Mulholland rose, went to the door to his reception room, and pulled it open.

Major Sara Weatherby braced. "Good afternoon, Mr. Ambassador."

Mulholland stared at her as though he were seeing her for the first time.

MAGNOLIA HOUSE, RIVER ROAD, HIGHLAND SPRINGS, VA

10:30 A.M.   Air Force Captain Howard Baylor and Sergeant Glenn Woodward climbed the steps to the porch of the decaying antebellum mansion and knocked lightly at the door. They waited for an answer; there was none. They opened the door, removed their hats and stepped into the foyer.

Softly Baylor called, "Mrs. Petrovsky . . .?"

In the timbered parlor beyond the archway, the grandfather clock chimed the half-hour. Baylor could see an old woman in a blue organdy dress standing before a wall of photographs, her back to him. The photographs were five generations of soldiers—Matthew Brady daguerreotypes of stiff-necked Civil War officers, tiny photographic calling cards that had been the late nineteenth-century rage, formal portraits of doughboys from World War I, and World War II officers in rustic bivouacs. The woman was decorating one of the photographs.

"Mrs. Petrovsky?"

Without looking back she said, "Come in, please." And when they approached her she said, "What can I do for you, gentlemen?"

"Mrs. Petrovsky, I'm Captain Baylor. This is Sergeant Woodward."

She turned to face them. "Yes, Captain?"

"Ma'am, I regret to inform you . . . Colonel Steven Petrovsky met his death this morning."

Her gracious, welcoming smile never wavered. "Thank you, Captain. And good day." Then she turned and gave a final touch to the last photograph in the line.

Baylor and Woodward looked at each other, then at the framed photograph of seven American prisoners of war surrounded by their Vietcong captors; it was already hung with red, white, and blue bunting.

AMERICAN MISSION, 11 ROUTE DE PREGNY, GENEVA

4:33 P.M. "And the marine security detachment has been alerted," Mulholland said. "If Handlesman makes a move, they'll arrest him. Understood?"

"Of course, sir," Sara said. "Will that be all?"

"For now."

She rose from her chair.

Then Mulholland said, "No."

"Sir?"

"Just . . . the way Jake relies on you. You always seemed so loyal."

"I am loyal, sir. Some would say I'm nothing if not loyal."

"Then I can count on you?"

"Yes, sir. But, can we count on the marines?"

"What do you mean?"

"Don't you find it odd that Colonel Wilding picked today for his annual inspection?"

Mulholland set his hands on his desk. "Colonel Wilding?"

"He's a Vietnam veteran. He was a prisoner of war."

"Are you suggesting—"

"No, sir. But he does fit the profile. Are you sure going ahead with the gala is a good idea?" She opened the door and let herself out.

For a moment, Mulholland sat, shaken. Then he reached for the phone.

HELICOPTER MARINE ONE, ABOVE WASHINGTON

10:43 A.M. The chopper swung in off the Potomac and turned due east. Sam Baker shaded his eyes against the strong November sun and looked down at the streets of the District. Among the spotty traffic, tour buses had begun shuttling down Independence Avenue from Capitol Hill past the four white boxes of the Air and Space Museum, the curious beige doughnut of the Hirshhorn, the red brick spires of the Smithsonian. The city was easing back to life, breathing a sigh of deep relief. The Lincoln Memorial slid beneath him, a brilliant cube of gleaming granite; he could see knots of tourists climbing its steps. As the media began to spread the word that the alert would end at 11:00 A.M., life was creeping back toward normal. Only the presence of army Jeeps among the traffic and scattered patrols of national guardsmen in battle dress gave any hint the nation's capital was still under martial law.

As the helicopter turned north and settled lower, the pyramidal tip of the Washington Monument glided past the window. At the base of the monument a bright ring of flags flapped boldly in the wintry breeze and a long, curved queue of mufflered parents and bundled children waited to ride the elevators to the observation windows. Sam Baker looked down at a typical Veterans Day: busy commerce, happy families, bright sunshine. It was an extraordinary sight—a testimony to the resilience of life.

Then, abruptly his mind flashed to the bombers thundering toward fail-safe. What if the planes didn't obey the recall order? What if they flew past fail-safe toward their targets? What if the Soviets thought they had no choice but to retaliate? He saw the city under nuclear attack—the sirens wailing out their terror, the pale sky gashed by fiery warheads streaking out of the ionosphere, enormous fireballs expanding like a searing dome of hell, consuming in one appalling breath the great shrines and monuments, the whole fabric of the American government, the lives and fortunes of six hundred thousand inhabitants, all sixty-seven square miles of office blocks and homes, parks and factories, schools and hospitals, all incinerated in one scorching bolt of madness.

Then the vision vanished.

Yet, as Sam Baker stared out at the gleaming dome of the Capitol, he saw the reality of the thermonuclear nightmare forty-five years of the Doctrine of Deterrence had begotten. And he realized how blind he had been.

He had always believed civilized nations would never use nuclear weapons against each other.

But, until today, he had never understood *men* might.

The helicopter descended over the Ellipse, and Sam Baker looked down at the White House. Along the tall iron perimeter fence armed Secret Service men stood in an unbroken line. On the South Lawn a ring of men in dark suits waited for the helicopter, their hair and neckties thrashing in the downwash of the prop. The District went about its Monday morning, but the White House had become an armed camp. The struggle was not over; within the next quarter of an hour the future might be won or lost.

Sam Baker walked quickly down the steps of the helicopter. On the ground, six men surrounded him, moved with him as a living shield to the white canopy of the south entrance. As they passed the Rose Garden he caught sight of the West Wing and the Oval Office. Windows and doors were shattered where firemen had hacked their way inside. The delicate white walls were charred where flames had leapt out of the ventilating ducts from the air defense room. Inside the Oval Office, a cleaning crew was at work under the sharp eye of Shirley McIlhenny; she looked up as she saw the president pass, nodded once, smiled bravely. On the lawn, black body bags lay in ranks while teams of firemen trundled gurneys toward morgue vans waiting in West Executive Avenue.

"We're in the East Wing," Harris said. "Ground-floor library."

The library was small and low-ceilinged as were all the ground-floor rooms; its elegant paneling was painted gray and rose. Above the mantel hung one of Gilbert Stuart's life portraits of Washington. Sam Baker followed Harris inside; the phone was ringing. Harris grabbed it.

It was Mulholland. "Ted, I've got to call off the gala."

"What? No way!"

Mulholland's voice was anxious, desperate. "We have the Soviet delegation and half the Geneva diplomatic community downstairs. If there were an incident . . ."

"An incident? What do you call DEFCON2—a picnic in the park?"

Sam Baker said, "Ted, what is it?"

Harris covered the receiver. "Mulholland. Wants to call off the reception."

"No! He mustn't!"

But Mulholland wasn't backing down. "Just to be on the safe side—"

"The safe side?" Harris said. "Craig, you're in the middle of neutral Switzerland with a whole platoon of marines to protect you. You're probably safer right now than anybody on this planet. Just maximize security and—"

"What if the marines are part of the conspiracy?"

"That's crazy!"

"Ted, I'm worried. Suppose—"

"Goddammit!" Harris shouted. "I'm giving you an order!"

"Fuck your order! I want to talk to the president."

"He's busy."

"I insist."

"No!"

"Ted, either you let me talk to the president or I'm going downstairs right now and clear the mission of all but essential staff!"

Harris stood steaming. "Hang on." He punched the telephone on hold, turned to Sam Baker. "He insists on hearing it from you."

Sam Baker took the receiver and punched in on the line. "Craig?"

"Mr. President, I—"

"Craig. Listen to me. There's no time. You must go on with the reception. If you disrupt things now, the Soviets may interpret it as a prelude to an attack."

"But, Mr. President, I can talk to Karpov. We can agree to reconvene tomorrow. There's no necessity—"

"Yes, there is." Sam Baker drew a breath; it was a bitter confession and a painful one. "Craig, we cannot allow the diplomatic community of the world to believe I've lost control of the armed forces of the United States."

There was silence on the line. Then, softly, Mulholland said, "All right, Mr. President. I understand."

"Good luck, Craig," Sam Baker said. Then he hung up and turned to Harris. "Where's Hernandez and the OSI team?"

"Down the hall. Conference room number two."

"That lieutenant—Russoff?"

"In the air. Be here any minute."

"What time is it?"

Harris checked his watch. "Quarter to eleven. I'd better go down there and—"

"Ted—" Sam Baker reached out and caught Harris by the arm. "The bombers—"

"What about them?"

"The men flying them—will they obey the recall code?"

Harris stared at the president; in seven years together, it was the first time he had ever seen him afraid. "Of course they will. Why wouldn't they?"

Sam Baker's grip tightened on his arm. "Suppose they don't?"

"Sam." Harris laid his hand on the president's. "Those men took an oath. They will obey."

For a moment, Sam Baker hesitated. Then he released his grip. "All right. Call the Soviet embassy. Ask Ambassador Volokin to come here and stand by."

"Stand by for what?"

"I wish I knew."

★ ★ ★

Outside, on the South Lawn of the White House, the helicopter from Andrews flared to a landing. Two SP guards hustled Christy out the door and into the arms of waiting Secret Service men.

"Hold on there!" Shapiro shouted over the downwash of the rotors. "Where are you taking her?"

But two Secret Service men seized his arms and roughly dragged him off in the other direction.

Ted Harris opened the door of conference room #2 and stepped into the low-ceilinged, spartan room. He waited until Tweed, Wheeler, and the other OSI staffers filed out and shut the door. The long table was covered with files and papers, telexes and dossiers; blown-up individual ID photographs of the conspirators were pinned to the corkboard on the wall. At the far end of the table, Hernandez sat alone. He rose.

"All right," Harris said. "Where's this Captain Shapiro?"

"The Secret Service is holding him in the next room."

"Get him."

Hernandez went to the side door, opened it, and beckoned. Shapiro entered; among the towering older men he looked like a boy playing dress-up.

"Captain," Hernandez said, "this is Mr. Harris, the president's chief of—"

But Shapiro didn't wait for him to finish. "Colonel, I protest being separated from my client against my will. And I may as well tell you I intend to move for acquittal on the grounds of violation of the constitutional protection against self-incrimination and—"

"Captain Shapiro!" Harris snapped. "No speeches—please! And no lectures on the Bill of Rights. We have a crisis on our hands." He reached past Hernandez and slammed the door. "Now sit down and shut up!"

The spring went out of Shapiro's legs; he sat. Harris stood over him.

"Captain, what we have here is a monstrous crime against the government of the United States, conceived and executed by serving officers. They may be planning one more attack. And I want to know what it is." He leaned over Shapiro. "Do you understand me?"

Shapiro's voice quavered. "I—I'm not sure I do."

"We need your help to frustrate this conspiracy."

"Sir, my responsibility is to defend Lieutenant Russoff, not—"

"Forget that! By the time the press gets through with your client, the country will be screaming for her blood."

"Excuse me, sir, but Lieutenant Russoff is not guilty."

"That doesn't matter. Somebody's got to pay for this. And she's got the short straw." Then Harris leaned back against the table and his tone changed. "Captain, do you plan to make a career of the air force?"

"That . . . was my intention."

"Well, what you have here is a career opportunity. Play it right— you have your career. Play it wrong—your career's over."

"I'm sorry, sir, play what right?"

"The plan of the last attack. We need that information. And we'll pay your price to get it."

For a moment, Shapiro sat as he was. Then he pushed his chair back from the table and stood. "Mr. Harris, you don't have anything I want." He started toward the door.

"You're not dismissed, Captain!"

Shapiro turned, came to attention. Harris stalked toward the trembling little man, his index finger thrust before him like a bayonet. "That bitch knows the plan! And you're going to get it for me in the next five minutes." He stood before Shapiro, towering over him like a thunderhead. "Or, as God is my judge, she'll die with a rope around her neck, and you'll curse the day you ever dreamed of wearing captain's bars!"

Harris leaned into Shapiro's face; menace gleamed through his voice. "Now. One last time, Captain. Do we understand each other?"

"With the—" Shapiro's voice cracked. "With the colonel's permission . . . Mr. Harris . . . you can go fuck yourself."

Ted Harris's hands closed into fists.

Behind him, Hernandez barked, "That's all, Captain. Dismissed!"

Shapiro stepped back, turned, and went out.

When the door closed Hernandez didn't even try to hide the contempt in his voice. "Are you satisfied, Mr. Harris?"

Harris sighed. "Now there goes a fine young man."

The phone rang; Hernandez answered it. "Yes? Yes, he is." He held the receiver out to Harris. "For you."

Mike Marden sat in the back of an NBC News mobile video van parked across the street from the White House on Jackson Place. "Ted—Mike Marden."

"You sonofabitch! You have the nerve to call me after—"

"We're putting a piece of old film footage on the *Nightly News* tonight. Think you ought to see it before it goes on the air."

"I've got no time for—"

"It's your seven conspirators being repatriated from Vietnam in 1973."

"*What?*" Harris remembered those televised homecomings. Honor was etched in the faces of the war-ravaged men who had stood before the microphones; love of country burned in their simple words. Ted Harris had wept as he watched those homecomings; the nation had. "Dammit, Mike! You put those patriotic speeches on television, you'll turn those bastards into folk heroes!"

"In the NBC mobile unit on Jackson Place. Be there." Marden hung up.

Harris slammed the phone down. "That sonofabitch Handlesman! He planned it down to a fare-thee-well. . . ."

AMERICAN MISSION, 11 ROUTE DE PREGNY, GENEVA

4:50 P.M.   At the end of the receiving line, an anxious Ambassador Mulholland and a smiling Viktor Karpov flanked the Swiss foreign minister and his wife. Invited and uninvited guests were still swarming into the mission to join the gala reception—accredited European diplomats in business suits, African and Asian diplomats in dashikis, turbans, robes—all eager to celebrate the end of the alert. Even the Swiss band had turned up to play cha-chas and two-steps. In the foyer, the security team worked feverishly to check credentials and clear new arrivals for admittance. In each corner of the reception room marine guards stood at parade rest.

On the crowded dance floor, Lieutenant Colonel Robert Wilding cut a dashing figure in his Dress A uniform and saber; he held Sara in his arms.

"So you were busy tonight. . . ."

She grinned. "And you were jealous."

"Am I a fool?"

"A tender fool."

"Is there room in your life for me?"

"No, Bob."

"Not an inch?"

"Not a micron."

A marine corporal stepped onto the dance floor beside them. "Pardon me, Colonel. I have a message for the major. Dr. Handlesman's compliments, ma'am. Would you join him in his office, please?"

"Right away."

"No you don't," Wilding said and held her. "Corporal, tell Dr. Handlesman he'll have to wait until after we've had our dance."

"Bob, please. I—"

But Wilding swept Sara away.

WHITE HOUSE SUBBASEMENT, WASHINGTON

10:51 A.M.   Shapiro entered the windowless concrete room in the subbasement dormitory known as Stalag 17. He waited until the Secret Service man had locked the steel door behind him; then he leaned against it, grim.

Christy looked up from her place at the bare wooden table. "Well? What now?"

"You've got five minutes to give them the plan of the final attack or . . ."

"Or *what?*"

"If the attack succeeds, they'll railroad you to the hangman."

The corner of Christy's mouth spiked up in an edgy smile. "So it's come to that." She looked at Shapiro; there was no fear in her. "Can they do it?"

"Christy, I got that from the president's chief of staff."

Her voice hardened. "I said, *can they do it?*"

"They can exterminate all human life from the face of the earth. They can kill you without a twitch."

"All right," she said. "I understand."

She sat with her manacled hands in her lap. So it was true. Her tormentor was not the air force. As incedible as it might seem, her ruthless mistreatment was the policy of the civilian government of the United States.

Christy remembered the blustery January morning in 1989 when she and Bryan had stood together on the parade ground in Monterey, watching the pageant of the winter term graduation exercises and listening to the marching band play "Stars and Stripes Forever."

Christy was halfway through her year of studies; both knew they were nearer to the end of their affair than the beginning.

"I don't want to leave when my semester ends," Christy said. "I want to stay here . . . with you."

"We'll both be leaving. Besides, you have your whole career before you. You have the calling."

Christy grumbled, "I know, I know. Duty-Honor-Country."

"Don't ever say those words in that tone of voice. Duty-Honor-Country isn't just a motto—it's a path. It's the way."

"The way to what?"

"To becoming a real soldier. Isn't that what you want?"

"How can I be a soldier if my government won't let me fight?"

"There are other ways to prove your courage. Besides, the government isn't infallible. They're only politicians. You're sworn to defend the Constitution, not the government."

Christy stared at Bryan, stared into those gray, impassive eyes and realized a distinction she had never clearly understood. A voice behind them rang out, "Attention to the colors!" Together—side by side—they braced and saluted as the color guard marched by.

And Bryan whispered, "Remember, it's the flag you follow. The government is only men."

Now Christy sat at the table in the subterranean cell and understood. She was alone—more alone than if she were in solitary confinement. Her government had repudiated and disowned her, had brutalized her with a cruel indifference to military law. Now the president's chief of staff was threatening her murder. That told her how deep the tide of panic was running through the men of the American government; the Soviets must be at the edge of hysteria as well. On two sides of the world, the military and political leaders of the great superpowers were staring at their plotting screens—muttering curses, mouthing prayers, waiting desperately for the moment when the men flying their strategic bombers would either obey the recall or fly on toward their targets and drag the whole world into flaming Armageddon. Christy saw those screens and saw the men clustered before them. She saw the terror in their eyes, felt the dismal horror creeping through their souls. Could they grasp the lesson of *Point Paradox* that Bryan had so brilliantly conspired to teach them? After all, behind the poppycock of ceremony, behind the ostentatious titles and rococo uniforms—they were only men.

Shapiro came to the table, pulled his chair in close, and sat beside her. "Christy, forgive me—I have to ask . . . Do you know the plan of the last attack?"

She stared at him. He was a man like the rest of them. A frightened man. A well-intentioned man. Perhaps even an honest man.

But just a man.

"No."

In the navigation bay of the lead B-52H of Charlie flight, Lieutenant Arnold Boyce finished recalculating their flight time. "Eight minutes to fail-safe, Major."

On the flight deck, Major Cutler tapped in on the intercom. "How are we against plan?"

"Picked up a little time. We're looking good."

Copilot Eddie Foyle leaned in beside Cutler. "Marv . . . all of a sudden, I got a bad feelin' about this. What if we get the *go* code?"

Cutler opened the precombat checklist on his lap. It was a question he had often asked himself. If the *go* code ever came, would he really fly into nuclear combat? Now his bomber was eight minutes from fail-safe and he still did not know the answer. He toggled the intercom. "Attention, please. Prepare to prearm. On my command—execute." He snapped up the arming sequence gate on his left side panel and threw the switch.

In the navigation bay, bombardier Lieutenant Harry Blackburn toggled the master arm to ON. "Weapons systems enabled."

Beside him, Boyce pulled a steel lever; the safety bolt that held the bomb bay doors retracted; the DOORS ENABLED light began blinking on his console. "Doors are live. I say again—doors are live."

One by one, Blackburn flicked up the toggles that prearmed the bomber's twenty air-launched nuclear cruise missiles. On the weapons panel between the men, each orange light burned in the semidarkness like a tiny sun.

In the tiny rose-and-gray ground-floor library of the White House, the president of the United States sat alone, his old hands resting on the bentwood arms of a stately Sheraton chair. He was staring at the bookcase on the east wall, staring at the curious antique lighthouse clock that stood there, listening to the soft tick of its escapement. It was a strange, brass-footed clock—inset with a medallion of Lafayette, the dashing Frenchman who had come at the last moment to turn the tide of revolution for General Washington and his ragtag Continental army. Infinitesimally, the clock's minute hand crept toward eleven o'clock. This morning, Sam Baker knew there would be no Lafayette to save the day.

First Step had been a mistake. In compromising defense to economics, he had blundered into fateful folly. Yes, disarmament was the only hope for the future. Yes, the massive conventional armies had to go.

But not before the strategic nuclear missiles.

Sam Baker understood that now. No man—no group of men—should ever be allowed to control weapons so monstrous that their power brought civilization to its knees as the missiles had this day. Somehow, Colonel Petrovsky and his band of conspirators had understood what the president and all his wizened advisers had not: that SALT, START, and First Step had ratified the existence of strategic nuclear missiles, had hallowed and exalted them, had left the world no choice but to rely on them to keep the peace for decades to come. And the conspirators had demonstrated that in time of crisis the mighty deterrent missiles were not a shield, but became themselves the blade of the guillotine.

Sam Baker's hands tightened on the arms of his chair. How could he have failed to foresee that? How could the brightest minds of civilization have labored ceaselessly for generations to build unconscionable weapons of mass destruction in the absurd belief that the monstrosities would somehow guarantee the peace?

After four decades of public life, after seven years in the Oval Office—at last Sam Baker saw the whole history of nuclear deterrence for what it was: a global suicide pact conceived in fear, sealed by suspicion, written in the blood of generations never to be born.

And no new round of START talks could provide the answer; the conspirators had been right about that, too. Nine years of bitter wrangling in Geneva had produced nothing but a cynical agreement to reduce the two superpowers' stockpiles of strategic nuclear warheads from fifty thousand to twenty-five thousand—a ludicrous travesty in light of the morning's events. If fifty warheads delivered against key urban targets in either nation were sufficient to terminate the national lives of those states, what difference if the rivals had one thousand warheads? Or one hundred thousand?

No difference.

Sam Baker saw now that what was needed—what was indispensable to the survival of the human race—was not strategic arms *reduction,* but strageic arms *elimination.* And the way to accomplish that was not through another ineffectual decade of START, but by joining with the Soviet Union and other nuclear states to first suppress the spread of nuclear weapons technology, and then to systematically eliminate the massive city-killer intercontinental missiles from the armories of all mankind.

That was what must be done. And the world must act *now*. Because the morning's events had only too painfully demonstrated that if the weapons ever fell into the hands of madmen or zealots, humanity would pay an unimaginable price.

How long would it be before some renegade nation developed a rudimentary nuclear capability?

Two years?

Five years?

Surely before the end of the twentieth century the world would face the reality of nuclear terrorism, unless all nuclear nations acted now in concert to ban these weapons and to enforce the ban by all possible means, even, if necessary, by force of arms. The new spirit of cooperation between the United States and Soviet Union had even created a basis for that action. All that was lacking was the will.

How could Sam Baker have failed to recognize that?

He knew how. Because it was cheaper to reduce the nation's conventional armies and rely on the deterrent missiles to keep the global peace. Because it was popular with a Congress that was obsessed with its own reelection, and a public more concerned with inexpensive gasoline and lower taxes than with the legacy of terror they were passing on to their children and grandchildren. Because it was expedient.

Because it was the easy way out.

The lighthouse clock ticked down toward eleven. The bombers flew toward fail-safe. In a few moments, the world might be at war. And there was nothing—absolutely nothing—the president of the United States could do to stop it now.

Even the most powerful man in history stood naked and defenseless before the golem of deterrence.

Slowly Sam Baker raised his hands and rested his forehead against his fingertips. And for the first time in a very long time, he prayed.

NBC MOBILE VIDEO VAN, JACKSON PLACE, WASHINGTON

10:54 A.M. Just across Pennsylvania Avenue from the front entrance to the White House, Lafayette Park was crowded with news crews and photographers swarming behind police barricades. Mobile network video trucks and microwave transmitters were parked up and down both side streets, and the pavement was a snake pit of transmission lines and power cables.

In the NBC production van, three technicians sat before the cramped switching console. On the raised platform at the rear, Hernandez, Tweed, and Mike Marden sat in swivel chairs.

Ted Harris paced behind them. "Well? When does this damn miracle happen?"

"Should have the satellite signal any time now." The TD punched in on the line. Bars and tone appeared on the center monitor; below them the legend

NBC SATELLITE NEWS
NEW YORK

The TD toggled the talk-back line to the third floor at 30 Rockefeller Plaza. "We have bars. Roll tape."

"About time." Harris dropped into a chair.

The bars disappeared; an old film countdown leader began to roll. Marden referred to a fax of faded production notes. "This was February 14, 1973. The thing speaks for itself."

The monitor cut to a washed-out image of an honor guard beside a MAC transport plane parked on the taxipad at Andrews Air Force Base. A long red carpet led from the steps of the plane to a bank of microphones. Behind velvet cordons tied with yellow ribbons, a crowd of chattering, flag-waving civilians—mostly women and children— clustered among news camera crews. The crowd fell silent as an air force captain came down the steps of the plane and limped slowly toward the microphones.

Marden said, "See anyone you know?"

Like the others, Hernandez squinted at the screen. The officer was a young man in his mid-twenties. He was pale and gaunt, his skin speckled yellow by malnutrition. But he was unmistakably Steven Petrovsky.

Petrovsky stopped at the microphones, stood a moment looking at the crowd, at the reporters. Then he raised his eyes and looked directly into the lens of the camera. "We have come through. We have come home. We are unbeaten. We are unbowed. And we have won peace with honor." He saluted.

The crowd cheered. Alone, Petrovsky limped away.

"A real patriot," Harris said bitterly.

A slender, ruddy-cheeked young first lieutenant took his place behind the microphones; his right hand fingered a rosary.

"The only thing—" O'Neill's voice cracked; he paused, gathered himself, began again. "The only thing that pulled us through was faith. Faith in our president and our country. Faith in our blessed Savior, Jesus Christ. God bless you all."

The crowd applauded. A woman and a pensive, dark-haired young girl rushed out to embrace O'Neill, then led him away.

Harding took his place. He was perspiring, trembling, near tears. His voice quavered as he spoke. "Thank you, Mr. President. For bringing us home to peace with honor. And to the brave women who waited for us and never lost hope."

A chubby young Beth Harding stepped forward and took him in her arms.

In the semidarkness of the production van, John Hernandez stared in wonder at the images on the monitor. In spite of what these men had done today, in spite of the outrages they had committed—in 1973 they had not been the betrayers, but the betrayed. The flickering ghosts before him had carried the flag in a war as pointless and corrupt as the politicians and generals who led them. The returning POWs were men whose heroism had been the stuff of legend, whose sacrifice had been the trials of saints, whose fidelity had humbled those who had debriefed them. Petrovsky and the others had suffered nobly, had never surrendered their ideals. All through the long years while the nation had been torn apart by bitter anti-war protests, these men had languished behind bamboo barricades, clinging for life itself to the old ideals of Duty-Honor-Country.

In the end, they had not been liberated by friendly forces but discarded by their North Vietnamese captors. The American government had dressed them in new uniforms, decorated them with medals, and told them a cynical, bald-faced lie about winning peace with honor. Now the scrawny, disoriented men stood parroting that lie to a foolish, credulous nation—a nation that would show them neither gratitude nor pity. Hernandez watched Granger push Logan's wheelchair to the microphones, and the greatest mystery of his career began unraveling before his eyes.

"Willie and I thank you all for this reception," Granger said. "And for bringing us home to America, to a new life and to peace with honor." Granger looked down at Logan. "Willie?"

Logan shook his head. "You said it, Cholly."

As the crowd cheered, a red-headed woman bounded forward,

grabbed Granger around the neck, and kissed him. Then she shook hands with Logan and they moved away.

Hernandez glanced at Harris; there were tears in the older man's eyes.

"What the fuck are you looking at?" Harris snapped. He wiped his nose with the back of his hand.

Then, from the end of the carpet, a solitary figure in an air force captain's uniform limped toward the microphone. He was gaunt, emaciated, barely able to walk; his arms and shoulders shook in spasms. But there was great dignity about him.

The men in the video van held their breath; there was no mistaking the figure on the screen. Hernandez whispered, "Bryan."

The young air force captain stood before the microphones. The wind ruffled his thinning, blond hair and his soft eyes scanned the joyful, flag-waving crowd. One by one, as though rebuked by his eyes, the onlookers stopped their cheering and fell silent. Even the busy news crews and reporters broke off their chatter and stood still.

When Bryan spoke, his voice was a whisper, a torment of pain. "Do not think me ungrateful when I say . . . no one who was not among us . . . will ever know how dear this day was bought—how terrible a price was paid." Slowly his eyes picked through the crowd. "Our leaders tell us . . . we have won peace with honor. Is it true? Will there be lasting peace? Can honor be found in hideous and brutal war?" Some women clutched their handkerchiefs; some clutched their infants to their hips. Well-fed men in civilian business suits turned their faces from Bryan's stare.

Then Bryan smiled—a dim, ironic smile. "How strange . . . our gentle nation should seek peace by learning war."

And then, quite suddenly, John Hernandez knew what the warrior prisoners of Chu My dreamed.

They dreamed of a world without warriors.

When Bryan spoke for the last time, his voice was no louder than the wind.

"God bless America . . . with peace."

The men in the van sat in profound silence.

Tweed muttered, "How the hell do patriots like that turn into traitors?"

No one moved to answer.

But Colonel Hernandez knew; Bryan had solved the mystery. Hernandez knew who was guilty, who had driven the prisoners of Chu My to despairing rebellion: a succession of strutting governments who had mocked their sacrifice by pursuing peace with ever-more-lethal arsenals of weapons. And a complacent nation which had learned nothing from their pain.

He whispered, "God forgive us." Then he covered his eyes with his hand.

"Wait," Marden said. "Watch this."

Slowly Bryan turned from the microphones; a marine corporal stepped forward to assist him. But Bryan pulled away, stood rocking on his heels, struggling to keep his balance and his pride. And then— each step a paroxysm of pain—he began to limp away. The crowd stood mute and motionless; a woman stepped from among them.

She wore the uniform of a United States Army ROTC cadet. Bryan saw her, stopped.

The woman braced, saluted.

Bryan stared at her uniform—at her.

Straight-backed she stood, proud shouldered; as if to challenge him, she held her salute and waited.

Slowly, agonizing, Bryan drew himself up to attention. His face twisted with suffering as he struggled to raise his palsied arm. But he could not raise his hand above his shoulder. Instead, he bowed his head to meet his quavering hand—a pathetic mimic of the woman's sharp salute.

The faces of the watchers in the edit bay were mirrors of his pain.

Finally Bryan lowered his hand. Then the woman stepped forward and enfolded him in her arms. And he laid his head on her shoulder as an exhausted man passes on his burden.

The woman stood erect, straight as a ramrod, the incarnation of strength and courage, the figure of indomitable resolve.

The film cut to a close-up of the two. Then the woman turned her gallant face toward the camera.

Marden said, "According to our production notes, her name is Cadet Lieutenant Sara Weatherby Bryan. She's his wife."

Suddenly the film ran out; the screen went blank. A technician snapped on the overhead lights.

Hernandez gasped. "That's—that's the Intel officer who's been watching Handlesman. Jesus Christ, we've been looking for a man."

The room was still—that momentary and eternal stillness that falls between a flash of lightning and the detonation of its thunder.

Then truth exploded among them.

Harris jumped to his feet. "My god! It's a woman! It's her! IT'S HER!"

Hernandez grabbed Marden's sleeve. "I need a telephone! Now!"

A technician handed him a receiver, punched through to the switch-board at station WRC.

"Operator? Operator!" Hernandez shouted. "Get me Geneva!"

AMERICAN MISSION, 11 ROUTE DE PREGNY, GENEVA

4:57 P.M.   The sound of dance music followed Wilding and Sara upstairs to the reception area outside Jake's office. Miss Green announced them through the intercom, and Jake pulled open the door and stuck his head out.

"Come in, Weatherby," he said. "Miss Green, you needn't stay. Go down and enjoy the celebration."

"Thank you, Doctor." She gathered her purse and hurried away.

"Please have a seat, Colonel," Jake said to Wilding. "I won't keep your dancing partner long."

Jake followed Sara into the inner office and shut and locked the door. "The bombers are three minutes from fail-safe. SAC is about to issue the recall code. I thought we might wait for the outcome together." He offered her one of the chairs before his desk.

"Thank you, Doctor." She sat.

"What do you think, Weatherby—will the men flying our bombers obey the recall?"

"Doctor, you know we're not permitted to discuss the deployment outside the bubble."

His smile chided her. "Weatherby, the world may be coming to an end. Surely this once you needn't stand on ceremony?"

Sara gazed at him in silence. Then she said, "They must obey."

"Well, a gleam of independence. Good for you, Weatherby. And let us hope you're right." Jake paced to the window; the setting sun gilded his face, suffused the scruff of his beard with a warm bronze glow. Through the glass roof of the Winter Garden five floors below he could see the party-makers moving around the buffet tables, filling their plates, laughing, chattering. "Even if the bomber crews obey, the damage may have already been done. Behind their glad-handing, the Soviets are vacillating so much the whole room is vibrating. The constructivists want to continue the negotiations. The hard-liners want to pull out and go home. Fascinating. Do you think they'll break off the talks?"

"They're at the height of suspicion," Sara said. "One more attack might turn their suspicion into panic. That would be the end of First Step. Perhaps even the end of START."

Jake chuckled. "Weatherby, you're uncanny. Sometimes I think you're a witch. Tell me"—there was a twinkle in his eye—"do you believe there's mischief afoot? Some last violent act by our military that will wreck the talks?"

Sara folded her hands in her lap. "Time will tell."

In the NBC video van Hernandez was shouting into the phone. "Hurry, operator, hurry! It's a matter of life and death!"

Jake went to the bar and picked up the bottle of Power's Irish whiskey. "Join me?"

"I will, thank you."

"Good, Weatherby." He poured for both of them. *"L'chaim."*

Sara raised her glass. "Long life."

They drank.

Jake took the chair opposite her. He cupped his glass in his hands to warm the liquor. "Weatherby, may I ask you a personal question?"

"Of course, Doctor."

"Why were you so determined to work for me? You gave up a promising career at the Naval Postgraduate School. Admiral Trost told me your course in Problems of Intelligence and Threat Analysis was quite remarkable. Particularly given your youth and . . ."

"And the fact that I'm a woman?"

"Yes. You know, they might have kept you on as a tenured professor."

"I didn't join the army to be a teacher."

He sipped his whiskey. "Why did you? A woman like you—beautiful, intelligent—you could have made a great success in government or business."

"To keep a promise."

"A promise? To whom?"

"A man who died."

"I see." Jake nodded, and understood. He, too, had made a promise to the dead, a promise he had struggled to fulfill these many years and had yet to keep. "Then why work in arms control?"

"I think he would have wanted me to."

"But why did you particularly want to work for me?"

"I read what you wrote about deterrence in the Survey of Strategic Bombing."

Jake chuckled sadly. "Many did. In those foolish early days, none of us could imagine that deterrence would become a tyranny. Once we began that road—"

"There was no turning back."

"No." He sighed softly. "Even now, it seems. No turning back."

Silently a light on the telephone began to flash.

"Ah!" Jake clapped his glass down. "Perhaps we have the answer to the riddle of the bombers." He rose and went around his desk.

But as he reached for the receiver Sara said, "Ambassador Mulholland believes you're part of the conspiracy."

The words washed Jake like a cold wind; his breath caught in the draft, and the muscles in his arms and back went rigid. He had always known he would be called to account for the treachery of Hakodate; he had never expected to escape retribution. But to hear the words of accusation spoken now by one so close to him, so suddenly and flatly, chilled him with a terror beyond knowing.

Slowly, carefully, struggling to moderate his voice, he said, "Me?"

"Yes, sir. Your phone is ringing, Doctor. Shall I—"

"Leave it!" Then he caught himself. "Did . . . did Mulholland say *why* I'm suspected?" Sara looked up at him; even now, even in the moment she had accused him of treason, he could see no emotion in her eyes.

"Because you told Lermontov about Hakodate," Sara said.

Jake swallowed hard; he could feel the noose of shame closing on him. "I did that?"

"Yes, Doctor. We both know you did. On Secretary Littman's instructions. Do you deny it?"

He rested his fingertips against the desktop to conceal their trembling. "Should I?"

"No."

"So, you believe I'm one of them?"

"No. In any case, that's irrelevant now."

The conviction in her voice surprised him. "Why not? Why don't you suspect me?"

"Doctor, shouldn't you answer the phone?"

"In a moment." Jake came back around the desk and stood before her. "Why *don't* you suspect me? You know I oppose First Step."

Sara finished her whiskey and set the glass down. "Yes. But you're on your own. A free-lance. Besides, you know a game of guile can't be won by force of arms."

Jake smiled and shook his head in admiration. "Weatherby, you are the most remarkable woman I have ever known." Behind him on the desk, the telephone light blinked on and off, ignored.

Hernandez stood in the video van, clutching the receiver, listening to the hollow ringing on the line. Above the monitors, the digital clock blinked past 10:58:23.
The operator said, "I'm sorry, sir. There's no answer."
"Keep trying, operator! Try again!"
"I'm going back to the White House!" Harris shouted. "Keep me informed!" He rushed out the door.

Jake stared at Sara, his eyes shining. "You are a singular woman, Weatherby—a human paradox. You have an extraordinary mind. And yet I've never known anyone who was more completely a soldier, more completely *theirs*. From the top of your head to the tip of your toes, everything regimented, everything regular army. Everything except"—he reached out and touched her sleeve—"except this old bracelet." He fingered the brass bangle at her wrist.

Lieutenant Colonel Wilding sat in Jake's reception room, holding his scabbard across his knees and staring at the ringing phone on Miss Green's desk, wondering if he should answer it.

"Why are you so attached to that old bauble?" Jake said.
Sara fondled the bracelet. "When I was in college, all the ROTC cadets wore these. For our MIAs and POWs. Each bracelet had a soldier's name. You wore the bracelet until your soldier came home."
"And your soldier? Didn't he come home?"
"Yes. But a week later he died of meningitis."
"I'm sorry to hear that."
Sara stared at the name etched on the bracelet; the years had worn the letters smooth. They were barely visible, but she remembered them. "He spent three years in a Vietcong prison. They beat him every day. His name was Captain Daniel Peter Bryan. He was twenty-eight years old when he died."
"Tragic. So you never met the man."
"On the contrary. He was my husband." Then Sara released the bracelet. "Excuse me, Doctor. Do you have the time?"
Jake glanced at his watch. "Exactly one minute to—" Then the name registered and he looked up. "Did you say Captain Bryan was . . . your husband?"

★ ★ ★

At last Wilding picked up the receiver of the ringing phone. "Dr. Handlesman's office. This is Lieutenant Colonel Wilding."

Slowly Sara rose from her chair. "The sun *will* come up tomorrow."

Jake stared at Sara. Then, suddenly the room seemed to pitch and yaw as though a great convulsion of the earth had rocked the building to its foundations. His hand shot forward and he clutched the edge of the desk against the dizzying, sickening swell. "Then, it's not the men flying the bombers."

"No, Doctor."

"It's you." He was breathless. "You . . . are the last conspirator."

"Yes." Sara took the .22-caliber Beretta automatic pistol from her purse and flicked off the safety.

Jake could feel the pounding rising in his heart; he clutched a hand to his chest to still it. "And I? I am the final episode?"

He clung to the desk against his vertigo and peered through the swirling tumult of reality into the one fixed, unmoving point— the opaque stillness of Sara's eyes. And in their unblinking stare the enigma began to unfold like a black-winged butterfly. "So . . . our military has silenced the enemies of First Step without. And now they will silence its enemy within."

"Yes, Doctor."

He gazed at her in awe. "A magnificent endgame, Weatherby. Even I never guessed."

Sara cocked the pistol.

Jake raised his hand. "Wait! One question, please. You and the others—you of all people—why do you oppose First Step? Weren't those poor, despairing wretches themselves victims of war?"

"Doctor, I'm surprised at you. You've missed the point entirely."

"Missed the . . .?" But even as he began to frame the question Jake knew the answer. "My god, it wasn't just First Step. It's START."

"Yes, Doctor."

"And all of this . . . was an exercise in terror?"

"Yes."

"A way to show those fools what the world would be like if madmen ever control the weapons of annihilation?" Jake's eyes widened with excitement. "Brilliant, Weatherby! By god, you are brilliant! For twenty years I've been telling them that if this day ever came there would be no options or negotiations. Then the bomb would dictate terms!"

Then, abruptly, he caught himself. "But . . . they didn't listen, Weatherby. You heard them yourself downstairs in the bubble. They didn't understand."

"Doctor, *you* expected the Americans to understand. I never did."

"Then who—" And then the ultimate revelation thundered through his brain. "The Soviets. . . . My god! Of course! All day *they've* been trying to keep their lines of communication open with *us*. They sat out a DEFCON2 alert. They even came to our gala! I've been staring at it all day but didn't see it. They must be terrified! We can't believe our armed forces are out of control but Gorbachev and his Politburo can. And if you kill me . . . they'll have to believe it!"

Wilding began pounding on the door. "Sara! Dr. Handlesman! Open the door!"

Slowly, Jake lowered his hands. "Are you going to shoot me?"

Her voice was gentle. "I'm sure you can see it's for the best."

The final irony was not wasted on him. "So I will achieve in death what I could not achieve in life?"

Wistfully, Sara smiled. "Let us hope so, Doctor. Now please turn around."

But Jake hesitated. He could not leave this world without a final glimpse of her. He stayed, and gazed at her one lingering moment. She was as always beautiful beyond his fantasies: blond and tall, smartly turned out in her uniform, her insignia and ribbons catching the glow of the setting sun. In the elegant curve of her fingers, she held the automatic pistol lightly. And behind her cool gray eyes, a mind of awesome magnitude reposed. He saw her then for what she was. Beautiful. Intelligent. Unyielding. Lethal. A woman and a soldier; giver of life—and taker; a triumph and a perversion; the crowning paradox of humankind. And he loved her with the very fiber of his soul, as he loved paradox itself.

"Thank you, Weatherby."

"For what, Doctor?"

"For giving me a way to atone." Still clinging to the image of her, he turned to face the sliding glass doors and murmured, "*Sh'mah Yisroel. . . .*"

Then he remembered Hiroshima; *that* was the last vision that lit his consciousness. And he knew it was his punishment and his damnation.

He cried out, "Please, Weatherby! Not my back!"

Sara fired.

The crashing rain of debris on the glass roof of the Winter Garden silenced the party-makers below. A hundred pairs of eyes looked up in time to see Jake lurch through the shattered sliding doors, stand swaying on the fifth-floor balcony. There was a huge exit wound in his forehead where the bullet had passed through his skull. His body leaned against the railing of the balcony and his dead face stared down at the crowd with a bizarre expression of contempt. Then he tipped forward over the railing and plummeted downward, turning end over end and crashing through the glass enclosure amid the screams and cries and horror of the diplomats. Marine guards drew their sidearms and hurried to surround the body.

A lieutenant pointed upward, shouted into his walkie-talkie, "Fifth floor! North corner office! Move out! Go!"

Lermontov stood looking down at his dead friend's body. His face convulsed in rage and grief. Then he shouted, "IT IS FINISHED!"

The lock on the door to Jake's office shattered and Wilding burst into the room. "I heard a shot! What's—"

Sara turned and leveled the pistol at him.

"Sara? What the hell is—" Then he saw the shattered glass and realized the room was empty. "My god—Sara! Did you shoot Doctor Handlesman?"

"Step aside, Bob. I don't want to have to hurt you."

"Damn you, Sara. Goddamn you!" With one sweep of gleaming steel, Wilding drew his saber; its blade glittered deadly in the ruddy light. He started toward her.

"Bob," she said softly. "If you take another step, I'll kill you."

Two marine guards rushed in from the reception area, knelt at the threshold of the office, their M-16 rifles leveled at Sara.

"Hold your fire!" Wilding took a step forward, one hand held open before him, the other gripping the sword at his side. "Sara. Give me the gun."

She backed away, but there was no fear in her.

"The gun, Sara—"

Sara stepped backward through the shattered sliding doors onto the balcony. On the flagpole in the mission driveway—in the freshening evening breeze off Lake Geneva—she caught sight of the colors standing stiffly at half-staff, saluting the veterans of America's wars. Westward, the sun was sinking behind the mountains, as it was setting on her life. She was joining them now—the hallowed souls of faithful men—the prisoners who had survived Chu My and risen to fight again as patriots to the world. Soon they would all be shades together. And when the politicians began their finger-pointing and name-calling ... when the partisan recriminations and the whitewash began tomorrow in Washington as it surely would . . . she wondered—would the world learn the truth that she and Petrovsky and the others had fought and died for? Or would their sacrifice be buried under new lies about how the deterrent missiles had won the nation another honorable peace?

Sara thought of Christy. She saw her as she had seen her for the first time—a dark-eyed girl in a freshly pressed second lieutenant's uniform, peeping through a classroom door in Monterey, bursting with curiosity and expectation, overflowing with noble ideals of Duty-Honor-Country. Now, on Christy's dainty shoulders the legacy of the prisoners of Chu My rested—as did, perhaps, the fate of nations. Did she understand all that had happened? Did she know how much depended on her? However the government might try to distort or dissemble—would Christy parrot their lies? Or would she see through their deception to the truth?

Sara Bryan smiled. She could not have found a safer repository for the testament of patriots—not in all the warriors she had ever known. In honor, she had never met a better soldier.

She raised her head—raised her pistol and pointed it at the marines.

Wilding shouted, "Sara! What are you doing?"

She squared her shoulders. The twilight's last gleaming wrapped her ashen hair in flame, and her gray eyes stared out from the corona like the accusations of the dead. "Bob, don't try to stop me from dying for my country."

"Sara! No!" In desperation, Wilding flung his saber aside and lurched toward her.

Sara fired over the heads of the marines. Instinctively they fired back. The two bursts struck her in the chest, lifted her off her feet and flung her backward off the balcony.

Her body cartwheeled through the air, smashed through the glass roof of the Winter Garden, crashed down beside Jake Handlesman. She lay, staring into the last glimmer of the darkening sky, her gray eyes impassive as they had been in life.

ARLINGTON NATIONAL CEMETERY, WASHINGTON

11:00 A.M.   The honor guard lieutenant shouted, "Fire!" A corporal yanked the lanyard and the flame and bellow of the howitzer boomed out across the gently rolling hills, boomed out across the endless ranks of headstones and the open grave of Captain Daniel Peter Bryan, rolled down the riverbank and across the wide Potomac. One by one, the guns saluted the moment of the veterans, and their warlike thunder echoed over Washington. It boomed through the empty hallways of the Capitol. It rang amid the graceful columns of Lincoln's colonnade, detonated against the granite of the Washington obelisk, shuddered the windowpanes of the White House. And when the guns fell silent a lone trumpeter before the Tomb of the Unknowns blew taps.

Sam Baker sat in the ground-floor library of the White House, his head bowed in solemn penance. He was listening, but he did not hear that trumpet sound; instead, he heard the thunder of a thousand turbofans driving deadly bombers through the stratosphere.

In the bookcase on the east wall the lighthouse clock began to chime the hour.

Outside, throughout the city, church bells tolled the knell.

In the Strategic Air Command battle staff room buried deep beneath the front lawn of SAC headquarters in Omaha, Nebraska, the plotting screen twinkled with lights that were American and Soviet bombers streaming toward fail-safe. General Lee Butler noted the time—1600 Zulu. Then he turned to the colonel at the comm console beside him. "You may issue the recall code."

The colonel looked at Butler. Then he began to laugh. Then slowly he lowered his head and rested his forehead in his hand.

In the missile operations center of SSBN-726 *Ohio,* three hundred feet below the surface of the Adriatic, Rear Admiral Henry Beame and Captain Wellesley hung their launch keys back around their necks. About them, officers and crewmen sat smoking, limp after the breaking of prolonged tension.

"You may stand down, Mr. Wellesley," Beame said, and turned to step out the open hatch.

"Until when, sir?"

Beame stopped and looked back. "Until next time, I suppose."

Sixty feet beneath the snowbound flatlands northeast of Cheyenne, Wyoming, the alert light went dark in Launch Control Center T of the Ninetieth Strategic Missile Wing. Captain Dallas Thompson looked down the length of the console; Lieutenant Steve Kranz sat staring back at her.

"No light," Dallas said.

"Me either."

"Okay. On my command—disable. Now."

Simultaneously they toggled down.

Abruptly Kranz jumped to his feet. " 'Scuse me, Captain. I gotta take a leak."

"Hold it, Kranz!" Thompson snapped. "Ladies first."

She shot past him into the john and pulled the curtain closed.

In the lead B52-H of Charlie flight, navigator Lieutenant Arnold Boyce looked up from the dead reckoning computer and tapped in on the intercom. "We are at fail-safe. I say again, we are at fail-safe. Right on schedule, Major." Beside him, the communications printer whirred to life. "Message from CINCSAC coming in. This could be it."

In the cockpit, Major Marvin Cutler sat at the controls, staring out at the undifferentiated darkness of sea and sky. Somewhere in that darkness—beyond Kyushu and Hiroshima—beyond the shrouded, storm-torn waters of the Sea of Japan, lay the nightbound, icy shores of Vladivostok and the headquarters of the Soviet Pacific Fleet. The digital clock on the panel before him read 1600 Zulu. He had brought his bomber to fail-safe on time; they were fifty minutes from their cruise missile launch point. As he waited for the coded message, Cutler realized that—including the flight time of his AGM-86B nuclear cruise missiles to their targets—the whole history of civilization had little more than an hour to run. And he understood that if the message on the printer contained an eight-digit battle code, the darkness before him stretched to eternity.

Boyce scrambled up the three steel steps to the flight deck and handed his clipboard to copilot Eddie Foyle. "Well, whaddya know." Foyle signed the clipboard with a flourish and held it out to Cutler. "Marv?"

But Cutler sat staring. Because in that moment he knew the answer to the question that had dogged him all the years he had commanded a nuclear bomber.

If ordered, he *could* fly on to Armageddon.

And he would.

"Marv?" Foyle said again, and pushed the clipboard against Cutler's chest. "It's the recall code."

Cutler looked down at the board. Then his eyes shifted to his copilot's, and Foyle could see the horror in them.

Gently Foyle laid a gloved hand on Cutler's shoulder. "Come on, Marv," he said softly. "Let's go home."

★ ★ ★

Ambassador Craig Mulholland stood in his office at the Geneva mission holding the telephone receiver. On the desk before him, a personnel file lay open. "Yes, Mr. President," he said. "By his aide— Major Sara Weatherby Bryan. When she left the naval school for Geneva, she filed a personnel request and took her maiden name again."

Sam Baker stood in the ground-floor library of the White House. "I see."

"The Soviet delegation has left the mission. Karpov says they're breaking off the talks and flying back to Moscow tomorrow morning."

"No! Craig, you've got to—"

Suddenly, the library door flew open; it was Harris.

Sam Baker slapped his hand over the telephone. "Ted, the bombers?"

"They've responded."

"All of them?"

"Yes, Sam. Yes! They're turning back."

"Thank God Almighty." Sam Baker clutched the receiver in both his hands. "Craig, the alert's over! Talk to Karpov. Stop them! Stall them."

"I've spoken to Karpov, Mr. President. It's too late."

"Not yet. They haven't left yet. Try again! Tell them—"

"Mr. President," Mulholland said softly. "There's nothing to talk about anymore. The Soviets believe America's armed forces are out of control."

In a cold concrete cell in the subbasement of the White House, Christy sat at the bare wooden table, her manacled hands before her. "Captain, what time is it now?"

Shapiro checked his watch. "Eleven."

Christy leaned back in her chair and stared blankly at the ceiling. The hour had come. It was the moment of the veterans, the time of the warriors. She had been brought to the White House for some purpose. But what purpose? She was locked in a windowless prison in the bowels of a government that had sequestered her from the outside world, alienated her from her comrades, deprived her of the insignia and privileges of her rank, humiliated and betrayed her, and threatened her with murder. What other malicious acts against her could they be planning?

Warily, she looked about the cubicle; it was a peculiar room to find in the basement of the White House.

"Captain, what is this place? Some kind of jail?"

Shapiro sat down on the cot and loosened his tie. "It's a bunker. They call it Stalag 17. Kennedy and McNamara slept down here during the Cuban missile crisis." He stretched out on the bare mattress, put his hands behind his head, and shut his eyes.

He did not hear the great, soft sigh that rose from Christy's lips. He did not see her push back her chair and stand and press her palms against the concrete wall. And even if he had—he didn't know why Sara Bryan had conspired to force mankind to confront a nuclear paradox of its own devising . . . to terrify the Soviet government with the specter of an American nuclear army out of control . . . or to imprison an ordinary air force intelligence clerk who might be able to see the alert through Russian eyes.

Shapiro knew none of this.

But Christy knew. Her captors had done their worst, but her spirit was unbroken. Even she could no longer doubt herself. She *was* a soldier. If the battle found her, she was ready.

Her education was complete.

Her day had come.

And a world was ripe for shaking.

HEROES

I, (name), having been appointed a (grade),
United States Air Force, do solemnly swear
(or affirm) that I will support and defend the
Constitution of the United States against all
enemies, foreign and domestic; that I will bear
true faith and allegiance to the same; that I
take this obligation freely, without any mental
reservation or purpose of evasion; and that I
will well and faithfully discharge the duties of
the office upon which I am about to enter, So
help me God.

OATH OF COMMISSIONED OFFICERS,
UNITED STATES AIR FORCE

11:08 A.M.

In the tiny control room of the NBC mobile video van parked on Jackson Place, Mike Marden sat alone before the switching console. A tense, hollow-eyed image of Tom Brokaw stared down at him from a dozen monitors.

> BROKAW
> I repeat—a Kremlin spokesman has announced that the START talks have been abandoned. The Soviet delegation will leave Geneva tomorrow morning. NBC News will bring you live coverage of President Baker's emergency address to the nation at noon eastern time. Now back to Garrick Utley in Washington.

"Hello, nightmares," Marden whispered. He flipped the master switch; the screens went black.

"Who gives a shit?" Fat Beth Harding pulled the ring tab on another can of Bud, leaned back in her Barcalounger, and zapped to *I Love Lucy*.

The tall white walls of the Soviet mission on the Avenue de la Paix were painted red by the sinking alpine sunset. In the cramped START offices on the second floor, harried diplomats were stuffing documents into shipping cartons, packing laptop computers, and shredding papers.

Mikhail Lermontov shuffled through the commotion toward his dormitory bedroom, looking neither left nor right, a zombie.

Ted Harris lowered the receiver to its cradle. "NBC's reporting the START talks have broken off. It's all over the network news."

Before him in the ground-floor library, three graying men sat in silence. The room was small—no larger than a sitting room in a suburban home. But at that moment it contained the executive branch of the government of the United States.

"Well, that's that," Charlie O'Donnell said. "The Cold War's on again. And after what those uniformed fanatics pulled today, by the time Congress gets through cutting the Pentagon budget, we'll be lucky if we can afford a National Guard."

Secretary of State Arthur Coleman got to his feet. "Gentlemen, let's not lose sight of what's at stake here. The START talks aren't the problem."

"Then what the hell is?" Harris said.

Coleman shot him a withering look. "The credibility of the command-and-control system of our armed forces. Have you any idea the effect this insanity has had on our allies? On world opinion? On the American public?" He turned to the president. "Sam, for three hours this morning you lost control."

Where the November sun cut down at a hard angle through the delicate lace curtains, President Samuel Baker sat with his head bowed forward, his hands clasped in an attitude of mournful prayer.

There was much to mourn. Zack Littman and Simon Whitworth were dead, as were their families and dozens of servicemen and servicewomen. And the conspirators had trapped the president in a final double paradox. Just as he had been given to see that disarmament must begin with the elimination of strategic nuclear missiles, the Soviets had been driven from the bargaining table in Geneva. First Step was a mistake, but reneging now might set off another round of the arms race. And how could he hope to persuade the Soviets to relinquish their precious deterrent missiles when the world had come so close to war?

The sword of paradox also cut the other way. Even if he could persuade the Soviets to consider eliminating strategic nuclear missiles, how could he persuade Congress to sustain America's conventional armies at full strength until the weapons were negotiated away? What legislature would support a military establishment that might turn on the nation again?

"The issue," Coleman said, "is not what has happened but what will happen. And what *must* happen is that we must get First Step back on track."

Softly and without looking up, Sam Baker said, "Not First Step."

"We've got to—" Coleman paused. "Sam? Did you say something?"

"I said, not First Step."

Puzzled, Coleman looked to Harris.

"Why not?" Harris said.

"Because First Step was a mistake. I was wrong."

"Sam, don't start that again."

"They were right, Ted. Whitworth. Littman. The conspirators. Strategic nuclear weapons must go first."

"Is that what you're going to tell the nation in your televised address at noon?"

"Yes."

Behind the president, Coleman and O'Donnell exchanged a startled look.

"Now, wait a second," Harris said. "Let me get this straight—" He came across the room, stood directly in front of the president's chair. "You're going to get up in front of two hundred million Americans and tell them that seven lunatics understood our strategic defense better than the president of the United States?"

"Yes."

Coleman said, "Sam, you're not serious?"

"Yes, Arthur. Dead serious."

"What about Littman?" Harris said and his voice was rising. "Are you going to tell them your Secretary of Defense violated our no-nukes treaty with Japan? Are you going to tell them that?"

"Yes, Ted. I am."

O'Donnell ran his hand back through his shaggy white hair. "Mary, Mother of God. . . ."

Harris was coming to a boil. "Well, while you're on the subject why don't you tell them Littman and Handlesman were guilty of treason?"

"I intend to," the president said.

"You *intend* to? Jesus Christ, Sam! You do that and our whole system of government will come crashing down around our heads!"

In the silence that followed, the president stared at his chief of staff. "Ted, what choice do we have?"

Neither Harris nor the others moved to answer.

But Sam Baker sensed their intent. "You're not suggesting we try to cover this up?"

Harris put his hands in his pockets. "No. Not exactly. Just—you know—put the best face on it we can."

"Ted, be realistic. There's bound to be a congressional investigation."

"Sure there is." Harris turned to O'Donnell. "Charlie? What do we do about that?"

"We can handle it the same way we handled the John Tower hearings in '88. All the written reports in a locked reading room in the Capitol attic. All the hot testimony in closed executive session." O'Donnell smiled at the president. "Not saying we won't get our hair mussed, Sam. But we'll survive."

Sam Baker took hold of the arms of his chair. He could feel the spider of expedient politics beginning to spin its ugly web about him. Once more he felt the solid earth of honorable judgment beginning to shift like quicksand beneath him.

"No." The president got to his feet. "No, this is madness! We can't tell the country a lie and persuade the whole world this never happened. Arthur, surely you don't go along with this?"

Deliberately, Coleman weighed the question. "Frankly, I don't care what you tell the country, Sam. What matters is what we say to the Soviets. And either we find a way to convince Gorbachev and the Politburo that our armed forces are and always were under control, or you can kiss our whole foreign policy goodbye."

"Arthur, do you realize what you're saying?"

"Sam, the Soviets need First Step as much as we do. If First Step is a way to get them back to the bargaining table, let's make the most of it. We can talk about eliminating strategic nuclear weapons—"

"When?" the president demanded.

Coleman opened his hands and smiled. "Why, down the road, of course."

Sam Baker had heard enough. "What's the matter with you people? Has everything that happened this morning meant nothing? My god, we almost lost the republic!"

"Sam, you're being melodramatic."

"Melodramatic?"

"Sam, be practical."

Then the president boiled over. "Goddammit. I've *been* practical! I ordered our air force into combat! I lied to the Russians about the missiles in Hakodate! I followed standing orders and sanctioned a DEFCON alert! For god's sake, we almost turned the world into a cinder by being practical!"

Abruptly, Sam Baker straightened. The three men were staring at him strangely. He looked down; his hands were shaking uncontrollably. He was losing his grip on his emotions and the moment. He reached out with one trembling hand and took hold of the mantelpiece. Then he leaned against it, struggling to catch his breath.

Behind him, his advisers exchanged an anxious glance. Coleman motioned Harris to the president.

Gently Harris laid a hand on Sam Baker's heaving shoulders and leaned close to his ear. "Sam—pull yourself together," he whispered. "It's over. The danger's past. Let's not turn a crisis into a tragedy. Let's do what we have to."

The president didn't answer.

Harris shot a worried look at the others; Coleman tapped the crystal of his wristwatch urgently.

"Sam, please," Harris said. "The clock is ticking. We need a decision. And you *are* the president."

But Sam Baker hesitated. He leaned against the mantel, feeling the eyes of the wise and powerful men observing him, knowing they were measuring him, beginning to doubt his strength of will. How could they be right? The truth seemed so clear and unassailable?

And yet, how could they be wrong? The authority and prestige of the presidency had to be maintained before the community of nations and the American people. Perhaps there was one desperate chance. And perhaps it was a chance he had to take.

At last he raised his head. "All right, all right. . . ." He turned to face them and cleared his throat. "Forgive me. For a moment there—"

"No problem," Harris said.

"Could happen to anyone," Coleman said.

"We've all been feeling the heat," O'Donnell said.

The three men smiled.

"All right," Sam Baker said. "We'll do what we have to." He clapped his hands against his flanks. "Starting now, we go on the offensive. Ted, where's Ambassador Volokin?"

"In the Vermeil Room."

"And Colonel Hernandez?"

"Conference room number two."

"Get Hernandez in here. Now."

"Yes, sir." Harris grabbed the phone.

The president turned to O'Donnell. "Charlie, you go up and work the Hill. Damage control. Cut our losses any way you can."

O'Donnell seized the president's hand and pumped it. "On my way. And, Sam, you won't regret this."

The president turned to Coleman. "Arthur, you're on a plane to Brussels tonight for a NATO ministerial to reassure the allies."

"Yes, sir." The two shook hands.

As Coleman and O'Donnell went out, Hernandez entered. "Yes, Mr. President?"

"Colonel, that Lieutenant Russoff—is she guilty?"

"I don't know, sir."

"Why the hell not?" Harris said.

"Mr. Harris, if you'd asked me that question an hour ago, I'd have said absolutely—yes. Now . . ." Hernandez shook his head.

"You said yourself she lied about Captain Bryan being the mastermind behind the plot."

"I was wrong. When Lieutenant Russoff was at the naval school in Monterey, Major Weatherby was known to her as Captain Bryan."

"She murdered that Sergeant Kulikov. You said they found the gun in her desk."

"Yes. Ballistics confirmed it was the murder weapon."

Harris jammed his fists against his hips. "Well? What more proof do you need?"

"Lieutenant Russoff's fingerprints weren't on the gun."

"Maybe she wiped them off."

"Colonel Petrovsky's fingerprints were."

That stopped Harris.

"What do you make of that?" Sam Baker said.

"We can't be sure," Hernandez said. "But it appears the conspirators wanted us to arrest Lieutenant Russoff. And detain her until the evidence exonerated her and we had to let her go."

The president's eyes narrowed. "Why? Why would they do a thing like that?"

"I think they wanted us to know she wasn't part of the conspiracy."

"Oh, for chrissake," Harris growled. "Russoff's one of them and that's that! She's guilty as hell!"

But Hernandez wasn't backing down. "Then why didn't they erase her service record?"

"Who cares? Maybe they forgot. Maybe they—"

"Hold on," Sam Baker said. "Why didn't they erase it?"

"I think they erased their service records as a way of separating themselves from our armed forces," Hernandez said. "So that their dishonor would be their own. But they left Lieutenant Russoff's record intact—"

"Yes?"

"—to indicate she was loyal to her oath."

Harris snorted. "Now that's the most harebrained load of nonsense I ever—"

Hernandez didn't let him finish. "Mr. Harris, whether you like it or not, there is absolutely no hard evidence to connect Lieutenant Russoff to any criminal act."

"Now just a goddamn minute," Harris said, his patience exhausted. "Are you telling us that all the power and the glory of the United States Air Force can't hang one little first lieutenant for treason?"

"No, Mr. Harris," Hernandez said. "I'm telling you that I harassed and persecuted Lieutenant Russoff on your order. But if you want to murder her, you're going to have to get someone else to do it for you!"

Before Harris could answer, Sam Baker stepped between them. "Colonel, you think she's innocent. Don't you?"

"Yes, sir. I do."

"Then what possible purpose could they have for involving her in all this?"

Hernandez shifted uneasily. "Mr. President, I'd rather not speculate about—"

"Dammit man, I want an answer!"

"I think . . ." Hernandez took a breath. "I think they were afraid the civilian authorities would try to cover up what really happened. And they wanted someone they could trust to tell their story after—"

"After what?"

"After . . . they were dead."

Sam Baker cleared his throat. "I see." He glanced at Harris. "Well . . ." Then he took Hernandez by the arm. "Does Lieutenant Russoff know she's been exonerated?"

"No, sir."

"Good. See that she doesn't." The president steered Hernandez toward the door. "Colonel, the Soviet ambassador is waiting in the Vermeil Room. I want your staff to brief him about this conspiracy. Everything we know—nothing held back. Particularly the evidence exonerating Lieutenant Russoff. Make sure Volokin understands that she's a loyal serving officer. Can I could on you to do that?"

"Yes, sir." Hernandez let himself out.

Sam Baker looked at his watch; it was 11:15 A.M. Time was short. There was much to do. "Ted, get the Secretary of the Air Force over here. On the double. I need him to sign some papers." He started across the room.

Harris barred his way. "Wait a second. What is it, Sam? What's the plan?"

"First, we convince Volokin this whole thing was the work of a handful of fanatics."

"Sure, but how?"

"Then we prove to Congress and the public that our military broke the conspiracy themselves."

"*What?*"

"And then I make both announcements when I speak to the nation at noon."

"Sam, you're asking for a miracle!"

"No." The president clenched his fists. "Just a patriot."

The door to the subbasement cubicle opened; two Secret Service women entered, showed Captain Shapiro out and locked the door behind him. One of the women carried a new dark blue dress uniform and shoes, the other a cosmetics case, hairbrushes and underwear.

When she had dressed, Christy held out her hands for the manacles. But instead the Secret Service women took her by the arms, led her upstairs, and showed her into ground-floor conference room number 2.

The long table was scattered with files and worksheets. At the head of the table, an air force colonel stood waiting.

"Good morning, Lieutenant. I'm Colonel Hernandez of the OSI. The commander in chief wishes to speak with you about the conspiracy."

Christy braced. "Not until I see my grandmother."

"Your grandmother is at home," Hernandez said. "She was never arrested."

"But . . . I got a letter from the Immigration Service. They said . . ." Christy's voice trailed off into silence as she grasped the cruel hoax. She was among her enemies now—a captive deep in the enemy camp. She must be on her guard, prepared for any ploy or subterfuge they might use against her. She must accept neither parole nor special favors. She must keep faith.

Hernandez came around the table toward her. "You will receive a formal apology for the mistreatment you've suffered. I will also. . . ." But he broke off when he saw the look on Christy's face.

Slowly, moving softly as a sleepwalker, Christy stepped past Hernandez and stood before the seven photographs pinned to the corkboard on the wall. Through the angry red X marks the conspirators stared back at her—Petrovsky and Harding, Watkins and O'Neill, two naval officers who must have been Granger and Logan.

Her eyes moved to the last photograph.

The face behind the X was an army major—a fair-haired, square-jawed, gray-eyed woman. She was older than Christy remembered her; in the three years they had been apart, Sara Bryan had aged more than Christy could have imagined. There were lines of care about her eyes; their light had hardened and grown colder, more determined.

"Is she . . . dead?"

"Yes," Hernandez said.

The word cut through Christy like the icy steel of a bayonet. She felt her skin go cold and clammy; her stomach rolled. But she held herself rigid, fought the nausea and dizziness. She had come so far; she must not show any weakness now.

"Dr. Handlesman?"

"Dr. Handlesman, too."

Christy felt light-headed, faint, as though a wound had opened in her soul and the life were pouring out of her. She closed her hands, drove her fingernails into her palms until the pain began to bring her back.

"And the START talks?"

"Broken off."

Christy whispered. "God rest their souls."

"Lieutenant," Hernandez said. "Did Major Bryan ever speak to you about the plan of this conspiracy?"

"No. If she had, I would have reported her. She knew that."

"Did she ever discuss her views on strategic weapons with you or—"

"Not since the naval school in Monterey."

"Well, was there anything about your relationship that might suggest—"

"We were lovers."

Hernandez stiffened.

"Once upon a time." Christy turned to the row of photographs and stared into Sara Bryan's face. The cool gray eyes looked down on her with a valediction and a blessing. It was their last goodbye.

"Whenever you're ready, Colonel."

There was a harsh knocking at the library door. It was Ted Harris, carrying a leather folder. "All right, I've taken care of everything." He slapped the folder on the table before the president. "The paperwork on Russoff is in here. Volokin's been briefed on the conspiracy." He checked his watch. "And you're live on network television in twenty minutes."

Sam Baker fingered the document in the leather folder. He had no choice but expedience. And yet as he gazed at the sheet of paper headed with the Great Seal of the United States he saw that the words written there reproached him.

"What is it, Sam? Something wrong?"

"Just that we keep trying to lie our way out of—"

"Sam. Please. There's no time for moralizing. Volokin's been briefed and Russoff's waiting in the hall. We have to act—now." Harris went to the door. "And, Sam—" His face tightened. "This had better work."

Sam Baker let the cover of the folder drop closed. "All right. Send her in."

"Twenty minutes," Harris said. Then he went out.

A young woman in a dark blue dress uniform entered, braced, and saluted. There was a large angry bruise on her right cheek as though she had been struck a terrible blow.

"As you were," the president said. "Lieutenant—" Then he caught himself. The woman who stood before him was an air force first lieutenant. But she was a small woman, delicate and almost child-like—her skin pale, her hair black, and her eyes Slavic and strange.

"Are *you* Lieutenant Russoff?"

"Yes, sir."

"How old are you, Lieutenant?"

"Twenty-eight."

"I didn't realize you were so . . . young." Sam Baker felt the tension in his shoulders ebb; she was a young girl—he was the president of the United States; he had the controlling hand. "Well, Christy—may I call you Christy?"

"Yes, sir."

"Colonel Hernandez tells me the evidence against you is equivocal. There's a possibility you might be innocent. Would you like to have a chance to prove that?"

Christy blinked in surprise. "Well . . . yes, sir."

"I'm going to give you that chance, Lieutenant. A chance to do a great service for your country. And if you cooperate, you'll receive a presidential pardon."

"A . . . pardon?"

The president turned and paced. "You and I know what happened today was the work of a handful of disaffected office.s. But the Soviets are convinced our military was out of control. You're the only living eyewitness. If you can help me convince the Soviet ambassador this insanity was the work of seven misguided fanatics, perhaps he'll urge President Gorbachev to allow their delegation to stay in Geneva and reopen discussions on First Step. Help me do that and you'll be pardoned. Now how does that sound?" He stopped before her, waiting for an answer.

Christy stared at the smiling man before her. After all that had happened, the President of the United States was still committed to the madness of First Step and offering her a pardon to help him persuade the Soviets to accept it.

"Lieutenant, I asked you a question. Do I have to remind you of your oath of allegiance?"

"No, sir. I understand."

"Good." Sam Baker pressed the button on the intercom. "Katherine, have Ambassador Volokin join us."

The door opened and Volokin entered, suave and unruffled in his dapper pin-striped suit and bright silk tie. His hulking interpreter, Gregor Malkin, came in behind him and took a seat on the sofa between the windows.

Instantly Sam Baker brightened; he clapped his hands together. "Well, Vassily, you've been briefed. The mutiny's been crushed. The conspirators are dead. I think it's time we got back to business as usual. Don't you?"

"Perhaps. But . . ." The cagey Russian smiled. "They said you had an eyewitness?"

"Yes, we have." The president beamed with confidence. "The air force officer who detected and reported the mutiny. And will confirm everything you've been told." He opened his hand toward Christy. "Mr. Ambassador—Lieutenant Russoff."

Christy braced, saluted; Volokin nodded condescendingly.

"Now, then." Sam Baker leaned against the table and crossed his arms. "Lieutenant, you are to tell Ambassador Volokin everything you know about the events of the past twelve hours. And answer any and all questions he might put to you. That is an order."

"Yes, sir."

Volokin folded his hands before him, waiting.

Christy stared at the grotesque tableau before her. Instead of clinging together for the sake of their mutual survival, a Russian and an American stood posturing and puffing, each trying to bluff the other with fatuous macho prattle—just as their two nations had done for the past forty-five years. But beyond the cocky pretense, she saw the men for what they were: two desperate creatures, prisoners of their sex, reeling from the aftershocks of Sara Bryan's masterpiece of terror.

Christy's heartbeat quickened. The three stood in no-man's land and the air was tuned for battle. She thought of Colonel Petrovsky's haunting question about the Cuban missile crisis. *Lieutenant—do you remember what Kennedy said that made Khrushchev and his Politburo blink? The threat that made them back down?*

Christy remembered; Bryan had instructed her to write her thesis on it—"Disinformation as Deterrent: A Case Study in Fear." A military coup against the government of the United States might seem inconceivable to the American people. But Robert Kennedy's insinuation that the American army might overthrow their government had struck a terror into Khrushchev and his Politburo that John Kennedy's ultimatum of all-out retaliation had not.

Military historians disagreed about whether Khrushchev believed what Robert Kennedy said to Soviet Ambassador Dobrynin in Washington on October 27, 1962. But history recorded that, on the following day, Khrushchev *had* blinked—and negotiations toward resolving the crisis began.

Christy remembered. And she knew what these strutting politicians feared.

She raised her head. "Sir, may I speak in Russian?"

The president looked to Volokin; he nodded. "If you wish."

When Christy spoke, she spoke softly.

But as she did Malkin's face went slack. Then, suddenly, he started to his feet. A snap of Volokin's fingers stilled him.

When Christy finished, Volokin's smile had vanished. Haltingly he said, *"Ochen' khoroshii . . .* a very good report."

Christy and Volokin stood, eyes locked, neither moving, neither giving ground. But behind Volokin's eyes Christy could see the old Russian habit of suspicion of their military churning, grinding. She could feel the doubt creeping up his spine. Dead-eyed and relentless she held his stare. It was not what she had said, but what *she was* that she must make him believe.

Sam Baker looked back and forth between them. Something was amiss; something was wrong. "Vassily? What is it? What did she say?"

Malkin began, "She says—"

Sharply, Volokin raised a hand for silence. "She says this military plot has been broken. But there will be others. She says the conspiracy reaches into the highest levels of the Pentagon, and they will try again and keep on trying until you are dead and the United States is ruled by a junta of the Joint Chiefs of Staff, the director of the FBI, and the director of the CIA."

"What?" Sam Baker gasped. "That's insane! Vassily. There are no more conspirators! She's lying! For god's sake, don't believe her!"

"Of course I don't believe her." Volokin shot a look of scorn at the president "Any more than I believe your lies about your army being under control."

Sam Baker caught Volokin's sleeve. "Vassily, I assure you . . ."

Roughly, the ambassador pulled away. "No more lies, Mr. President. No more!" He pointed at Christy. "All day long in my country we have struggled with fanatics like her. Monsters urging us to launch our missiles—strike first before you strike at us." Volokin turned on the president, his eyes a fury of indignation. "This is where your American obsession with deterrence brought us. To the brink of insanity and extinction!"

Bewildered, Sam Baker groped, "I—I don't understand. . . ."

"Do you not see the truth when it stands before you and defies you to your face? Look at her!" Volokin commanded. "Look at her and tell me you can stake the world's survival on whether governments can control these traitors! Don't you see? If we rely on strategic nuclear missiles to keep the peace—if we permit these weapons to exist and spread—sooner or later we are all doomed!"

Sam Baker took hold of the back of a chair. "Vassily? What are you saying?"

Volokin swept the room with an angry wave of his arm. "First Step and START are finished! Our negotiating team is flying home to Moscow for new instructions. If you wish to negotiate with us again, you must renounce your demented worship of deterrence. You must join with us to call all nuclear powers to the table. And somehow find a way to eliminate the missiles before it is too late!"

"But, Vassily—that's exactly what I want to do!"

"Then we must begin. Now." Volokin stepped close to Sam Baker. "And we must not fail, Mr. President. For if we fail"—he glanced at Christy and in his eyes now there was only dread—"we know who we will have to reckon with." His voice became a snarl of bitterness. "In many countries there are such . . . such patriots."

Then, abruptly Volokin made a tense little bow. "Now you must excuse me. *Das-vedanya*, Mr. President. I will call again tomorrow to discuss arrangements for a fresh start in Geneva. *Das-vedanya*." He beckoned to Malkin; the interpreter followed him out the door.

"Am I pardoned?"

Like a man waking from a dream, Sam Baker murmured, "What?" Then his eyes focussed on her. "Lieutenant! Have you any idea of the damage you might have done with that stunt?"

Christy's voice was steady, cold. "First Step was dangerous. You knew that. How else could I stop you? I said—am I pardoned?"

He peered at her in awe. "My god . . . what kind of woman are you?"

"I'm a soldier. And I'm sworn to defend my country from all enemies—foreign *and* domestic."

Sam Baker straightened at the insult. "Stand at attention!" Then he caught himself; she had suffered much and done great service to the nation. Besides, it was almost noon and he had things to do.

He went to the table and uncapped his pen. "All right, Christy. As we agreed—you and Sergeant Browning are pardoned—on one condition." He signed the sheet of paper and handed it to her.

Christy could feel the president's indignation. She had grown accustomed to resentment in men's eyes. It had become the price of honor. She looked down at the paper in her hand and went rigid.

"Yes, you have one more duty to perform today, Christy," the president said. "And I think you'll find it a pleasant one. You're going to help me restore the confidence of Congress and the American people in our military." He opened a drawer in the table and lifted out a small velvet box. "In a few moments I will present you to the press as the courageous young officer who uncovered the conspiracy and helped her superiors to crush it—and preserved the honor of the armed forces of the United States." He raised the cover of the box. The Air Force Cross gleamed on the pale blue velvet.

Sam Baker pinned the medal to the left breast of Christy's uniform, and spoke the traditional words. "For extraordinary heroism in military operations against an armed enemy of the United States. Congratulations, Captain Russoff."

Christy looked down at the medal on the freshly pressed new uniform and thought of the ragged prisoners of Chu My. "But . . . they weren't the enemy. . . ."

"No? Then who was?"

She fingered the medal. "And I wasn't a hero. . . ."

Then she understood. She stepped back; her voice rose. "You're going to use me to cover up what really happened. Aren't you? You're going to say they were criminals and use me to make the country believe our military broke the conspiracy!"

"Captain!" the president snapped. "There's more at stake here than your pigheaded code of honor!"

Christy braced, fell silent.

Sam Baker lowered his voice. "Christy, please—try to be reasonable. Everything's turned out well. You got a pardon and a medal. The television audience gets a hero. The Congress and the taxpayers will get the deficit relief they need. Even the conspirators got what they wanted. Someday—God willing—we may actually rid the world of strategic nuclear missiles. Now just keep quiet and be glad you're going to face the press instead of a firing squad."

She lifted her chin, defiant. "Never."

Sam Baker shook his head. "Christy, you don't seem to understand your situation. Either you walk out that door a hero with a long and glorious career before you . . . or you spend the rest of your life as an outcast trying to find someone—anyone—who'll believe a crazy story about seven conspirators who murdered fifty people and brought the world to the brink of nuclear war because they thought they were saving mankind."

Christy stared hard at the man before her. He was the president of the United States. But in the deadly game of disinformation he was no match for a soldier. "I'm not going to tell that story," she said softly. "You will."

"*I will?* I hardly think so."

"Volokin believes I'm a traitor. If you go through with this charade the Soviets will never believe anything you say again. And the whole cycle of deceit and mistrust will repeat itself—first with lies, then with weapons. And, one day, that armed enemy will come again. And next time there may be no patriots to stop him. Mr. President, you can tell the truth because you want to . . . or because you have to. But you *will* tell it."

For a moment, Sam Baker stood silent. Then, abruptly, he turned away, walked to the window, and drew back the curtain. "Captain, you're dismissed. Now go upstairs to the Green Room and wait for me so that I may present you to the press."

Behind him, he heard her feet shuffle on the carpet, hesitate, and then the sound of the opening door. "A moment, Christy. You have your pardon. Just for the record . . . Were you one of them? Were you part of the conspiracy?"

Christy looked back at the president; in the fall of light through the window, he was an old man, stoop shouldered, worn and weary. As the years had bent his body, compromise had bent his soul. She had never understood the president of the United States could be so vulnerable. She had never considered the fact that even he was only a man.

"Yes, sir," Christy said. "In the end, I suppose I was."

The hall door swung shut.

The side door opened; it was Ted Harris—breathless. "Well? Sam? How did it go?"

Sam Baker stood looking out the window at the bright midday sun gleaming on the city, on the Capitol dome and the great shrines of Washington. "Taken care of," he said absently.

"Volokin believed her?"

"In a way. . . ."

"And the talks? Sam, what about the talks?"

"The Soviets will return to Geneva."

"My god! Sam! You got your miracle!" Harris clapped his hands and rubbed them together and glanced around the room. "Where's the girl now?"

"I sent her upstairs. To the Green Room."

"Perfect." Harris checked his watch. "You've got ten minutes to get a suit on while I—" He broke off. "Sam? What's this? I thought you were going to give her the medal down here."

Sam Baker let the curtain fall. When he turned, Harris was holding the blue box. The Air Force Cross lay where Christy had left it— tossed on the pale velvet.

Harris snapped his fingers in delight. "Hell, this is even better! Here." He thrust the medal into the president's hand. "You can pin it on her live in front of the television cameras." Then he hurried to the door. "Come on, Mr. President. It's show time! Don't keep the American people waiting!" He went out.

But Sam Baker didn't follow. He stood a moment in the close and silent library. The little woman in the lieutenant's uniform had been right. Perhaps he could lie to the nation. But he could not lie to the Soviets. And he could not lie to himself.

First Step was dangerous. He had been wrong.

The conspirators had died to show him his error.

Who, then, was the criminal?

He looked down at the Air Force Cross gleaming on its velvet cushion. And he knew the name of the armed enemy who had threatened the life of the United States.

Him.

NOON

By the slanting rays of sunlight that descended through the cupola of the United States Capitol, the bare catafalque stood empty, awaiting the caskets of Margaret and Simon Whitworth. Four men in uniform stood at the four points of the compass—a marine corporal, a navy seaman, an army sergeant, an airman first class.

Before the altar in the flickering candlelight of the chapel of St. Mary-in-the-Woods, Sister Mary Patrick O'Neill knelt on the cold stone floor, her arms held stiffly away from her body in the shape of a cross, her face streaked with tears, her lips moving silently in words of thanksgiving for the life of her father, for the nation's answered prayers.

The door of the security police headquarters at Andrews Air Force Base opened and Tod stepped out, blinking in the midday glare, picking his personal effects from a manila envelope. The November air was cold; involuntarily he shivered.

The bedroom was empty in the bachelor officers' quarters at Oceana Naval Air Station. The orderly had stripped the bed and turned the mattress back. A navy pilot's duffel waited on the floor, as if the owner were moving on.

In his tiny bedroom in the Soviet mission at 15 Avenue de la Paix, Mikhail Lermontov sat on the edge of his bed in the gathering darkness, his tie hanging loose at his collar. On the table before him a portable chessboard lay open, its men frozen for eternity in a last unfinished game.

Two marine guards stood at parade rest before the door of the utility room in the basement of the American mission at 11 Route de Pregny. Inside the narrow, unheated room two bodies draped in white sheets lay close together, side by side. On one, someone had carefully arranged a threadbare, careworn tallis and a leather pouch of phylacteries. Beside the other body, Lieutenant Colonel Robert Wilding brushed the army crest on the officer's hat with his sleeve, then laid it on the breast of Major Sara Weatherby Bryan.

And in the drafty parlor of Magnolia House, to the slow ticking of the Seth Thomas long-case clock, photographs of five generations of American soldiers hung shoulder-to-shoulder as though gathered in parade. A single candle guttered before the bunting-draped photograph of seven prisoners of war—the last in a long line of patriots.

★ ★ ★

In the East Room on the first floor of the White House, President Samuel Baker stood at the podium facing the reporters, the massed television cameras, the still photographers, and flashing strobes. He announced that a new round of multinational talks would soon convene in Geneva under Soviet-American sponsorship to begin negotiating the elimination of strategic nuclear missiles. He spoke eloquently of a new era of international cooperation, an end to forty-five years of nuclear terror, the promise of a lasting peace. The reporters squirmed impatiently; they had heard this kind of fluff before.

But when the president told them about the missiles of Hakodate, about Zack Littman and Jake Handlesman, when he listed the names of the patriots who had spent their lives in a desperate crusade to show him the error of First Step, the reporters could hardly believe their ears.

Outside the White House, Christy pushed through the security gate at the south end of West Executive Avenue. She stood a moment, squinting in the brightness of the sun. Then she set her cap and followed the path around the Ellipse to where Constitution Avenue crossed Fifteenth Street.

On the Mall, the Marine Corps band was playing, and a long queue of families waited to ride the elevator to the top of the Washington Monument. Christy stood a moment, watching, listening. The November breeze stiffened the flags that ringed the obelisk and swelled the tunes of glory.

Quite suddenly Christy felt her eyes dampen. Self-consciously she dabbed at their corners with her hand. After all that had happened, was an old song and the snap of flags to reduce her to a young girl's silly tears? Embarrassed, she peeped about.

But she need not have worried. No one took notice of her. It was Veterans Day—and the city was full of real soldiers.

EPILOGUE:
HOMECOMING

Arlington National Cemetery
Saturday, November 16, 1991
7:48 A.M.

There were only five flag-draped coffins; Granger and Logan had been lost at sea. The air force burial detail wore dark blue, the army detail forest green. Under the terms of the posthumous presidential pardon, the five were to be buried with a minimum of ceremony; whatever their motive, their crimes were intolerable under military law. There were no salvos from riflemen, no fly-by of jets, and the Memorial Drive gates of the cemetery were closed against the news crews and the curious.

A small gathering of civilians ringed the gravesite. Among them, Christy recognized only Mrs. Watkins; the others were unknown to her. But as the flags were lifted from the coffins, folded, and presented to the mourners, Christy understood the nun was Colonel O'Neill's daughter; the elderly lady with blue, piercing eyes was Colonel Petrovsky's mother; the chubby, bleached-blond woman who never stopped crying was Lieutenant Colonel Harding's wife.

Then the lieutenant of the army burial detail stood before Christy and offered her the flag from Sara Bryan's coffin. Christy looked down at the tightly bound stripes of red and white, wrapped as they were around stars—and it was as though Sara, not the lieutenant, stood before her.

"Thank you," Christy said.

The lieutenant stepped back and saluted. Then the mechanisms hissed and the five caskets began their descent into the receiving earth. As Christy watched, her thoughts drifted back to Monterey, a still night, a driftwood fire.

"What we do isn't about medals," Sara said.

"I know, I know. Duty-Honor-Country."

"And sacrifice."

"And what do you get to show for that?" Christy demanded.

"Knowing those you honor, honor you."

Christy crossed her arms and pressed the flag to her breast. And they both knew it was safe there.

THANKS

To editor Robert Loomis. To expert advisers Roland Starke, Norman Sandler, Jimmie Butler, Dr. Paul R. Sohmer, and Jack Peters. To research wizard Jill Rosenfeld. And to early commentators Elizabeth McKee, Jonathan Matson, Mark Wells, Deidre Hall, Martha Zuckerman, Radi Kushnerovitch, Raymond Sternthall, Raeanne Hytone, Abraham Tetenbaum, Kenneth Johnson, Gary Crutcher, Leonardo Bercovici, Rod Browning, Gregg Coffey, Andrea Merkel, and Martin Cutler.

The author also wishes to express his appreciation to the men and women of the United States Departments of State and Defense who made possible the technical authenticity of this book. Their help, of course, should not be considered an endorsement of any of the themes of the book.

UNITED STATES DEPARTMENT OF STATE AND EMERITUS

To the many distinguished diplomats who graciously contributed their time to help an innocent begin to understand the complex and awesome responsibilities of American and Soviet arms negotiators: Ambassador Paul Nitze, Ambassador Max Kampelman, Ambassador Paul Warneke, Ambassador Edwin Rowny, Ambassador Henry Cooper, Dr. Stanley Riveles, Robert Simmons.

UNITED STATES DEPARTMENT OF DEFENSE

STRATEGIC AIR COMMAND: Offutt AFB, NB, Gen. John T. Chain, Jr., commander in chief
NORTH AMERICAN AEROSPACE DEFENSE COMMAND: Petersen AFB, CO, Gen. John L. Piotrowski, commander in chief
UNITED STATES AIR FORCE ACADEMY: Colorado Springs, CO, Lt. Gen. Charles R. Hamm, superintendent
SOUTHEAST AIR DEFENSE SECTOR CONTROL: Tyndall AFB, FL, Colonel Arnold R. Thomas, Jr., commander

AIR FORCE OFFICE OF SPECIAL INVESTIGATIONS: Bolling AFB, Washington, DC, Brig. Gen. Francis R. Dillon, commander
USAF OFFICE OF PUBLIC AFFAIRS: the Pentagon, Washington, DC, Brig. Gen. Michael P. McRaney, director
125TH FIGHTER INTERCEPTOR GROUP: U.S. Air National Guard, Jacksonville, FL, Col. Don Garrett, commander
AIR FORCE RESERVE OFFICERS TRAINING CORPS: Detachment 55/ UCLA, Los Angeles, CA, Colonel George P. Pehlvanian, professor of Aerospace Studies

In particular: Colonel Frederick W. Morgan, Colonel Thomas A. Hornung, Colonel Richard Law, Colonel William Harwood, Colonel William Campbell, Colonel Donald Cook, Colonel Timothy Kinnan, Colonel David R. Zorich, Lt. Colonel Jacob Huffmann II, Lieutenant Colonel George Peck, Lieutenant Commander Steven Golle, Major Kathleen McCollom, Major Dave Moore, Major Charles Merlo, Major Michael E. Gentry, Major Richard Caldwell, Major Suzanne Randall, Captain Bill Stephenson, Captain Carolyn Hodge, Captain Barbara Austin, Captain Ray Kirby, Captain Rick Rankin, Captain Dave Uzzell, Captain Tom Neiman, Lieutenant James Brooks, Lieutenant Judy Wiser, Lieutenant Julie Colson, Lieutenant Larry Gatti, MSgt. Mike Grinell, Mr. Will Ketterson, and Lieutenant Colonel Samuel Carter, who gave me the F-16 ride of my life.

And to Major Ronald D. Fuchs, USAF Office of Public Affairs/ Western Region, without whose leadership, friendship, and hard work, the writing of this book would simply have been impossible. And without whose example of character and dedication, this would have been a very different book indeed.

About the Author

STEVE SOHMER served as president of Columbia Pictures and as writer-producer of the acclaimed dramatic television series *Mancuso FBI*. His first novel, *Favorite Son,* has been published in fifteen languages and twenty-two countries. He lives in California and in Shipton-under-Wychwood, a village in rural England.